SHADOW SONG

Terry Kay

WHEELER
PUBLISHING, INC.

★ AN AMERICAN COMPANY ★

Published in Large Print by arrangement with
Pocket Books, a division of Simon & Schuster, Inc.
in the United States and Canada.

Wheeler Large Print Book Series.

Set in 16 pt. Plantin.

Library of Congress Cataloging-in-Publication Data

Kay, Terry.
    Shadow song / Terry Kay.
        p.   cm.—(Wheeler Pub. large print book series)
    ISBN 1-56895-157-4 (hardcover)
    1. Large type books. I. Title.
[PS3561.A885S48   1994b]
813'.54—dc20   94-42481
                                                          CIP

Shadow Song

A few years ago, two friends—cohorts in the business where I was then employed—appeared in my office not long after the publication of one of my novels, and they said, in jest (or maybe half-jest), that they did not understand the story I had written, that it was interesting but complex. They wanted me to write a novel of romance for them. I promised that I would. Someday, I said. When I found an intriguing story. Two years ago, while visiting the Catskill Mountains of New York for the first time since 1957, I found that story. It had to do with an opera singer named Amelita Galli-Curci and some wonderful ghosts from three summers of working in a resort hotel.

And, so, this book is dedicated to:
Patty and Elaine
Because a promise is a promise.

1

On the morning that he died, Avrum Feldman came calling. He said he would, and he did. He had promised it would be his last act on earth before meeting that old faker, God, and, as he often reminded me, I, of all people, should know how eager he was for that encounter. God had been hiding from him long enough, up there in his smoke screen of clouds and in his dazzling cluster of stars, pulling off his cosmic tricks like a cheap magician.

"But before I find this God, this Houdini, I will try one last time with you," he had said repeatedly. "One last time to see if you will listen."

When Avrum came calling, it was in a ghost-whisper, a premonition. He came in a warm shiver that swept over my shoulders and neck like a sudden puff from the sun on a bright and cheerful morning.

I remember because I arched my shoulders to nuzzle against the shiver.

It was early morning. I was in the art studio of the private school where I taught, watching a gifted young man intently studying his painting of the leaves of autumn. The painting was beautifully, brilliantly colored, rendered in rich, thick swipes of oil that seemed to lift up and curl off the canvas, as leaves of autumn do when they first touch the ground.

And I was thinking of Avrum. Or I could have been.

The last time that I had seen him—nine months earlier—the leaves of autumn in the Catskill Mountains were curled on the ground, beautifully, brilliantly colored in their cups of red and yellow and orange, looking very much like the painting by the gifted young man who stood before the easel, his darting eyes searching for a spot to put the one glistening dot of oil that was on the tip of his brush and in the center of his imagination.

And the warm shiver that struck my shoulders and neck—the knowing before the knowing— was Avrum's way of gently teasing me with his dying, telling me about it in the instant that Brenda Slayton, secretary to the headmaster of the school, said from the doorway of the studio, and in a voice so soft I knew something was wrong, "Bobo, you've got a call from New York that you need to take."

When I speak of Avrum's death in the years still before me, I will say, "Yes, I knew." And it will not be a lie, or a fancy thought, because, in life, Avrum had had a wondrous power to be where he wanted to be merely by wishing himself there. If such power had been so simple in life, getting around in death would have been a trick as effortless as a finger snap to him.

"It is easy to do, *ja*," Avrum had boasted. "So easy."

I have never argued that such claims by Avrum sounded anything but crazy. They did—his claims and his stories. And he was called that—called crazy—by a lot of people who knew him, or thought they knew him. I was one of them. When I first saw him, I mean.

He was sitting on a sidewalk bench made of concrete and heavy timbers in the small village of Pine Hill, New York, in the Catskill Mountains. His eyes were closed, his head tilted back. A soft smile was on his ancient face. He was listening, Harry Burger told me, to Amelita Galli-Curci.

"Who?" I asked.

"An old opera singer," Harry explained.

"I don't hear anybody," I said.

"So? Do I hear her? Does anyone hear her? Only Avrum. What can I say?"

The people who knew him, or thought they knew him, muttered smugly that Avrum was an old fool preoccupied with romantic nonsense. Who could hear a voice when there was no voice? Who? It was nothing, they declared. Nothing but Avrum Feldman's way of getting and keeping attention, this hearing of voices. An old man's begging to be seen. Nothing more.

But the people who scoffed at him, who ridiculed him, did not know of Avrum's wondrous power to be where he wanted to be merely by wishing himself there. He could do that—could

3

transport himself—as freely and jubilantly as a dreamy child. He could will himself back through memory, leaping time like a joyful, streaking star, back to a night when all that he had been and all that he was and all that he would become gathered in serene harmony, and a voice—one that was both within and without, one that entered him and surrounded him—spoke with such absolute command, Avrum could only obey it.

That night was January 28, 1918, one day past his thirty-first birthday. Because he loved the opera, his wife of eighteen months had presented him with two tickets in the least-expensive section of the balcony at the Lexington Opera House in New York City to hear Amelita Galli-Curci sing the title role of Giacomo Meyerbeer's spirited *Dinorah*.

Avrum's wife was a Polish immigrant who had Americanized her name to Marina. She disliked the music of the opera. "I would play my recordings and she would complain," Avrum reported. "'Such squealing,' she would say, and I would tell her, 'You do not listen. Listen, and the voice of the music will speak to you.' But she would not listen. She did not believe in the voice of the music. If you do not believe, you cannot hear."

On January 28, 1918, sitting beside his annoyed wife, listening to Amelita Galli-Curci sing the *Ombra leggiera*—the "Shadow Song"— the voice of the music spoke to Avrum, and the

4

power to wish, to dream, was released in him and he became another man, a man that people would call crazy and an old fool preoccupied with romantic nonsense.

When he spoke of that night—as he often did during the thirty-eight years I knew him—it was always as though he were living it for the first time, as though the experience were something that had occurred only hours earlier.

It was a cold night, he remembered, a night whipped with snow and sheets of rain and wind that howled out of the lungs of Manhattan skyscrapers. After the performance, standing outside the theater, with his wife quarreling about the thinness of her winter coat, Avrum heard the voice of the music again. The voice ordered him to walk away, and he did, leaving his wife shouting angrily at him as passersby shook their heads in disgust.

Avrum did not return home that night. He wandered the streets dazed, with the echo of Amelita Galli-Curci's magnificent voice ringing joyfully in his memory. Twenty-four curtain calls for the "Shadow Song," he vowed emphatically when he told the story. He had counted them. And sixty for the final curtain. Yes, sixty. And Geraldine Farrar, the great prima donna, had stood in her seat in the theater and cheered.

"And my wife, my wife. Do you know what she said?" Avrum would hiss. "She said, 'So much money for such squealing.'" And then he would add, in a bellowing of anger, "She would not stand for the ovations."

In the morning, at sunrise, taking coffee in a small coffee shop, Avrum read the reviews from newspapers left on tables by other readers. The critic from the *Times* had written: "The voice that this shouting audience heard for the first time is one of those voices that 'float.' At the end of its principal demonstration last night it wasn't a woman's voice but a bird's swelling throat . . ."

After his coffee, Avrum folded the newspapers under his arm and went home. Marina had left early for the bakery where she worked. She had placed a note on the kitchen table against the sugar dish: *Where did you go? What did I do?* Avrum tore the note in half and went into the bedroom and packed his belongings into two suitcases and left.

It was what he had to do, he explained. It was what the voice of the music told him to do.

I never tired of hearing the story, though he told it always in the same manner, with the same words, the same intonation, like a script memorized and perfected over many performances. It was romantic and bizarre, the kind of story that old people are likely to tell when they have locked onto a solitary moment in their life, allowing that moment to seize and command them. Still, there was always something compelling about it. Over time, I began to believe that Avrum repeated it because he wanted me with him when he made his leap back to that night. I think he wanted me to understand something that he believed essential for the good feeling of happiness, or contentment. In everyone's life, he instructed, there was one moment of change—one grand, undeniable moment of change—that was so indisputable and consequential it never stopped mattering.

And with Avrum, that moment was the night he heard Amelita Galli-Curci sing at the Lexington Opera House, and the voice of the music spoke to him.

Until he died on July 12, 1993, at the age of one hundred and six, Avrum Feldman devoted his life to the celebration of that moment. It was a life of innocent fantasy and sweetly endured anguish.

It was, as Avrum often confessed, a life wholly wonderful, but not quite complete. "It is very painful," he would warn me, "to love someone and believe you can never be with them."

He would add, with a sad smile, "I chose the right person, but I am the wrong man."

The caller was Sol Walkman, administrator of the Highmount Home for Retired Citizens, where Avrum had lived for thirty years. I knew Sol's voice immediately—a thin, almost impersonal voice. Though I had met him a few times during my visits with Avrum and he had tried to be pleasant, I had never really liked him, because I have never understood why people who have

7

no apparent compassion choose to work in a profession that begs for it.

Sol told me that Avrum had died at some hour between midnight and dawn.

He said, "According to Mr. Feldman's records, you were to be notified of his death. There's nothing to indicate it, but I must ask: Are you his son?"

"No," I answered. "Just a friend. He had no children, or any other relatives that I'm aware of."

"I see."

"I can be there tomorrow morning," I suggested.

"He was very specific about his wishes. He wanted to be taken immediately to the crematory. It's very clear in his instructions, very clear. I've just finished reviewing them."

"Then take him," I said.

There was a pause. "You don't wish for us to wait until you arrive? Is that what I understand? I spoke to the funeral director. He—"

I interrupted. "It's all right. Do as he wished."

Again, there was a pause, then Sol said, curtly, it seemed, "Very well. It's not a Jewish custom, but as a gentile I thought you may wish to view the body."

"I have no reason to," I replied.

"You probably wouldn't know him. Frankly, he looks bad."

"I'm sure he does. He was old."

"Yes," Sol sighed. "Old and helpless. He required a lot of special attention."

"He was a special man," I said.

I could hear Sol Walkman inhale, then he countered, "All of our residents are." His voice was barely controlled.

"I'll be there tomorrow," I told him.

The telephone clicked into a hum.

By late afternoon, I was at the airport in Newburgh, New York, slightly off-balance and groggy, like someone awakening from a disturbed sleep. The day had been a blur—arrangements at school for a substitute to take my classes, flight reservations, hurried packing, the expected and irritating argument with Carolyn, my wife. She had complained about my rush to leave, about the expense of the trip, about forcing her to juggle plans that included both of us. It had been an uncomfortable confrontation. I did not blame Carolyn and, yet, I resented her for not understanding. She had never accepted my friendship with Avrum. To her, it was an odd and ridiculous and embarrassing relationship. What could I possibly have in common with an old man who was as batty as the Mad Hatter? For years, she had accused him of using me, and she had accused me of not having the nerve to call an end to his demands.

"Now that he's dead, maybe you'll put all that nonsense behind you," she had said.

"I didn't know it was nonsense," I had replied.

"What else do you call it?"

"Friendship."

"Good God, Bobo," she had sighed.

I had wanted to call her immediately after talking to Sol Walkman. I had wanted to tell her about Avrum and how he had warned me by his presence in my classroom. I had wanted her to understand about the shivering and to reply, in her softest voice, "I'm sorry, Bobo. I know he meant a lot to you."

I could not make the call then because she could not give me the answer I needed. Carolyn was the last person I had called.

The quarrels between us over Avrum were ancient and tiresome.

I rented a car at the Newburgh airport and drove to Kingston and checked into a motel. I had dinner in a small, nearby restaurant, then bought a bottle of brandy from a package store and returned to the motel. In my room, I poured a shot of brandy over ice and took the complimentary Kingston newspaper and propped against the pillows of the bed.

There was a story on the front page of the newspaper about Avrum's death. It did not reveal much about him. It said he had been born in Germany in 1887, that he had immigrated to America in 1907, that he had worked as a peddler, a furrier, a teacher, and, finally, as an interpreter for the United States Immigration Service at Ellis Island. It said he had retired to the Catskill Mountains and had died there in the Highmount

10

Home for Retired Citizens, which was supported by Jewish charities. It said he had been the Home's oldest resident and, perhaps, the oldest citizen in the state of New York.

The story was six paragraphs long.

I thought: Newspapers know so little about people.

I wanted to read that Avrum Feldman loved music as other people love God, that he could recite passages from the librettos of operas as easily as schoolchildren could recite the poetry of Kipling, that, though he could not read music, he could be seized by its power and, in a stroke of inspiration, lift a twig from the ground and conduct imaginary orchestras with such conviction and tenderness that passersby—even those who thought him crazy and an old fool preoccupied with romantic nonsense—would stop and watch and become so enthralled by the majesty of his performance they would believe they heard violins from the voices of birds.

I wanted to read that Avrum had had a gift of insight that was rare and astonishing in its simplicity and in its accuracy. At least, it had been with me.

I wanted to read that when people had laughed at Avrum, the sound of their laughter was the sound of fear, that their voices had trembled because he made them uneasy. I wanted to read that when they walked away from him, they had stopped and lifted their faces and listened, wondering if they, too, could hear the voice of Amelita Galli-Curci.

I wanted to read that Avrum Feldman had accepted as his friend a boy of the rural South, barely seventeen, and that he had declared it destiny that we should meet. What else could it be? he had reasoned. Why would he, a Jewish immigrant from Germany, almost seventy at the time, meet, and like, a boy of the rural South? And in the Catskill Mountains of New York? Why? Destiny, Avrum had pronounced.

He had heard horror stories, he told me that summer, in 1955, of Southern men in white bed-sheets burning the cross of their Christ on the lawns of the Jews. He knew, as fact, that Jews had been lynched for nothing more condemning than the sounds of their names. He had read of it, he raged. He had heard the rabbis speak of it. He knew that, in the South, Jews were ostracized, that their rights, like the rights of the Negroes, were denied them.

"And," he had cautioned, "you are of the South. You must learn how other people live, if you are to live yourself."

What Avrum did not, or could not, understand was that I knew nothing of the atrocities against the Jews that he described with stubborn certainty. In my home, atrocities against any race, or faith, were not celebrated or tolerated. When they were discussed, which was seldom, it was always with regret and sadness.

"No one is such an innocent," Avrum had protested.

But he had been wrong. I was such an innocent—the fifth child of a farming family with an Irish and English heritage, settled from more than a hundred years of wandering from Pennsylvania through Virginia and the Carolinas and finally into Georgia, to the fertile bottomlands of the Savannah River. There was pride in the heritage and in the wandering and in the settling. Pride and tolerance and patience. And quietness. Quietness, too, was part of our nature. The silence of work, as my father had believed, was a great teacher. "A quiet man does not carry the weight of his tongue," he had advised. I would later learn that people who did not know us—people who were not of the South—thought we were lazy and passive because we were quiet. We were not lazy. We were not passive. We were Southerners.

And for a Southerner, for an innocent, it had been a great leap to go from the green, humid foothills of northeast Georgia to the cool, majestic mountains of the New York Catskills—from the loblolly pine to the hemlock, from red clay to dark forest soil. But it was more than a leap of miles and scenery. It also had been a leap of culture, a leap so mighty that I am still in awe of it.

Avrum Feldman had been there, in Pine Hill, in the Catskills, when I landed, bewildered and frightened. He was sitting on his sidewalk bench, an old man who was thought to be crazy, a fool preoccupied with romantic nonsense.

And we had become friends. Destiny, Avrum had called it.

And long ago he had chosen me to close out his life, to recite his kaddish.

It was a strange request and I had tried to decline it. Many times, I had tried. I would say to him, in a plea, "But I can't do a kaddish. I'm not Jewish."

And Avrum would smile in his old-man way—mischievously—and reply, "So? Neither is my kaddish. You will see. You will see."

I never insisted on an explanation. I knew he would be right.

I wanted to read in the Kingston newspaper that Avrum Feldman's kaddish would be recited—performed—by his friend, Madison Lee Murphy, who was also known as Bobo.

I wanted to read that Avrum Feldman had not been crazy, or a fool, but blessed, because he understood something the rest of us could not understand.

But I knew I was being unfair. How could the writer of six paragraphs—six obligatory paragraphs, acknowledging the wonder of a man living one hundred and six years—know that Avrum Feldman believed in the power of one grand, undeniable moment of change, and in the voice of the music?

It was late and I turned off the lights of the room and settled into bed and thought of Avrum.

Death refreshes memory, pushes away the clutter of years. It is like finding an object, a keepsake, in a stored-away box, and by the simple act of touching that object, that keepsake, you remember vividly the time you first touched it, and whatever you felt, whatever it was that made you put it into a stored-away box, you feel again. And perhaps it haunts you.

There was, in my memory of Avrum, a stored-away box, one that made me understand the stories of Amelita Galli-Curci were more than gossip on the streets of Pine Hill and in the other towns and villages of the Shandaken Valley.

One night, in the summer that I met him and after he finally told me of Amelita Galli-Curci, Avrum insisted that I accompany him back to his room in the small hotel where he then lived. I thought he was not feeling well and was afraid of being alone. I asked if he needed to see a doctor.

"Doctor?" he said, puzzled. "Why should I see a doctor? What's a doctor got to do with anything?"

I apologized to him. "I just wondered. I thought if you wanted somebody to walk you back to your room, maybe you didn't feel too good."

He spit a laugh into the air. "*Mein Gott.* I'm not

one of those old people at the place you work," he declared robustly. "I want that you should see something."

In his room, which was sparse and drab, he directed me to move a chair to the front of the door, blocking it, and he instructed me to sit in the chair and watch him. "Ask me nothing," he warned. "Nothing."

He went to a trunk at the foot of his bed and opened it and removed an ornate mahogany box and took it to a table beneath a window and unlocked it with a key that he kept in his vest pocket, a key that he often fingered absently as he walked the streets of Pine Hill. He lifted from the box two candlesticks of beautifully cut glass and two white candles. He pushed the candles into the candlesticks and placed them on the table, and then he carefully, ceremoniously, took from the box a framed photograph of a woman with a severe, but distinctive, face. He did not tell me, but I knew it was Amelita Galli-Curci. He leaned the frame against the candlesticks, balancing it, and then, in front of the photograph, he placed a sheet of music with a signature scratched across the face of the page, and on the sheet of music, he placed a necklace of costume jewelry.

I thought he was going to say something to me, offer an explanation, but he did not, and I watched as he sat in the chair at the table, his eyes locked on the photograph. A smile settled warmly into his face. I could see his lips moving

16

in a soundless whisper, like a soft, begging prayer. After a few minutes, I slipped the chair away from the door and quietly left the room.

I did not tell anyone about that night, about the candlesticks and the candles and the photograph and the sheet of music and the necklace of costume jewelry.

People would have laughed. They would have said Avrum had made an icon of an old opera singer. They would have said it was proof that Avrum was crazy, a fool.

And I have never told anyone that during that same summer and for many years afterward, there was a photograph that I, too, kept locked away until I could no longer bear not seeing it. And, like Avrum, I would take it out of its hiding and place it before me—not as Avrum did, not with the candlesticks and the candles, but on a bare table. Then I would hold a blue stone that the girl-woman of the photograph had given me and I would sit, as Avrum did, and look at the face that smiled back at me with bright, giving eyes. I would believe that I could hold her again, touch her mouth with my mouth, feel her hands on my hands. I would make her name with my lips, say it again and again, and my soul would send soft, happy prayers of longing to her.

But I am not as brave as Avrum was. I did not quit my life for an impossibility. I did not risk hearing voices. I still had the photograph and the stone, and there were times when I looked at them and remembered, but I no longer performed the ritual of loneliness.

Avrum was not crazy, or a fool.

He was in love with Amelita Galli-Curci.

And he taught me the joy of such love.

That is why we were friends, and it is what I have never been able to tell Carolyn.

And I think it is why, long ago, Avrum chose me to close out his life, to perform his kaddish.

Avrum knew about the photograph that I kept hidden. He knew who it was and why I had it.

I did not have to tell him. He knew.

2

I always go into the Catskills with melancholy and gladness. I go slowly, following Highway 28 out of Kingston. I do not want to take the mountains in a gulp. I want to sip them, to hold the taste of seeing them again as I would hold the taste of a surprising, perfect wine. I like to say aloud the names of the towns and villages as I slip past them—Stony Hollow, Glenford, Ashokan, Boiceville, Phoenicia, Allaben, Shandaken, Big Indian. I think of the streams where men cast lines as light as spider's silk over the waters and the whiplash of the lines' curl before settling for the chase of the trout that glide in the cold spills of the Beaverkill and the Neversink, the Delaware and the Esopus. The names of the towns and villages, of the trout streams, are like poems to me.

I like the feeling of the mountains rising up from the valley of the highway and cupping me in their walls of hemlock and oak, of birches with white, peeling trunks, of rhododendron and laurel, of scrub bushes and wild grasses on the knolls. It is wondrous to see the trees. I have always wanted to stop on the roadside and take canvas and oils and to paint frantically, to find in the touch of a brushstroke what I see, and sense. But I think the trees cannot be painted. Their colors flow with the sun—pale and dark greens, scratches of white, red, and amber blossoms. Their colors flow and I think I can see them moving on the sunriver, their high faces lifted in exuberance and their muscular tree arms stretching like dancers of the ballet embracing the music of their dance.

I wondered if this would be the last time I would take the slow, melancholy drive into the Catskills, past the towns and villages and streams with names like poems. Since 1955, I had returned every few years to visit Avrum. At least, that is what I had told myself. I may have lied. Avrum was my friend and I loved him for that friendship, but perhaps I had used him as an excuse to make the drive that fills me with awe.

Carolyn has always believed there was some reason, some calling, for me to return to the Catskills that was more alluring than friendship. She has always been suspicious of the trips and of my insistence on taking them alone. I had argued that Avrum would be uncomfortable if she was with me. It was a childish and transparent suggestion, but I could not think of anything else to tell her. "I could stay at the hotel while you're with him," she would protest, and I would answer, "Maybe next time. We'll talk about it." But there was never a next time. Finally, we had stopped discussing it. I would leave and Carolyn would be bitter. I would return home and nothing would be said.

There is part of me—my social conditioning, I suppose—that made me believe I should suffer guilt because of the trips and leaving Carolyn, but I did not. I think of the Catskills as my moment, my one grand, undeniable moment. *Mine.* Not Carolyn's. Not mine and Carolyn's. *Mine,* alone. How could I feel guilt over something that changed me forever, even if I had never expressed that change?

It was different in 1955. I wanted Carolyn with me. We even talked about it before the summer. The two of us working together in a resort in the Catskills, hundreds of miles away from our hometown. It would be fun, we said. And romantic. "I want to go with you," Carolyn told me then. But it was only talk, a kind of dreamy prelude to the separation that we both knew would happen.

That separation was on the morning of May 27, 1955. It is one of the few dates in my life that I cannot forget. We were in New York City on the first stop of the high school senior trip, but I would not go with my classmates to Washington, D.C., and from Washington back to our home. I would say good-bye to them at Penn Station, would watch the train heave forward and take them away, with Carolyn waving to me from a window, crying and mouthing, "I love you." And then I would walk back to the hotel where we had stayed and wait for my brother, Raymond, to find me and drive me to Pine Hill to begin work that day in the Pine Hill Inn.

It was Raymond who had arranged for me to work at the Inn. He was studying for his doctorate at New York University and was serving a circuit of small parishes in the Shandaken Valley for the United Methodist Church. One of his parishioners was named Nora Dowling. Her late husband, Morris, had owned the Inn. Morris was Jewish, but Nora was Lutheran. Because there were no Lutheran churches in the area, Nora attended my brother's services. She liked him. When he told her about me, she offered a job for the summer.

I do not remember that first drive into the Catskills with Raymond, except for a herd of deer on a knoll. I must have sat forward in the car seat, as would a child who is excited. I know that Raymond slowed the car and said, "You'll see a lot of them up here." Then he added, "Bobo, everything up here is different," and he began to tell me the stories of the Catskills, from the early settlers to the resort industry. "Once it was believed that Catskills would be the new Jerusalem. There's a rich Jewish heritage here. You'll find that out at the Inn."

I have thought of that first trip over the years and wondered why I have no impression of the mountains and trees and the towns and villages and streams. Perhaps I was too young, or too tired. We had been in New York for two days. On the last night with my classmates, Carolyn and I had stayed together until late, and then I had joined some of the boys in one of the rooms

22

and we had talked long after midnight. I did not know it then, but I was trying to tuck away my time with them as fully, as completely, as possible. Coy Helms called it "Bobo's last night as a human being."

Coy. Coy is another person I always remember when I am in the Catskills.

The last thing Coy said to me on May 27, 1955, was, "Keep it pointed toward the ground, Bobo. They's Yankees all over the place up here."

His exact, last words were those.

I laughed at Coy and took his offered hand. "Sure, Coy," I said. There was great strength in his handgrip. He looked away, then blinked his eyes rapidly, then licked the dryness from his lips. He shrugged the way Coy always shrugged when he wanted to appear nonchalant—a casual roll of the muscles across his shoulders. Coy was large and powerful, the strongest boy-man I knew. He had played tackle on the football team. One night, enraged because an opponent had threatened me, Coy broke the boy's leg. Yet, Coy was also gentle and caring. If he liked you, Coy loved you. In a good way, I mean. With his soul, with the fluttering that bubbles up in a person's chest when that person has sensed, or witnessed, something too splendid for the chest to contain. When Coy said to me, "Keep it pointed toward the ground, Bobo. They's Yankees all over the place up here," I knew it was not what he wanted to say. What he wanted to say was, "I love you, Bobo."

I remember thinking, as I watched Coy stroll

away and board the train, "I love you, too, Coy. Thank you for breaking legs for me."

The train left and I stood watching it slide away from me. They are going one way and I am going another, I thought.

And out of that swimming, dizzying morning of leaving, with Carolyn clinging to me and Mazie Herndon, who taught English and was a chaperone, warning me about the meanness of the street people of New York, it has always been Coy Helms I remember most clearly.

It was a few minutes after ten when I arrived at the Highmount Home for Retired Citizens. The name was a polite sham. Avrum had called it, cynically, the Highmount Hilton. It was a converted resort hotel and from the outside had the appearance of being large, but, inside, it was not. Inside it was crowded and always in need of repair. The rooms were too small and never thoroughly cleaned. There was a smell of medicine and urine mixed with the damp, cool odor of death. It was not, as its brochure advertised, "a community of senior citizens engaged in the common joys of life." It was a holding place for people who had no other home. They had been left there by their families, like children who are left overnight with a baby-sitter and a promise: "We'll see you in the morning." At the Highmount Home for Retired Citizens, morning never arrived. "Old Jews," Avrum had muttered. "Who wants us?" For years I tried to persuade him to move, but he would not. He was near Sul Monte, the summer home that Amelita Galli-Curci had occupied.

The receptionist guided me into Sol Walkman's office. A small man with a pinched, pale face, Sol tried to be professional, but I knew he wanted to be finished with the business of Avrum Feldman, the eccentric.

He invited me to sit in a worn leather chair in front of his desk.

"Let's see now, Mr. Feldman's file. I have it here," he said, leafing through some papers on his desk. He looked up at me. "I'm sorry. You are . . .?"

"Lee Murphy."

He tried a smile. "Oh, yes, here it is." He pulled a page from a folder. "We handle so many people, and, unfortunately, I've never been very good with names. I know we talked yesterday, and I know we've met briefly a few times, but I drew a blank."

"That's all right," I told him. "Avrum may have noted my name as Bobo. That's what he called me."

A smirk crossed Sol's face. "Bobo?"

"It was—well, still is to most—my nickname," I explained.

"I see," Sol said. He looked at the page. "We have it as Madison Lee Murphy."

"That's official."

"Of course."

25

"I assume Avrum's wishes have been carried out," I said.

Sol nodded vigorously. "Just as he instructed. His ashes will be available later."

I did not reply. Sol studied from a sheet of notes he had made.

"You know that he became extremely ill just before his death," he said after a moment.

"No. But I don't doubt it, being as old as he was."

Sol nodded again, again vigorously. "The oldest person we've ever cared for. Frankly, it was remarkable how strong and alert he was until the last few weeks."

"He always amazed me," I said. "When I first met him, I thought he would only live a few years. That was thirty-eight years ago."

"He's certainly been an interest to the media. We've had a lot of calls about him. I think it must be true, what they say."

"What's that?"

"That you automatically become a celebrity if you live to be a hundred. Everyone in New York seems to want to know about him."

"What do you tell them?"

Sol blinked in surprise. "Tell them? I tell them he was one hundred and six years old, that he had lived here for thirty years."

"Nothing else?" I said in a purposely flat voice.

"What else could I say? It's all I really know, except for the records of employment, previous addresses, that sort of thing." Sol settled back into his chair. "As I said, Mr. Murphy, we handle a lot of people. It's impossible to get to know them very well, especially at their age. So many of them who are placed here by their families seldom talk at all. They're at that stage of their life, as you may imagine. They're forgetful, and they know it, so they choose not to talk, or they get confused by being left by people who used to care for them—or so they thought—and they don't know how to explain it, to themselves or anyone else. They don't know what to say."

"Was Avrum that way?"

He again tried to smile. "Mr. Feldman was, well, different," he replied slowly. "Sometimes he could be extremely difficult, but I'm sure you know that. For example, he occasionally insisted on playing his opera recordings at odd hours, and at full volume. We would have to take his records away until he promised to be more considerate. He could be very stubborn, Mr. Murphy, and, if he wished, he could be mean." Sol picked up the file before him and held it up for me to view. It was crammed with papers. "You can see the number of complaints we received over the years."

I suppressed a smile. I knew the file of violations and warning that Sol Walkman held was Avrum's last, proud protest against the Highmount Home for Retired Citizens.

"A lot of people used to think he was insane," I said.

Sol's eyes narrowed in thought. "Most of the

doctors who attended him over the years would probably agree with that," he said after a moment. Then: "What do you think?"

"I think he was brilliant. And, sometimes, that can be mistaken for insanity."

Sol frowned.

"I assume the media have come and gone," I said.

"For the most part," Sol replied. "A couple of television stations doing specials on the aging have called about coming up." He glanced around his office. "We've been busy tidying up."

"That should give you a chance to put in a good word about the treatment of old people," I suggested.

"Yes, I suppose."

"I know that Avrum was concerned about it," I added, baiting him. "He talked about it a lot, when I visited."

Sol fingered the file before him for a moment, thumbing the papers like a deck of cards, and then he lifted his eyes to me and said, "Mr. Feldman was well cared for."

"I'm sure he was. Are his affairs in order?"

Sol shifted in his chair. He pulled a sheet from an envelope and pretended to examine it.

"There's no outstanding bill, if that's what you mean. Apparently, Mr. Feldman invested well in his younger years, and, of course, if his estate wishes to make a contribution to the Home, it would be greatly appreciated."

"Perhaps," I said. "I'll have to study his

accounts. We seldom discussed his financial condition. I have no idea what he was worth, if anything."

"Ummmm," Sol murmured. He again leaned back into his chair. I could hear the wood of the chair creaking. The features of his face gathered in discomfort. "You do understand, Mr. Murphy, that Mr. Feldman's request for cremation was absolutely against Jewish law. In fact, to many, it would be considered a sacrilege."

"Yes, I know. I tried to dissuade him a few years ago, when he first mentioned it to me. I disagreed with his decision, but he wouldn't listen."

"Why did he do it?" Sol asked earnestly. "I'm not orthodox, but I find it very difficult to understand such a decision."

I remembered the day that Avrum had told me in a spilling of anger and passion why he had chosen cremation. His last relative, a cousin, had been cremated in Treblinka, in Hitler's fiery purging of the Jews. Cremation was to be Avrum's gesture of grief, his last ceremony of honor to an extinct family.

"Do you know?" Sol asked again.

I did not want to share Avrum's celebration of death with Sol Walkman, like gossips talking about strangers.

"No, I don't," I lied. "It was his wish."

"I see," Sol said heavily. "One other thing, Mr. Murphy, and this is rather delicate. It indicates in our records that Mr. Feldman wanted you to

29

conduct his kaddish. That's not permitted, you understand. There will be no kaddish, since he had no relatives."

I remembered the shining in Avrum's eyes as he told me about his kaddish, that it would not be from the Jewish ritual. His eyes were those of a prankster delighted with himself.

"I understand that I cannot exercise a Jewish rite," I said deliberately. "I think Avrum used the word *kaddish* merely as an expression. I believe we both understand that his concept of a kaddish was as likely inspired by the Mardi Gras as by God. I know he left some instructions for me, and when I read them, I'll know what his wishes were."

I could feel my voice rising in anger. "I must tell you, Mr. Walkman, that Avrum Feldman meant a great deal to me. He taught me a lot. And though I don't want to offend anyone, I am duty-bound to carry out his instructions."

To my surprise, Sol did not argue. He wagged his head and I realized, for the first time, that he had heard such stories before and that he cared for the old people who could only die at the Home. He picked up a sealed envelope from the desk.

"This must be what you're talking about." He stood and handed it to me. "I don't know what's in it. I would never violate the trust of such documents."

I thanked him and told him that I would read

it as soon as I was settled, and that I would visit him again before I left.

"I'd like that," he said.

When I am in the Catskills, I always stay at the Pine Hill Inn, not for comfort, but out of loyalty.

Once it was a hotel of charm and subdued elegance, as one of those ancient mountain inns in Europe would be. It was meticulously clean and the service was gracious and reliable and disciplined. The food that Nora Dowling and her sisters, Gretchen and Olga, prepared was considered the best of the nonkosher establishments in the Catskills. It was a place where the guests were made to believe they belonged, and to them, belonging was important; most were Jewish refugees from the First and Second World Wars. They understood what it meant to be displaced, and they understood, even more keenly, what it meant to belong.

Since 1983, the Inn has been owned and casually operated by a man named Sammy Merritt, who imagines that he is a sculptor, but he is not. He is, I sometimes think, a psychopath with hammer and chisel who pulverizes stone out of an antediluvian urge for destruction. He escaped New York City, he once told me, because it stifled his creative growth; I have always thought he was thrown out in a conspiracy of annoyed art dealers. Yet, Sammy is not easily discouraged. He is always eager to exhibit his recent work for me, explaining with juvenile enthusiasm the deeper meaning of each piece. I offer exaggerated praise, which sends him leaping back to hammer and chisel. It is unfair of me to lie so blatantly, but it is the only way to stop Sammy from lingering and blithering. Often, at night, after I had examined his pieces, I would hear him at work and I would imagine him puffing like bellows to keep the flames of inspiration burning at blue heat.

Sammy's wife, Lila, is pretty and thin-bodied, but with great, protruding breasts, the kind that heave like water buoys in romance novels. She wears tight clothing and excessive makeup and a perfume that is almost offensively sweet. Still, there is an eloquence about Lila that is like an instinct. She has a soft voice, but she uses profanity easily and often—at least in my presence—and I think her greatest pleasure, when I am visiting, is in teasing me. "Just once, Bobo," she will say. "Just once, let me ball a real artist."

There is one cook and one chambermaid (never the same from year to year) at the Inn. If any other services are required, Sammy and Lila may, or may not, provide them.

For years, the hotel has needed painting and repair. It is crowded with the junk of cheap collectibles and with Sammy's sculpture. There is a stale, musty cigarette odor in every room. Even with the windows open, the air refuses to circulate.

Once, there were more than a hundred guests at the Inn during the summer season. Now, Lila told me as I signed the register, there were seven, counting me. "We're getting crowded, Bobo," she said flippantly. She looked at me and winked. "But we're glad you're back. I know that I am. Gives me another chance."

I asked her about the winter ski season.

"It was a bitch," she said casually. "Sammy was working on a piece—big, fucking deal; he's always working on a piece—and he left me holding the bag, as usual. I brought in a couple of kids from the city to pretend to be waiters. Before it was over, we made out like bandits."

"I'm glad to hear that," I told her. "Still, it feels strange not seeing people around in the summer. The place used to be full."

She reached for a key from a rack behind the desk. "Yeah, well, they were old. They died. Everybody died. This is a ghost town, Bobo, or haven't you noticed? Three more hotels closed last year." She handed me the key.

"Sad," I said.

"Look, where did you see the last McDonald's on the way up?" she asked. "This side of Kingston, right? Up a few miles, maybe. That should tell you. You don't find a McDonald's, you find a ghost town. People can piss and moan all they want about those fast-food emporiums, but where they are is where life is. Believe me. If you ain't got the Golden Arches, they're about to shovel dirt over your ass."

"I guess you're right," I said. "Never thought about it."

She looked at me tenderly. "You know, Bobo, every time you come here, you talk about how it used to be. Those days are gone. You've got some kind of weird idea that when you're here, it's going to be the way you remember it. No way, Bobo. No way."

I was embarrassed that she was so right.

I asked, to change the subject, "How's Sammy?"

"Sammy? Sammy's Sammy. He went to Kingston this morning to pick up a block of marble, or granite, or something. I think he's over his Brancusi stage."

I smiled. A year earlier, during my last visit with Avrum, Sammy was convinced that his medium was wood. He had babbled incessantly about Constantin Brancusi.

"He'll be glad to see you," added Lila. "He's got a few tons of new stuff. Rented the old Ellis Drug Store down the street to put it in. You remember him, Bobo? Arch Ellis? He died earlier this year."

"He did? I'm sorry to hear that. I liked him a lot."

"Yeah, me, too. Anyway, Sammy's beating the hell out of his rock collection in there now," Lila said. She leaned across the registration desk. I could smell her too sweet perfume. She whispered, "Tell me, Bobo, is Sammy any good? I mean, is he any good at all?"

I could feel myself swallow, which is something

I must do before I lie. "He's not bad. I think he may be a little too impatient."

Lila cackled a laugh. "He's a mental case, and we both know it." Then: "Are you having lunch with us?"

"Sure. Why not?"

"I like brave men," Lila replied. "Turns me on."

In my room, I put away my clothes and sat on the bed and opened the envelope that Avrum had left for me.

There was a single, folded sheet of paper and a second, smaller envelope. Across the front of the second envelope, written by Avrum's shaking hand, was a message: *Avrum Feldman's kaddish. To be opened six days after his death. A.F.*

He had noted the date beneath his initials: 6–11–80. He would have been ninety-three, I thought.

I unfolded the single sheet of paper and read:

Dear Bobo,
  I am dead.
  When you read this, I will be face-to-face with God. He won't get away this time.
  You are as close to being my son as I have ever had. Go be my son and do away with me. Bury my ashes on the sixth day where I told you. Go do your service that you want to do. Do it three days after I am dead. You

35

*know why. No requiem music. You know
why.*

*My kaddish is in the other envelope. Do not
listen to the rabbi. Do what I say.*

Give away everything I have left.

I love you, my son.

It was signed, *Avrum Feldman*. The date was
the same as on the second envelope: 6–11–80.

3

Before I left my room for lunch, I called Carolyn. She works in a small computer store, a job she accepted after our children—Rachel and Lydia and Jason—were gone from home. She does not like the job, but does not dislike it enough to search for another. She makes good money— more than I do—and she has a good arrangement and she knows it. If she wants to take off for a day, to shop, or do nothing, she tells Darby Bailey, who is her employer, and he nods permission. Sometimes she gets annoyed that Darby is so accommodating. She believes he doesn't want her around. I tell her she would be more distressed if, one day, he refused her request.

Darby answered the telephone. "Yeah, Bobo, she's here. Just a minute." Darby's voice is kind, a voice that people like.

Carolyn did not say, "Hello." She said, bluntly, "I thought you were going to call me last night."

"Did I say that? I thought I said I'd call you when I got here. I stayed in Kingston last night. Went to bed early."

"Never mind," she said. "We're busy. Where are you? At the Inn?"

"Yes. You've got the number."

"How long will you be there?"

"I don't know," I answered. "Maybe a week. It'll take some time to settle things."

"A week?"

"Maybe less. I don't know."

"What's there to do? He's dead. You said he was going to be cremated. How long does that take?"

"That's already been done, as far as I know. But there are other things. A memorial service. Some paperwork. You remember how it was when your father died. It's not simple."

Her voice became soft. I knew she was thinking of her father. "I know," she said.

"I'll take care of things as fast as possible," I promised.

"You know where I am," she said.

"I'm sorry about this, Carolyn."

"At least it's finally over," she said. "The great Catskill getaway just ran out of excuses."

"Jesus, Carolyn—"

"I didn't mean it that way," she countered. "Look, I've got to go."

"Did you tell the kids what happened?"

"Of course I did. They said they were sorry. Jason will probably try to call you tonight."

"Call me if you need anything," I said.

"I won't," she replied.

There is a ritual when I go into the dining room of the Inn. It began the first year that Sammy and Lila took ownership. In the ritual, Lila takes me by the hand and, in a loud, cheerful voice, announces to anyone present that I am a former waiter and before I will eat, I insist on a sentimental tour of the kitchen. People smile, because they do not know what else to do, and then Lila pulls me through the swinging doors into the kitchen.

The kitchen is always as I first saw it, only older and more cluttered. The ovens and stoves are the same, the dishwasher is the one that I used on May 27, 1955, the dishes that I washed are the dishes stacked on the shelves, the preparation tables are exactly as they have always been.

Lila always says the same thing: "Well?"

And I always answer the same way: "It's still here, isn't it?"

And, still grasping my hand, Lila leads me back through the swinging doors to a table.

There was only one couple in the dining room when I entered. Lila was serving wine to them. She turned and smiled, then crossed to me, extending her hand. I took it. She said to the couple, "This is Bobo Murphy, the famous Georgia artist. He used to be a waiter here and I know what he wants to do; he wants to look at the kitchen before he eats. He loves nostalgia."

The couple smiled.

We completed the ritual of the kitchen and Lila led me back to a table on the far side of the dining room, away from the couple. "You want some wine?" she asked.

"I don't think so," I said. "What was that

splendid aroma from the kitchen? Wiener schnitzel?"

"Baked chicken," Lila answered. "Or, that's what it damn well better be. Take some wine."

"I don't think so," I said again.

She leaned forward, her great breasts near my face. She whispered, "You'll need it. The chicken's always tough. Anyway, it's from their bottle." She flicked her eyes toward the couple. "The good stuff. They have a case of it with them. Besides, they won't know. All they're doing is screwing."

I could feel a blush rising in my face. "You can be remarkably eloquent at times, Lila."

"Take the wine, Bobo."

"All right."

She started to leave the table, then turned back. "Oh, by the way, I forgot to say anything about your friend dying. I'm sorry. He was really old, wasn't he?"

"Yes, he was. Thank you for remembering him."

"Does this mean you won't be coming back?"

"I don't know. Maybe not."

She looked at me for a long moment. "I'd miss you," she said softly, then she left.

No place I visit affects me as deeply, as severely, as the Pine Hill Inn. When I am there, I experience moments that strike me like strobe lights, and each flash is hypnotic in its power.

I came to the Catskills as a seventeen-year-old

40

boy from Georgia, whose neighbors were named Ginn and Carey and Skelton and Winn and Dove. I had never heard a foreign language spoken. I knew only one Jewish family—the Blumenthals, who owned a clothing store. I bought my first suit there, a blue, double-breasted gabardine. In Pine Hill, I met people named Rosenberg and Kraus and Reichmann and Mendelson and Berenstein. They spoke German and Yiddish. Their religion was puzzling and mysterious. They ate food I had never heard of people eating.

Food. When I am in the dining room of the Inn, food is always the first flash of the memory strobe.

Raymond drove me directly from New York City to the Inn. It was a few minutes after one when we arrived. Dessert was being served in the dining room. It was Memorial Day weekend, which Nora Dowling used as a rehearsal for the official summer season beginning in mid-June.

I followed Raymond into the kitchen through a side door that opened to a platform-porch built to hold garbage cans for pickup. Raymond stood at the door until Nora Dowling noticed him. I saw him smile nervously as she crossed the kitchen to us.

Nora Dowling frightened me. She was tall and thick and, I believed, very strong. Her hair was the color of a dried-blood red and it held to her head as though it had barely survived a raving argument with the rest of her body. Her deep green eyes were squinting. She glared at me in a scowl. I could see disappointment quivering in her heavy jowls.

"This is my brother, Bobo," Raymond said pleasantly. "Bobo, this is Mrs. Dowling. She owns the Inn."

Timidly I said, "Hello."

Her eyes covered me. After a moment she said heavily, "He is such a baby." She sighed, then repeated, "Such a baby."

I knew she had surprised Raymond. He laughed good-naturedly and said, "Well, you can't let his looks deceive you. Under those dimples, you'll find more than a boy." He reached and touched my shoulder, in part to calm his own uncertainty, I thought, and in part to assure me. "Back home, he ran the farm by himself last year when our father was sick."

The scowl on Nora Dowling's face deepened. She tilted her head to inspect me. A frown of pain furrowed in her brow. I knew what she was thinking: So this is what my own minister brings me, a baby.

"You'll find he's a good worker," Raymond said confidently. "And he knows why he's here. He either has to make some money for college or go back to the farm. I think he had enough of that last year."

I could hear the unfamiliar sounds of the kitchen—the murmuring of voices, the swishing and clicking of the swinging doors leading into the dining room, the dull bell-ring of pots and pans, the fragile glass-against-glass pinging. I could feel the heat of the stoves and ovens. A scent of rich foods swam in the trapped air.

Nora Dowling crossed her arms and continued to stare at me with disappointment. A boy my age, maybe older, passed too close to her carrying a tray of dishes and she glared at him irritably. Then she turned to face me. "So, what is all this college for? What will you do with it? Be a man of the cloth like your brother?"

"Plenty of time to make that decision," Raymond said quickly. "He's a very talented artist. That may be his calling." He squeezed my shoulder. I was glad he was touching me.

Nora Dowling sighed again and rolled her eyes dramatically. Her face changed from scowl to resignation. She had made a promise; she would keep it.

"Well, there's work to be done," she said. She dismissed Raymond with a look. "Come back for him around eight."

"I'll be here," Raymond replied. His hand rubbed across my shoulder, signaling me that I would be all right and that he would return. "Do a good job," he said to me. "We've gotta show them that Southerners know how to work." Then, to Nora Dowling: "We're grateful to you."

Nora Dowling tried a smile, but it did not fit her face.

Raymond left through the side door—in a rush, I thought. He did not look back.

"Did you have lunch?" Nora Dowling asked.

I swallowed and lied: "I had a sandwich at my brother's house. We stopped by so I could see my sister-in-law, Linda."

She rolled her huge shoulders and I thought of Coy Helms. "They's Yankees all over the place up here," Coy had warned. He had no idea how right he was.

"A sandwich is not lunch," Nora Dowling proclaimed. "You need food. Come."

She led me to a table near the side door and motioned for me to sit. She did not introduce me to anyone, and no one approached me. But I knew they were watching. I could feel their eyes. Their eyes were bullets.

In a few moments Nora Dowling returned with a bowl of soup. *"Kartoffel suppe,"* she said.

"Thank you."

She nodded once and left. Her voice boomed instructions across the kitchen. People ducked to their work.

I sipped the soup. It was delicious. I did not know what *kartoffel suppe* was and I wondered if my mother, who was a renowned cook in our community, would like it. I thought she would. I was hungry and I finished it quickly.

"So, was it good?" Nora Dowling demanded.

"Yes, ma'am," I answered politely. "What was it?"

She looked at me in amazement. *"Kartoffel suppe?* It's potato soup. That's what it means."

"Oh," I said. I did not know that people made soup from potatoes. In my family, we did not.

We ate the potatoes. "It's one of the best meals I've had in a long time."

Nora Dowling's sullen face flashed with amusement. A laugh bubbled from her abundant bosom. *"Ach du lieber Gott,"* she exclaimed. "Meal? That's not a meal. That's soup."

In that moment I experienced the first memorable cultural bewilderment of my life: there could be more to a meal than soup. In my family, on the farm, soup *was* a meal. Soup and cornbread. My mother made the soup with meats and vegetables and a sweet beef broth that stayed in the mouth with a filling aftertaste. We loved her meals of soup and cornbread.

"Now, you have the meal," Nora Dowling crowed. She pivoted to the people in the kitchen. "He thinks soup is a meal," she announced in a roar. A hard, sharp laugh dropped from her mouth. She muttered again, *"Ach du lieber Gott."*

The meal that Nora Dowling placed before me was astonishing, grander than any I had ever eaten anywhere, the kind of meal that I had imagined in reading stories of banquets in foreign countries. I thought of my mother as I ate. I wished she were with me.

The baked chicken that Lila served was, as she had warned, overcooked and tough, but it was better than the asparagus and carrots. I was glad for the wine.

Lila sat at the table with me and occasionally glanced toward the couple huddled at the other

45

table. She seemed fascinated by them. The woman was young and radiantly pretty, the man obviously older. His hair was gray, but he was slender, with the athletic look of a man who plays racquetball three days a week.

"Lord, Bobo," Lila said behind her hands. "You should see that bed after they've been at it. Looks like elephants have wallowed in it."

"Don't you think that's personal?" I asked.

Lila flicked away my righteousness with her fingers. "I'm not complaining," she whispered. "Tell you the truth, it turns me on. You can smell sex in there after they leave. The place reeks of it."

"Maybe they're honeymooners," I suggested.

Lila giggled. "Sure, that's it. Where do you keep your head, Bobo? In the sand or up your ass? They come up here once a month. He's a big-shot stockbroker in the city, she pretends to be a high-grade socialite. They're both married. His wife's a cokehead, her husband's a Superior Court judge. They have no idea I know who they really are, and I don't plan on telling them. They tip twenty percent. Anyway, they've been pounding on one another for years." She paused and inhaled deeply. "To be honest, Bobo, I envy them. Most days I think I'd do the same thing if I could find somebody to do it with." She rolled her eyes at my disapproving frown. "Hey, remember, I'm married to Sammy. The hardest thing about him is his chisel."

I bit from the chicken and chewed.

"So, how're the wife and kids?" Lila asked.

I nodded that everyone was fine. The chicken seemed to expand in my mouth.

"That's good," Lila said. Then: "How's the chicken?"

I nodded again.

"That bad, huh? I've got to fire that bitch. She stays drunk half the time and tries to sober up the other half. I think I'll hire a Chinaman and buy him a wok. You can't screw up stir-fry."

I swallowed the chicken and took some wine.

"How long you going to be here, Bobo?"

"A week. I hope that's all it takes."

Lila brushed an invisible something from her blouse. I could see her breasts shudder. "Don't like our company, is that it?"

"No, that's not it, and you know it. I have some things to do, some arrangements relating to my friend's death, then I'll have to get back to the classroom."

Lila adjusted her bra strap with a hitch of her shoulders. "What was his name? I read the story, but I don't remember."

"Avrum Feldman."

"Oh, that's right," she said. "I've always heard he was crazy."

"I guess it depends on what you think it means to be crazy."

"Somebody said he heard voices," Lila replied.

"He did."

"I think that's crazy."

"And I think it's a miracle."

47

Lila smiled warmly. "You know, Bobo, that's what I like about you. You could smell roses in a shithouse. God, I'd love to take you to bed."

"Maybe in our next life," I said.

"Then I'll die tonight," she sighed. "You bastard."

"I'm sorry," I said.

"Oh, no big deal," she replied flippantly. She looked toward the couple at the far end of the dining room. "All I want is to have that expression one more time."

"What expression?"

"The one on her face. What do you think it is, Bobo?"

I looked at the woman. She was leaning forward at the table, gazing at the man. A halo of light from an overhead fluorescent tube rested on her blond hair. She fingered the stem of her wineglass. She seemed mesmerized.

"I think she's . . ." I hesitated.

"What, Bobo?"

"It's trite."

"Try me."

"Glowing," I said. "I think she's glowing."

Lila exhaled a soft sigh. "Yes. That's it. Glowing. That's what I want, Bobo."

"I hope you get it, Lila."

"If I do, I think I'd better start looking for a big-shot stockbroker. You artists are all alike, somewhere between fatigue and fag. I can't understand for the life of me what I see in you."

"We need mothering," I said.

"Bullshit," Lila replied.

After lunch, I went outside, across the street from the Inn, and sat on the bench that I think of as Avrum's bench. It was an afternoon of sun filtered through a casual breeze that slid from the branches of the hemlocks and pines, the oaks and birches. I thought of the first time that I saw the village, saw it in its charm and simplicity. A narrow street, which had once been the main highway, curved out of the mountain in a gentle, downward slope, rose slightly at a bridge that crossed a narrow stream of water called Mosier Creek, then curled into and through the village. When I first saw the street and the few shops and stores of the village nudged up close to it, there were many elderly people on the sidewalks, moving in drag-steps or standing in bubbles of sunlight, or under tree limbs that waved above them like exquisite fans. To me, on that day, the first day that I saw them, they had seemed sedated, frail, like windup toys clicking to a stop. Now, as Lila had correctly observed, they were all dead. Avrum had been the last of them.

I also remembered seeing Avrum for the first time, remembered Harry Burger's amused voice when he pointed toward Avrum with his cigar and told me that Avrum was listening to Amelita Galli-Curci.

Harry explained that Amelita Galli-Curci had once had a summer home in the Catskills—a place called Sul Monte. In late afternoons she would stand on the porch of Sul Monte and sing, and her voice would be heard for miles. When she sang, everyone stopped what they were doing and listened. Everyone. She had the voice of an angel, Harry admitted.

"There is a story," Harry said, "about some workmen. One day, after she had finished her singing, there was a knock at her door and the workmen's boss was there, telling her he needed to speak to her about her singing. 'Do I disturb you?' she asked. 'No,' the workmen's boss told her, 'but next time would you please not hold that last note so long. My men quit for the day.'"

Harry chuckled at his story and then bit into his cigar and gazed sadly at Avrum. "Avrum, he was in love with her. Foolish old man. Followed her up here every summer, just to sit and listen. Now, he stays. And still he hears her. Nobody else does. Only Avrum." He clucked his tongue. "Look at him," he added quietly.

And I did look. Closely.

Avrum Feldman's wonderful face was transfixed, enraptured by the splendor of a voice that only he could hear.

"Come on," Harry said. "Leave him in peace. You will meet him later." We walked a few steps. "Poor bastard," Harry mumbled.

I am not sure I would have met Avrum if not for Harry. I may have spent the summer walking past him, as others did, with wary, over-the-shoulder glances that tried to measure him for

50

acts of sudden absurdity. But Harry and Avrum were friends in an odd way. They argued constantly, especially about God. Avrum contended that God caused as much grief *for* humankind as he suffered because *of* humankind. Harry accused Avrum of being a blasphemer and declared that he was greatly offended by Avrum's disregard for tradition. I was never sure that Harry believed what he said, or if he was merely pretending. It was not easy to tell with Harry. He loved attention and argument, almost as much as he loved to aggravate. When he really wanted to bother Avrum, Harry would sit beside him as Avrum listened to the imagined voice of Amelita Galli-Curci and he would sing lively German folk songs in a harsh, off-key baritone. Avrum's face would twist in pain.

I encountered Harry the day that I arrived at the Pine Hill Inn. Other than Nora Dowling, he was the person who frightened me the most.

It was midafternoon. I had been led to the back of the kitchen by Nora Dowling and given a brief demonstration on operating the dishwasher, a strange, rounded-top machine that rolled open like the mouth of a rhino. On a wide aluminum rack in front of the dishwater were the dishes and glasses and silverware from lunch. Huge sinks were filled with pots and pans.

"Get these done by five," Nora Dowling had ordered. "We need them for dinner."

The next three hours were the most horrible I had ever lived. I became soaked. My hands shriveled into a disease of wrinkles, the skin of my arms sagged, my face burned with the detergent the machine spit on me. The floor became too slippery to stand on. The heat of the kitchen became steam.

And I was lonely. More than anything, I was lonely.

I knew that in Washington, D.C., my high school classmates were at the Lincoln Memorial, and their laughter was so shrill I could hear it in the Catskill Mountains over the churning sound of the machine and the clicking of glasses being washed in a stream of hot, hissing water. I thought of Carolyn and wondered if she missed me as much at that moment of loud, shrill laughter as she had at Penn Station. Or had the tears dried quickly? Had she found the waiting shoulder of Gary Reeder, offering a tender, pretended comfort? She had dated Gary before dating me and he had slipped into the seat beside her on the train as she was waving to me. I saw him smile triumphantly. His hand shot up and he flipped a bird toward me.

The memory of Carolyn's body against mine, her arms tight around my back, her hands stroking my shoulders, the warmth of her breath on my face, made me shudder. I dropped a glass and it shattered at my feet.

A voice snapped at me, *"Was ist los?"*

I turned to see a man standing in front of the swinging door. He was dressed in oversize trousers, a wrinkled shirt, and cardigan sweater that drooped far below his belt. He had narrow shoulders and a slender chest and a soft, pillowed belly. His hair was gray and thinning and he had it oiled and plastered in a straight backward combing, except for a few curls over his ears. He wore a hard, accusing stare on his face. A long, unlit cigar dangled in his hand.

"*Was ist los?*" he said again.

"Ah, excuse me?"

"*Mein Gott,*" he growled.

"I—I don't speak German," I said.

"*Dummkopf,*" he mumbled. He pointed with his cigar at the glass on the floor. "*Ker das auf.*"

"Sir?"

He made a sweeping motion. "*Ker das auf.*"

"Sweep it up?" I said.

The sweeping motion became more vigorous, pulling him toward me. He said again, "*Dummkopf.*"

I nodded rapidly. "Yes, sir. *Dummkopf.* Sweep it up." I mimicked his motion and pointed toward the glass.

A glimmer flashed in his eyes. "*Ja, ja. Das ist gut.*"

I knew that *ja* meant "yes." It was in the way the man's head bobbed when he said it.

I said, "*Ja.*"

I thought I saw him bite a smile. He bit, instead, his cigar and he looked at me pitifully. "*Dummkopf,*" he muttered, then turned and pushed through the swinging door. The door slapped gently at the jamb—twice, three times,

53

then stopped. I thought I heard a giggle from behind the door, but I knew I was mistaken. Madmen did not giggle. I hurriedly found a broom and swept up the glass.

It was almost five when I finished the washing and putting away of dishes and glasses and silverware and pots and pans and had mopped the slime from the floor. I was covered in soap water and perspiration. My hands and arms were numb.

I went to one of the swinging doors and pressed my ear against it. I could not hear anything and I opened the door slightly and looked inside. I did not see anyone, but the dining rooms seemed cool and fresh and inviting. Each table was perfectly dressed with a pressed, white tablecloth, and white cloth napkins trimmed in a narrow pink border were at each place setting. The napkins were folded to look like the sails of sailing ships. There was a sweet, clean scent of laundry in the air.

It was quiet in the dining room.

I went out of the side door onto the platform-porch, which was crowded with huge garbage cans, and I sat wearily on the steps. My muscles ached. I could smell the detergent caked into my shirt. I leaned back against the railing and looked up at the mountain behind the Inn. I saw a deer, a buck crowned with a majestic rack of antlers, standing beside a white birch tree. The deer was beautiful and I knew instantly that I would never forget him. He was like a painting that I had done in another time, another existence. I thought the deer was studying me, asking with his deer eyes, "Who are you?"

A quivering sadness fell over me. I thought: I am Madison Lee Murphy—Bobo Murphy. I am from Georgia, the son of William and Coretta Murphy. I am a Southerner. People speak English where I live. They are not mean, like these Yankees.

The deer lifted his head as if he had heard me. He stroked the wind with his face.

I closed my eyes. The warm, late-afternoon sun struck the steps where I was sitting and it felt good across my head and shoulders. It was like the sun of the Georgia fields. My body began to surrender to the begging need for rest. I could hear my classmates' laughter from Washington. Laughter and one weeping voice: Carolyn. I wanted to be with her, to lace my fingers with her fingers. On our last night together in New York, I had confessed that I wanted to marry her, and she had held to me and cried joyfully and had whispered, "Yes, oh, yes . . ." The memory of that moment swam around me. It was as warm as the sun on my head and shoulders. And then I slept.

A hard bump jarred me awake and I stood quickly.

A large truck with a steel body was there, backed against the platform-porch. I had not heard it drive into the side yard. I watched as a man got out of the cab and lit a cigarette. He was tall and lean-muscled. A scar angled from his temple to his cheek. He was wearing jeans and a flannel shirt and a trucker's cap. The belt at his waist had a bronze, snap-open buckle with the face of a bear stamped into it. There was a dangerous look about him.

He drew from the cigarette and let the smoke seep from his lips. He stared at me coolly. From behind him and across the side yard, I saw a group of men—all young—approaching. They stopped several feet away. I recognized one of them as a busboy from the Inn.

The man beside the truck said, "You the cracker?"

"Excuse me?" I said.

"The cracker, the Georgia boy. You him?"

"Uh, yes, sir."

He drew again from the cigarette and pulled himself up to the body of the truck and stepped over inside it.

"Why you up here?" he asked roughly.

"To work," I replied.

"People around here need jobs," he said evenly.

I did not answer. I looked at the group of men. They were amused. I turned to go back into the kitchen.

"Where you going?" the man demanded.

"Back to work," I told him.

"You got some work right here."

"Here?"

"Right here. Hand up them garbage cans."

I stood, looking at him, wondering how he knew me.

"You the dishwasher?" he said.

I nodded.

"The dishwasher helps load the garbage truck." A smile crept into the man's face. "That right, boys?" he called.

The busboy from the Inn answered, "That's right, Ben."

I stepped to the nearest garbage can and caught the handle and pulled it. I could hear rocks rolling inside it.

"Maybe you better ask some of these boys for some help," the man in the truck said. "You don't look like you got it in you to pick up one of them cans."

"That's all right," I said.

The man wiggled the cigarette in his mouth. "I'm waiting."

And then the door opened and the man from the kitchen who had bellowed at me in German stepped outside. A pleasant, calm smile rested on his face. He said, in perfect English, "Hello, Ben."

The man in the truck mumbled, "Harry."

"I've been looking for this young fellow," Harry said in a strong voice. He moved close to me and reached into his pocket and pulled out a ten-dollar bill. "Wanted to be the first to give him a tip in his new profession. Glad I've got some witnesses." He handed me the bill, then stepped back. He said gently, but with warning,

"I think you should hand those cans up to Mr. Benton."

"Yes, sir."

I tilted the can that I was holding by the handle and caught it at the bottom and I lifted. I thought of Coy Helms, imagined that I was as strong as Coy. My muscles burned from the weight and I knew that I was straining, but I lifted the can and pushed it up to the truck, and I could see the expression on the man's face change. He took the can and rolled it over the truck gate and emptied it. The rocks tumbled across the steel flooring.

"All that leftover food, it gets heavier every year. Am I right, Ben?" Harry said cheerfully. "*Ja, ja.*" He went back into the kitchen.

"I'll give you a hand with the rest of it," Ben said quietly.

I was throbbing with pride and anger. I said, "I'll do it."

And I lifted the cans, each of them, and handed them to the man named Ben. He emptied them without speaking. The group of men who had been watching from the side yard began to back away. I could see Harry's face in the shadow of one of the kitchen windows.

When the last can was emptied, Ben crawled down from the truck body. He pulled a long drag on his cigarette and flipped it away. He studied me for a moment, then he tucked his thumbs into his belt and flexed the muscles of his arms.

"My name's Ben Benton," he said, "and you

are one strong little son of a bitch." His voice began to rise. "Anybody wants to give you any trouble up here, you tell them you're Ben Benton's friend. Won't nothing happen to you."

"Excuse me," I said. "What trouble?"

"Don't go fucking it up by asking questions," Ben answered easily. "I got to go. We'll get a beer later. Tell Harry I'll see him."

"Who's Harry?"

Ben looked at me curiously. "The man that just gave you ten bucks for washing dishes. Harry Burger." He glanced at the window and smiled. He said in a low voice, "Watch that old fart. Nobody never gives a dishwasher a tip. He'll have that ten bucks back before sundown."

Harry Burger died in 1958 and was buried in Pine Hill because he believed Pine Hill was where he belonged. Avrum told me about Harry's death in one of the three telephone calls he made to me in the thirty-eight years that I knew him. He sobbed when he said Harry's name. The second time Avrum called was a year later. He was worried, he said. It was the day before my wedding to Carolyn. He begged me to wait. He said I had given up too easily. "She is not the one," he advised. "Listen to me. I know." He told me again about the terrible pain of loving someone and believing you could never be with them. "It is not always true," he said. "Why do you not listen to me?" I told him that I was fine, that I was doing what I had always wanted to do.

He said nothing more. The telephone went dead against my ear. The third time he called was in 1963. He said simply, "She is gone." The next day, I read that Amelita Galli-Curci had died in California.

It was ironic, or maybe it was the power of Avrum's bench, but sitting there, remembering the calls from Avrum, I heard Lila from the front porch of the Inn: "Bobo, you've got a call. Some woman from a television station."

For a moment, an eyeblink, I thought she said that Avrum was calling.

In a way, he was. In a way.

4

The reporter was a freelancer, a stringer for CNN, an aggressive, but pleasant, young woman named Dee Richardson. She said she was calling from Margaretville, a few miles north of Pine Hill, and she wanted to schedule an appointment with me.

"I've called a dozen places to track you down," she said. "They told me at the Home that you were taking care of Mr. Feldman's affairs."

"I suppose that's right. It was something he asked me to do a long time ago, but I'm not sure I can tell you why. We weren't related."

"The why doesn't interest me," Dee Richardson replied. "I want to talk about his age and his obsession with Amelita Galli-Curci. We've been here shooting some background at the Galli-Curci Theater."

I remembered the theater. It had been dedicated to Amelita Galli-Curci in the early twenties, when she vacationed in the Catskills. Supposedly, she attended the grand opening, sang two selections accompanied by her husband, the pianist Homer Samuels, and never returned.

"Does that still operate?" I asked.

"It's part of what I would call antique row, but

the name's still there. Will you have time to see me?"

"I suppose," I answered. "May I ask you a question?"

"Ask."

"How did you know about Amelita Galli-Curci?"

"I was at the Home about an hour ago," she said. "I saw the mess in his room, all those broken records. They were all Amelita Galli-Curci. The director—what's his name? Walkman. Sol Walkman. He told me the story. He said Feldman was in love with her."

"What broken records?" I asked.

"You don't know?" Dee Richardson responded with surprise. "The old folks trashed his room."

"They did what?"

"Trashed it. It looked like a war zone."

"I can't believe it," I said.

"Trust me. I used to work in the city. I know trash when I see it."

"I think I'd better go over there," I told her. "Why don't I meet you about three-thirty. Here, at the Pine Hill Inn."

"I'll be there," she promised.

I hung up and called the Highmount Home for Retired Citizens and asked to speak to Sol Walkman.

"I just got a call from a television reporter," I told him. "What's this about Avrum's room?"

"You should see it for yourself," Sol said

62

tensely. "I would have called you, but I didn't know where you were staying, and I've been busy trying to get to the bottom of things."

"I'll be there in a few minutes," I said.

Avrum's room had been destroyed. The cheap, flimsy curtains at his window had been pulled away and torn, his bedcovering and mattress ripped with his own scissors. The foam stuffing of a pillow bloated open like the gut of a slaughtered animal. His phonograph, ancient and priceless, had been smashed. His clothing had been yanked from the closet and from the drawers of the dresser. Shreds of paper from my letters to him, and from articles he had clipped and saved, covered the floor like confetti. His prized collection of Amelita Galli-Curci recordings peppered the room in tiny, shining black shards.

I said to Sol, "What the hell went on here?"

"I don't know, not at this moment." His voice quivered. I knew he was either furious or fighting to control a bewildered hurt.

"My God," I whispered. "These people couldn't have done this. They're too old. This is savagery."

"You don't work with them. It's wrong to believe they're too old. They're never too old."

"But why would they do this?"

"They were afraid of him," Sol said softly. "It's the only thing I can think of. They thought he was evil. A lot of them whispered about him.

Maybe I can even understand that, because he was different, but I can't explain this."

"Everything?" I said. "Did they ruin everything?"

"I'm sure some of it was stolen. Some of our residents have very little and they steal when they think they can get away with it," Sol answered. "But everything else, yes, they destroyed." He paused. "No," he corrected. "Not everything."

He went to the dresser and opened the top drawer and removed Avrum's mahogany candlestick box.

"This," he said, holding it, "they would never touch."

"Why not?"

"I can't answer that," Sol said. "I think Mr. Feldman let them believe that it contained something of, well, a supernatural power." He looked at the box for a moment, then admitted, "I inspected it once, after a complaint. It had nothing in it but some candlesticks and candles and a few other things."

"A photograph?" I asked. "Was there a photograph?"

"Yes. I assumed it was of her."

"You mean Amelita Galli-Curci?"

"Yes."

"It was," I said. "Does that strike you as strange?"

Sol hesitated for a moment. "No. Not if he cared for her as it was rumored."

"He did," I said forcefully. "You can damn well bet on it."

"Would you like to inspect it?" Sol asked.

"Yes, I would," I said. "By the way, when you looked in it, were there any audiocassette tapes?"

"I don't remember. It's been a couple of years since I looked at it. Why?"

"I made copies of Avrum's records a few years ago. I thought it would be easier for him to use a tape recorder than his record player, but he didn't like the recorder and he put the tapes in his box."

"Then maybe they're still there," Sol said. "I have the key. I found it on the floor."

He placed the box on the sliced mattress and handed me the key and I opened it. Everything was there—the candlesticks wrapped in purple velvet, the white candles, the white sheet of music, the costume jewelry, the photograph of Amelita Galli-Curci, and the six audiocassette tapes I had given him.

"I think you should take possession of this," Sol said. He looked over the room, shaking his head. "I'm truly sorry, Mr. Murphy. It's a desecration. I think if his body had been in here, they would have mutilated it as well."

"You could be right," I said.

Sol picked up a broken piece of a record and turned it in his hand, then he tossed it on the bed. He said hesitantly, "It may be an imposition, but I'd like to ask a favor."

"What?"

"When I got to the room, there were three people still in it. I had them escorted to my office. Will you talk to them?"

"Me? Why?"

"I'm not sure I have an answer. Something tells me it would help. Maybe they'll say something to you they won't say to me."

"Who are they?" I asked.

Sol named them—Carl Gershon, Leo Gutschenritter, Morris Mekel. They were in their mid to late eighties.

"They've been here a long time," Sol explained. "Never a minute's trouble from any of them."

"What kind of mood are they in now?"

"Frightened," Sol said. "Leo was crying when I left the office. He was afraid I was going to call his son and his son would yell at him." He inhaled slowly and nibbled at his lip. I saw a shiver run through him. "And the son of a bitch would have yelled, if I had called him. He would have been here in three hours, screaming about dignity, something he knows nothing about." He sighed a soft, cynical laugh and looked at me. "I'm sorry. I don't like such people. Will you speak to them?"

"I will. If you think it'll help."

Sol shrugged.

He led me from the room and down the corridor toward his office. The doors to the other rooms were closed and the only sound that could be heard was our footsteps on the wood flooring. An attendant, a muscular young man dressed in hospital whites, stood at the end of the corridor. He had a military bearing.

"Is everything all right?" Sol asked the attendant.

"Yes, sir," the attendant answered. He added, "Mrs. Fisher had to have some medicine. The nurse is with her."

Sol turned toward one of the rooms, hesitated, then turned back and continued toward his office. I followed, carrying Avrum's candlestick box.

The three men had pulled their chairs close and they were huddled, waiting for the punishment they were certain they would receive. I knew Leo Gutschenritter instantly. He was sitting between the other two men. His eyes were red and damp. He trembled. I could hear the rasp of labored breathing deep in his thin chest. He seemed too brittle to be alive, and I thought of my grandfather, who had died when I was twelve. My grandfather had fought against death until his strength was gone, and one day he had announced, simply, "I can't do it anymore," and he closed his eyes and died.

The men looked up, first to Sol, then to me. So old, I thought. So very old. And I remembered an illustration I had seen in an art exhibit—aging dormice attending a puppet show, their narrow shoulders sloped forward, covered in shawls. They were watching without expression as puppets with painted-on smiles danced on strings before them. I had asked the illustrator why he had given the dormice such tired, suffering faces.

"Oh," he had answered, "don't you see? They're being treated as children, but they are not children. What is a puppet show to them? It's a cheap illusion, a nothing illusion. Why should they care? They've lived the illusion of life." It was the most profound explanation of a work of art that I have ever heard.

Sol stood for a moment, his eyes fixed on them. Then he said, in a surprisingly soft voice, "Gentlemen, I want you to meet someone."

A gasp, like a cry of fear, flew from Leo. His body curled in his chair and he closed his eyes. His hands crossed at his throat.

"Don't be afraid, Mr. Gutschenritter," Sol said. "This isn't a policeman. I'm not going to call the police, and I'm not going to call your families."

One of the men sitting beside Leo Gutschenritter reached and patted his arm. "Don't worry, Leo," he said in a bold voice. "No worry." He looked up at Sol with a proud, defiant gaze.

"Yes, Mr. Mekel, there's no need to worry." Sol looked at me, then back to the men. "Gentlemen, this is Lee Murphy. Mr. Murphy, meet Morris Mekel, Leo Gutschenritter, and Carl Gershon."

The men stared at me and at Avrum's candlestick box. They did not speak.

"I'm pleased to meet you," I said.

"I've asked Mr. Murphy to talk to you for a few minutes," Sol explained. "He was Mr. Feldman's friend. He arrived from Georgia this morning to settle Mr. Feldman's affairs."

"He was a crazy one," Morris Mekel said angrily. "Crazy." He leaned forward in his chair. His head bobbed with his words.

"A *meshuggener*?" I said.

Morris Mekel's eyes narrowed in surprise.

"I can understand why you think that, Mr. Mekel," I said. "That's why I knew the word. Avrum used it to describe himself." I held the candlestick box up in front of them. "Do you know what this is?"

The three men stared at the box.

"Devil's box," Carl Gershon whispered. Morris Mekel's head nodded agreement.

"Is that what you call it? The devil's box?" I said. I put the box on Sol's desk and opened it and removed the candlesticks and held them up and turned them in my hands. The light from the room struck the glass and splintered in delicate blades of soft flashes.

"Do you know where Avrum Feldman got these candlesticks?" I said. "From Germany. He ordered them because he remembered that his mother had had candlesticks like them, and he wanted something that would remind him of his mother and his homeland."

I saw the men exchange quick glances.

"You think he used them for some devil worship, don't you?" I continued. "Something mystical. A *meshuggener* at work. He didn't." I paused and placed the candlesticks on Sol's desk.

"Let me tell you what he did with them. He had a photograph—wait, I'll show it to you." I took the photograph of Amelita Galli-Curci from the box and presented it to them. "You know who this is, don't you? You've heard the rumors of Avrum and Amelita Galli-Curci, that he was in love with her? Am I right?"

"The singing," Leo Gutschenritter sneered. "Over and over, he played it. Nobody could sleep. Nobody could think. Always the singing."

"He did, didn't he?" I said. "I used to tell him he was like a teenager listening to rock and roll music, the kind that gives you headaches. But the truth is, Avrum actually was in love with Amelita Galli-Curci. In his way, he was."

I placed the photograph of Amelita Galli-Curci against the candlesticks, as Avrum had done. "This is what Avrum did with the candlesticks and the photograph. Just this. A photograph against candlesticks. Then he would put some white candles in the candlesticks and he would place a sheet of music and a piece of costume jewelry before the photograph—a little like an offering, I guess you could say. And he would sit and look at the photograph and the candlesticks and he would remember the two women he most loved—his mother and Amelita Galli-Curci. He would sit and look and remember and wish."

Morris Mekel glared at the photograph against the candlesticks.

"Mr. Mekel, do you have a wallet with you?" I asked.

He moved his eyes to me. *"Ja."*

"Could we see it?"

He curled his lips insolently. His eyes darted from me to Sol to the photograph of Amelita Galli-Curci, then he pulled his wallet from his pocket.

"Do you have any photographs in it?" I asked.

He opened the wallet slowly. "My daughter. My grandchildren." He offered the wallet to me. A faded color picture of a plain-faced woman and two children—a young boy and girl—was tucked into a plastic photo covering.

"When you look at that picture, how do you feel?" I asked. I handed the wallet back to him.

"They are my family," he answered quietly.

"When I saw Avrum looking at the picture of Amelita Galli-Curci, I saw love on his face, and I liked that," I said. "I think that is true of you, Mr. Mekel, when you look at this photograph of your daughter and your grandchildren. Am I not right? Is that not how all of us feel when we look at the photographs of the people we love?"

Morris Mekel turned his wallet to look at the photograph, then he closed it.

"I want to tell you something," I said to the men. "Avrum Feldman was my friend. I loved him for that friendship. He taught me many things, or tried to, but it was not easy. He was an immigrant who knew the world. He spoke five languages, as all of you probably do. I was a Southern boy from the fields. I only knew a little about Georgia. I barely spoke English, and what

71

I did speak was hard for Avrum to understand because of my accent."

I saw Carl Gershon smile.

"But what I learned from Avrum, and from others—like you—helped me make enough money working as a waiter to get into college. I did it by trying to speak German and Yiddish with a Southern accent. I did it by saying such things as, '*Guter morgen*, y'all.' It was a trick that a man named Harry Burger taught me."

The smile burrowed deeper into Carl Gershon's face.

"And I want to tell you something that I always knew about Avrum: he could be stubborn. He was that way with me many times. I used to say to him that I was glad I didn't have to live with him."

I paused and looked at the three men, and I thought of the illustration of the dormice and wondered if I was nothing more than a puppet show to them, another cheap illusion.

"I'm not going to lie to you. What happened to Avrum's room angers me," I said. "It's hard for me to believe it. I think it's wrong to destroy a man after he is dead, and that's what happened, but I can't change that. The only thing I can do is tell you that Avrum Feldman was my friend. And I don't believe he was *meshugge*. He was who he was, a man who knew he was different and was proud of it." I studied the faces of the men sitting before me. They gazed shamefully at the floor. "Is there anything you want to ask me?"

No one spoke.

"Maybe they'd like to know if you're going to press charges," suggested Sol.

"Of course not," I said. "But I would like for them to do one thing."

"Tell us," Sol said.

"Because of our different religions, Avrum used to tease me about what would be done for his death. Once I made the mistake of asking if he would like a memorial service, as many people have. He thought it was funny, and he thought it was something from my own church. He told me I should do it—to please me, not him—and he left it in his instructions. So, that's what I'm going to do. I'm going to hold a memorial service for him in two days, and I'd like for them to attend."

"Where will it be?" asked Sol.

"I don't have a place yet," I told him.

"Then do it here, in the dining room."

"You wouldn't mind?"

"I insist on it," Sol said. He looked at the men. "We'll have a good showing, won't we?"

Again, the men did not speak.

"Now, gentlemen, why don't you go back to your activities," Sol said.

The men left in silence. I watched as each passed the candlesticks and the photograph of Amelita Galli-Curci. I saw their eyes wander across the photograph, as though looking for something they had never before seen.

Sol thanked me for talking to the men—"the

73

ringleaders," he called them. He assured me that what I had said would be known by everyone in the Home within the hour.

We agree on a time for the memorial service—eleven o'clock on Thursday morning. "I'll take care of everything," promised Sol. "But if you think of anything you need, call me." He apologized again for the destruction of Avrum's room.

"You couldn't help it," I told him. "In a way, I suppose I understand it."

"You know what surprised me?" Sol said. "That young woman from the television station. She didn't shoot anything in the room. And she's sharp. I could tell that from her questions."

"I've got an appointment with her in a few minutes," I said.

"Hope it goes well."

"Me, too."

On the way out of the Home, I passed Carl Gershon. He was near the front door, leaning on an aluminum cane. He raised his head slowly, as a turtle would. He said, in a strained voice, "*Guter morgen*, y'all." And he laughed softly. So did I.

I was surprised when Nora Dowling asked to speak to me on Sunday afternoon, May 28, 1955, my second day of work at the Pine Hill Inn.

"Come in the dining room," she said in a tired command as she pushed open the door and walked out of the kitchen.

"Yes, ma'am," I replied, but the door closed on my words.

"Oh, shit," Carter Fielding whispered. Carter was at the dish rack, depositing a tray of dessert plates. He was a busboy, and the only person in the Inn who had spoken to me. That morning, after breakfast, he had helped me stack the dishes. He had a quick smile and bright eyes and he talked constantly. I did not know it then, but Carter would become the best friend I would ever have.

"Am I in trouble?" I asked.

"Jesus, who knows?" Carter said. He shrugged his shoulders in a thought, then added, "Naw. She'd be yelling. But you'd better get your ass moving. She hates waiting."

Nora Dowling was in a mellow mood. She told me she had learned of the trick with the garbage cans and that she had discovered it was a conspiracy between Ben Benton and her own busboy, a test to drive me back to the South.

"Ben, I understand," she sighed. "Ben's such a man, a bully. But he's a good man, too. Nobody ever believes it, but he's on the city council."

She said of the busboy, a young man named Al, "He will never again work for me, but you will. In his place. I'm going to take you from the dishwasher and make you a busboy."

"Ma'am, I can't do that."

"And why not?" Her voice was sharp, demanding.

"I can't speak German."

"We will teach you," she countered.

"How?"

"You will see," she promised.

Early the next morning, Nora helped me dress in the uniform of a busboy. She declared that I was handsome and ready to begin my training.

"But, we don't have any guests," I said. "They all left, didn't they? Carter said—"

"Not everyone," she told me. "Come."

She led me into the dining room. Sitting there, alone, was Harry Burger, an unlit cigar dangling from his mouth. He was reading a newspaper.

"You know Mr. Burger," Nora said.

"Yes, ma'am."

"He does not go home. He stays through the summer."

"I'm too rich to run away," Harry said.

Nora laughed. "No one else will have him." Then, to Harry: "He's yours. Teach him."

"*Ja*. He will be the headwaiter before I finish with him."

"Make him a busboy first," Nora advised. She looked at me with doubt, then left the dining room.

I stood before Harry Burger, waiting. He studied me from a squint.

"So," he said after a moment, "you are from where?"

"Georgia," I answered nervously.

Harry nodded. He rolled his cigar between his thumb and forefinger. "That's in America?"

"Yes, sir," I mumbled.

76

"It's still there?"

"Uh, yes, sir."

"I thought it was all 'gone with the wind,'" he said gruffly.

"Uh, no, sir."

"Do you know Jews in Georgia?"

I told him about the Blumenthals, who operated the clothing store.

"All good clothes come from the Jews," he declared proudly. "My ancestor was a tailor on the exodus from Egypt. Such a *mensch*. He made the robes for Moses. His name was Haber. Every time Moses got a rip in his robe, he would call for my ancestor, Haber, and my ancestor, Haber, would go running to him. Haber's family called him a dasher. That's where the word *haberdasher* comes from."

"Sir?"

"*Haberdasher*. You know this word?"

"Uh, no, sir."

"It's a man who deals in men's clothing. It was what I did in the city. Harry's Haberdashery. I sold clothes to all the rich Jews and to the goys who wanted to look like rich Jews."

I did not know what to say. I nodded nervously.

"Do you believe this story about my ancestor, Haber, the dasher?" Harry asked.

"Uh, yes, sir."

Harry rolled his eyes. "*Oy, mein Gott,*" he muttered. Then: "All right. Now, I teach you. Now you will learn."

And he did teach me. He taught me the names of foods in German and Yiddish. He taught me simple expressions—*guter morgen*, *danke schön*, *bitte schön*. He explained serving rotations, drilled me in table settings, demonstrated how to pour soup from serving cups into bowls with a twist of the wrist to catch the dribblings and hold them on the lip of the cup. He timed me in folding table napkins to look like the masts of sailing ships. He made me walk the length of the dining room balancing filled plates along my arm, or filled coffee cups stacked high from the fanned grip of one hand.

I was Harry's project and Harry was relentless in his instruction. Nothing pleased him as much as watching me struggle with German or Yiddish. I never knew which I was speaking; Harry never told me. He would point to an object and say its name and make me repeat it. Then he would speak the word in a sentence. "Say it," he would roar. "Say it, *dummkopf*." The words were impossible in my mouth. They would clog on my tongue and I would spit them, and saliva, into the air, and Harry would howl with amusement. He would shout, *"Dummkopf!"* and order me to try again. And the *dummkopf* would try. It was needless to argue with Harry.

But it was because of Harry's enthusiasm, and his prankish nature, that I eventually met Avrum.

One afternoon we were walking from the Inn to the swimming pool across the street. Nora

Dowling had ordered me to clean the pool, and Harry decided he would sit and watch and teach me new words. "Slave words," Harry called them, joyfully.

Harry saw that Avrum was sitting on his bench, reading. He whispered to me, "You see that old man I told you about, the one who hears voices?"

"Yes."

"I want you to go over to him and say this: '*Guter morgen, Herr Feldman. Wo ist dein arsch?*'"

I remembered Ben Benton's warning about Harry. "I don't know," I protested. "I don't think I should."

"So, tell me why not? He's not crazy all the time. He won't hurt you. Besides, you need the practice with somebody else."

"What does that mean, what you said?"

Harry acted irritated. "You know what *guter morgen* means: 'good morning,' *ja*?"

"Yes, sir, I know that. What about the rest of it?"

"*Herr Feldman* is 'Mr. Feldman.' *Wo ist dein arsch?* means 'What are you reading?'" Harry replied. "Say it. Say, '*Wo ist dein arsch*'"

I repeated the phrase slowly, hesitantly.

"*Gut, gut,*" Harry said proudly. "Now, go speak to him. He'll be a pleased man. I know him well. We're great friends. He likes young people. Maybe he'll give you a big tip for being so nice. Say 'y'all' to him. He'll like that." He urged me forward.

"What will I do if he says something back to me in German?" I asked.

"Don't be such a worry one. I'm right here. I'll take over. Anyway, he speaks English."

I approached Avrum. He looked up at me and frowned. He did not seem pleased. I said awkwardly, *"Guter morgen, Herr Feldman. Wo ist dein arsch?"* I smiled nervously.

Avrum's face flooded with a rush of blood. I could see violence in his eyes. His lips quivered. I heard Harry behind me, laughing. Avrum's eyes moved from me to Harry, then back to me. He closed his book and patted the bench beside him. "Sit down," he said quietly.

I sat.

He said, "That man you're with, that Harry Burger, is a son of a bitch." His voice rose suddenly and he spit the words at Harry. "He's old and he's mean and when he dies, I am going to piss on his grave, right on his ugly face."

I said, "Sir?"

Harry laughed harder, sucking for breath.

Avrum nodded his whole-body nod. "What you said to me was, 'Good morning, Mr. Feldman. Where is your ass?'"

"I did? I thought . . ." I hesitated.

"So, tell me, what was it that mean old son of a bitch told you you were saying?" Avrum asked calmly.

"He said it meant, 'What are you reading?'"

"Ah, yes," Avrum whispered. He nodded with

his body again, his forehead furrowed in thought. Then: "And did he tell you who I am?"

"Well, yes, sir. Before now, I mean."

Avrum sat forward on the edge of his bench and glared at Harry. He said in an angry bellow, "My name is Avrum Feldman and I am the crazy man! I am *meshugge!*"

Harry was leaning against an oak, his arms wrapped around his chest. He was laughing uncontrollably. Little strings of tears streamed from his eyes.

I was terrified. I stood.

Avrum again patted the bench beside him. "Come, come," he said gently. "Sit down."

I sat again.

"And you are the boy of the South. Georgia."

"Yes, sir. My name's Bobo Murphy."

"Irish?"

"I—I guess so," I stammered.

"You do not guess. You should know," Avrum said forcefully. "Tonight, you will write to your people, and you will ask them. You must know who you are."

"Yes, sir."

Harry pushed from the tree and crossed to the bench and sat heavily beside me. He rubbed his face with his hands. Giggles rolled from him.

"Got you, Avrum," Harry said after a moment. "A good *vitz, ja?*"

"*Schmuck,*" Avrum hissed.

Ben Benton's garbage truck passed on the street. It slowed and Ben stuck his head out of

81

the window and looked at us in surprise. His hand flipped up in greeting. I wondered how we must have appeared to Ben.

"The book I am reading, Bobo Murphy, is about the great opera star Enrico Caruso," Avrum said evenly. He kept the book closed in his lap. "He was a man the old son of a bitch Harry Burger knows nothing about, because he knows nothing of music. He can fart better than he can sing. He knows dirty jokes, and that is all."

"Mein Gott," Harry exclaimed. "You better go to work on the pool, Bobo. This old fool's about to let his mouth outrun his mind."

"Excuse me?" I said.

Harry pushed at me gently. "Go on. I can see Nora looking out to the window. She'll be out with her meat cleaver in her hand in a minute and she'll use it on both of us."

I stood and said to Avrum, "I'm glad to meet you, Mr. Feldman."

He looked at me and blinked once, slowly. "I will tell you about the great opera singer Enrico Caruso another time, without the old son of a bitch Harry Burger."

"Yes, sir."

I walked away. I could hear Harry laughing. He said to Avrum, "Did I ever tell you, Avrum? I used to sleep with Amelita Galli-Curci. What a woman she was."

And then I heard only their voices in argument, speaking German. Or Yiddish.

That night, Harry confessed to me, "I like that old man, Bobo."

"I don't think he liked what I did," I said.

"Avrum? It was the best part of his day," Harry insisted. "He'll be talking about it for weeks."

When Dee Richardson asked me about Avrum's passion for Amelita Galli-Curci, I wanted to tell her about Harry's prank, but I did not. I told her about the night Avrum attended *Dinorah*. She thought it was a touching love story.

The interview was hurriedly conducted. She began it by looking into the small, glass face of the camera and saying quietly, "Amelita Galli-Curci no longer sings in the Catskills." I would think about her lead-in many times over the next few days. It was the perfect summation of Avrum's life. When she introduced me, she asked only about Avrum's fascination with Amelita Galli-Curci. I volunteered the information about the memorial service.

"That's not a Jewish practice, is it?" she asked.

"I'm not Jewish, but I don't think it is," I replied. "But it isn't a religious occasion, just something that I once told him I would like to do. It was as much a joke as anything. We were discussing death. He later wrote and insisted that I have the service—not because he wanted it, but because he thought I did. It was also in the instructions that he left for me."

"I understand he was cremated," Dee said. "That's not a Jewish custom, either, is it?"

"It's not supposed to be done, but sometimes it is, I understand."

"And the ashes? What will you do with them?"

"Bury them."

"Where?"

I swallowed. I was not ready to tell anyone where I would bury Avrum's ashes. It would have been, for anyone other than me or Avrum, a foolish answer. "I'm not sure yet," I lied. "Certainly nearby."

"Interesting," she said. "All of it."

And then the interview was over. I was surprised that she had not mentioned the destruction of Avrum's room, and I asked her about it.

She took me by the arm and led me away from Avrum's bench, where she had positioned me for the taping.

"Look," she said, "don't say anything about that. I'd get my tail kicked for not making something out of it. The fact is, this is a much nicer story, and sometimes I think nice gets lost in the shuffle. Let's just say there are times when enough is enough. He was one hundred and six years old, for God's sake. He was a man who knew something about love. Why spoil that? Besides, I won't get this kind of story again for another five years, and I'll have a dozen of the others before the week is out."

"You know, Dee Richardson, you've almost restored my faith in journalism," I said.

"And you've almost restored mine in friend-

84

ship," she replied. "I hope you get a chance to see this."

"Me, too," I told her.

Watching her drive away, I wondered how many people would watch Dee Richardson's love story of an old man and care. I wondered how many would laugh.

5

It was four-thirty when Dee Richardson left. A slip of cool air funneled through the village and followed the street out into the valley. Three blocks down, I saw a young girl skipping rope. I could hear the slapping of the rope on the sidewalk, as rhythmic as a calm pulse beat, and I wondered if there was any joy for her in her solitary dance.

I crossed the street and went into Dan Wilder's Coffee and Pastry Shop, which is also part of the ritual of returning to the Catskills. Dan's Coffee and Pastry Shop used to be The Cave. At least, that is what we called it. It is where I had lived in 1955, with three other young men—Carter and Joey Li and Eddie Grimes. The four of us slept on two bunk beds in the long, crowded room. Dan had purchased The Cave from Sammy and Lila and had renovated it, making the room deeper and installing a kitchen and pastry bar, and then he had placed several small tables along the walls. In winter, during the Belleayre ski season, it is Pine Hill's most popular place. Dan's pastries are as sweet and delicate as sugared air, or as thick and rich as heavy honey. He vows he can tell what a customer will buy before the customer asks for it. It is in the way their lips react, Dan contends, when they see the pastry they will have. "The lips move," he says philosophically. "It's like the beginning of a kiss. It's an involuntary thing. They can't help it." He may be right. I have never fooled him, but I am a predictable customer. I always ask for the crumb cake, because it is a recipe from Nora Dowling.

I like Dan. Everyone does. He is a short man with a great, rounded girth shaped by years of sampling. The apron he wears fits over his chest and stomach like a sheet that has been tightly tucked. He is always smiling. Always. He has a voice that comes from his girth, a voice laced in laughter. When he is truly happy—when the shop is filled with people glad to be there—his voice is a bellow. Occasionally he will break into a lively Bavarian bar song and the crowd will sing with him.

Dan knows the table I prefer, and why I prefer it. It is the kind of sentiment he enjoys. The table is beside the wall where my bed used to be. One night, in 1955, I killed a fly on the wall and it stuck there. I drew a circle around it with a pencil, and beside the circle I wrote, *Bobo Murphy kilt a fly on this spot, July 10, 1955*. Dan swears he remembers seeing that circle and reading my declaration when he was renovating in 1985. He also swears the carcass of the fly was still there.

There was no one except Dan in the shop when I entered. He got my coffee—a special blend from Kilimanjaro, he said—and crumb cake and sat with me at my table. We were talking about

Avrum's death when Sammy Merritt pushed through the door and cried, "Bobo, what in hell's name are you doing in this pigsty?"

"He's having coffee, asshole," Dan said easily. "Good coffee."

"He can get that at the Inn," Sammy snorted.

"This is coffee, Sammy, not chicory," Dan replied.

Sammy extended his hand in greeting and I took it. "He's lying, Bobo. You know that, don't you?"

"How's that, Sammy?" I asked.

"He buys my leftover grind and runs hot water over it and gives it those shitty exotic names and overcharges for it." Sammy laughed at his own joke, then added, "So, how are you, Bobo?"

"Good, Sammy. And you?"

"Never been better," he answered enthusiastically. He pulled a chair from another table and sat.

"You want a cup of your leftover grind, Sammy?" asked Dan.

"Why not?" Sammy said. "And give me Bobo's bill. It's on me."

I did not want to be put in debt of Sammy's generosity. I said, "Oh, no, Sammy. I've got it. You want something to eat?"

"Eat? Here? Jesus, Bobo, I do have a little respect for my body."

"Yeah. Shit," Dan said. He struggled from his chair and wandered away to get Sammy's coffee.

I knew Sammy was excited. His thin, fierce

face was flushed with energy. His eyes were shining like the surface of a blue lake when the wind is skimming it. I could see perspiration at his hairline and rock dust in his long, pulled-back hair. His smile was a child's smile.

"Lila tells me you've been busy," I said.

"Like a goddamn one-armed paperhanger, Bobo," Sammy replied cheerfully. "Damn, I'm glad you're here. I was thinking about you a couple of weeks ago. Thought I'd take some shots of the pieces I've been working on and send them down to you, but this is better. You get a firsthand look."

I swallowed. "I'm looking forward to it, Sammy."

"Did Lila tell you I'd rented the old Ellis Drug Store?" he asked.

"She did," I said. "Good idea. You needed a place. That back room at the Inn was getting a little crowded."

"Crowded? Bobo, I couldn't think in there anymore," Sammy said profoundly. "That was my trouble, and that's what I've discovered about my work. It's a breakthrough. Art is thinking, Bobo. All that waiting around for inspiration is bullshit. You've got to think it through, and I was too crowded to think. You have to have the right place to work, but, hell, you know that. I got to stumbling over stuff in that back room and I knew I had to bust up all that junk and sell it for gravel, or move out. I got a great deal on Arch's old place, so that's where I am. Took my tools and my rocks and started over, but this time I can think, and that's the key. I guaran-damn-tee you all the great ones have been thinkers, from Michelangelo to Norman Rockwell."

"Well, it sounds good," I said.

"Best move I ever made, other than getting out of the city. I think I may have a small exhibit down in Woodstock this fall. It's being talked."

"An exhibit?" I said. "Good."

Dan handed Sammy his coffee and refilled my cup. He looked at me and winked. "I've been telling Sammy he should open his own studio. Redo that old drugstore. Get the right person behind it and this place could be another Woodstock in a few years. We're right off the main highway."

Sammy blushed slightly. "I don't think I'm the right one for that."

"I don't know," I said. "Sounds like a good idea to me. We used to go over to Woodstock all the time." I thought of Lila. Lila would kill me, and Dan, if she knew we were encouraging Sammy to expand his dreams.

Sammy tasted the coffee. He tilted his head back and stretched the muscles of his neck as a tired man does. "I don't know," he said. "I don't know."

"Think about it," I suggested.

"I could use the business," Dan added. "So could the Inn."

"Yeah, well, it sounds good, but like I said, I just don't know," Sammy mused. Then, to me:

"Sorry to hear about your friend, Bobo. We thought you'd probably be coming up when we read about his death."

"Thanks," I said.

"You remember that old man, Dan?" asked Sammy.

"We were talking about him before you came in," Dan said. "Yeah, I saw him a few times. Carla Jarvis used to work at the Home. She'd bring him down once in a while, even after he got past a hundred. Sometimes he'd come in here, but most of the time all he'd do was sit on that bench. Carla would come in and get coffee and stand at the door and watch him. Said she never knew what he might do next."

I agreed: "That was Avrum, especially in his later years."

"Lila mentioned you were going to have a memorial service for him," Sammy said.

"On Thursday," I told him.

Sammy sat forward suddenly. An earnest, inspired expression was on his face. "You know, Bobo, I've got a piece I finished about a month ago. Took me a long time to figure it out. I call it the *Old Man*. I'd be honored to dedicate it to your friend and let you use it for the service."

Dan smiled at me sympathetically and walked away with the coffee pot. I could feel my face mugging the pretense of serious consideration. "That's kind of you, Sammy," I said. Sammy twitched modestly. "No, it is," I insisted. "But, to tell you the truth, I don't know what kind of service it's going to be. Not at the moment, at least. I'm going to work on it tonight."

Sammy's expression did not change. "If you want it, it's yours," he said brightly.

"I'll certainly think about it. I promise."

"You do that," Sammy urged. He nodded and paused to sip from his coffee. "So, when can you see what I've been doing?"

I knew there was no reason for delay. "When we finish our coffee."

"Great, great," Sammy bubbled. He began to rock anxiously in his chair. "You know, Bobo, I found some old fishing flies in a box when I was cleaning up at Arch's, stuff I think he must have tied himself. Maybe you'd like to have one for a souvenir."

"I'd like that, Sammy. I had some great times at Arch's."

"Yeah. It was still going pretty good when I got here," Sammy sighed. "Still hard to believe Arch is dead."

Arch Ellis' Drug Store—Arch's—had been one of the old-fashioned kind. Arch had filled prescriptions and sold over-the-counter drug needs, a few gift items, postcards, stationery, maps,and, because he was a fisherman, an impressive selection of fishing equipment, including his own hand-tied flies. Yet, for the townspeople of Pine Hill and for those who worked in the resort hotels, Arch's was more highly regarded as a place to gather than as a drug-store. For the gatherers, Arch sold coffee and soft drinks and sandwiches and packaged crackers and malted milk shakes that were the best in the Shandaken Valley. In summer, at night, the booths and tables in Arch's were always filled until he declared a closing hour.

Arch, like his store, had a warm, comfortable personality. He was a pharmacist by heritage and by training, but he did not like being a pharmacist. He liked telling stories, and no one knew the legends of the Catskills as well, or told them as wonderfully.

Someone would call out, "Story, Arch, story."

And a burst of applause would bring him from behind the counter of the soda fountain.

"Maybe you've heard this one," Arch would begin, "but I was thinking about it just this morning . . ." And he would move about the store, like a strolling actor delivering a passionate soliloquy, and every eye would be on him.

He told of the days of the tanning companies, which stripped the bark of the hemlocks to tan the skins of animals for leather, and he told of the great plank road constructed from the hemlocks and of a stagecoach robbery by thieves who put fire to the road. He told of the murder of a midget from a traveling carnival, of the hanging of a wealthy landowner by his own children, of the ghost of a beautiful woman who had been drowned on the Esopus Creek.

His favorite story—and mine, and I believe,

the favorite of all who heard him—was about a giant Indian warrior named Winnisook.

"Winnisook was seven feet tall," Arch would whisper dramatically, his hand drawing the height above his own head, "and he was proud, but most of all, he was in love with Gertrude Molyneaux, a white girl, the daughter of one of the early settlers."

The story of Winnisook and Gertrude was a classic story of regret and anguish and, finally, romantic sacrifice.

"Now, Gertrude Molyneaux loved Winnisook, also, but her parents would have none of that," Arch would explain. "No, not that. Not a white girl married to an Indian. They forced her instead to marry a man named Joe Bundy."

Arch would pause and his face would contort into a snarl and a growling sound would vibrate from his throat. "A mean man," he would say, dragging the word *mean* across his store.

We, his listeners, knew the cue. We would answer with a chorus of hisses.

"Beat her," Arch would add. "Treated her like a dog. Even worse."

More hissing, stopped by Arch's spreading hands.

"But one day, Gertrude had had enough and she ran away with Winnisook, ran away to live in the woods with his people, with the Indians. They were married in an Indian ceremony and she became the mother of his children."

94

"And where was Joe Bundy?" someone would always shout.

More hissing.

"Ah, Joe Bundy," Arch would reply profoundly. "Joe Bundy was still around, hating Winnisook. Hating him worse than he hated anything, and Joe Bundy was a man who made hate his profession. And then one day, years later, in a fierce battle between the Indians and the settlers, Joe Bundy saw Winnisook—he was hard to miss, being seven feet tall, as he was—and he raised his rifle and fired and shot Winnisook in his great chest. Winnisook slipped away, blood pouring from him, and hid in the hollow of an ancient pine tree."

In a whisper that had the sound of wind with a voice, Arch would add, "And there Winnisook died, standing up. And there he was found by Gertrude, who buried him under the shade of the tree. And there Gertrude lived the rest of her life, with her children, near the grave. That place is now called Big Indian."

When he told this story—when he performed it—the power of his melodrama would always bring cheering, and Arch would go behind the counter with a pleased smile and announce, "Half-price on the malts." The story of Winnisook became known as the "Half-Price Story." We urged him to tell it as often as he would.

Sammy's madness was out of control. In the gutted-out building that had been Arch's, he had mounted dozens of pieces of battered stone to wood pedestals, and he had handwritten the title of each on an index card. Some of the pieces had the appearance of concrete broken apart by street workers bent over jackhammers. There was not a single work of merit—even with the generosity of artistic forgiveness—among the entire collection.

"Well?" Sammy said eagerly.

"Jesus," I mumbled.

"What?"

I recovered and swallowed. "This is—well, incredible."

Sammy beamed. "You like what you see, Bobo? I mean, do you really like it?"

I nodded professorially and wandered to a piece and touched its rough surface. I read the title: *Suffering*. Yes, I thought. It is.

"Like I've said before, Sammy, sculpture's not my medium, but this is—"

"Different, right?" Sammy suggested eagerly. "It is, Bobo. At least it is for me. I picked it up from listening to some skinny-assed poet over in Woodstock. He was reading some free-form stuff—you know, putting down whatever word popped up when he was holding the pen—and it struck me: that's what I should try. Free-form sculpting. But it's not as simple as it looks, Bobo, or as I thought it would be. When I first started doing it, I'd take my sledgehammer and whack the shit out of a piece of stone until it started to look like something, and then I'd take the chisel and clean it up a little." He tapped his temple with his finger. "That was before I started thinking," he emphasized. "You know what they say about something being buried in every piece of stone? Well, you can't just knock it out. You've got to *think* it out. You've got to see what's in there before you start. And you know how you do that, Bobo? You do it by seeing the weak stuff, the stuff that you're going to take off. When it's gone, what's left is what you were thinking. Now I guess I could polish it up a little bit, like the Italians, but I like the original, rough look. What do you think? It's different, right?"

"Definitely," I said. I could not tell the difference between Sammy's thinking and his whacking.

"Let me show you the piece I was telling you about," Sammy urged. "The one for your friend's memorial, if you want it."

He led me across the shop to a piece of granite that was two feet high and had the shape of a grotesque head, like some petrified evidence of disease.

"You see it, Bobo?" Sammy asked proudly. "All the knots of pain. You get that in this free-form, thinking style." He stepped back and looked lovingly at the figure. "I remember the night I did it. Lila had been bitching at me for spending too much money on my work. I told her to kiss my ass. She has no idea what it is to be an artist."

I thought of Carolyn. Once she had loved my paintings, had watched in awe as I created them in the small studio-room of our first home. Now, she only glanced at them. Or so it appeared. She seldom talked to me about them. To other people, she described them proudly and in detail, often with enthusiasm that even I did not have, and it made me wonder if she stood before them, alone, and studied them, perhaps searching for the celebrations that we had shared, freely and joyfully, in the discovery years of our youth.

"I suppose that wives and husbands of artists put up with a lot," I suggested to Sammy.

"Works both ways," Sammy countered. "Sometimes I think all Lila wants to do is fuck." He paused and looked away and forced a casual laugh that had pain in it. "I think she's made it with some of the guests. In the ski season."

"I'm sorry," I said.

Sammy touched the grotesque face that he had titled *Old Man*. He said, too easily, "She'd probably take you on in a minute, if you'd let her, Bobo."

"Oh, come on, Sammy."

He smiled sadly. "Hey, don't worry about it. I know you're not about to do that, but with you, I'd almost think it was all right." He patted me firmly on the back. "Hell, I like you. If you don't come back—I mean, after this time—I'll miss you." I felt his hand tremble. "I can't get nobody else to talk to me about my work, Bobo. Nobody."

I did not know what to tell him. Again, I thought of Carolyn's silence. "You're not alone in that, my friend," I said. "Not many people talk to me about my work, either. I think that's the way it is with what we do."

Sammy laughed and the old flash of optimism blinked in his eyes. He pounded my back. "Well, this is what I think: fuck 'em. Com'on, let me find those flies that Arch tied."

I followed him back to the front of his shop, where a row of booths still lined one of the walls. I stopped to look at them.

"Brings back old times, doesn't it?" Sammy said. He wiped his hand over the back of one of the booths, smearing the thin layer of stone dust that clouded the store from his mad hammering.

"Yeah, it does," I admitted. "I had some good times in here."

"Let me show you something else," Sammy said. He turned and crossed to a corner of the room and pulled a dingy sheet off the jukebox that Arch had had. "Mint condition," he bragged. "Some fellow in one of those antique shops offered me a couple of hundred for it, but I told him he could kiss my skinny ass. I like playing it. I bought a bunch of old forty-fives and loaded it up." He reached into his pocket and took out a quarter and dropped it into the slot. "Let's see," he mused, "you were here in the fifties, right?"

"That's right. 'Fifty-five."

Sammy studied the list of records that he had coded. A smile coiled across his face. Then he pushed a button. "How about this one?"

A record slipped out of the stack and settled on the turntable and the arm holding the needle lowered over the record. The Four Lads began to sing *"Moments to Remember."*

"You must have danced a few miles to that one," Sammy said.

I nodded. The music filled the room.

"That's great music, Bobo, not like the shit they've got today. Listen to those lyrics. Poetry, Bobo, poetry."

Sammy held up his hands like a dancer and began to move around in a slow dance step.

"God, I wish I'd been here in those days. We'd of been a pair, me and you, Bobo."

He whirled his imaginary partner across the floor, then dipped her and pretended to drop her. He laughed and said, "You know what we ought to do, Bobo? We ought to have a party in here before you leave. I could sweep up the place a little and we could drink some good wine and dance to some good music. What do you think?"

"Sounds good to me," I told him.

"We'll have to find you a partner," Sammy suggested.

"That's all right. I'll play the records."

"I'll talk to Lila. She'll come up with somebody."

"I think I'd rather just sit in here with the two

of you," I said. "Wallow in the memories, you know."

The last note of the song faded and disappeared and the metal arm of the record changer reached out and cupped the record and lifted it and slid it back into the stack.

"Yeah, I know," Sammy said quietly. He draped the sheet over the jukebox. "Shit, what kind of memories can you have with a bunch of strangers around?" He looked at me and smiled. "Hey, while you're here, anytime you want to come in and listen to a few old favorites, the place is yours."

"Thanks, Sammy."

"I've got a feeling there's a lot of history in this place for you," Sammy added.

"There is. Yes."

"I'd like to hear about it sometime, Bobo. I love the old times."

6

My history in Arch's was Amy Lourie.

It was where I discovered her one night, following dinner, two weeks after the regular season had begun in the Inn. I had gone into Arch's to buy envelopes to mail a letter to Carolyn. Amy was sitting in a booth with Carter. He saw me and motioned me over.

"Bobo," he said, "this is Amy Lourie. You're going to be serving her breakfast in the morning. Amy, this is Bobo Murphy, your waiter and my boss, and if you understand anything he says, you'll be among the few. He's from Georgia, way down yonder in Dixieland."

Amy Lourie flicked a smile to me. She was the most beautiful girl I had ever seen.

"Hi," she said.

I nodded a reply and forced a smile.

"Why are you called Bobo?" she asked.

I blushed. "One of my sisters gave it to me. She couldn't say *brother*. She called me Bobo and it just stuck."

"You're really our waiter?"

"I—I don't know." I looked at Carter.

"You are," Carter said. "They always sit in the middle dining room." He moved in the seat of the booth. "Come on, take a load off."

I sat beside Carter and looked away from Amy Lourie. I was uncomfortable.

"They just got in," Carter explained. "Amy comes up every year with her folks. They spend the summer."

"My parents love it here," Amy said softly.

"You don't?" Carter asked.

She moved her hand to touch the milk shake in front of her. Her hand and her fingers were as beautiful as her face. She looked around the store, then said, "I like it, but it can get a little boring." Her eyes covered me. "Have you ever been here?"

"I've never been anywhere, until a few weeks ago," I said.

I could see the flash of delight in her eyes. She said, "You really are, aren't you?"

"Excuse me?" I replied.

"From the South."

"I told you he was," Carter interjected. "Come on, Bobo, say 'y'all' for Amy."

I blushed again.

"Leave him alone, Carter," Amy said. "I love the accent."

"You better get used to it," Carter told her. He grinned. "You should see the look on old Mrs. Mendelson's face when Bobo tries to speak German."

"Carter, that's mean," Amy said. She was still looking at me. "How did you get to be our waiter?"

Carter chuckled. I knew it was a tender matter

with him. He had been at the Inn for two years as a busboy, and I had been promoted from dishwasher to waiter in three weeks.

"I'm not sure I know," I answered.

"Jesus, Bobo," exclaimed Carter, "don't be so uptight." He said to Amy, "Al Martin—maybe you remember him from last year—got fired and Mrs. Dowling gave his busboy job to Bobo. Then Connie Wells found out she was pregnant and her husband didn't want her to work, and that opened up a waiter's job. Bobo got it, and that's fine with me. I don't mind being his busboy. Jesus, who wants to be a waiter, anyway? People always yelling at you, giving you grief. Jesus. I didn't even think I was going to be here this summer, but I changed my mind. My car needs a new motor. Anyway, Harry Burger taught him the ropes, and you know Harry. He pulls some weight—most of it in silver dollars."

"Mr. Burger?" Amy said. "He's back?"

"Did he ever leave?" Carter said. "He's like your folks. They couldn't live without this place."

Amy smiled patiently, ignoring Carter. She said to me, "I'm glad to meet you, Bobo. Will you keep something warm for me in the morning? Sometimes I sleep late."

Carter laughed.

"I'm sure we'll find something," I said.

"Don't y'all know it," Carter drawled, mocking me.

Later, in The Cave, Carter strolled from the bathroom after his shower. A towel was wrapped around his waist and an amused smile was lodged at a crooked angle in his face. He took a cigarette from the night table and lit it, then he sat on the edge of my lower bunk bed and gazed at me through a veil of smoke that steamed from his nose. I closed the writing pad that I had balanced against my knees.

"Bobo," he said.

"Yeah."

"What color are her eyes?"

"Who?"

"You know damn well who: Amy."

"I don't know."

"Bullshit," he snorted. "You're the artist. Artists see things like that. What color, Bobo?"

"Aqua. Violet. Something like that."

Carter laughed. "Are they the prettiest eyes you've ever seen?"

"I don't know," I mumbled. "They're pretty."

"What color is her hair?"

"Brunette," I said.

"No, Bobo, black-gold," whispered Carter. "You've never seen hair like that, have you?"

"Sure, I have."

There was a pause. Carter drew from his cigarette and nudged a smoke ring from his lips. The ring twirled over my head and scrubbed against the mattress of the top bunk.

"You're lying," Carter said easily. "You've never seen eyes or hair or lips or arms or hands or fingers or legs or feet, or anything else like Amy Lourie. Wait until you catch her in a bathing suit. You're going to faint, Bobo. Arch will have to get you up off your little Rebel ass with a gallon of smelling salts. All you'll want to do is put your face between those babies, and she's got them, Bobo. She makes Elizabeth Taylor look like she's deformed. And you tell me you've seen women like her? Not on the best day of your life, Bobo. You're from Georgia, for Christ's sake. All you've ever seen are field hands."

"So?" I said. "Some of them are pretty."

"Maybe," Carter replied. He leaned close to me. "But I'm talking beautiful," he whispered conspiratorially. "There's a difference."

"She's very pretty," I admitted.

Carter flicked ash on the floor. He bobbed his head in thought. "I can see it now. In a couple of weeks, you'll be trying to get her to strip naked and pose for you."

"My God, Carter."

"If you do, I want to buy whatever you draw," Carter replied. "You can have the whole damn summer's take on my tips."

"Why are you telling me this?" I asked.

"Because, Bobo, you are going to fall in love with her, and I guarantee that. You're going to cream in your jeans over her. When you close your bloodshot eyes at night, you're going to see her looking at you." He sighed and inhaled

106

slowly. "Yeah, yeah, you will. You're going to be staring at those little aqua-violet sunspots and you're going to want to lick them off her face. You're going to be in love, Bobo. I'm an expert at this sort of stuff, and I watched you tonight. I know the signs. I ought to. Last year, I went through the same thing you're going to go through. But I'm a politician at heart, and I know when to cut and run. You're an artist. You'll never have any sense. But I like you, Bobo. Damned if I know why, but I do, and I've got to warn you: she's got a boyfriend back home, in the big city. Adam. That's his name. He'll probably be up before the summer's over. He was last year. Comes from more money than you'll ever see, and I don't care if you take a tour of the U.S. Mint. But you know what the real pisser is? He looks like a goddamn movie star. When I saw him last year, I folded the tent, and Amy and I became friends. I figured if I couldn't have it one way, I'd settle for the next best thing—just being around her."

"So?" I said.

"So, I just wanted you to know. Don't come around whining, saying I didn't warn you. You're going to be surprised at how right I am." He stood and stretched. "What are you doing, anyway?"

I opened the cover of the writing pad. "Writing Carolyn."

Carter laughed and pulled himself up to the bunk above me. He smoked and giggled and talked aloud about Amy Lourie, talked of her beauty, of the sound of her voice, of the way she touched a napkin to her lips in the dining room. And every time he said her name, I could see her face.

"Yep," he sighed, "that's the kind of woman that scares a man to death. Too damn pretty. Take one look at her and you know you don't have an ice cube's chance in hell with her. Not her."

In my letter to Carolyn, I wrote:

> *I'm not sure if I can last through the summer with the boy in the bunk above me. He's my busboy. His name is Carter Fielding and he lives in a little town not far from here called Phoenicia, but he stays here during the summer. He says it's because Mrs. Dowling wants him to stay here, but I have a feeling it's because his parents don't want him around. He talks too much and he seems a little girl-crazy, if you ask me, but he's good in the dining room. He's kept me from making a fool of myself a few times. Maybe he's all right. He's just different from the people I know. By the way, if you see Coy, tell him I said he was right about Yankees being all over the place.*

Above me, a snowflake of cigarette ash drifted down and landed on my writing pad. Carter said, "Yeah, Bobo, that's the kind of woman that scares a man to death."

The next morning, Nora Dowling led Amy and her parents, Joel and Evelyn Lourie, into my dining room and seated them at a circular table in the middle row. She motioned me to the table and introduced me, as she did with all new guests, telling them—or maybe warning them—that I was from the South, from Georgia.

"Oh, yes, we've heard," Joel Lourie said pleasantly, extending his hand to me. "Our Amy tells us you're quite charming, a gentleman. You must be, or she wouldn't be here for breakfast. She does like to sleep late on vacation."

Amy did not blush. She gazed at me confidently from her aqua-violet eyes and smiled. He black-gold hair hugged her face. And I knew Carter had been right in his assertion: Amy Lourie scared me to death.

At dinner, I sat with Sammy and Lila. The stockbroker and the judge's wife were not in the dining room. "Room service," Lila said with an exaggerated sigh when I asked if they had left. The other two couples were there, seated at a table near the lobby door. Both couples were older, both recently retired and traveling together, according to Sammy. "Taking the cut-rate, senior-citizens' tour of America that they've been saving for since God was a baby," he said. "They're worse than the Japanese. They take pictures of everything that moves. Talk about bored. Can you imagine their families when they get home?"

We had liver for dinner, which was only a slight improvement over the chicken for lunch. Lila cut wedges of apples for us and we drank more wine from the stockbroker's cache. Lila confided they had switched to chilled champagne. "Her choice," Lila said. "It's her turn-on. Give her a couple of bottles and she tries to tear his dinger off."

"Jesus, Lila, don't talk like that in front of a guest," Sammy complained.

"What guest? This is Bobo."

"Is he paying?"

"Of course he is."

"Then, goddamn it, he's a guest."

"And guests need some entertainment," Lila shot back. "Which is exactly what we've got in Hump and Bump upstairs."

"You make it sound like a whorehouse," Sammy mumbled.

"Honey, she ain't charging," Lila hissed. "She's giving. I call that life."

"And I call it a joke," Sammy countered.

Lila laughed cynically. "You would," she said triumphantly. She turned to me. "Am I offending you, Bobo?"

"No, of course not," I said.

"Good." She leaned to Sammy. "Then, you can kiss my ass," she whispered.

After dinner, after the running, word-swatting argument about the stockbroker and the judge's

110

wife, I went with Lila and Sammy to the front porch of the Inn and we sat in padded rocking chairs with our wine, and I listened as Sammy talked hopefully of his Woodstock exhibit.

"All I need is a foot in the door," he said. "I'd sure like to sell something." He paused. "Well, something else."

"You've been selling some pieces?" I asked.

"A couple," Sammy said nonchalantly. "A guy down in Jersey—Vinnie Paulsen—bought a couple of things last winter when he was skiing."

I saw Sammy look at Lila. She pulled on her cigarette and stared at the empty ghost-town street. I knew she heard the accusation in Sammy's voice.

"He said he had one of those modern apartments," Sammy continued. "Said what I did would go perfect in it."

"That's good," I told him. "It's a start, a good one."

Sammy smiled painfully. "I guess. I need all the help I can get."

Lila picked up her wineglass and sipped from it. I wondered if she had bartered with Vinnie Paulsen to buy Sammy's curious sculpture, and if she had, was it for Sammy or for her? I knew she loved Sammy, but I also believed she was lonely.

"So, you're going to let me know if you want the *Old Man* for your service?" Sammy said.

"Of course," I replied. "And that's something I should go up and get started on."

Sammy tried to sound cheerful, but there was begging in his voice: "Just let me know." On the porch, in the rocker, Sammy looked tired and desperate.

"Look, why don't we put that to rest now," I suggested. "I think it'd be nice, having the piece. Something that Avrum would have liked. Let's use it."

Sammy shifted in his rocker. He nodded relief. "You're sure, Bobo? I don't want to push it on you."

"You're not doing that. I'm glad to have it." I stood and thanked them for the wine and the company at dinner.

"The company's our pleasure," Lila said. "You need to thank the stockbroker and his playmate for the wine."

"It's a good vintage. I hope they stay for a week," I replied.

Lila laughed and beckoned me to lean to her for an embrace. She whispered, "Thanks, Bobo. By the way, I've got a little surprise for you upstairs."

I knew the surprise when I saw the two empty champagne bottles at the doorway leading to the suite next to my room: by Lila's arrangement, I would be forced to listen to the stockbroker and the judge's wife making love. I knew that, downstairs, Lila was pleased, and I knew that she would greet me at breakfast with a wink.

I took paper and pen from my briefcase to

make notes for Avrum's memorial service, but I knew the notes would be useless. It would be a short, informal ceremony. I would thank those who appeared—if any did—and I would tell them about meeting Avrum, and how our friendship began, and then I would tell them a story I had never told anyone. I did not know what I would say about Sammy's *Old Man*.

I began a letter to Carolyn, but the words were heavy and listless and I wadded the paper and dropped it into the trash can. In 1955, I had written to her daily—at least in the beginning—and she had written to me daily. I wondered if she ever thought of that summer of letters and of the confusion that eventually found its way into my words. The confusion was over Amy Lourie. I could not tell Carolyn about Amy. I had wanted to tell her, yet I could not. And in the years after the summer of letters and confusion, I had often wanted to say to her, "Look, there was a girl in the Catskills. Her name was Amy Lourie . . ." But I knew what Carolyn would say and how she would say it: "Oh, really? And why are you talking about the Stone Age? Did something happen I need to know about?" She would try to say it teasingly, but there would be a touch of arrogance in her voice.

That has been the one constant about Carolyn: she has an answer for every mood, and her answer can be as soft as a kiss or it can be delivered on the tip of a dagger. She permits very little silliness in her life, and maybe that is why our children have always relied on her when they needed protection. She has been—is—the warrior for them, and it did not matter if the foe was a neighbor or an umpire in a Little League baseball game. Carolyn was—is—a lioness in the face of threat against her family, including me. I have heard her bully art dealers who expressed a so-so attitude about my work, even when the work did not impress her.

Still, I think Carolyn suspected something must have happened that summer. In one of her letters, she had asked, *Are you dating anybody?*

I answered with a lie: *No.* I explained there was a group who would sometimes go to a movie or take walks together or meet in Arch's to have milk shakes and to talk. I told her the only date I had had was not a date at all, but a favor for Harry Burger, and he had paid me for the experience. And it was true. It was also the reason that I began to be with Amy.

Harry had been raving about his two teenage nieces, who were to visit him for a weekend. They were beautiful, he assured me. I would be begging to take them to a movie, he predicted, but I would agonize over which to choose. "Angels," Harry sighed with pride. "Like models in great magazines."

Carter knew them. He laughed foolishly and said, "Bobo, you are talking about the two ugliest girls in the state of New York, and, just possibly, the northeastern United States. They were here last year."

114

"Harry said they were beautiful."

"What did you expect him to say? They're his nieces, and he's Jewish."

"What's that got to do with it?"

"Maybe you haven't noticed, Bobo, but the Jews tend to have a little pride. If those girls weren't Harry's nieces, he'd swear they were freaks from a sideshow, but blood, like love, is blind, boy, blind. Harry thinks he's got Jane Russell and Betty Grable on their way here."

"Harry wants me to take them out," I told him. "He said to find somebody to go with me and he'd pick up the tab."

"And you're asking me?" Carter said suspiciously.

"No," I replied sarcastically. "I thought I'd ask Ben Benton."

"Ben would slit your throat," Carter said. He pondered a moment. "All right, I'll do it, but this is what you've got to tell Harry: twenty bucks apiece, plus expenses."

"I can't do that," I protested. "Not after all he's done for me."

Carter shook his head and laughed cynically. "Believe me, he's been setting you up for this little adventure since day one. That ten bucks he gave you for washing dishes, it was just a down payment. All that waiter training was for one thing: his nieces. Remember, Bobo, I've seen them. Twenty bucks. That's the deal, or find somebody else—if you think you can. I'm telling you, last year every eligible male in a twenty-mile radius went into hiding the weekend they were here. Twenty bucks apiece. All you've got to do is say it to him like you're kidding him. He'll pick up on it. You don't know Harry. He'll go for a bargain like a trout after one of Arch's flies, and that, my friend, is a bargain. Trust me."

Carter was right, as usual. The next day I said to Harry, "We need to talk about this date with your nieces."

"What's to talk?" Harry said irritably. "I offer you a night out with beautiful women and you want I should talk about it?"

"I figure twenty bucks each for me and Carter, plus expenses," I said, grinning.

Harry did his dramatic sigh, the one where he rolled his head and his eyes in exasperation. *"Ach du lieber Gott,"* he muttered. He wagged his cigar like a swagger stick. "You're a thief, Bobo Murphy, an Irish *no-goodnik*, but, all right, all right. If I didn't like you so much, I'd find somebody else for two such beauties."

Harry gave me the money up front. He said it was because he was an honorable man. Carter said it was because he didn't want me to renege on the arrangement.

Carter, again, was right.

Harry Burger's nieces were beyond ugly. They were tragic. Thin, pinched faces, no chins, beaver teeth, tiny eyes behind thick eyeglasses. Coy Helms would have said of them, "You'd have to hang meat around their neck to get a dog to play with them."

They were waiting with Harry on the porch of the Inn, having arrived an hour earlier, after dinner.

"Take your pick," Carter mumbled as we approached him.

"I'll take Harry," I whispered.

Carter giggled. "Damn, Bobo, you just did a funny."

"So, boys, you're in good spirits, I see," Harry called cheerfully.

"Great," Carter said.

"Good, good," Harry chirped. He beamed a smile of joy.

We reached the porch.

"Boys, I want for you to meet Charlotte and Erin," Harry said. He indicated the girls. Then: "Girls, this is the Georgia boy I've been telling you about—Bobo Murphy. He didn't know a *schnitzel* from a *schnook* when he met me. Now, he's a waiter." He looked at Carter." And Carter you know already. He's the one who dropped the fruit cup down your back last year, Erin."

The girls smiled.

I thought: Oh, my God.

"Hi," Carter said brightly. "You still mad at me, Erin?"

Erin tilted her head to Carter, like a long-necked bird inspecting an insect. She shook her head timidly.

"Hi," I said weakly.

"Well, boys, what's it to be?" Harry said in a loud voice. "A movie? A little stroll under the moon, maybe? Yes? Why don't you make the start down at Arch's? I told him you'd be there, to put whatever you wanted on my bill."

"Uh, I—I think we'd better get on to the movie," I said.

"So, what's the hurry?" Harry replied in a firm voice. "No, no, Bobo. The girls love Arch's. There, first."

"Suits me," Carter said flippantly. "Come on, Erin, why don't you go with me? I owe you."

"Sure," Erin said in a small voice. She stepped off the porch to stand with Carter.

"And that leaves lovely Charlotte with Bobo," Harry said proudly. He pushed at his niece. She moved hesitantly toward me.

"Have fun," Harry crowed. He wiggled his finger at her. "No hanky-panky, boys."

Carter coughed down a laugh.

"No, sir," I promised emphatically.

We began the long, tortuous walk to Arch's.

I saw Avrum on his bench. His head was tilted back and his eyes were closed and he was not aware of us. I wondered if he was listening to the ghost-voice of Amelita Galli-Curci, or if he was faking a nap.

Ben Benton was waiting to turn into the side yard of the Inn for his garbage pickup. He looked at me in astonishment, then shouted from the window, "Hey, Bobo, finally found you a woman, did you?" He ducked his head in laughter.

Mrs. Mendelson, slow-stepping up the sidewalk, paused and smiled. *"Gut, gut,"* she squeaked.

We walked into Arch's. It was early and only a few people were there. One of them was Amy. She was sitting alone in a back booth, writing a letter.

Carter called to her, "Hey, Amy."

She looked up, first to Carter, then to me. She saw the girls and a shudder of surprise touched on her face. She tried to smile, but the smile faded quickly. She got up and walked past us and out of Arch's. She did not speak.

"Look, girls, why don't you grab that booth back there?" Carter said. "We'll get some Cokes and be right there with you."

The girls dipped their heads in agreement and walked away. Carter whispered, "I think you just screwed up, Bobo."

"What?"

"With Amy. She was pissed. I could tell."

"Why?"

"I was wrong, Bobo. I hate to say it, but I was," Carter sighed. "She's got a thing for you."

"Me?"

We were at the counter of the soda fountain. Carter said to Jeannie Ellis, who was Arch's daughter and occasional counter girl, "Four Cokes, Jeannie, and a pack of Marlboros. Put it on Harry Burger's bill."

"Sure," Jeannie replied. "He was in earlier. Said to give you whatever you wanted."

"Make it a carton of Marlboros," Carter said,

"but, Jeannie, do me a favor: make it show up as sandwiches or something."

Jeannie smiled. "Sure." She reached for the glasses on a rack behind her.

"What do you mean, she has a thing for me?" I said to Carter.

Carter looked at me sadly. "You stupid, dumb redneck hick. The most beautiful woman you'll ever see is dragging around like she's got lead in her ass because of you, and you're out with Miss Ugly of Nineteen Fifty-five."

"It was your idea, not mine," I reminded him.

"So, I was wrong again," Carter said. "Sue me. Jesus, Bobo, it's been a year since I saw them. I thought they might improve." He took the carton of cigarettes from Jeannie and tucked them under his arm and then he picked up two of the Cokes. "Come on, let's get this over with."

It was a night I remember only in pain. In a private whisper as we were getting into his car to drive to Margaretville, Carter offered me his twenty dollars to kiss Charlotte—fifty if I would touch her breasts. I told him. "If there's any kissing going on, you can do it, and you know where you can start." He laughed maniacally.

We attended a movie in Margaretville, then drove to the base of the ski lift at Belleayre Mountain and walked in the cool air under a full moon that was like a lamp dimmed for sleeping. Carter told absurd stories about me—that Harry had almost persuaded me to convert to Judaism, that I was a great-grandson of a Confederate general who had fought at Gettysburg and lost his leg, and that my ambition in life was to be a country music star like the great Little Jimmy Dickens. He begged me to sing for them. I refused. "He's shy," Carter explained to the girls. "He knows nobody can understand him, so he doesn't say much." He looked at me and winked and he added, "You'd think his mind was somewhere else, wouldn't you?"

Carter knew.

I was thinking of Amy Lourie.

Amy did not appear for breakfast the following morning. Her parents said she had not slept well. I asked if I could prepare a plate for them to take to her, some muffins or cheese or fruit. "If she wants something, she'll come down," Evelyn Lourie said gently. "But thank you for offering, Bobo." I knew she was watching me carefully. When I served Harry and Charlotte and Erin, suffering Harry's jesting about his nieces being in love with me, I could again sense Evelyn Lourie's eyes, which were as beautiful as Amy's.

At midmorning, I looked from the back window of the kitchen and saw Amy. She was walking alone on the mountain behind the Inn, climbing toward a birch tree where I would often go at night to be alone. I had found the birch on advice from Avrum not long after meeting him. He had said, "Look up to the hill and find you a place, and go to it. Make it yours. Get a tree. A tree is best." I had selected the birch because

121

I could look down on the village and up to the stars. For some reason, it was not so lonely to be there, at the birch, between the village and the stars.

I told Carter, "I need to get away for a few minutes. Can you cover for me?"

"Sure," Carter said. He glanced around the kitchen. Nora Dowling was not there. "I saw her, too," he added. "I don't blame you."

Amy was at the birch, under the canopy of its limbs. I knew she had seen me approaching, but she looked away, as though something in the valley, something far off, had captivated her.

I said, "Hi."

She turned to me. Her face was calm, controlled. "Hello."

"You missed breakfast," I said.

"I wasn't hungry."

I waited for her to say something else, but she did not.

"I like this tree," I told her. "Sometimes at night I come up here and look at the stars."

"I know," she said.

I was surprised. "You do? How?"

"I've watched you."

"You have?"

She said nothing. She sat on the soft grass beside the tree.

"Mind if I sit with you a couple of minutes?" I asked.

"It's your tree," she said.

I sat near her, but not near enough to touch. "It's pretty up here," I said.

"Yes, it is."

"Are you—well, mad at me, or something?" I asked.

"No. Why should I be?"

"I don't know. You act like it. I thought you were mad last night, in Arch's."

She moved her head and the wind caught the thick curl of her black-gold hair and made it flutter across her shoulder.

"How was your date?" she said after a moment.

"Date?" I said. "That wasn't a date. We were with Mr. Burger's nieces. You know that. He wanted us to take them to a movie."

"I call that a date," she said firmly.

"Well, I don't," I countered. "I'd consider it a job. He paid us."

"He did what?"

"He paid us."

"Do you know what that makes you?"

"No. What?"

"A gigolo," she said.

"I don't know what that is," I confessed. "Is it a German word?"

"No, it's not. It's English. A gigolo is someone who gets paid to—to escort women," she explained.

"Then I guess I am one," I conceded.

Amy ducked her head. The sun coated her hair. Her lips puffed into a smile. She said softly,

"Bobo, it's not a compliment to be a gigolo, so don't tell anyone you are."

"I didn't know what it was," I said. "First time I've ever heard the word."

She looked at me. The brightness was back in her eyes. She asked, "Are you really an artist?"

"Did Carter tell you that?" I replied.

"He said you were good. Really good, I mean."

"I draw some. It's something to do."

"Will you draw a picture of me?" she asked.

I wondered if Carter, in his disregard for anyone's privacy, had found the pictures I had been drawing of Amy—quick sketches penciled in moments of solitude and hidden away among my things. I wondered if he had told her about them.

"Will you?" she repeated.

"I'll try," I said. "But I'm not very good at faces. Not from memory."

"I'll pose for you," she offered.

I thought of Carter, of the torment that Carter would heap on me. "I don't think that would be a good idea."

"What about a photograph?" she asked. "Would that help?"

I shrugged uncomfortably. "I guess."

"I'll get one for you. It's new, a school picture."

"Okay," I said, "but give it to me at Arch's."

Amy leaned toward me, almost close enough to touch. "You don't want my parents to know, do you?"

I looked away, to the Inn. I could see the old

124

people moving about on the lawn, ambling to tables with umbrellas cupped open against the sun. They would sit and play their games of cards until lunch.

"Do you?" Amy said again.

"It doesn't matter to me," I told her.

"They think you like me, you know," Amy said quietly.

"Well, I—"

"They also think I like you," she added.

I did not know what to say to her. I wanted to reach and touch her hand, to feel her hand living in my hand. I could hear the easy rhythm of her breathing.

"I do," she said gently.

I looked at her. I could feel her mysteriously entering me, slipping past caution. I thought she could also feel it. She smiled at me.

"Would you take me to a movie if my father paid you?"

I could feel my heart rushing. "I wouldn't do that. I'll take you, but not for money."

"I'm glad," she said. There was a pause. "I feel better. Thank you."

In the room next to me, the stockbroker and the judge's wife were making love. She was begging, in a voice muted by the wall that separated us, "Please, please . . . Now, now . . . Oh, yes. Yes, yes yes." There was a sudden, furious slapping of the headboard against the wall. The judge's wife cried once. I could hear her inhale against the pouring from her body. The sudden, furious slapping of the headboard stopped.

I wondered if somewhere, nearby, Lila was smiling and breathing deeply, trying to catch the scent of sex.

7

I slept, finally, sensing that I was somehow more exhausted than the stockbroker and the judge's wife. I believed I would dream of them, see them as a voyeur watching erotic movies in a dark room. I would peer at them as they caressed and moved over one another like powerful animals at sex play. I would see the oils of their skin shining in candlelight. I would watch their mouths at feast.

I did not dream of them. I dreamed, instead, of Amy Lourie. And in the way of dreams—surreal moments so startlingly clear you know they have happened or will happen or should happen—I was sitting with her in the Galli-Curci Theater in Margaretville and her hand was in my hand, milking my fingers with her fingers. It was two days after being with her at the birch tree on the mountain.

Carter had arranged it in the bold manner that was his personality. A group of us were going to the movies on Tuesday night, he had said to Amy in the presence of her parents as we served lunch. Would she like to go?

"Why don't you?" urged Joel Lourie. "Get away from the old people for a night."

"And who would be going?" Evelyn Lourie asked quietly.

"Just a group," Carter replied. He glanced at me as I served coffee. "Me, two or three others who work at some of the other places around here. Bobo, I think. Are you still going, Bobo?"

"I don't know," I said. "Maybe."

"We do it all the time," Carter added casually and pleasantly. "We never know who's going. Whoever shows up at Arch's."

"Oh," Evelyn Lourie said. She smiled at me. Her eyes lingered, questioning.

"I'd love to," Amy said cheerfully. She did not look at me, but she knew what Carter was doing.

That night, in The Cave, Carter leaned over from his top bunk and said, "I've been thinking about it, Bobo. You owe me for tomorrow night."

"I know. And I'm sure you won't let me forget it," I replied.

"No, you don't know. Not yet," Carter said. "I plan to slit my wrists in front of both of you. You'll be sorry when I'm dead." He leaned back on his bed. I saw a cloud of smoke from his Marlboro rolling toward the ceiling.

"Carter?"

"Yeah."

"Do you think her mother believed it?"

"Believed what?"

"That story you fed her," I said.

"Of course not. She's a mother," Carter answered.

★ ★ ★

I have never remembered the movie we saw, and even in my dream I knew nothing about it. We were at the theater, holding hands, and then we were walking at the base of the Belleayre ski lift, where we had been with Harry Burger's nieces—Amy with me and a girl named Rene Wallace with Carter. Rene worked as a chambermaid at the Greenleaf Lodge. She and Carter had been dating since the first week of the summer season.

I did not know what happened to Carter and Rene. We were all walking together, and suddenly, they were no longer with us, and I said to Amy, "Maybe I should find them."

"They're all right," she said. "They just want some time alone. Are you afraid of being with me?"

"Of course not. I just wondered—"

"Bobo, it's all right," she insisted softly.

We walked past the gate leading to the ski lift. There was a sharp chill in the air, like the late-autumn nights in Georgia. I thought I heard the call of an owl somewhere from below us. Far off, I could see the feathered rim of the mountains and the murky purple of the horizon under the moon. We passed a hemlock and Amy took my hand and pulled me into its shadows. She said, "I'm cold. Will you hold me for a minute?"

She moved to me and I embraced her. She curled her arms around my waist and rested her face on my chest. I could smell the delicate scent of flowers in her blackgold hair. Her breasts were soft against me.

"This is nice," she whispered. "You're warm."

"You, too," I said.

After a moment, she asked, "Do you have a girlfriend back home?"

I knew it was a test. Carter had told Amy about Carolyn, as he had told me about Adam. Carter loved the entanglements of romance.

"There's a girl I dated when we were in school," I answered.

"What's her name?"

"Carolyn."

"Oh. Do you write to her?"

"Some. Yes, some."

"You must get lonely, being so far away from home."

"A little," I confessed. I added, "It's not as bad as it was."

"Do you think I would like your home?"

"I doubt it. It's just a farm."

"I've never been to a farm," she said. "Not a real one."

"What about you? Do you have a boyfriend?"

She lifted her face to me. "I don't know," she replied.

I tried to be flippant, as I thought Carter would be. "Did you forget?"

A tiny smile, almost a shadow, moved on her lips. "We had a fight before I left."

"Why?"

"He's spoiled. He thinks he can get anything he wants simply because he has money."

"I don't know anybody that rich," I told her.

The smile moved again, off her lips, into her face. "It's nothing special, Bobo. It's just money."

I did not speak and she again nuzzled her face against my chest. "He wouldn't do this," she said softly.

"Do what?"

"Hold me to keep me warm. He'd want to go to the car and turn on the heater. He's not a warm person."

"He'd miss a great view," I mumbled.

I felt her mouth touch my shirt. "Of what?" she asked lightly.

"Well, a lot of things," I replied. "The mountains."

She raised her face and her hand moved from my waist to my neck and she pulled me gently to her and kissed me. I could feel the heat of her tongue tipping my lips and I turned my face away.

"Carter said I would have to kiss you first," she whispered. "He said you would be afraid. Are you? Are you afraid, Bobo? Did I scare you?"

I shook my head.

"Maybe you're not," she said, "but I think I am. I think I scared me."

"Don't be," I begged. "Please—"

She kissed me again, her tongue finding my mouth. Her body trembled. She pulled back and burrowed her face against me. I could feel her heart racing.

"Do you want to date me, Bobo?"

I nodded.

"It won't be easy," she said.

"I know," I replied.

"There'll be so many things against us."

"What things?"

She did not answer. She stood close, holding me. Then she said, "I have something for you."

"What?"

"It's in the car, in my purse."

"Your picture?"

She nodded. "I hope you like it."

"Can I keep it?" I asked.

Her head moved against my shoulder.

"I mean, after you leave?"

Her head moved again.

Joel and Evelyn Lourie were sitting on the front porch of the Inn with Nora Dowling when we returned. I walked with Amy across the lawn to them.

"Well, here they are now," Nora said in a relieved voice. "We were beginning to worry."

"We got a Coke in Margaretville and then Carter had to drive a couple of the other kids to the Greenleaf," Amy lied cheerfully.

"Did you have a good time?" her father asked.

"It was great," Amy said. She turned to me. "Thanks for letting me tag along, Bobo."

I was nervous and I knew it was obvious. I said, "Sure. Anytime."

Joel Lourie reached for his wallet. "Well, let me pay for the tickets," he said in a kind voice.

"No, sir," I replied too quickly. "I couldn't do that."

"But I should," he said.

"No, sir, I really couldn't accept that." I glanced at Amy. She was biting a giggle.

"Put the money away, Joel," Nora said. She looked at me tenderly. "He's a Southerner. They're gentlemen. I think, next year, I'll have all Southerners working for me."

Joel Lourie laughed easily. He slipped his wallet back into his pocket. "I'm sorry," he said to me. "I didn't mean any offense."

"There wasn't any," I replied. I again glanced at Amy. "See you in the morning."

"Good night, Bobo," Amy said.

I heard Nora Dowling say as I walked away, "Such a nice boy. So nice."

Carter was waiting for me outside The Cave. He was smoking a cigarette and watching the smoke curl in blue ribbons against the haze of the sky. "Come on," he ordered. "Let's go for a little walk."

I followed him across the street and beside the annex to the swimming pool. We sat in lounge chairs. Carter was in a languid mood and he did not speak until he had finished his cigarette and crushed it against the ground.

"Hell of a night, wasn't it?" he said, leaning his weight against the back of the chair and gazing into the sky.

"Yeah, it was nice," I agreed.

He rolled his head to look at me. "So, tell me: how did you do?"

"What do you mean?"

"I mean, what happened? Jesus, I gave you enough time, didn't I? I almost froze my balls off."

"Nothing happened," I said. "What happened to you?"

"Got my hand on it," Carter chortled. "God, Bobo, it was warm." He paused and whistled softly and twirled his lucky hand in the air above his head. "And wet. I think I'm in love, Bobo."

"I'm glad," I told him. "Look, it's late."

An evil grin crawled into his face. "Yeah, I forgot. You've still got a letter to write, haven't you?"

"What letter?" I demanded.

"To Carolyn."

"Come on, Carter, Don't bring that up."

"A joke, Bobo. Just a joke," Carter said. "Don't be so damned tense. Tell me what happened with the most beautiful woman you'll ever see."

"We walked, we talked," I said.

"That's it?"

"I hugged her."

"Did you kiss her?"

"Yes," I said after a pause.

134

"You son of a bitch. I hope your tongue falls out," Carter sighed. "Was it good?"

I smiled. "It was nice."

"Nice?"

"Nice," I repeated.

"That's it? Nice? You kiss that woman and you call it nice? Bullshit," he snorted. "Next thing you know, I'll be renting a tux and standing up with you before your preacher brother and some pissed-off rabbi, and you'll be seven months away from being a daddy."

"Don't start it, Carter," I said.

"Okay, okay," he mumbled. "Joke, Bobo. Joke." He laced his fingers in his lap and crossed his legs at his ankles, a pose imitating the old people who used the lounges in the heat of the day. "But we need to talk about something," he added after a moment.

"And what's that?"

"About Amy."

"What about her?"

"I haven't said anything about it, because I didn't think I'd have to, but sometimes, Bobo, you're such a goddamn hick you miss things."

"And what have I missed?" I asked.

Carter again turned his head to me. "That little remark about your brother and the rabbi. I think you missed it."

"What about it?"

"Bobo, Amy's Jewish."

His voice was uncharacteristically deliberate and serious, and it surprised and angered me.

"I know she is," I told him.

He sat up on the side of the lounge, facing me. He rested his elbows on his knees and let his hands dangle between his legs. "Do you know why I want to be a politician?" he asked.

"No, I don't."

"Part of it is because my daddy's a lawyer and I want to take it one step more up the ladder," he answered. "But the real reason is because I think I can read people. It's a little like you when you draw somebody. You see them from the outside, but I see them from the inside, see who they are. I think people who can do that should be politicians or priests, one of the two. I like politics better than pulpits."

"What does all of that mean?" I asked.

"With Amy, it means you know she's Jewish, but you don't know what being Jewish means. Not up here," he advised quietly. "And I'll bet you don't even know what it means back in Georgia. You asked me if I thought her mother believed the story about all of us going to the movies, and I told you she didn't. I meant that. Why do you think her mother's so nervous around you? She knows what's going on, Bobo. I don't know how she knows, but she does, believe me. Maybe Amy told her. But after tonight, she'll be watching you like an eagle."

Carter fumbled for another cigarette and lit it. He fell back into the lounge chair and flipped small smoke rings into the night air with his tongue. He said pleasantly, "Does it get this cold at night in Georgia?"

"Not in the summer."

"Then I think I'll move down there," he mumbled. "I hate freezing my ass off."

"Down there, you sweat it off," I told him. Then I asked, "Carter, what does it mean to you—Amy being Jewish?"

"What it means, Bobo, is that nothing is ever going to happen between the two of you. Nothing more than tonight. Oh, you may diddle with her, and love it, but that's as far as it goes. Some things just don't happen. New York Jew and Georgia redneck, that's one of those things. Not in your lifetime."

I thought of Amy's warning: "There'll be so many things against us."

In the dream, I saw Carolyn sitting in the lounge chair where Carter had sat. She had an irritated expression on her face. She looked at me. "You lied to me. How could you lie to me?" she said.

I awoke suddenly with Carolyn's words in the room with me.

And with Lila.

She was sitting on the edge of my bed, lightly rubbing my arm.

I started to speak, but Lila touched her hand to my mouth.

"Keep it quiet," she whispered. She motioned

with her head toward the wall separating my room from the room occupied by the stockbroker and the judge's wife.

"What time is it?" I asked.

"One-thirty, maybe two," she said.

"What are you doing here?"

She smiled easily. "I came to tuck you in. It's a new service for favorite guests."

"Come on, Lila, don't do this."

"I said *tuck*, Bobo. I'm not doing anything. Just sitting."

The light from the window flowed into my room like a dull sunrise. Lila's face and body were silhouetted against it.

"Where's Sammy?" I asked.

"Don't you know? He's in his shop."

"You shouldn't be here," I told her.

"Don't make so much of it," she replied. "I came up to get the bottles and dinner tray from next door, and I thought I'd check on you. I was just watching you sleep. Were you dreaming?"

"I guess," I said.

"I thought so. Must have been a good one. You were smiling."

"I don't remember it, I had some trouble getting to sleep. The next-door entertainment committee gets a little rowdy."

Lila smiled with delight. "They're something, aren't they?Usually when they're here, I sneak into this room and listen. I get a kick out of screamers, and she's a screamer."

She slipped from the bed and moved carefully, silently, to the window and looked out.

"I really think you should leave," I said.

"I will in a minute," she replied softly. She pulled open the curtain with her fingers. "He's still working. I can see his shadow on the street when he moves around. He'll be there for another hour, at least." She dropped the curtain and looked back at me. "You do know he does that when you're here, don't you, Bobo? I don't think he could stand it if he didn't think you were impressed with him."

"I am," I told her. "He has a great passion."

"But no talent," she whispered. She moved back to me.

"The passion matters," I said.

Her look told me that I had missed something in their relationship. "Of course, it does," she said. "That's why I stay with him. My God, Bobo, I divorced a Wall Street lawyer to marry Sammy. He was the most handsome son of a bitch you ever saw. He had a face that looked like it had been peeled off the cover of a fashion issue of *Esquire*. We drank champagne that would make that stuff the judge's wife guzzles taste like swill. I had more money hidden in a Tampax box in my bathroom than Sammy and I have in the bank. But, do you know the truth, Bobo? I'd rather live a lifetime with Sammy, even when he's being a shit, than twenty minutes with my ex-husband."

"I'm sorry," I told her. "I didn't mean—"

Her raised hand interrupted me. "Do you know the Mountainside Playhouse?"

I shook my head.

"It's a kind of honky-tonk just off the highway near Shandaken. Sammy likes going there. Different kinds of bands. Some country, some rock, some jazz. And they've all got one thing in common: none of them are good enough to make it. They play their ass off, Bobo. I mean, when they get onstage, they work harder than Michael Jackson, and when they finish, everybody sits around and tells them it's a goddamn pity they're not on tour in chartered jets. Sammy's always in the middle of it, always leading the cheers. Do you know why?"

I did know. It was the story of Sammy's life, his own dream being exercised by others. Still, I lied to Lila: "No."

"Birds of a feather," she said.

"Look, I don't mean to—"

Again, Lila raised her hand to interrupt. "It's all right. I know what you think. You think that if Sammy's so passionate, what am I complaining about? You think I must be a nymphomaniac to be with a passionate man and still carry on about getting laid. There's all kinds of passion, Bobo. Sammy's like you. His passion is in his soul, and, honestly, sometimes I miss the kind that's in the sheets, but I'd rather have the soul." She smiled at me sadly. "I'll bet Carolyn and I are a lot alike in many ways, putting up with the two of you."

140

I had never thought of Carolyn and Lila being at all alike.

"I don't know," I said. "Maybe you're right."

She gazed at me for a moment, then she said, "No, I just said that. I don't believe it's true. You and Sammy would have to be alike to make it true, and you're not—except for your souls. He wants to be what you are, but he won't be. Ever. He's just not good enough, but he tries, Bobo. Oh, my God, he tries." She inhaled and turned to look at the window, then she turned back to me. "I want to ask a favor."

"Ask," I said.

"Sammy wants to give you the piece you're going to use for your friend's service. That's what he's doing now. Getting it ready for you, putting it on another base."

"He wants to give it to me?"

"Yes." She paused, closed her eyes slowly, like swallowing something painful, then she opened them again. "I want you to accept it. Please. I don't care if you dump it on the road back to Kingston, but take it."

"Of course I will. Happily."

She came to me and leaned and kissed me softly on the lips, a brush kiss. "Thank you," she whispered. "It's funny, isn't it, Bobo? We both have loved insane people in Pine Hill." She touched my face with her fingers. "Sammy told me what he said to you about the two of us making love, and how he'd understand."

"He was just talking."

"I know. But I think about it sometimes."

"I take that as a compliment," I said.

"It is. Good night, Bobo. I love you."

"And I love you, Lila."

I did not dream again, but I did not sleep well enough for dreams. I lay awake and remembered, and perhaps that is the same as dreaming. I think it is.

I have always had such nights when returning to the Catskills. It is as though I am again seventeen and in awe of all that I see and experience. Each moment is a visit with the ghost of who I used to be, and with the ghosts of the people I knew. When Lila speaks of Pine Hill as a ghost town, she means it is an empty place, a once-crowded village that has been bypassed by the highway that used to run through it. To me, it is a ghost town because ghosts are in it. I see them. They are walking in their toddling steps on the sidewalks and they are sitting in the fold-out lounge chairs beside the neglected ruin of the swimming pool. They ask me for water— *"Wasser! Wasser!"*—in the dining room of the Inn when I am having breakfast or lunch or dinner with Sammy and Lila. They push hurriedly through the swinging doors leading into the kitchen, balancing trays of dishes like circus performers. They are red-faced at the stoves and ovens, and the kerchiefs tied around their necks are stained with perspiration. When I am in Dan's Coffee and Pastry Shop, sitting at the table where

142

my bed used to be, I can smell the Marlboros that Carter used to smoke in the bunk above me. I can stand on the sidewalk in front of Arch's, where Sammy now smashes stone in the name of art, and see apparitions floating in and out of the store.

Privately, secretly, I want to think these ghosts wait for me to return to the Catskills—that, somehow, I am a medium for them. When I am in Pine Hill, they go about happily, being what, and who, they were. They do this for me, I believe, because they know I am aware of them.

Once I asked a friend, a psychologist, about such sensations. We were at a cocktail party and perhaps he was only trying to be clever, but what he said satisfied me: "It's reenactment. Your mind is simply forcing you to relive moments that were memorable, for one reason or another."

I started to tell him about Avrum's theory of the one grand, undeniable moment of change, but I did not. The cocktail party was too lively. No one was thinking about change: they were simply trying to keep up.

It didn't matter. Reenactment was the word I needed to know, because it was the correct word.

It has happened to me many times.

There is a place, a precise spot, on the sidewalk in front of Arch's where a young man who lived on the mountains pulled a switchblade knife against me. We had been kidding, or so I thought, about the Civil War, about the Yanks and the Rebs, and I had made some remark about the

South rising again. I do not remember what I said, but it infuriated him. His hand shot into his pocket and out again and I heard the snap of a steel blade locking. He growled, "You son of a bitch," and he drew back his arm. Ben Benton was there. He grabbed me by the shirt and flung me aside and then he stepped in front of the young man and crossed his arms and, in a blur, slapped his hands at his waist. I heard a fluttering of leather pulled through cloth—it was the sound of a covey of birds rising on frightened wings— and when Ben extended his arms, he was holding his belt with the bear buckle. He twirled it near the man's face. "You want to die?" he hissed. The man turned pale. He folded the knife and walked away.

Whenever I am at that place, on that precise spot, I see the reenactment of Ben Benton, and I know he is there, not in the coffin marked by the headstone bearing his name.

There are many such places, like stage settings for the theatrics of memory.

In 1955, there was a pay telephone booth outside Arch's. The first week that I worked as a waiter, with only a few guests, I earned exactly one hundred dollars. I got change from Arch and went to the pay telephone and called home and my father answered the call. "What's wrong?" he demanded. "Nothing," I told him. "I'm just celebrating. I made a hundred dollars this week." There was a pause, a heavy, long-distance pause, and then my father said, "Am I paying for this call, or are you?" I said, "I'm paying for it, Daddy. I wouldn't charge you for my celebration." There was another pause, heavier, more distant, and my father said in a blunt voice, "Well, you don't have a hundred dollars anymore, do you?" And he hung up. It took me a long time to understand, but my father had taught me an important lesson: he had made me angry and determined to prove myself. My father knew I was lonely and homesick. He knew he had to challenge me.

When I am at the place where the pay telephone used to be, I remember my father. And I miss him. He was never in the Catskills, but he, too, is a ghost for me.

So many places, so many little stage settings of memory.

Avrum's bench. Sitting there with him, listening to him, amazed at what he knew.

The mountain birch tree, where Amy and I began to meet at night.

The swimming pool, where Carter and I would go to talk when either of us wanted to say something private.

The theaters in Margaretville and Fleischmanns.

The base of Belleayre ski lift.

Woodstock. Big Indian. Shandaken.

In every place, there is something to remember.

And Amy Lourie is everywhere. Everywhere.

I have never been able to tell Carolyn about the ghosts. It is the reason I never wanted her

8

Carter Fielding is an attorney, with offices in Phoenicia. He has been twice married and twice divorced, and the political career he wanted as a busboy at the Pine Hill Inn has been sacrificed to what he refers to as "hardearned scandal."

He is philosophic about it: "Damn it to hell, Bobo, I love love and I wouldn't give it up to spend the rest of my days in the White House, or to be crowned king of England."

Over the years, while visiting in the Catskills, we have always had dinner, and he has always told whichever companion he was with at the time about our summer of working together.

"There was this girl," he would begin.

And I would have to suffer the story of Amy Lourie—not as I knew it, but as Carter had elected to remember it.

In Carter's version, he was heroic. Depending on his consumption of alcohol, he had either prevented me from committing suicide or had persuaded me that a love relationship and possible marriage to a Jewish girl in the fifties— "the tight-assed fifties," as he called them— would have been a disaster.

"She was beautiful," Carter would say. "God, she was that."

I have never corrected Carter, even when his story was absurd, as it was the night he declared to a striking blonde named Billie that he had watched as I made love to Amy under the hemlock at the base of Belleayre ski lift.

"I didn't know you were there," I said. "That embarrasses me."

He had been expecting my call, Carter told me, after reading about Avrum's death.

"I came in yesterday, but things got crowded," I said.

"No sweat; I knew you'd call," he replied. Then: "I thought he was going to outlive God."

"He gave it a try," I said.

"Well, sorry about it, Bobo. I know you were fond of him. So was I, even if I thought he needed to sleep in a straitjacket. We're going to have dinner while you're here, aren't we? You're not on a pop-in, pop-out schedule, I hope."

"No, I'll be staying a week at least. And dinner's at your convenience, but, actually, I need to do some business with you."

"You mean the kind of business where somebody pays somebody else a ton of money?"

"If you're that kind of lawyer, and I don't know one who's not."

He laughed. "What do you need, Bobo?"

"I've got to settle Avrum's affairs."

"Get you ass down here. I specialize in that."

"I thought you were a real estate lawyer."

"That, too. When can you get here?"

148

"After lunch, say around one."

"Good. I've got an opening."

"Business that bad, Carter?"

"Bobo, I'm a lawyer," he answered in his mock Southern accent. "Business ain't never that bad."

I spent the morning reviewing Avrum's papers and interpreted them as he had written in his note: everything had been willed to me, with the instruction that I immediately dispose of it. To others, it would confirm that Avrum was, indeed, insane; I knew that he simply did not want to make decisions, for some of them would have been bitter to him. Better to let someone else do it. To Avrum, dead was dead. Only the mind and the imagination could keep someone alive, as he had kept Amelita Galli-Curci's voice alive in the Catskills.

Sol Walkman called midmorning to tell me Avrum's room had been cleaned and that a mood of contrition was evident among the Home's residents.

"One of them came to see me this morning," he said. "He told me he knew about some personal items that had been taken from Avrum's room, and he gave me some names."

I asked if he had checked the report.

"He was right," Sol answered. "I knew he was, but they all had the same story: whatever they had, Mr. Feldman had given them as gifts."

"That's imaginative," I said.

149

"They're afraid of what may happen to them," Sol told me.

"It doesn't matter," I said. "Let them keep whatever they've got. In a way, I think Avrum would have admired their spunk."

I could hear relief in Sol's voice. "It'll be easier that way." He paused. "Did you watch television last night?"

"No, I didn't. Why?"

"You should have. You came across very well."

"They used some of the interview?" I asked.

"Mostly, that's what it was. We've had a couple of calls about the memorial service."

"From?" I said.

"I don't really know." Sol answered. "The desk took them. Media, I suppose. They were just confirming time and place of the service."

"I hope they won't be disappointed," I replied. "By the way, you're going to have a delivery from Sammy Merritt. It's a piece of sculpture that he wanted to dedicate to Avrum."

"Really?" I knew by Sol's voice that he had seen Sammy's work.

"Let's just say it's one of those things I had to do, and keep it between us," I told him.

"I understand," Sol said.

Carter is a man who has aged gracefully, even with the abuse he imposed on his body in his younger years. His hair is graying, but still thick, and he is twenty pounds heavier, but it is muscle from tennis and jogging. He gave up smoking many years ago, yet he swears he longs for a cigarette every moment he is awake. A minor heart attack in his early forties remains a frightening memory, however. His vice now is good wine and single-malt whiskey. He is convinced good wine and single-malt whiskey keep his blood thinned.

The office that Carter occupies—his father's old law office—is too stately and too pretentious for Phoenicia. Its walls are of thick paneling, the carpets are lush and deep, expensive and large furnishings are placed with a decorator's touch, the artwork is splashy, and Carter knows I find it offensive. It is the office of a corporate executive or of a well-supported politician, and perhaps that is why Carter is comfortable in it. If he cannot be the politician, he can live like one. Still, I have always suspected that Carter's office is a liability, that he has lost business because it has the appearance of richness and, therefore, exorbitant fees. The truth is, his first wife was wealthy and it was she who decorated the office. She willingly surrendered its contents to Carter in the divorce after he discovered the affair she was having with one of his former partners.

"Bobo, they used to ball on top of my goddamn desk," he once declared to me. "I mean, right on top of it. I wondered why she bought one that was so goddamn big you needed an intercom to talk across it. But what goes around comes around. She later caught the son of a bitch humping her own sister. I had him disbarred."

Carter was waiting for me in his reception area, talking to a young woman I had never met. He introduced her as Libby Blister, his new secretary-receptionist. I did not have to ask if there was more than a professional relationship between them. The look on Libby Blister's face was an announcement.

In his office, with the door closed, Carter poured coffee from a silver service and announced with pride that he had, at last, met someone he truly loved.

"Isn't she a little young?" I asked.

He handed me the coffee. "Christ, Bobo, you could be decent enough to let me keep you in suspense a few minutes. Does it show that much?"

"On her," I said. "And you don't look too unhappy."

He plopped into a chair near me. "Yeah, I guess you're right on both counts."

"How serious is it?" I asked.

"It's getting there, And, by the way, before you ask, she's twenty years younger than I am, but she thinks it's fifteen. I lied and you're not to give me away. We worked together in 1960, not 1955." He lifted his cup in a salute. "To love, in all its glory, Bobo."

"To love," I said.

We drank from our coffee.

"And are you learning anything about love up at the Inn?" Carter asked lightly.

"What's that supposed to mean?"

"The word's out."

"What word?"

"The stockbroker and the judge's wife," Carter said. "They're back."

"You know about them?" I asked in surprise.

Carter laughed. "We may be humble mountain folk, Bobo, but we've got our little underground, our little network of gossip." He grinned. "A little like you rednecks."

"I always knew we were alike," I told him. "So, what should I learn from the stockbroker and the judge's wife?"

"A lot of things," Carter answered philosophically. "What it's like to have balls, for one. Arrogance, for another. I saw them in a restaurant one time. They were at the table next to me, and you know me—just naturally curious, I guess. I listened. They were talking about some loss he'd taken in the market. She asked him how much it was and he told her, 'Seventy thousand.' You know what she did, Bobo? She took off her ring and her watch and put them on the table in front of him. 'That would cover it,' she said. I wanted to get up and smack the shit out of her, the pretentious little bitch."

"Sounds like she's managed well," I said.

"Yeah." Carter replied. He laughed at the memory of the judge's wife, then he said, "Let's get the business out of the way. What do you need?"

"I want to leave you all the papers dealing with Avrum," I told him. "Everything's been left to

153

me, but I want you to do whatever legal mumbo jumbo necessary to have it all transferred to the Home."

"All of it?"

"Take out your fee, but everything else, give it to the Home," I said.

Carter waved away the remark. "This one's on the house, Bobo. Hell, I liked that old man. He was crazy as a loon. Besides, if it hadn't been for him, you wouldn't have been coming back all these years."

"Thanks, Carter," I said. "The Home can use whatever it can get. I've changed my mind about that place. I used to think they didn't give a damn, but I was wrong. They do."

"How much is in his estate?" Carter asked.

"I have no idea," I told him. "I didn't even look at his financials, just his instructions."

"Okay, I'll check it out. Maybe we should bargain for an Avrum Feldman Room, or something."

"No, don't."

"Your call," Carter replied. "Don't worry. I'll take care of it. Are you sure there's nothing you want?"

I thought about Avrum's room and the thievery of old, desperate people who were afraid of a candlestick box.

"I have a mahogany box that he kept some things in," I said. "I'd like that."

"Keep it," Carter advised easily. "All right, business over?"

154

"As far as I'm concerned. You know where to find me if you need me."

Carter stood. "Let's go," he said.

"Where are we going?"

"Bobo, you're too damned curious. Always have been." He touched a button his intercom. "Libby, we're going out for a hour or so. Can you hold down the fort?"

A voice sweetly answered, "Sure. Be careful."

Carter smiled at me and winked. "She loves my ass, Bobo," he whispered.

We drove to Woodstock, which had been a small artists' colony in 1955, but had become a mecca for young people in search of a subculture that existed more in their appearance and in their fantasies than in their longing. For years, tourists had flocked to Woodstock to see them and to pick among the good and bad of their art and their trinkets. There was always talk of the rock festival that became legend.

"It's amazing, Bobo," Carter said as he drove slowly through the town. "Used to be a great place, didn't it? Now it's as gaudy as a New Orleans whore. Damned rock concert changed it. What a ball-buster that was."

"You went?" I asked with surprise. "I didn't know that. You've never said a word about it."

He shrugged and drummed his fingers on the steering wheel of his car. "Never been exactly proud of it," he confessed.

"Why not?"

Carter mugged smugly. "I'm a lot more conventional than you think."

"Sure, you are," I replied. "I've always thought that was your most remarkable quality, Carter. In fact, I thought that part of your nature, alone, would get you to Washington."

Carter laughed easily and slowed the car for a girl wearing cutoff jeans and a slip-top to cross the street. The girl's hair was braided in a pigtail that dangled to the small of her back. Her breasts bounced freely under the slip-top.

"Damn," Carter muttered. "You see the tits on that, Bobo? Did anybody have tits like that when we were young?"

"What are we doing here?" I asked.

"I want to show you something," he answered, "but not here. I just thought you'd like a drive-through for old times' sake."

"There's nothing old-time here," I said. "At least not much that I recognize."

"You forgot about us, Bobo," Carter replied. "We're here." He laughed again.

We drove northeast out of Woodstock, climbing into the mountains. Carter talked aimlessly about Libby Blister. She had vacationed the summer before in Phoenicia, separated from her husband. Carter had met her one afternoon while tubing on the waters of the Esopus and she had asked to see him concerning matters of her divorce. She was, he enthused, the world's most fantastic woman in bed. She was also bright, sophisticated, humorous, patient, and beautiful.

"She is, don't you think, Bobo? Beautiful, I mean?"

I assured him she was beautiful and told him I looked forward to having dinner with them.

"Tomorrow night?" he said. "That all right with you? I've got a meeting with a client tonight. A bankruptcy thing."

"Fine," I said.

We continued the slow drive and Carter began to talk about the closing of the resort hotels in the Shandaken Valley. He sounded like Lila. It was, he reported, a sad sign of the times. He personally had handled a half dozen closings in the bankruptcy courts, and there was about to be another. Great old places, he said of the resorts. I recognized two or three of the names.

"If you ever want to pick up something cheap and get back up here, let me know," he advised. "Now would be the time, but who knows if anybody could make a go of them. Jesus, everybody goes to Europe now, or out west, or down to Florida. There was a time you came to the Catskills because it was paradise."

He slowed his car and turned off the road at an unmarked mailbox that was wrapped with a flowering vine. The driveway was graveled. It twisted through a dense stand of hemlocks and ended at a large, secluded cedar ranch house.

"What do you think?" asked Carter.

"Impressive," I said. "Why are we here? Is it yours?"

Carter did not answer. He got out of the car and motioned for me to follow.

At the front of the house, Carter lifted a stone and pulled out a plastic Ziploc bag with keys inside it. He went to the front door and opened it and stepped inside.

"I suppose you have a legal right to do this," I said.

"Sure do, Bobo. It's on the market in an unlisted sort of way. A new client of mine. I keep the keys under the rock because I don't want every sleazeball agent in the valley having his go at the lockbox, but I've got a cleaning lady coming in once a week and she needs to get in."

I walked inside. The house was astonishing. It had a great room that only an artist could have designed, with a rock fireplace and bookcases and wall space for the display of a series of remarkable paintings that seemed somehow familiar, though I knew I had never seen them. Off the great room, I saw a studio streamed in light. I turned. A wide stairway circled up, and I knew it led to a master bedroom that would be as unique as the great room. I turned again. I saw a kitchen and a corridor leading to back bedrooms.

"You look pleased," Carter said cheerfully.

"My God, Carter, who owns this place?"

"Someone you may have heard of," Carter answered: "Jean Archer."

"The artist?"

"One and the same."

"Of course I know her," I said. "Who doesn't?

158

That would be like somebody in the car business not knowing about Henry Ford." I moved about the room, looking at her paintings. I could feel the tension of awe that always strikes me when I see great art.

"She's good," Carter said.

"She's brilliant," I corrected. "But I've never seen these in anything—a show or a magazine, anything."

"My understanding is all this stuff is private," Carter said. "You're one of the few people who's ever seen them. She's pretty close to being a recluse."

"You know her?" I asked in amazement.

"Well, she needed a lawyer," Carter said simply. "She wants to sell and move to New Mexico."

"I'll be damned. How long has she been here?"

"Three or four years. She moves about, I understand," Carter answered.

I wandered to a painting hanging near one of the bookcases. It was of a young man in a field, on his knees, pulling weeds from around a tomato plant. Jean Archer's work had always reminded me of the Old Masters in its clarity of expression. Carter said nothing. He watched as I studied the paintings.

"I can't believe this," I said at last.

"No, you can," Carter said quietly. "But what I'm about to show you, you won't believe. Come on."

He led me up the stairs and into the master

bedroom. The room was huge and commanding. It had a separate fireplace and a sitting alcove on the left side as one entered. On the right was a dressing area that led into a bathroom. The only thing that seemed odd about the room was the absence of color, and the sudden, drab sensation of loneliness. Single skylights on opposing sides of the beamed ceiling directed shafts of light across a kingsize bed that was against the far wall.

Carter stood away from me, watching as I scanned the room.

"Do you see it?" he asked.

"What?" I said.

"The painting."

I looked up. A single, large painting was hanging over the bed. The painting was of a woman sitting alone in a train station. She was wearing a peasant's clothing, shades of brown and gray. The shaft of light from the skylights skimmed over her head. I stepped forward, to the foot of the bed. It was a peasant's setting, but not a peasant's face.

"Am I wrong, Bobo?" Carter asked quietly. "Who is it?"

"My God," I whispered.

"I knew it," Carter said. "I knew it."

The face of the woman in the painting was Amy Lourie's.

On the drive back to Phoenicia, Carter explained that he had discovered the painting only a week earlier while doing a photographic inventory for insurance. At first, he believed the likeness between Amy and the woman in the painting was coincidental, a quaint deception of memory, but the face in the painting had haunted him and he had returned twice to study it.

"I found some old pictures, Bobo. From that summer. There was one of Amy by the swimming pool, a close-up, and one of you and Amy in Arch's, and one of the three of us sitting on the porch of the Inn. Maybe you remember that one. It was a day or so before Amy left. Rene took it. Jesus, we were young. Babies, Bobo, babies. And innocent. I swear, I don't think there's ever been a generation as innocent." He paused and shook his head over the memory. "Anyway, after looking at those pictures, I knew it had to be the same person, but it's been so damn long. Yet, when you looked at it—Christ, you should have seen the expression on your face—I knew for certain. No doubt."

I asked why he had not called me.

"I thought about it," he said, "but what was I going to say? 'Hey, Bobo, I found your old girlfriend.' Come on, I know how things like that cut to the quick. Jesus, you're worse about her than Avrum was about that old opera singer."

"Why do you think that?" I said irritably. "We were kids. It was a summer thing."

Carter snorted a laugh. He wagged his head and then glanced at me. "I was there, Bobo. Remember? And you've been coming back up here so damn long, looking for her, I get a fresh view of it every couple of years."

"You bring her up, not me," I argued.

"Only because you don't have the guts, old friend."

We rode in silence, bypassing Woodstock. I knew that Carter believed I was thinking of the painting, but I was not. I was thinking of Carter and how well he understood me. It had been that way from our first meeting. He had a gift of certainty, of reading the wavering of moods. We saw each other only when I was in the Catskills, yet I was more comfortable with him than I was with my own brothers.

"How do you feel?" Carter asked after several minutes.

"All right," I answered. "Curious, I guess. I'd like to know why she posed for it."

"If I get up the nerve, I'll ask Archer the next time I see her—if I ever do," he said.

"Couldn't you call her?" I asked.

Carter laughed easily. A deer sprinted to the side of the road from an apple orchard and Carter braked and slowed the car. The deer tensed, then turned and bolted back into the orchard.

"Bobo, that is one strange woman," Carter said carefully. "You don't talk to her, not that one. You ask permission to speak. In fact, I don't even know where she is. I go through her agent, some shitty little whiner in New York. What do you know about her, by the way?"

"Not a lot," I admitted. "Not her private life,

at least. She's in her late sixties, I suppose. I think she was in one of the Jewish ghettos in Poland, or somewhere, during the war. I read a retrospect on some of her drawings from those days, when she was just a child. All I know is, she's brilliant."

"And rich," Carter added. "She gets a shitpot full of cash for those things."

"In this case, it's deserved," I said.

"Is she really that good?" Carter asked. "I mean, I like her stuff, but I like your stuff better, Bobo. That's why I keep it at home, instead of at the office."

Over the years, I had given Carter four or five of my favorite paintings to celebrate moments of friendship. I always had the feeling he kept them stored away in closets until I visited.

"And I thought you didn't want to be embarrassed by displaying them in public," I said.

"Bullshit," Carter mumbled. "I had a guy try to buy one of them from me five or six years ago. He was at the house for dinner. Went bananas over the one with the pasture scene. He was from Alabama. Said it reminded him of the place he'd lived."

"And you didn't sell?"

"Of course not. What kind of question is that? I'm telling you, I like your stuff better than hers."

"Carter," I said, "you're a friend and I appreciate what you just said, but compared to Jean Archer, I draw stick figures in the mud."

"Sure, and Amy Lourie is the queen of the trolls," Carter replied.

163

We reached the bridge crossing the Esopus Creek at the east end of Phoenicia. The creek was dotted with floaters nestled into the puffed rubber of large inner tubes. They bobbed like leaves on the swift, cold water. Carter had said it was the only thriving business in the area. "Think of it," he had grumbled, "they're making a fortune off people who're doing nothing more than cramming their ass in a tire tube and then freezing it off in ice water." Then he had added with pleasure, "But it is one hell of a place to meet women."

We sat in Carter's car in front of his office. He said, "Well, old friend, I hope this didn't short-circuit the wiring."

"There's nothing to short-circuit, Carter. It was what I said it was—a wonderful summer, a great memory, the kind of love that everyone ought to have at least once in their life. It had a great impact on me, and I know it. It changed my life—or almost did—and I think about it more than I should, but I suppose I am, as Carolyn constantly tells me, a pitiful romantic."

"Pitiful romantic?" Carter said. He arched an eyebrow in mock disapproval. "Not kind, my friend. Not kind."

"She doesn't mean anything by it. It's sort of a thing between us. You know: one of those husband-wife exchanges. In fact, I like it, and she knows it. Anyway, it's better than being called a wimp, I suppose."

"Not much," Carter judged. He glanced at his watch.

"I appreciate the time you've given me," I said.

"No problem." He opened the car door, but sat for a moment. "I'll try to find out what I can, Bobo, to make sure it's her. We could be wrong. It could be just a—what do they call it? A doppelgänger. Is that the word?"

"A look-alike?"

"Yeah. Whatever. I'll ask the agent."

"Only if you want to," I said. "Are you coming to the memorial service tomorrow?"

"Of course," he answered. "There's got to be somebody there to listen to your bullshit."

It was midafternoon and on the drive back to Pine Hill, I stopped at a roadside restaurant for coffee. I carried my briefcase inside with me and opened it and took out the photograph and the blue stone that Amy Lourie had given me. I had kept them hidden for thirty-eight years—kept them from Carolyn, from our children, from everyone.

The face in Jean Archer's painting was the same as the face in the photograph, only feathered with age. The brilliant, warm violet eyes were the same. And the lips—slightly opened and moist. The cheeks were soft and tender.

"Want cream?" the waitress asked.

"No, thank you."

"You need a refill, just wave."

"I will," I told her.

I remembered my own drawing of Amy. She had praised it, and her parents had praised it, but it was not good. It was an overdone effort by a young, untrained artist too anxious to perfectly create the perfect face. Only someone as gifted as Jean Archer could draw, or paint, Amy Lourie.

I put away the picture and the stone and drank from the coffee, and I thought of a night on the mountain, late in the summer, only a few days before it would end with Amy. I was holding her under the covering of the birch and she whispered to me, "I love you, Bobo." And then she did something she had never done. She pushed her body gently against mine, searching with her body, until she felt the pressure of the erection I could not stop. I heard her whimper and her arms tightened around me.

"I love you," she said again.

"And I love you," I told her.

"Do you think this is wrong?" she asked.

"I don't know."

"Do you feel guilty?"

"Sometimes, yes," I said.

"I do, too. I think about—about others."

I did not reply.

"Do you want to talk about them?" Amy asked.

"Not now," I said. "Later. Not now."

"All right," she replied. "Later."

We both knew it was something we would avoid as long as possible.

9

Lila was in my room, cleaning it, when I returned to the Inn. The chambermaid, she grumbled, had failed to report for work. "Happens every month. If I had cramps as bad as she does, I'd call a plumber with a Roto-Rooter," she said irritably.

Lila was not meant to be a chambermaid. The bedcovering was crooked on the bed and the pillows smashed flat. She had not hung towels. They were stacked on the back of the commode. I could tell by the tracks on the carpet that she had only pushed the vacuum cleaner up and back once. The only thing in the room that was different was the cut-glass flower vase. It had three large jonquils. Their yellow trumpet mouths seemed to be playing a concert of color.

"Very pretty," I said, putting down my briefcase.

She smiled a teasing smile. "I thought they'd brighten things up. But don't get any ideas, Bobo. It's not a pass. I took them from next door. They always have them. He stops at Dorrie Kincaid's flower shop in Phoenicia and picks them up. Dorrie swears there's a turn-on about those flowers. She tells me the only time she ever makes love is when she gets his order. It's been going on for so many years now, she finally had to tell her husband the truth."

"Won't they miss them?"

"They checked out," Lila said. "Same schedule every time. Monday through Wednesday."

"How do they get by with it?" I asked.

She flipped a dustcloth at the top of the table, then rubbed hard at a spot that had been burned by a cigarette. "He's supposed to be meeting with some well-heeled clients. For her, it's an uncle over at the Home, but it's a weak excuse if you ask me. He's a turnip. She goes by, pats him on his bony little head, gets an orderly to snap a couple of pictures, and then she roars over here to hit the sheet with Dow Jones." She tossed the dusting cloth at the cleaning cart. It missed and she picked it up. She looked at me. "I've heard her on the phone a couple of times, talking to the judge, I guess. She claims she's practically living at the Home, says she thinks the old boy feels better when she's around."

"To each his own."

"God, Bobo, I love it when you get profound."

"Yeah, me, too."

Lila dropped the cloth into the cart. "Let me show you something, Bobo. You want to see what turns them on?"

"Not particularly."

"Sure you do."

She pulled a magazine from the cart and handed it to me.

168

"I found it under the bed," she said. "They're always leaving them behind. I think they're trying to tell me something."

I fanned the magazine quickly and handed it back to Lila. It was, as I knew it would be, a magazine of sexually explicit poses.

"Embarrass you?" Lila asked.

"No," I told her. Then: "Okay, so it does—a little. It's not on my subscription list." I sat on the side of the bed.

Lila stepped toward me. "Would you look at it if I weren't here?"

I answered her honestly: "Maybe."

"Sure you would," she said.

"My God, Lila, I am human. I'm curious, like anyone."

"You don't have a great sex life at home, do you?" she said softly.

"It's—"

"Almost nonexistent? Is that it, Bobo?"

"I didn't say that."

"You don't have to. I can read the signs."

I could feel a blush coating my face.

Lila dropped the magazine on the bed. "Centerfold," she teased. "And, Bobo, if you're anything like that man, you couldn't lock me out of this room with the CIA standing guard. I'd kick the hinges off."

"I'm glad to know the Inn is now providing reading material," I told her. "Especially such inspirational literature."

Lila laughed gleefully. She stepped to the desk

and opened a drawer. "If you want inspiration, Bobo, read this." She sailed a brochure at me. It landed on the bed and I picked it up and examined it. On the cover, it read, JEWS FOR JESUS.

"We had a group of them in for a meeting a couple of months ago," she explained. "They left these things everywhere. No tips, but a lot of inspiration."

"I'll read it with interest."

"Sure you will, Bobo. The minute I close this door, you're going to grab that magazine and lock yourself in the bathroom. I know all about men." She winked. "What a waste," she sighed. "What a waste."

She stepped outside and closed the door. I waited. The door opened again.

"Yes, Lila?"

"You knew I'd do that, didn't you?"

"Yes, Lila."

"See you later, Bobo."

"See you, Lila."

She closed the door again. I could hear the cart squeaking down the corridor.

I slipped out of my shoes and took the magazine and brochure and leaned against the headboard of the bed.

Lila had not exaggerated about the centerfold. The picture was of a man with an enormous, erect penis, a blood-purple blush covering its gleaming head. He was sprawled awkwardly across a young girl clothed in a gown from the waist up. He had his left arm around her neck and shoulder, and his right hand was under her left thigh, pulling the leg up to reveal her vagina and the glistening mat of dark hair. In this position, his penis was about to penetrate her. In the background, as though suspended by wires, was an image of Elvis Presley standing in a garden.

I laughed. Someone at the magazine—or a freelance photographer—had a sense of humor. The pose was an imitation of a famous Japanese painting from the eighteenth century. I remembered it from a college art class taught by a shy, nervous man named Winfred Reed. I remembered the swimming giggles of embarrassment as Winfred Reed attempted a serious discussion of the painting's composition as we stared at the slide in a darkened room. He talked of its lines and its symbolism, its historical social message. It was, Winfred Reed, explained, the story of a young girl—a student, perhaps—being taken by an older man in permissive sexual abuse. There was persuasion, trickery, hollow promises in the scene. Not once did he mention what everyone was staring at—the penis-beast. The name of the painting was *Lovers in a Landscape Garden.*

I thought of the stockbroker and the judge's wife in the pose, imagining themselves as the couple of the centerfold, playing at power and submission, playing at the joy of conquering and being conquered.

I heard Lila say, "... you couldn't lock me out of this room with the CIA standing guard." And for a moment, a flash, I saw myself in the

171

same pose with Lila. She had been close to the truth about my sex life. It was not dead, but it needed more passion than acts of habit can provide.

I closed the magazine and tossed it aside, then picked up the *Jews for Jesus* brochure and scanned it. The rationale of its message had been carefully defined—ancient cultures stitched together with select threads of Scripture. There was urgency and joy, begging and celebration, in the words.

There had been another religious pamphlet in 1955. I never knew who slipped it into the pocket of my waiter's jacket. It could have been anyone. Harry Burger, enjoying his pranks. Mrs. Mendelson, trying to be helpful in her confused way. Nora Dowling, because she cared and because she understood what the pamphlet meant. Evelyn Lourie, who had a reason.

The brochure was about the risks of interfaith marriage, especially between Jews and Christians.

I took it to Avrum. He read it, then handed it back to me.

"Such nonsense," he mumbled. "Throw it away."

"Who do you think did it?" I asked.

He looked at me in his curious, questioning manner. "Why should I know such things? Better to ask yourself. Who do you think it was?"

He knew about Amy, that we had been dating. "Amy's mother," I said.

He did his whole-body nod. "So? She's a mother."

"She must be trying to tell me something," I suggested.

"*Ja,*" he groused. "Maybe she does not want her Jewish daughter to have Irish babies. Let her worry."

"Babies?" I said. "What babies?"

"It could happen," Avrum replied philosophically.

I stared at him in disbelief. "We're just friends. We're just seeing one another."

Avrum smiled wisely. "Yes, seeing. I know. I know. By the tree on the mountain."

I was surprised. "How do you know that?"

He pointed to his eyes with his finger. "I see what I see." He reached and patted my shoulder. "Don't be such a worry one. No one else looks. I would know if they did, wouldn't I? What do I do all these days? I look. I listen. I see everything. I hear everything. Everything."

"Nothing happens," I said defensively. "We just talk."

"Ah, talk," Avrum sighed.

"Talk," I repeated.

We sat for a moment without speaking. Avrum closed his eyes and raised his face, like someone happily warmed by the sun. I thought he was hearing the first, clear rush of Amelita Galli-Curci's voice. I started to stand.

"No, stay," he said without opening his eyes.

I sat back on the bench and waited.

"Do you not remember what I told you?" Avrum asked.

173

"Sir?"

"When I told you about her? Do you not remember?" His eyes were still closed.

I knew he was talking about Amelita Galli-Curci. In the first days of our friendship, he had not mentioned her name. He had talked of the operas he loved, of such performers as Enrico Caruso and John McCormack and Lily Pons, but not of Amelita Galli-Curci. And then one day he had said, casually, "So, did Harry tell you about me?"

"Yes, sir. Some things."

"Then I will tell you the truth, not the lies of that mean old son of a bitch Harry Burger," he had replied firmly.

His story of Amelita Galli-Curci had been Harry's story, almost verbatim. Yet, in Avrum's telling it was not the gossip that Harry had tried to make of it; with Avrum, it was real.

"So," Avrum said. "Do you not remember?"

"I'm not sure," I told him.

"Then I will say it again." He opened his eyes and looked at me. "It is very painful to love someone and believe you cannot be with them."

"Yes, sir, I remember," I said.

He closed his eyes again. A muscle trembled across his mouth. He licked his lips. A sad smile settled into his slender face.

"Do not be so afraid," he advised. "That is the only thing that can hurt you. Nothing else."

"What are you saying?" I asked.

"Do not be so afraid," he repeated. "I know. *Ja*, I know."

After I left Avrum, I went into the dining room, and with the blade of a dinner knife I made the faint imprint of the letter *T* in the tablecloth beside Amy's plate.

It was a signal that Amy had devised as a playful game the day following our first movie date in Margaretville—code letters pressed lightly into the tablecloth, like writing with invisible ink, almost indiscernible. The letters would tell me where she wanted to meet at night. *T* meant the birch tree. *A* meant Arch's. *S* meant the swimming pool. *B* meant the base of the ski lift on Belleayre Mountain. *R* meant room, or, to Amy, her room. The *R*, I told her, would never be used. I was not a fool.

It was a teenage thing of the fifties, the code letters, a kind of flirtation, like the passing of notes in a classroom. Still, in the giddiness of the game, it was as personal and as secret as a kiss.

The first time I saw a letter pressed into the tablecloth beside her plate, it was an *R*. When I removed her soup bowl, I deliberately scratched through it with my thumb-nail and she laughed. Her mother looked at her, and then at me, curiously.

"I'm sorry," Amy sputtered. "I thought you were about to drop the soup bowl."

Amy was waiting for me at the birch tree after dinner. She kissed me easily.

"Is anything wrong?" she asked.

"Why did you ask that?" I said.

"You hardly looked at me during dinner."

I handed her the brochure.

"What's this?" she asked.

"Something somebody left for me after lunch. I found it in my waiter's jacket."

She opened it and read it. She did not speak. She folded the brochure into a small, thick square and knelt and took a rock and clawed a hole into the ground. She pushed the wadded brochure into the hole and covered it with dirt and the rock, then she stood and glared at the spot. "Let it rot," she said bitterly.

"It's all right, Amy."

"No, it's not," she snapped. "People should mind their own damn business."

Her eyes burned. She hugged her arms tight across her chest and stepped on the rock and pushed hard with her foot.

"It doesn't mean anything to me," I said.

She whirled to me. "It should," she blurted. "It should bother you. I don't like people meddling in my life."

"You said there would be problems," I reminded her.

She looked away, toward the Inn, then turned and stepped quickly to me without uncrossing her arms. She leaned into me and I held her. I thought she was crying.

"It's just a piece of paper," I whispered.

"No, it's more than that," she insisted. She pulled her arms from her chest and wrapped me in them. "Do you know who did it?" she asked.

"No."

"Carter?"

"It couldn't have been. I left the jacket hanging on the back of a chair in the dining room. Carter was with me in the kitchen.

"Harry Burger? He's always pestering us."

"I don't know," I said. I faked a soft laugh. "Maybe it was your folks."

I could feel her body tense.

"I was kidding," I said. "It was a bad joke."

She raised her face from my chest. Her eyes studied me. "Maybe not. My mother knows I see you."

"How? Did you tell her?"

"I had to," she admitted. "She's been asking about Adam coming up, like last summer. I had to tell her why I didn't want that."

Carter had told me about Adam, and Amy had described him as being spoiled, yet she had mentioned his name only once, and only then to answer Carter's plaguing questions in Arch's. "Yes," she had said to him, "Adam and I still date, or we did." She had turned to look at me. "But we're not married, or anything like that."

"How did your mother take it? About us?" I asked.

"She wasn't surprised, if that's what you mean. My dad doesn't notice a lot, but my mom does. She's a little . . ." She paused. "Emotional."

"What do you mean?" I asked.

She pulled from me and crossed her arms again and again stepped on the rock covering the brochure, pushing her weight against it. "She worries," she said after a moment. "I've never told anyone about this, Bobo, and you'll have to keep it between us, but two years ago, my parents separated for a few months. I don't know why. They just did. My mother left and we didn't hear from her for weeks, then she came back. They live together now and they're nice to one another, but that's all." Her eyes became moist. "They don't even sleep in the same room," she whispered. "I don't know if you know it, but they have twin beds here. Sometimes—sometimes, I think it's all a show for me."

I could not imagine Joel and Evelyn Lourie living apart. Their relationship was the most tender I had ever seen.

"I'm sorry," I told her.

She reached her hand to me. I took it and moved to her and held her.

I could hear her voice against my shoulder. "She likes you. She thinks you're very talented. She loved the drawing you did of me."

"She was nice about that," I said. "So was your father."

"It's a Jewish thing, to worry," Amy said. "Especially about children."

"I understand," I told her.

"Bobo?"

"Yes."

"I love you."

"And I love you," I said.

Her face was damp from crying, her mouth hot on my mouth.

Sammy Merritt was overjoyed that I would accept his gift of the sculpture that he called *Old Man*. He asked if I knew where I would display it, in my office at school or at home. I told him I felt it would be more personal to keep it at home, that Carolyn had a place in her favorite bookcase where it would fit well. I could see Sammy's imagination at play in his furrowed brow and glad eyes—his sculpture among leather-bound books, a small pinspot lighting it. "Good, good, good," he muttered.

He had followed me on a before-dinner walk along a route that elderly guests of the Inn, the refugees at rest, had taken in 1955—past the untended swimming pool with its shallow, dark green pond of algae and leaf-rot, past the cemetery, then along a grass-covered roadbed where a rope-pull ski lift had once operated. It was the same route that Amy had taken to meet me at the birch tree.

I had not invited Sammy to join me. He had simply appeared from the Inn, jogging to catch up. He wanted to tell me about the gift of the

Old Man, he said, because he was too eager to wait until after the memorial service for Avrum.

I was glad that Lila had warned me, but still I tried to act startled.

"That's too generous," I told Sammy. "I'd love to have it, but why don't you let me buy it? You're an artist. You need to sell what you create."

Sammy was grinning like a child. "Bullshit. The next one, I'll sell. This one's for you, Bobo. After all the encouragement you've given me, it's the least I can do."

"Why don't we swap?" I suggested. "I'll send you a painting."

Sammy studied me suspiciously. A twitch fluttered over his left eye. His grin spread. He said quietly, "Jesus, Bobo, I'd like that, but I'm not in your league. It'd be unfair."

"No, believe me," I said. "I've thought about this before, having one of my paintings here. I want to do it." I remembered a landscape that I had had for years. Carolyn had advised me to paint over it. "It's dull," she had judged. "You're better than that." But I had liked the painting and had stored it. I knew that Sammy would hang it and tell enthusiastic lies about artists—real artists—sharing their art.

We walked leisurely and Sammy jabbered about his envy of my medium. He had tried oils and watercolors in the city, in art classes, he confessed, but he could never make his fingers do what his eyes were seeing, and that is why he turned to sculpture. He told me that the first time he chipped at a piece of sandstone with his hammer and chisel, he felt empowered, like a god making life.

"But if I could do what you do, Bobo, I'd throw the goddamn hammer in the creek," he vowed. "I mean it. I was looking at some paintings in Woodstock not long ago, and I—"

I interrupted. "Sammy, have you ever heard of Jean Archer?"

He stopped walking. "Heard of her? Bobo, I met her."

"Where?" I asked.

"Woodstock. Two or three months ago. I was over there to talk about my exhibit, and I saw a crowd of people hanging around this woman. I asked somebody who she was, and they told me. Well, hell, I'd heard of Jean Archer for years, so I pushed my way through the crowd to get to her and I introduced myself. Tell you the truth, Bobo, I think she was relieved. Goddamn punk kids, with their silly-ass dyed hair and earrings dangling out of their noses. Who the hell wants to be around those assholes?"

I asked him to tell me about her.

"Healthy woman," Sammy said with authority. "Looked like she'd just hiked the Appalachian Trail. Bluest eyes I ever saw. Bluer than Paul Newman's eyes, for Christ's sake. Didn't talk much, though. I asked her what she was doing in Woodstock and she just looked at me, like she didn't understand the question. She got away after that. Somebody told me she has a house around there. It was news to me."

I did not tell Sammy about Jean Archer's house. I knew he would press me to take him to see it.

"She stays to herself, I understand," I said.

"She must," Sammy agreed. "Hard to believe I didn't know she lived up here." He walked a few paces, remembering his meeting with Jean Archer. "Do you know her, Bobo?"

"No. Like you, I've known of her for years, but I've never met her. Even saw some works from her private collection not long ago. They were interesting, especially one or two."

"That right?" Sammy said. "I wish I'd had a chance to talk to her, maybe have a cup of coffee or something. You think it's true that she tried to kill herself?"

I stopped walking. "She did? I didn't know that."

"That's what one of the kids was saying," Sammy answered. "But, Jesus, Bobo, you know kids. They'll say anything."

"Do you remember anything specific?"

"Not really," Sammy replied. "Something about somebody walking in on her one day and finding her almost dead from an overdose of sleeping pills, or something. I guess they took her to the hospital and got her pumped out."

"Did they say who found her?" I asked.

Sammy thought for a moment. "Don't remember anybody giving a name, but I think they said it was one of her models." He clucked his tongue seriously. "You know, Bobo, I don't give a tinker's damn what people do, as long as they don't bother me with it, but I've got to tell you, anytime I hear things like that about an artist, it pisses me off. That kind of business gives the rest of us a bad name."

10

Marriage becomes predictable, a kind of routine that floats like a stationary buoy on moving waters. Its early, intensely wonderful drama becomes repetitive theater, the same lines rotely spoken, or mumbled, the same gestures instinctively offered from the drill of daily rehearsal. The anticipation of surprise following surprise eventually fades, then vanishes. It is not needed. How can you anticipate what you already know?

Once I called Carolyn, or thought I had.

I was busy writing a student evaluation and was not listening carefully.

"Hello," a woman said.

"Hi," I replied. "Everything all right?"

"Everything's fine. What about you?"

"Fine. Any mail?"

"The usual: bills."

"Any calls?"

"A couple of salesmen. Nothing else."

"How're the kids?"

There was a pause.

"What kids?" the woman asked.

"Our kids."

"Who is this?"

"Bobo."

"I don't know any Bobo."

We both laughed, this strange woman and I.

"Ain't marriage the pits?" she said. "You don't even sound like my husband, but you ask the same questions."

"And you don't sound like my wife," I told her, "but you have the same answers."

"You know, that's scary," the woman said. "Makes me wonder what happened. Now that I think of it, I—what's your name?"

"Bobo."

"Right. Bobo. Now that I think of it, Bobo, this is the first decent conversation I've had with anybody in a year."

"I could say the same, I suppose," I admitted.

"Well, thanks for the call," she said. "Hope the kids are all right."

I had been away from home for two days. I knew that Carolyn would call and I knew the call would come between five-thirty and six. She was—no; we were—that predictable.

There was nothing of importance in the mail, she reported. No phone calls that needed my attention. She had talked to each of the children. They were well. Nothing was different at her work, except for a summer cold that Darby was suffering.

"How much longer are you going to be there?" she asked.

"Probably through the weekend," I said. "I met with Carter about handling the legal stuff.

It'll take time, but I won't have to worry about it."

Predictably, she did not ask about details. She said, with an edge to her voice, "Well, I hope you're enjoying yourself."

"Carolyn, I'm not on vacation."

"Sounds like one to me, if you're just sitting around, waiting."

"Well, it's not. I've got the memorial service tomorrow. It takes time to put these things together."

I could hear her sniff restlessly. I knew she was pacing between the kitchen and the dining room, dragging the long extension cord with her. She said, "Mavis Rogers called to tell me she saw you on television last night. I didn't know anything about it."

"It was on down there?" I asked.

"Mavis said it was." Her words were measured, as though I had called Mavis Rogers personally, secretly, to inform her of the interview.

"I'm surprised," I said. "I didn't see it, either. But Avrum was over a hundred. I guess that interests people."

"Mavis said it had something to do with that opera singer you're always talking about."

"Look. I'm sorry about the interview," I told her. "I didn't know when it would show, or where. And you know who that opera singer is, and I don't always talk about her. Anyway, you know the story."

"I should," she replied bluntly, "I've heard enough about it. It still seems ridiculous to me."

"I'm sure it seems that way to a lot of people," I conceded. "It wasn't to Avrum."

"I've got to go," Carolyn said. "I forgot to pick up the laundry, and I may go to dinner with Andrea Wright tonight."

"Have fun," I said.

"I'll talk to you in a couple of days," she mumbled.

The two older couples had checked out of the Inn and were on their quest to see America by car, leaving me as the only guest in the care of Sammy and Lila Merritt. Because she wanted a night out before a busy weekend with a marriage-renewal group booked at the Inn, dinner, Lila told me, would be at the Dollhouse Lodge and Restaurant near Phoenicia.

"Our treat," she added.

"We'll argue about that later," I said. I was, in fact, glad to get away from the Inn. I had the memory of banquets for kings; in comparison, Sammy and Lila served food from the recipes of college cafeterias operating on low budgets.

We drove in my car, Lila sitting up front with me. It was early evening, when the mountains become ethereally beautiful. We did not speak for a few miles, and then Lila said, "Is something bothering you, Bobo?"

"No. Why?"

"I don't know. You seem preoccupied," she replied. Then, to Sammy, "Don't you think so?"

"Naw," Sammy said. He was curled comfortably in the backseat, a pleased smile embedded in his face. If anyone was preoccupied, it was Sammy. I knew he was dreaming of his work.

"Trouble at home?" Lila asked casually.

I shrugged.

"You always get this way when you come up here, Bobo. Do you know that?"

"What way?"

"I don't know. Irritated, I think."

"Carolyn's a little miffed, that's all," I told her. "And I guess I don't blame her. I did leave in a rush and there were a number of things she's had to handle. And to make matters worse, one of her friends saw the spot on CNN about Avrum. She didn't know about it and Carolyn's not one who loves surprises. I should have called her."

"Oh," Lila said.

We rode again in silence. In the rearview mirror, I saw Sammy close his eyes and lean his head against the headrest of the seat. His lips moved to some soundless tune.

"Has she ever been up here with you?" Lila asked. "Before we took over the Inn, I mean."

"Carolyn?" I said. "No. Except for the summer I worked here. She came up with my mother that year."

"Why hasn't she been back?"

For a reason that I could not explain, I wanted to tell Lila the truth—that I had never wanted

Carolyn to be with me. I said instead, "I told her about you. She's jealous."

Lila laughed easily. "I think I'll send her a picture of me in a bikini," she teased. She glanced at Sammy. He was oblivious to our conversation. "No, seriously. Why?"

"No real reason," I answered. "Money, for one thing. But mainly, it's always been a trip to see Avrum. Nothing appealing in that for her."

"What kind of person is she?" Lila asked.

I looked at Lila. She was pushed against the door, like a teenager on a date. She was watching me quizzically.

"She's a nice person," I said. "Strong-willed. Very strong. A good mother. A little blunt at times, a little too quick to give her opinion, more restless than she thinks she is, a soft touch when you'd never expect her to be. A really good person. A lot of our friends think she's the balance in my life."

"And she puts up with you?" Lila teased.

"She tolerates me, which is asking a lot, I suppose," I answered.

"Don't criticize it," Lila advised. "I've always heard there were three perfect possibilities in a marriage—perfect ecstasy, perfect misery, and perfect tolerance. I think most of us live the latter." Her eyes moved from me to Sammy. "It's not easy, is it?"

"Being married?" I asked.

"Being married," she answered.

"No, it's not," I admitted.

Her next question came so smoothly, I wondered if she had rehearsed it: "Do you ever think you're not married to the right person?"

I smiled and let the smile serve as a pause to search for an answer.

"Well, do you?" Lila probed.

"Doesn't everybody think that?" I said. "At least once in a while. But, to be truthful, I don't dwell on it. I think marriage becomes a kind of habit, something so familiar we feel more comfortable there, in it, than anywhere else. Every marriage I've ever seen—the good ones and the bad ones—all seem to become a habit. And maybe that's the way it's supposed to be."

"Some habits are better than other habits," Lila observed.

"Yes, I suppose," I replied.

I glanced at her. She was gazing at me, as though she wanted to say something else, something bothersome. Instead, she reached with her hand and stroked me lightly on the arm. "We're not going to fight about the check, are we?"

"No. It's on me," I said.

"But you've already paid for one meal, at the Inn. You just didn't get it."

"Then think of this as a tip."

"You didn't get enough service for what this is going to cost."

"Who cares?" I said. "It's the company that matters."

"Yes, it is, isn't it?" Lila replied.

The Dollhouse Lodge and Restaurant featured a collection of dolls from most of the countries of the world, as well as French cuisine from a couple named Paul and Maggie Charles. Paul was from Paris, Maggie from Kingston. They had met in Paris at a school of culinary arts and had operated a restaurant in San Francisco for many years before Paul became obsessed with the fear of earthquakes. They had chosen to relocate in the Catskills. Sammy and Lila—especially Lila—knew them well. In the Dollhouse restaurant, I saw in Lila a new person, someone zestfully young and happy. She and Sammy were warmly embraced by Maggie, who then called in a bright voice for Paul to come from the kitchen. Paul took Lila's hand dramatically and kissed it and spoke to her in French. To my surprise, and delight, she answered him fluently. I was introduced with the explanation of my occasional trips to visit Avrum, and then we were led to a table beside a bay window.

"You do not order," declared Paul, pulling the menus away from Maggie. "Tonight, I will decide, in honor of your guest." He rushed away, giving Maggie instructions about wine.

"That man's a work of art, Bobo," Sammy said giddily. "If I could sculpt like he can cook, I'd be in the Louvre. God, I love coming here."

"I didn't know you spoke French," I said to Lila.

"There's a lot you don't know about me," she

answered in mock haughtiness. "But I did go to college, Bobo, and French was my major."

"How could I know you all these years and not know that?" I said.

"Never any occasion to use it," she replied. "But that's one of the reasons I come here—the three Fs: French, friendship, and food. You're going to want to blow up our kitchen after this meal, Bobo."

"Damn right," Sammy agreed. "Maybe I'll help you."

Lila was right about the food. We had a small bowl of *aux chous* soup, then broiled trout with asparagus tips and marble-size new potatoes, and, afterward, a Caesar salad, then coffee and a dish of cut strawberries in cream. Maggie and Paul fluttered about us, perfecting each serving with excited consultation between them. It was a joyful experience and I regretted that, in the years of knowing Sammy and Lila, we had never been to the Dollhouse Lodge and Restaurant. I toasted them with the select chardonnay that Paul had insisted on serving and told them they had failed our friendship by keeping the restaurant a secret.

"And risk losing you?" Lila said. "My God, Bobo, you're our summer business. Anyway, you were always busy. But, to make you feel better, we did talk about asking you to come here with us. We just never knew when you'd be with your friend, and we didn't want to intrude."

"Now you've got another reason to come

back," Sammy insisted. "Lila, me, and the Dollhouse."

It was a good, comfortable evening with friends, and that was how I felt about Sammy and Lila: they were friends. Over time, we had become easy with one another, had learned the give and take of personality. Celebrating that friendship was not a task; it was a pleasure.

Still, there was something unsaid between Lila and me. I could sense it through the dinner. It was a question she had left in the car, on the drive from the Inn. When Sammy excused himself to go to the bathroom, Lila said it: "You can blame this on the wine, Bobo, but I've got to ask you something."

"Ask."

"Who are you looking for when you come up here? I've always wanted to know."

"I don't understand," I told her.

"Of course you do. I see you. I've watched you for years. You didn't know I was watching, but I was. I see the places you go when you walk, always the same, year after year. It's as though you lost something a long time ago—a lucky penny, a pocketknife, a set of keys, something— and you keep looking for it. I see you standing around, always in the same places, like you've told somebody you would meet them there, and you're waiting for them to pop up out of thin air."

"Lila, I walk a lot of places when I'm up here. I enjoy it."

She did not accept my answer. She shook her head and reached for my hand and held it. "I believe it's possible for people to pop up out of thin air, Bobo," she said quietly.

"And I believe it's hard to breathe in thin air," I replied.

"Who is she, Bobo?"

"Lila—"

"Tell me. Please. Who is she?"

I did not know why, but I wanted to hold Lila, and to be held by her. I wanted to cry into her shoulder. She knew. She had always known.

"Someone from my youth," I answered quietly. "Someone from a long time ago. She made me feel special."

"Did she have a name?"

I nudged the word out: "Amy."

"Did you love her?"

I paused, remembered Amy holding me. I said, "Then, I did. Yes. Or I think so."

Lila smiled. She leaned to me and kissed me softly on the cheek. She whispered, "That kind of then can last a long time, can't it, Bobo?"

I looked away. Sammy was crossing the restaurant from the bathroom. I blinked the dampness from my eyes.

"I envy her," Lila whispered.

"Why?" I asked.

"You're glowing," she said.

We left the Dollhouse Lodge and Restaurant and went to the Mountainside Playhouse after a brief argument between Sammy and Lila on how to finish off the evening. Sammy wanted to go to Arch's, to his workshop, and play old records and dance. It would be in my honor, he asserted. A trip down memory lane. Lila persuaded him that memory lane was too narrow for three people. Besides, she wanted to be in a crowd. Sammy eagerly surrendered. "This will balance things off," he promised. "All that French wine will rot a man's system, unless he chases it with a good cheap beer."

The Playhouse could have been a tavern in Georgia or in Alabama or Texas or Tennessee. It had a bar, a bandstand, a dance floor, a jukebox for band-break, a collection of assorted tables shoved close together, and the unmistakable odor of beer, popcorn, and cigarettes. It was crowded with a group that had just completed country-dance lessons at a local community center, and they were trying their steps to the music of Jack Cavalier's Merry Mountain Music Makers. The group consisted of Jack on fiddle, a woman named April Moss on piano, a drummer named Pete Capes, and a guitarist they called Sailor Parker. They were energetic and personable, but not very good, as Lila had cautioned. And as she had also cautioned, Sammy thought they should be playing for Dolly Parton in Nashville.

"Damn," Sammy complained, "I just don't understand it. They ought to be making a million dollars a year, Bobo, but they can't seem to get going. I'll bet they spend more money promoting themselves than they make, and this place is packed all the damn time when they're here, but they can't raise a fart in a windstorm outside of here."

Sammy drank beer and ate peanuts and bellowed hellos to people who wandered by. Lila laughed easily at the pawing of men she knew. She danced once or twice with Sammy, playing seductive and teasing bumps and grinds toward me. She tried to pull me onto the floor, but I refused and Sammy made her stop. "Jesus, Lila, leave the man alone. Maybe he's not in the mood to be dry-humped before a bunch of people he's never seen."

When we left and drove back to the Inn, Sammy and Lila were pleasantly drunk. They invited me to have a glass of brandy with them, but I told them that I wanted to take a nostalgic drive to Margaretville, to the Galli-Curci Theater, to spend some time thinking about what I would say at Avrum's memorial service.

"Shit, I forgot about that, Bobo," Sammy apologized. "We should have skipped the Playhouse."

"I'm glad we didn't," I told him. "I had a good time."

"One of these days you'll be able to say you saw the Merry Mountain Music Makers before they became famous," he declared.

Lila rolled her eyes in a didn't-I-tell-you look. She said, "Thanks for the dinner, Bobo. See you in the morning."

196

"Yeah, buddy, thanks," Sammy added. "Next time, I get the check, though."

"Next time," I promised.

I watched them walk inside the Inn, Sammy's arm locked around Lila's waist.

I did not drive to Margaretville. I went, instead, to Woodstock, to Jean Archer's home. I turned the car lights off at the driveway and followed the moonlit, silver bed of gravel to the yard. The house was dark. I sat, looking at it. Because it belonged to Jean Archer, it seemed more magnificent than it had before, somehow more imposing.

I turned off the car motor and got out and went to the rock that covered the key. I knew I did not have permission to go into the house, but that did not matter. I wanted to see Amy Lourie's face again.

I could not risk turning on the house lights, but there was no need for them. The moon funneled in from the windows, throwing dim pools of light across the rooms. I walked cautiously upstairs to Jean Archer's bedroom and stood in the doorway. The skylights in the roof filtered the moon to a color of dull pewter. The light fell in slats across Jean Archer's bed and glazed over the painting of the peasant woman. In the light, the woman's shadowed face looked at me with resignation and sadness. Her eyes asked me to touch her.

Lila knew, I thought. She knew.

197

I wanted Amy to appear out of Lila's thin air. Lila knew.

I had looked for Amy on every visit, waited for her to be there.

And now I was looking at her.

I thought of Carolyn and I wanted to say, "This is wrong." I knew it was what I should say, but it was not what I believed.

"No," I said aloud.

I remembered Amy's warnings about the problems, about the many things that separated us.

"I know," I had said to her.

"But not now," she had whispered. "Not now." And she had pressed close to me. "I want to be with you now," she had added in a voice so soft I could barely hear her.

The girl who had kissed me, who had rested against me, was the same woman in Jean Archer's painting.

Carter could ask, but it was not a doppelgänger. There could be no mistake. It was Amy.

11

Because he became my friend and I was often seen sitting with him on his bench, the young people of Pine Hill began to regard Avrum not as a threat, but as a harmless and interesting town eccentric. They loved him for his playful, humorous stories and they fretted over him during the dark, hypnotic moods that would fall on him like a coma. Older people—villagers and guests of the resorts—still mostly avoided him, believing his odd behavior was somehow contagious, and yet, they were also fascinated by him. Avrum knew this and through Harry Burger and one or two others who enjoyed his companionship in games of chess and casual, meandering discussions, he salted his reputation with deliberately outrageous tales.

He had once owned a Stradivarius violin, he claimed. It had been purchased either from a peddler friend he knew or from a member of the New York Philharmonic or from a descendent of Stradivarius, depending on Avrum's sense of drama during the telling.

He vowed with conviction that, as a young man, he had been a skilled boxer, a lightweight. He had won many neighborhood tournaments, he said, and once he had sparred with the great

Young Stribling—a story told for my benefit since Young Stribling was from Georgia. A broken hand had ended his promising career, he insisted.

He had flown in a hot-air balloon over a New Jersey field, he revealed to Harry. He described the sensation as one of being dangled by a string as he watched the earth roll slowly beneath him. He said he met the legendary pilot Charles Lindbergh on that same day.

He had won a dance marathon in Brooklyn, he bragged, dancing with a Lithuanian girl who later appeared in the chorus line of movie musicals directed by Busby Berkeley.

When he worked as an interpreter on Ellis Island, he often gave immigrants their new American names, he proudly announced.

Those who heard Avrum's stories, directly or indirectly, half-believed him because they wanted to believe him.

But the only truth from the stories was the truth of Amelita Galli-Curci and of the name-giving. Once, Avrum showed me age-yellowed letters from two families he had corresponded with for a short period after their arrival in America. He had named one family Montague and the other Capulet.

"I could see, easy," he had explained, tapping below his eye with his finger. "Two young people from the two families. Do you know? On the boat trip, they find love. *Ja*, Romeo and Juliet. They send me a wedding invitation." He had begun to sort through the letters. "Somewhere, I have it." I saw the invitation. The names were from the Montague and Capulet families.

I had not slept well, after returning to the Inn from Jean Archer's home. I had sat at the desk of my room, holding a pen over a sheet of paper, remembering Avrum's stories and again trying to make notes for his memorial service. There were no words from the pen tip, only a memory sketch of Jean Archer's painting of Amy, and in the background, on the same sheet, a small likeness of Avrum, sitting on his bench.

When I did sleep, it was a bothered, restless slumber, a dazed stupor. I dreamed—in one of those glimpse-dreams, a dream that is quick and leaping—of an afternoon when Avrum asked Amy and me to go to his room in his hotel and to find a book and to bring it to him.

"Amy doesn't have to go," I said hurriedly. "I'll get it."

"No, no, take her," Avrum insisted. "Show her my music records."

"Maybe later," I said.

"Are you ashamed of me going with you?" Amy asked.

I blushed. Ashamed? No, I thought. No. But I knew if anyone saw us going into the hotel together, there would be gossip in Arch's and in the Inn.

"That's not it," I argued. "I just thought you could stay here and talk and I'd—"

Avrum shook his head. He handed his key to

Amy. "Go, already. Take the young lady with you. I'm tired of talking. I need rest." He blinked his eyes to fake fatigue.

"Come on," Amy said boldly. "Don't be so afraid of everything."

Avrum smiled triumphantly.

If anyone saw us go into the hotel, no one ever said anything about it. I left the door to Avrum's room open, but Amy closed it. Then she came to me and put her arms around me and kissed me.

"Amy, we can't stay in here," I told her.

She smiled playfully. "You don't know what he just did, do you?"

"What are you talking about?"

"He just gave us a chance to be together, without anybody spying on us."

"Spying on us?" I said weakly. "Who?"

"Anyone. My parents. Carter. Especially Carter."

"We can't stay in here, not with the door closed."

"We can for a minute," she whispered. She held me, kissed me again, then she looked around the room. The room was not cluttered as it usually was. It was clean and orderly. A small vase of flowers was on Avrum's bedside table. "I like it," Amy said. "It's cozy. I feel safe."

"Well, I don't," I said. I took the book that Avrum wanted from his bookcase. "Let's go."

"One more kiss," Amy purred.

"One," I replied.

She kissed me passionately, a lingering, feeding kiss.

"All right," she said. "Now we can go."

I did not know why Amy understood what Avrum had done, but she did. She understood. When we returned with the book, Amy offered the key back to him.

He waved it away with his thin hand. "Keep it, keep it. I have another. You want to go and listen to the music sometimes, go. I'm always here."

Amy smiled. Later she told me, "Avrum wants us to have a place with a bed."

"Don't even mention it," I begged.

"Now, when I leave an *R* in the tablecloth, you'll know where to go," she teased.

In my dream—my glimpse-dream—Amy smiled from Jean Archer's painting.

The morning was clear and bright. A shivering, fresh-day chill lingered under the limbs of the hemlocks and flowed into my room through the opened window. From the window, I could see the young girl, the rope-skipper, riding a bicycle in the street, making slow, even figure-8 circles, like a lazy, contented bird swirling on currents of air. She seemed to be daydreaming, one dream rolling into another dream and then another and another, like the slow, even circles of her bicycle. Dreams lapping into dreams. I wondered if she ever tired of her loneliness.

I went downstairs to the dining room. It was

empty. In the kitchen, a plump woman in her midthirties sat at a work table, eating breakfast from a full plate. A cigarette burned in an ashtray near her. She looked up with a scowl when I pushed open the door and entered.

"You looking for the Merritts?" she asked.

"Have you seen them?" I said.

"They still asleep, I guess." She picked up her cigarette and pulled on it. "You staying here?"

I told her that I was.

"You want some breakfast?"

"Just coffee. I'll get it."

"Suit yourself," she mumbled. "I just started to eat."

"That's all right," I told her. "I know where everything is."

She studied me curiously. "You that fellow that used to work here?"

"Yes, I am."

"They always talking about you—them two."

I took a cup from the shelf and filled it with coffee from the pot on the stove. "They're friends," I told her. "I've been staying here, off and on, for a number of years."

"Yeah, that's what they said," the woman mumbled. She pushed the tip of her cigarette into the ashtray, smothering it. "It's my first year here."

"Is that right?"

She nodded and chewed on a piece of toast. "They tell me this used to be some kind of place."

"It was. But everything's changed."

"You can say that again," she grumbled. "Ain't no jobs nowhere around here."

"That's what I understand," I said.

"Nowhere," She sipped from her coffee and looked up at me. "You up here because of that old man? The one that died?"

"Avrum Feldman. Yes. He was a friend of mine."

She smiled suddenly. Her teeth were dark and uneven. "I knew I'd seen you. You was on the television, talking about him."

"Well, yes, I was."

"I thought it was you. When you come in the kitchen yesterday. I was busy and didn't pay much attention, but then when I seen you on the television, I thought I'd seen you somewhere."

I wanted to be pleasant. "I'm sorry I didn't introduce myself before, but I know how it is when there's work to be done."

She waved a hand in the air. "Not that much around here, I can tell you that. Just you, right now. Supposed to be a bunch coming in over the weekend, but you can't never count on that." She reached for another cigarette. "Tell me something. Was that old man crazy like everybody said he was?"

"Avrum? I don't know if he was crazy, but he was different."

She laughed a quick, hard laugh, a single, stabbing cackle. "Same thing, you ask me. Half my family's that way. Crazy. Different. They always up to something. Even got one or two of them that hears voices, just like they say that old man used to do."

"Is that right," I said.

She nodded vigorously, lighting her cigarette. "It's in the Benton blood."

"Benton?" I asked. "You wouldn't happen to be related to Ben Benton, would you?"

She looked at me in surprise. "You know him?"

"Yes, he was my friend."

"He was my daddy. I'm Shirley Benton. Used to be. Shirley Bagwell now."

I was stunned. I had remembered seeing Ben Benton's daughter in the late fifties, when she was a baby, a beautiful, blue-eyed child with a rolling, happy laugh. Then Ben had killed himself and I had been told that his family had moved away. It was impossible to believe that the woman sitting before me was the beautiful, blue-eyed child with a rolling, happy laugh.

"Well," I said, "this is something. Ben Benton's daughter. I'm glad to meet you. My name's Bobo Murphy."

"That's a funny name," Shirley said.

"I can't disagree with that," I told her.

"You really know my daddy?"

"I sure did. He was a fine man. We were good friends."

"I don't remember nothing much about him," Shirley said casually. "I got some pictures, but pictures don't tell you nothing. They all look the same. People smiling like Cheshire cats. It ain't the way people are if you ever find out anything about them."

"I guess you're right," I said.

"You sure you don't want something to eat?"

"No, thank you," I replied.

She nodded gratefully and drew from her cigarette. "We moved off after Daddy died." She paused, then corrected herself. "Well, after he killed hisself. Me and Roy—that's my husband—moved back last year. He works in a garage up in Fleischmanns."

"Do you like it here?" I asked.

She looked around the kitchen, then rolled her shoulders. "It's all right."

"Your father was an important man here. He was even on the city council," I told her. "He helped start the ragweed wars."

"What was that?" she asked seriously.

"I guess it does sound a little strange, doesn't it?" I said. "This area used to be famous as a haven for people with hay fever. If a ragweed came up, somebody yanked it out of the ground and destroyed it. Your father was in charge."

"He went around pulling up ragweeds? Is that what he done? I thought he drove a garbage truck."

"He did," I explained. "But he was involved in a lot of things."

Shirley nodded thoughtfully, as though she were trying to imagine her father in some official uniform that was neatly pressed and decorated with ribbons and medals signifying his heroism

207

against ragweed. After a moment, she nodded the thought away and looked around the kitchen again.

"Won't take but a couple of minutes to put some eggs on," she said. "I fry them sunny-up in butter and high-broil them for a couple of seconds. Best eggs you ever had."

I suddenly felt sorry for Shirley Benton Bagwell. She did not understand anything I had said about her father. He was dead. She did not remember him. That was all she needed to know.

"I think I'll pass," I said. "But I appreciate the offer. I'll just take my coffee and go sit on the porch for a few minutes. Take in the morning air."

"Suit yourself."

"Glad to meet you, Shirley."

"Same," she replied.

The girl on the bicycle was still in the street, still turning in slow figure-8 circles. I sat in a chair and watched her, but she did not look up. Her eyes were on the pavement in a mesmerized stare. She was graceful and pretty, her long blond hair billowing off her shoulders in the slight morning breeze, the daydreamer's look of monotony resting easy, and a little sad, on her face.

I remembered a girl from 1955 whose newspaper picture looked very much like the girl of the bicycle. She had been attending a summer camp near Pine Hill, and one day, she had disappeared while on a hiking trip. The men of the Shandaken Valley had searched for her for a week, but she was not found. It was Ben Benton's suggestion, boldly and loudly offered, that the girl had been kidnapped and taken away from the mountains. A year later, Carter wrote to tell me her skeleton had been discovered in a shallow grave not far from the birch tree where I used to meet Amy. No one knew who had killed her, or why, Carter said, but Ben had been questioned because he had tried so hard to convince everyone that the girl had been taken out of the valley. Ben was never charged with the crime, but, as Carter observed, he was forever judged by the harsh court of gossip.

It was an odd coincidence, I thought, that Ben's daughter, Shirley, was born less than a year after the young girl's body was found. As a child she, too, had been blond and pretty. I wondered if knowing that his own daughter would have to live with the gossip had caused Ben to pick up a gun one night and shoot himself in the temple. Or was it something more? Had Ben killed the girl, as the gossip ruled, and had seeing his own daughter—blue-eyed, blond, like the missing girl—tormented him and driven him to suicide? The fifties had been curious years. Some things— the murder of a child, or the rumor of murder— were not excusable. Some things were too great to bear.

I had liked Ben. He had accepted me after doubts. He had stepped in front of a switchblade for me. He had laughed with me. I did not want to think he had killed anyone.

Once, I saw Ben talking to Avrum. They were sitting on Avrum's bench and Ben was leaning forward, his elbows propped on his knees, listening and nodding as Avrum explained something to him, using his hands for exaggeration. Later, Ben told me that Avrum had said the most profound thing he had ever heard.

"What was it?" I asked.

"He was talking about God," Ben confessed. "He said men were fools to think that God worried a lot about them. You know what he did? He pointed up to the mountain behind the Inn and then he asked me what it was I saw up there. I told him I saw a mountain. Why, hell, I thought that was plain as day. And old Avrum, he said I was right, but he said there was more going on under one tree up on that mountain that God had rather worry about than what was going on in anybody I ever knew."

"Sounds like him," I said.

I remembered that Ben looked up at the mountain, looked at it as though he were seeing it for the first time. Then he said, "You know, Bobo, ain't nothing scary about that old man being crazy. What's scary about him is how smart he is."

I thought: Perhaps that is what I should tell the people at the memorial service. Perhaps I should tell them about Ben Benton and Avrum.

It would be a good story, one they would under-stand.

But I knew it was not the story they would want to hear. They would want to hear about Amelita Galli-Curci.

One last telling of Amelita Galli-Curci. A story they had not heard.

And I knew the story. Avrum vowed he had never told it to anyone but me, and I believed him.

The door leading into the Inn opened behind me and closed with a sharp bang, and I heard Lila say, "Bobo."

The girl on the bicycle stopped suddenly. She looked up, her eyes on my eyes, and she smiled, then she looked at Lila and her smile faded and her face became defiant. She pedaled away, down the street.

"What are you doing out here?" Lila asked.

I turned to her. She looked fresh and happy and content. The sweet odor of her perfume floated across the porch.

"Watching the world," I said. "Watching the world."

"And how goes the world?"

I looked back to the street, where the girl had been riding her bicycle. "Around in circles."

"You're strange, Bobo. Did you get break-fast?"

"Just coffee."

She fell into a chair near me. "I'm going to

fire that bitch," she sighed wearily. "Damn it, I can't get her to understand the first thing about this business."

"She offered," I said. "I just wasn't hungry."

"I'm still going to fire her," Lila declared. "She's a pig. She eats more than the guests and, for Christ's sake, it's her own cooking, which tells you she's got no taste whatsoever." Lila lit a cigarette and spewed smoke into the air.

"We had a talk," I said. "She's the daughter of a man I used to know."

"Who?"

"A man named Ben Benton. We were friends."

A puzzled frown crossed Lila's face. "Seems as though I've heard that name."

"Maybe," I said. Then: "Did you sleep well?"

Lila smiled from the memory of the night. She nuzzled against the cushion of the chair and, avoiding the question, said, "What time's the memorial service?"

"Eleven."

"Are you ready for it?"

"No," I said. "I think I'll have to wing it."

"You'll do great. Oh, by the way, that man from the Home called a few minutes ago."

"Sol Walkman?"

"Yeah. Him."

"What did he want?"

"You got me. I think he's as crazy as some of those old people he keeps locked up in his nut house."

"He must have said something," I said.

"He did, but it didn't make a lot of sense. He said somebody had sent a book of poems to him, with a note that it was for Avrum's service. He wondered if it was from you."

"Poems?" I said. "No, I didn't send him anything."

"He said one of them was marked."

"Did he say what it was?"

"Something about a child," Lila answered.

"From Walt Whitman?"

"Whitman? Yes, it was. I love his writing," Lila said.

12

I could hear Lila's voice: "Bobo?"

I knew that she was speaking to me, but I could not answer her. I tried to inhale. My lungs felt closed, blocked by a seizure in my throat.

"Bobo?" she said again, her voice rising sharply. And then she was beside my chair. I could feel her hands on my face, massaging me with her fingers.

"Goddamn it, Bobo, what's wrong?"

She pulled her hands from my face and rushed to the front door of the Inn and called, "Sammy! Sammy, get out here!"

Then she was back with me, again kneeling beside me. She had my hand in her hands, rubbing it.

"What is it, Bobo?" she pleaded. "Jesus, talk to me. Breathe, damn it."

Sammy bolted through the door. I could hear him ask in a worried voice, "What's wrong? What did you do to him?"

"Nothing, damn it," Lila snapped. "I don't know what's wrong. Look at him. My God, he's white as a sheet. Call a doctor, for Christ's sake."

The vise on my throat released and I sucked in a deep, quick swallow of air.

"Easy, Bobo, easy," Lila said. "Slow and easy."

My breathing calmed.

"I'll get some water," Sammy said. He rushed back into the Inn.

"Bobo, you all right?" Lila asked anxiously.

I nodded.

"What happened?"

"I don't know," I said. "Hyperventilation, I guess."

"Out of the blue?"

"I suppose so. It's never happened before."

"You scared the shit out of me, Bobo. I thought you were having a heart attack."

"I'm all right," I told her. "Sorry."

"For what? You can't help things like that."

"I guess not," I said.

Sammy returned with the water and I drank it. I apologized again to both of them. They dismissed the apology with an argument between them about the need to have a doctor examine me. Sammy insisted that I should go to Fleishmanns; he would drive me, he said. Lila told him that it was nothing, an involuntary thing. She informed him that many people hyperventilate, and it was never as serious as it seemed.

"Did you eat anything?" asked Sammy.

"No, thank God," Lila said. "We might be looking at his corpse now if he had."

"I'm fine," I told Sammy. "Lila's right. It just struck me. Besides, I don't have time to go to a doctor."

"If it happens again, you're going," Sammy declared. "If I have to hit you in the head with my hammer and drag you, you're, by God, going."

I promised I would, if it happened again.

"Why don't you go upstairs and rest for a while," Lila suggested.

"Not now," I told her. "I want to drive over to the Home."

"Now? It's only a few minutes past eight," Sammy argued.

"I won't be long. I just want to check on things."

"Want me to go with you?" Lila asked.

"No," I said. "I'll be all right."

"This happens again, Sammy can take you to the doctor, but I'm going to do some mouth-to-mouth resuscitation," she said. She winked. "And I hope it does," she teased.

"Shit, Lila, leave the man alone," Sammy grumbled.

As I believed that I sensed the death of Avrum before Brenda Slayton told me about the telephone call from Sol Walkman, I think that everyone, at some moment in his life, has been chilled by circumstance, by coincidence, by ironies as mysterious and eerie as déjà vu or telepathic messages from friends thousands of miles away.

Unexplainable things.

216

When our oldest daughter, Rachel, was very small, Carolyn and I were having dinner with Hart and Cathy Fisher, who were next-door neighbors. In the middle of laughter over a joke, Carolyn suddenly paled and bolted from the table, without explanation, and ran out of the door and across the lawn to our home. Sitting bewildered at the table with Hart and Cathy, I could hear her calling desperately for Rachel. We followed her. When we entered the house, we found Rachel choking and Carolyn pounding on her back, while the baby-sitter cried hysterically. Carolyn could not explain how she knew about Rachel. She said, "I knew. That's all."

A student once erupted into tears during the middle of a class and told me, with great agony and with great conviction, that his mother had just died. He was correct. At precisely the time he sensed it, his mother had died of heart failure in a hospital three miles away. "She passed by me," he vowed. I had thought of him, and of his mother, while walking to the office to receive the call from Sol Walkman about Avrum.

A friend, a colleague, who was deeply in love, called me late one night and in a trembling voice begged me to meet him for a drink. He told me that he knew the woman he loved was, at that moment, in bed with another man. "I know, goddamn it, I know," he cried. Later, he told me that he had been right; she had confessed it. I asked how he could be so certain. "I could feel it," he answered. "I was at home, watching television, and it hit me, and I knew what was happening. It was like being there and watching. I could feel it. I knew. I simply knew."

With me, Sol Walkman's telephone call about Walt Whitman's poem was not a mystic experience, not like Carolyn with Rachel or my student's mother or my friend's lover. It was merely a chill sweeping through me, a freezing and choking chill.

How could the book be there? I wondered. The poem of Whitman's Child was an old sharing between Avrum and me. No one else knew about that sharing.

One afternoon, as I was leaving The Cave for work, I saw Avrum beckoning to me from his bench. I crossed the street to him.

He was holding a book that he turned for me to see. It was an anthology of poems.

"I have found who you are," he said enthusiastically.

"You have?" I asked.

"*Ja, ja,* sit." He patted his hand on the bench beside him. "I must read this to you."

I looked toward the Inn. I could see Carter going up the steps of the platform-porch leading to the kitchen. "I've only got a minute," I told Avrum.

"Good, good. Only a minute," he said.

I sat beside him. He opened the book and began to read slowly:

"There was a child went forth every day
And the first object he look'd upon, that
    object he became,
And that object became part of him for
    a day or a certain part of the day,
Or for many years or stretching cycles
    of years . . . "

The poem was Walt Whitman's "There Was a Child Went Forth." As I listened, it immediately became my favorite of all poems. Its message was simple: there is a child in everyone and that child goes forth every day and becomes part of everything he sees or hears or experiences, and everything he sees or hears or experiences becomes part of him. Taking and leaving, leaving and taking, as Avrum explained it. It was what I had always instinctively believed, but did not know I believed until I listened to Avrum's reading.

When he finished, Avrum closed the book and smiled peacefully.

"Do you understand?" he asked.

"I think so," I said.

"Good, good. We will talk about it another time. Now, work. Go, go."

After that, Avrum would often call me Whitman's Child and he would say of himself, "But I am Whitman's Old Man."

And in his way of making logic fit his purpose, Avrum reasoned that only certain people were capable of being Whitman's Child. "Too many want to take, but not to leave," he would pontificate. "And what would they know if something good happened to them? Nothing. They would know nothing."

It was the discovery of Whitman's poem that encouraged Avrum to begin talking to me seriously about Amy. He insisted that it was not coincidental that I had traveled to the Catskills from a farm in Georgia to meet him and a Jewish girl from New York City. It was intended, just as it was intended that he would hear Amelita Galli-Curci at the Lexington Opera House. "Listen to yourself," he would urge. "Do not listen to others. I know you. You are like me. Listen to the voice. It will tell you. This Amy, she is for you."

I did not tell Amy or Carter or anyone about Whitman's Child. I believed the story would have amused them. Or, perhaps, it would have frightened them as, in moments, it frightened me.

Only Harry Burger seemed to understand what Avrum was saying to me. I could sense Harry's concern, could see it in the worried way he watched me. Occasionally, after I had spent time with Avrum, Harry would whisper to me in the dining room, "Take care, take care. Avrum, he likes to pull the strings. When you are old, the strings have all been pulled away. Not so, when you are young. The strings are many when you are young."

At the end of the summer, on the day that he left the Pine Hill Inn to return to his home on

Long Island, Harry took me aside. He said, "Go live your own life, Bobo Murphy. Live it without Avrum. When you leave for your Georgia, leave him on his bench. Leave him with his music. He is a dreamer and sometimes dreamers can be selfish. They want everyone to dream their dreams."

'But I thought he was your friend," I said.

"Ah, friend. Yes, yes, he is," Harry murmured. "And he is your friend, but friends are not always right. When they are wrong, you forgive them. When they are right, you love them."

"I guess so," I said.

He put his hands on my shoulders and looked at me tenderly. "Avrum, he wants to make himself young again. He wants to be young so he can go to Amelita Galli-Curci and tell her that he loves her. That is what he is doing with you—making himself young again. Do you not see it? He wants you to be him and he wants Amy, your Amy, to be Amelita Galli-Curci. She is lovely, yes, but she is not Amelita Galli-Curci. If you make her that, you will suffer. Always, you will suffer." He squeezed my shoulders with his strong hands. "Don't be such a *dummkopf.*"

The book that Sol Walkman held was Avrum's book. I recognized it immediately. It had Avrum's name, scrawled by his hand, on the title page.

Sol had no explanation for it. "It must have been delivered to the front desk, or left there by

221

someone. The receptionist brought it to me. She said she didn't see anyone leave it."

A typewritten note was in the envelope that had been slipped inside the book. *For Avrum Feldman's service. Please see the marked page.*

The marked page was "There Was a Child Went Forth."

"Do you know what it means?" asked Sol.

"Yes, and no," I answered. "I know about the poem. I know it was Avrum's favorite, but I have no idea who left the book. The last time I saw it, it was among his possessions."

Sol stroked his chin with his fingers. "Maybe one of the residents did it. They could have taken it when they destroyed his room."

I asked if any of them had a typewriter.

Sol shook his head. "No. I would know that."

"Could they have used one of the typewriters in the office?"

"Doubtful," Sol answered. "Someone's almost always around. Are you sure he had the book?"

"The last time I was with him, last October, he had it," I said. "It was one of his special possessions. He loved Whitman."

"He had good taste. I like that poem myself. Always have. Will you use it today?"

"I don't know," I told him. It was an honest answer.

"Do you need anything?" Sol asked.

"No, I don't think so."

"You're going to have a good crowd," Sol said.

"There's nothing mandatory about it, but I think everybody will be there, and there's at least one television station covering it."

I asked what he had done with Sammy's sculpture.

Sol smiled. "It's in a corner," he said easily. "Out of harm's way, so to speak. I wouldn't want anyone fooling with it. It could topple and hurt one of those old people."

"Good thinking."

I was glad I had been wrong about Sol Walkman. He was a good man in a job where death always won.

I returned to the Inn and placed a call to Carter. Carter had a lawyer's mind for reasoning the unreasonable, and though it often bothered me that he could be so dispassionate about passionate matters, it always impressed me that his thinking was clear and direct. If there was an explanation for the book of poems, Carter would find it, or he would make me believe he had found it.

Libby Blister told me Carter was in a meeting and would not return until after he attended the memorial service. "I'm sure I can find him, if you need him, though."

"No, it's all right," I said. "I'll see him at the service."

"We're looking forward to having dinner with you tonight," Libby said cheerfully. "Carter's talked a lot about you."

"Believe only half what you hear, and then take that with a grain of salt."

She giggled. "You must know him pretty well."

"Believe me, too well," I said. "Tonight, then?"

"Tonight."

It was nine-thirty. I sat at the desk in my room and read Whitman's poem of the child going forth. Whoever left the book at the Home had to know Avrum well. Avrum had imagined the poem was the story of his life, of his history. Childlike, he had filled himself with all that he had seen and heard and experienced, and he had tried to leave payments of himself for all those things that had mattered to him.

Yes, I thought: I will read the poem.

I rested and then went to Dan Wilder's Coffee and Pastry Shop and had coffee and a breakfast of crumb cake fresh from a morning baking. I left at ten-thirty for the Home. Sammy and Lila had promised to meet me there. Sammy was giddy. He had his camera. "I want to take some shots of you beside my *Old Man*," he said enthusiastically. I asked him to wait until after the service.

"Sure, Bobo, sure. I understand. That'll give us more time."

Lila looked at me and smiled empathetically.

Inside the Home, the old people were moving into the cafeteria, a slow, waddling, silent crowd. Some of them looked at me suspiciously; others smiled nervously. I saw Leo Gutschenritter and

Morris Mekel and Carl Gershon. They were sitting together, watching intently.

Sol was in the cafeteria, testing the sound system by tapping on the microphone with his finger. The dull, hollow thumping echoed in the room. He seemed relieved to see me.

"I think everything's ready," he told me.

"I hope you didn't go to too much trouble. I didn't even think about a sound system."

"Just takes a minute to put it up," he said. "We use it for formal occasions. The rest of the time we shout. Sometimes I wonder if they hear us either way." He nodded to the back of the room where a young man with a crewcut stood with a television camera balanced on his shoulder, taping people as they entered. The harsh glare of the lights made the people turn their faces and raise their hands, like children warding off a blow. "Your friendly television commentator's back there somewhere."

"I'm glad it's her," I said.

"Me, too." Sol gestured toward a chair behind the podium. "That's for you. You want a glass of water?"

"I don't think so. This won't take long."

I sat in the chair and opened Avrum's book of poems and scanned "There Was a Child Went Forth" and wondered again who had left the book at the Home. I was sure he, or she, would be at the service, but I did not know if I would know them.

"How are you?"

I looked up to see Dee Richardson. She was dressed in a pale blue blouse and gray slacks, an outfit very much like the one she had worn two days earlier. Still, there was something different about her and my expression must have been a puzzled one.

She laughed. "It's the hair. I had it cut."

In the interview at Avrum's bench, her hair—a rich, shimmering auburn color—had been shoulder length. Now it was cropped close to her head.

"Well, it's different," I said, "but I like it."

"Do you?"

"Yes. It looks very nice."

"Does it make me look more professional?" she asked seriously.

I confessed that I did not know about such things, but assured her that I liked the cut. Then I said, "I'm sorry I missed the broadcast, but I've heard good things about it from as far away as Georgia."

Dee Richardson smiled pleasantly. "We've had good response. The only complaint was about my hair, from some producer in Atlanta. That's why I got it cut."

"You're in a strange profession," I told her. "I always thought content mattered."

"To some people, content is how you look, not what you say," she countered. "And I don't disagree with you about the profession. We do use a lot of smoke and mirrors."

"What are you doing here today?" I asked.

"They wanted me to pick up some more footage. I think they're planning something on the elderly. You don't mind, do you?"

"Not at all. As long as it's not a question-and-answer session. I think I've had my few seconds of fame."

"Don't worry. We're just shooting for coverage. Will the lights bother you?"

"I don't think so," I replied. "I'll trust your judgment. If you think I'm squinting too much, you'll have to rescue me."

"Will do," she said. She turned away, then turned back. "I'm glad I met you, Lee Murphy. You've made this easy."

"I think it's Avrum's doing," I told her.

"Maybe. Who knows?" She smiled again. "Remember: smoke and mirrors."

13

As I waited in the chair for the crowd to settle, I thought of Avrum's instructions about his memorial service. Do it on the third day. You know why, he had written.

I did know. It was Avrum's last gently cynical swipe at Christianity. "If Christ can rise on the third day, and him being such a nice Jewish boy, so will I," he had boasted. "Such a story, such a story," he would say in his old-man chuckling. "You know, Bobo, your people, they're worse than the Jews, and this God, this God, he must be a hardhead."

I had tried to understand why Avrum was so intolerant of religion, but he would never tell me. He would sneer and look away, and then he would babble about some horrendous world condition and demand to know where my God was at such times. "Maybe on a holiday," he would thunder. "Maybe this is where he is. On a beach, sleeping in the sun. Huh? Could he be there?" Harry Burger believed Avrum's anger was from his agony over the death camps of World War Two. If God existed, how could he stand by and permit such things? But for Avrum, that was only one example. Wasn't it God who put Job to test when Job was the only man doing

228

everything God expected of him? And why? Because God had a little side bet going with Satan. What kind of God would do that? Avrum had railed.

But I did see Avrum in church once. He went with Harry Burger. They spent their time nudging one another and nodding toward me, smiling like children watching an amusing embarrassment.

And that is what they were watching.

My brother, Raymond, had asked me to speak at one of his small churches, permitting him an early break for a summer-long vacation in Georgia.

"I can't do that," I told him.

"Sure you can," Raymond assured me. "I've got a sermon already written. All you've got to do is read it. Everything else will be taken care of by the lay leader."

"But I've got to work," I protested.

"I talked with Mrs. Dowling about it," Raymond explained. "She said you could get off. In fact, she said she'd come to hear you."

"What?"

"She said she'd come. I think that's good. She likes you. She told me you were doing a great job."

"I don't think this is going to work," I argued.

"Come on, Bobo. Of course it will. It's a small church. Not many people even attend. It'd help me out if you'd do it. I've got to drive to Georgia. It'll save me three days."

Foolishly, I agreed and accepted the type-written sermon. Its title was "This Little Light of Mine" and it was about the power of every person—regardless of who they were or what they did—to penetrate the darkness of sin with the light of goodness. A lot of little lights make a blinding glow, Raymond had reasoned, long before George Bush got the idea.

"You're going to be one of those little lights for me," Raymond said proudly. "I'll be thinking about you while I'm on the road. I'll probably be in Virginia when you're speaking."

Raymond was a man of great faith. He did not consider that some little lights get snuffed out by the winds of absurdity.

The lay leader of the church, a man named George Arrington, stopped by The Cave early on Sunday, after breakfast, and gave me a ride to the church. We met the pianist. "Don't worry about a thing," George said confidently. "I'll handle everything except the sermon." We took our seats behind the pulpit while the pianist played softly. And then they came. Not the few my brother had promised, but a crowd so large they filled every seat and stood along the back walls.

"My heavens," George whispered. "Who are these people?"

The people were from the Pine Hill Inn, the guests who occupied my dining room. All of them. Nora Dowling and Carter had led them in. I saw Amy sitting with her parents, and Mrs.

Mendelson, who, that morning, had complained again of her boiled egg. I saw the Schwartzes, the Cohens, the Levins, the Garfunkles. All of them were there.

"Do you know any of them?" George asked.

I nodded nervously.

"Some of them look Jewish," George said.

"They are," I told him.

A worried frown crossed George's brow. Then he mumbled, "Well, they'll get a chance to hear about Jesus, won't they?"

I thought: Hear about Jesus? Not unless I do it in Yiddish.

Nora Dowling was overdressed. She sat proudly erect, knowing that she would be watched and imitated by the guests of the Inn. Harry and Avrum were sitting near her. Harry was trying to distract me and I determined not to look at him. I looked, instead, at Amy. She was beautiful. There, sitting behind the pulpit of a small, rustic church, I could sense her close to me, holding me. Her mouth was on my mouth, her body pinned to my body. I could smell the perfume of her hair. Her hands rubbed the muscles of my back.

"Praise Jesus," George said softly. He smiled at me. "Let us begin."

It was not a church service. It was a circus event. When I read my brother's sermon, I heard a high-pitched, rushing voice, not the Richard Burton baritone of Raymond. I tried to remember how Raymond appeared in the pulpit, how he would pause and curl the Bible in his hand, how he used his arms to scatter words into the congregation like a sower of truth, and I tried to emulate him. Harry later told me I looked like an addicted spastic begging for medication.

And then the oddest thing happened. When I finished the reading of the sermon, I stepped back, and suddenly, in unison, the congregation rose and began applauding. George was startled, and so was I. I wondered what Raymond would do, but I had never seen a congregation offer a standing ovation for Raymond. I did the only thing I could: I bowed slightly and sat down.

"Hallelujah!" George thundered. "Praise Jesus!"

Standing at the front door to greet the congregation after the service, I heard the voices— *"Gut, gut . . . Ja, gut . . ."*—and I looked into their confused, smiling faces. Nora Dowling and Mrs. Mendelson embraced me. Harry mumbled, "Praise Jesus." Avrum said, "I gave a dollar." Joel Lourie said, "Very nice, Bobo, very impressive. Your brother would be proud." Evelyn Lourie smiled. Amy touched my arm. I could feel the heat of her fingers through my suit.

Avrum's request that his memorial service— or my memorial service for him—should be held on the third day after his death was his teasing of that uncomfortable Sunday, as well as his mockery of religion, but I did not care. He had been my friend. I could accept the mockery. Avrum had also balanced his mockery with humor: no requiem music. And I understood that, too. Avrum despised requiem music. To him it did little more than bore the living and irritate the dead. "If you must do music, do one of your songs from the fields," he had said to me. "Just don't make it about Jesus."

At eleven o'clock, the cafeteria was filled. In one corner of the room, I saw Sammy and Lila standing beside Sammy's *Old Man.* He smiled radiantly and lifted his camera in salute and pointed to his sculpture. I nodded to him. Lila pulled his arm down.

I did not see Carter, but it did not surprise me. Carter was always late to events that he attended only out of obligation. "Last in, first out," he had often bragged. "Anything else is a waste of time."

Sol stood at the metal podium, waiting for the doors to close. The lights for the video camera struck him and I saw him blink and drop his head, then raise it again.

"Ladies and gentlemen," he said, "my name is Sol Walkman, and I am the director of the Highmount Home for Retired Citizens. I want to thank you for attending this special occasion honoring Avrum Feldman, who, for many years, was a resident with us. I admit that having a memorial service is, well, a bit unusual for us, but it's something that I gladly endorse.

"It was Mr. Feldman's wish that this service be conducted by a man whose friendship was as

233

bonding to him as that of a son, and I am now pleased to introduce that man: Mr. Madison Lee Murphy, who also happens to be one of the most admired artists out of the South." He turned to me. "Mr. Murphy."

Sol stepped away from the podium and I rose and walked to it, holding the book of poems. The beam of lights for the video camera was blinding. I could not see the faces of those people sitting in front of me, only the stilled silhouettes of their bodies.

I said to the silhouettes, "I have never done this kind of thing and I confess to you that I don't know if there is a protocol for such services. But, for those of you who knew Avrum Feldman, you will understand that protocol would probably be out of place anyway. I will emphasize this is not a religious service. It is meant simply to acknowledge that Avrum lived among us and that he was, in many ways, a very unique man.

"I am going to do two things. I am going to read you his favorite poem, and then I am going to tell you a story that Avrum swore he had never told anyone but me. It is about Amelita Galli-Curci."

I heard a quiet murmuring in the crowd.

"But before I do anything, I want to recognize a contribution by one of your fine local artists, Mr. Sammy Merritt. He has graciously permitted us to display a piece of sculpture that he has dedicated to Avrum Feldman's memory, a piece that he calls *Old Man*." I squinted into the lights. "Sammy, where are you?"

Sammy stopped forward and waved. The lights swiveled toward him. He was smiling happily. A mild scattering of applause rippled across the crowd.

"Please feel free to stop by where Mr. Merritt is standing and view his work when the service is over," I suggested.

The lights turned back to me.

"Avrum was convinced that Walt Whitman had written his poetic biography in the poem I am about to read," I said to the lights and to the silhouettes. "He thought this because Avrum did not believe in passing *through* life; he believed in living *in* it, and he knew that living in it was risky, more risky than simply being swept along on the current that he once described to me as 'the little waves called days.' I did not always agree with his thinking, but in this, I could never find any reason to disagree."

And then I read them the poem. I did not know how they accepted it. I could not see their faces. But I did know that it was quiet during the reading and when I finished, even quieter.

I closed the book and said, "Now, I want to tell you a story about Avrum, one that he shared with me only a few years ago on one of those melancholy days we all have—the kind of day that makes us remember something so clearly it becomes as real in memory as it was in reality. It is the story of how he could hear her voice, when no one else could. I think you will understand it."

I heard a cough and the almost whispery sound of movement, as though people were leaning forward in their chairs.

"All of you know that Amelita Galli-Curci built a summer home called Sul Monte, not far from here. The stories are legend about her singing from her porch, and how her voice would drift down over the valley, like a voice out of the skies, and how everyone would stop what they were doing and listen.

"Avrum followed her here, every summer, for the two weeks he had as vacation. He would sit on a bench in Pine Hill and he would listen to Amelita Galli-Curci sing, and he would be at peace.

"He told me that, one day, he gathered his courage and went to Sul Monte and hid in the woods nearby, in a spot where he could watch her house. He wanted to see her, as he had seen her from the opera houses of New York, or from the streets when she left the theater after a performance. He waited for many hours. Late in the afternoon, she came out onto the porch and began to sing the 'Shadow Song' from *Dinorah*—his favorite. In the song, the character, Dinorah, is wandering through a forest of birch trees under the light of the moon. She sees her shadow and imagines that it is a friend, and she invites it to dance and play with her.

"When she finished her singing, she did a small

bow to the mountains, and she turned to go back inside.

"That is when Avrum came out of his hiding. He had a bouquet of roses that he had picked from the roadside. He called out to her, 'Wait, please.' She turned back to him and he crossed the lawn of her home and handed her the roses.

"She took them, looked at them, and then she threw them at his feet. She shouted at him, 'Leave me in peace.' And Avrum hurried away. He did not know she had heard the stories of a man who worshiped her, who followed her each summer to the Catskills. He would not know that until years later, when he read an account of it in an interview that was published in an opera magazine.

"That night, Avrum took his collection of recordings by Amelita Galli-Curci and he wanted to smash them. He wanted to destroy all that he had ever felt for her, but as he raised the first record to strike it against a chair, he began to hear her voice, and he put the record away."

I could hear whispers from the silhouettes.

"I do not know why he heard her voice," I said, "but he did. I have never doubted that. The mind, obsessed by very great caring, is a marvelous thing, I think.

"And this is the last thing I want to say: When you think of Avrum Feldman, think of him as a man who had a gift, not a burden. He told me he was Whitman's Old Man. I think he was

Whitman's Child. And it is my hope that that child will rest in peace."

I moved away from the podium.

There was no response from the audience, only the sound of labored breathing. Sol walked to the microphone and said, "This ends the memorial service for Mr. Feldman. Thank you for attending. You may return to your other activities now."

The glare of the camera lights pivoted to scan the leaving audience. Sol extended his hand. "Very nice," he said. "Very warmly done."

I could see Dee Richardson flash a thumbs-up approval from the back of the room. Sammy and Lila were standing beside the *Old Man* sculpture. Sammy was aiming his camera at me. The flash spit light and I blinked at the glare. I felt someone touch my arm and I heard a voice.

"Bobo."

I knew who it was before I turned.

Amy Lourie.

Carter was standing beside her, beaming.

14

I wanted to speak Amy's name, but I was numbed by disbelief. She was dressed in a dark blue pants suit, with a simple white silk blouse that buttoned at her throat. She wore a delicate silver necklace with a blue love stone, like the one she had given me, set in a oval of thin silver. She was as beautiful as she had been on the first night that I saw her in Arch's.

"Jesus, Bobo, don't you know who this is?" Carter prodded.

I nodded and Amy stepped to me and embraced me politely, almost formally. Still, I thought I felt her body tremble. She whispered, "Hello, Bobo," She pulled her face back and looked at me. Her eyes were shining.

"You look wonderful," I said.

"You, too," she replied.

Carter crowed happily, "I can't stand it. I love this." He threw his arms around us and pulled us to him in a powerful hug. Then he called across the cafeteria, "Sammy, get a picture of this and print it up life-size. I've been waiting almost forty years for it."

Amy was caught in a wedge between us. Sammy rushed close and the flash from his camera blinked. "One more," he said. And the flash blinked again.

"I couldn't believe it, Bobo," Carter said exuberantly. "I was coming in and I saw her standing outside. I couldn't believe it."

"Nor can I," I said.

Carter embraced Amy joyfully. "Still the most beautiful woman I've ever seen," he exclaimed. "God, I hope you're up here looking for a husband, because I'm available."

Amy laughed the girlish laughter of 1955.

We left the Home and returned to the Inn at Sammy's and Lila's insistence. "For lunch, on us," Sammy commanded. I did not have the heart to protest, though I knew the meal would be a disaster. Surprisingly, it wasn't. Lila supervised Shirley Bagwell in the cooking and the food was pleasing, complemented by wine from the stockbroker and the judge's wife.

I learned little about Amy during lunch. She lived in New York, was married and had three children, all daughters. Her husband was named Peter Meyers, a lawyer who represented foreign business investments. He was often in Washington, lobbying to snip away the red tape of regulations. Two of their children were away from home. One was married and pregnant, the other had been married and divorced and was studying interior design. The daughter who still lived at home was a senior at New York University, studying anthropology.

I realized later that we had talked of our families quickly, almost obligatorily, almost as an act to accommodate the expectations of Carter and Sammy and Lila. Amy asked about Carolyn, calling her by name, and it surprised me. "She's fine," I said. "She's survived me all these years." Amy smiled. "And your children?" she said. "Tell me about them." And I did, reciting their names and ages. Amy listened and again smiled. She did not offer to show me pictures from her purse and I did not offer to show pictures from my wallet.

Only one question seemed to make her uncomfortable: "And what about your parents?"

Her answer came after a pause, a quick glance away to the table they had occupied as a family during their summers at the Inn. "My father lives in Florida. He's still healthy, still active." She paused again and looked back at me. "My mother died six months ago."

"I'm sorry," I told her.

She did not respond. A sadness wandered across her face.

After lunch, Carter announced that he was late for a meeting. He hugged Amy quickly, whispering something private to her. She smiled and nodded and Carter rushed away, crowing his praise of the lunch to Sammy and Lila.

"The two of you, go visit," Lila commanded.

"Why don't we all go for a walk?" Sammy suggested cheerfully. "It's nice out."

"My God, Sammy, where are your manners?" Lila said. "Leave them alone."

"Jesus, Lila, you don't have to snap my head off," Sammy complained. "I thought if Amy wanted to see—"

"Sammy, you can be a real pain in the ass. Do you know that?" Lila hissed.

Sammy blushed with anger.

"I don't have much time," Amy said.

"You're not going back to the city today, are you?" I asked.

"No. I have to meet some people," she answered. "I own a house near Shandaken. I'm having some work done on it."

"You do?" I said. "You have a house here?"

"It belonged to my mother. She left it to me."

"Go, go, you two. Have fun," urged Lila, motioning us out of the dining room. She looked at me. "After all these years, you've got some catching up to do."

We walked outside into the warm sun-bright day. Down the street, the girl of the jumping rope and the bicycle was tossing a ball against the side of the abandoned fire station. The thump of the ball was the only sound in the village.

"Where to?" I asked.

"Why don't we just walk," Amy suggested.

"Like the old people used to?" I said.

"Yes. Like the old people."

She slipped her arm into the cradle of my arm and we began our slow walk down through the village.

242

She said after a moment, "Do you get the feeling that he's still here with us?"

"Avrum?"

She nodded.

"I'm sure he is," I said. Then: "You left the book of poems at the Home, didn't you?"

She nodded again.

"When did you get it?"

"Last year. He gave it to me."

"You saw him?" I said in surprise.

She turned her face to me. "Yes, Bobo. Almost as often as you did over the past few years. Maybe more often. After my mother moved here, I came to visit two or three times a year. I read about him living at the Home the year he turned a hundred and I went to visit him. The last time I was with him, he asked me to read the poem to him, and then he told me to take the book. He said you had given it to him."

"No, I didn't."

She smiled. "I didn't think you had. It was his way of reminding me of you, and he was always finding ways to do that. Anyway, when I saw the interview with you, and you were talking about the service for him, I knew the poem had to be part of what you did—because of what he told me about it."

We passed Dan Wilder's Coffee and Pastry Shop. I could see Dan through the window. He was stacking boxes on his counter.

"Why didn't you call me? You must have known I was at the Inn," I said.

"Yes, I knew. I knew you were here last year, also. I saw Avrum the day before you arrived."

"I really wish you had called," I told her.

"I didn't think I could see you," she said simply. "Last year, when Avrum told me you were coming, I left that afternoon and drove back to the city. I don't know why, really, but I did. I thought I might accidentally see you, I suppose. Even driving back, I kept looking into every car that I met, wondering if the driver would be you. And this morning, I didn't think I could go to the service, but I changed my mind. I knew I had to see you this time, or risk never seeing you at all."

We approached the abandoned fire station. The girl stood watching us, holding the ball she had been bouncing against the wall. She was wearing a woman's dress hat, a style from the twenties that had a wide ribbon band and a bow over her left ear. The hat was cupped humorously on her head. Amy waved to her, but the girl did not return her greeting. She turned back to the fire station and bounced the ball. It skipped once, struck the wall, and careened back to her. She caught it easily, lazily.

"She's pretty, isn't she?" Amy said.

"Yes, she is," I replied.

"Let's go back to Avrum's bench," Amy said.

"All right."

We crossed the street and walked back toward the Inn. At Arch's, Amy stopped and looked at the window that still carried the sign with his name bordered in chipped gold paint: ARCH'S. She said, "A lot of memories are in there, Bobo."

"Sammy still has the jukebox," I told her.

A shimmer of delight skipped in her face. "He does?"

"Still has some of the records from the fifties."

"Maybe we can get him to play some for us before you leave," she said.

"Knowing Sammy, he'd restore the place if we asked him."

Amy dropped her arm from my arm and took my hand and laced her fingers with my fingers. She tugged at me and we turned from Arch's and continued walking up the sidewalk.

"I can't believe Avrum never said anything to me about you," I told her.

"I asked him not to. It was an understanding between us. I insisted on it."

"I wish I had known," I said.

"What good would it have done, Bobo?"

"I would have learned something about you. Where you were, how you were."

She glanced at me. Her eyes were shining. "Do you know what you would have learned? You would have learned that I was a wife and mother, married to a man preoccupied with success and money and a man very, very talented at gaining both. You would have learned that I serve on a half dozen socially acceptable—some think necessary—civic and art committees in the city. You would have learned that I sometimes work in a boutique that I invested in twenty years ago

245

just to have something to keep me occupied. You would have learned that I have never used my college major, which was philosophy, for the good of anything, unless you count the tending to children, and I do. In fact, I think they're the true accomplishment of my life. I love them passionately. You would have learned that I have seen the same counselor twice a month for the past eight years and only recently declared myself cured of whatever malady it was that made me carry on before him like I was a talk-show host." She turned to me and smiled softly. "You would have learned how ordinary I really am."

"None of it sounds ordinary to me," I said. "Still, knowing Avrum, I'm surprised he didn't find some way to tell me about you."

"He wanted to. He argued with me about it, but I wouldn't let him. I knew he understood, even if he disagreed."

We reached Avrum's bench and sat. She took my hand into both of her hands and began to massage it gently. She seemed peaceful, comfortable.

"And Carter? You never saw Carter?" I asked.

She shook her head. "I wasn't ready to see him, either. When I visited my mother, I stayed with her most of the time. Once or twice we drove here, just to see the Inn again, and the village. But even that was hard to do. There were too many memories for both of us."

"I know," I said.

We sat for a moment, not speaking. The slow

rhythm of the young girl's ball hitting the wall of the abandoned fire station two blocks away was like a laborsome ticking of time.

"Have you noticed how deserted it is here?" Amy asked.

"Yes," I said. "I sometimes think that I'll come here one day and everything will be closed. Everyone will have died or moved away."

Amy lifted her face to the sun and closed her eyes. Her thumb stroked the back of my thumb. She said softly, "I went to the cemetery this morning, to Arch's grave. I think he and Avrum were the last two people of that summer." She opened her eyes and looked toward the mountain behind the Inn. "Our tree's gone, too, isn't it?"

"Several years ago," I said. "A storm, I think."

"I thought it would last forever."

"Me, too."

"I wonder if it missed us." she said.

I tried to be casual—wanted the words to sound casual: "I don't know about it, but I did."

Her hands tightened on my hand.

"Your necklace," I said. "It's the stone, isn't it?"

Her eyes searched me in surprise. "Do you still have yours?" she asked.

"It's in my briefcase."

"It is?"

"Yes."

She lifted her head again, nestled it against her shoulders. A smile eased into her face. "It's really childish, isn't it? But I've never been without it.

Never. I wore it in my wedding. You know—something blue. My mother wanted me to wear a blue garter, but I wouldn't. I wanted the necklace." She pulled one hand away from my hand and touched the stone with her finger. "I think my mother knew why."

"I used to keep mine in my pocket, but I was afraid of losing it," I told her. "That's why it's in my briefcase. I told my children that it was my magic eye, that before I could paint anything, I had to look through it. I said it so often, I think I began to believe it myself. But you know kids. Eventually they told me it was nothing but a rock."

She did not reply for a moment. She was again gazing at the mountain, at the place where our tree had been. Then she said, "My girls are the same way. Sometimes I think I used up all their magic, that I didn't have any left to pass on to them. And that's a horrible thing to do to children." She paused and looked at her hand in mine. She opened her fingers, closed them again around my hand. "Do you know I'm having dinner with you tonight?"

"No, but I'm glad. I was going to suggest it."

"Carter insisted."

"Carter. Our friend Carter," I said. "He's in love again."

Amy laughed lightly. "I thought so. He told me I would like his date, but to be vague about his age."

"He hasn't changed very much over the years,"

I said. "But he didn't need to. I think he was always a step ahead of the rest of us. I have my friends in Atlanta—some good ones, some good people—but he's Carter and that puts him in a special place."

"I think it's mutual," she replied. She lifted her face to look at me. "Do you know that he wrote to me before your wedding, asking me to call you?"

"He did? Why?"

"He didn't want you to get married. Not then. He thought I could stop it."

I was puzzled. Carter had met Carolyn only once, in 1955, and he had been pleasant to her, but he had seldom mentioned her to me again.

"I didn't answer his letter," Amy said.

"Why didn't you?"

"It was the one letter I didn't want to receive, I suppose," she answered. "That was a long time ago, wasn't it, Bobo? Everything was either wonderful or painful. The wonderful was too wonderful to imagine; the painful was too painful to take." The smile returned to her mouth, but it was a melancholy smile. "We were very young, weren't we?"

"Yes. We were."

Amy left a few minutes later. She gave me directions to her home—"Unless you want me to meet you at Carter's," she said.

"No. You're with me."

"What do we call it? A date?"

"Why not? That is, if I don't have to ask anyone's permission."

She laughed. "Not this time. And I don't think you'll have to be afraid of anyone seeing us on the front porch."

"This time, I don't care," I said.

I watched her drive away. She waved from her car window as she passed Arch's and she pointed to the store with her finger. I knew what she was saying in her sign language: *Do you remember the date?*

Each summer, Arch Ellis closed his store on one night to everyone but the young people who worked in the resorts, and their dates. He moved the tables and display counters from the center of the room and made a dance floor, and then he provided coins dabbed with red fingernail polish for the jukebox. Every refreshment was half-price, but Arch did not allow the drinking of alcoholic beverages, regardless of how it was disguised. His reasoning was sensible: "I want mamas and daddies to know they can trust me. If their kids are with me, they're safe." His attitude was material for poor humor, but we were all glad that he meant what he said.

Arch's Night was the highlight of the summer for the youth of the Shandaken Valley, and even the owners of the resorts honored it by serving light dinners and permitting kitchen work to go undone until the following morning.

On Arch's Night, 1955, I had my first official

date with Amy. It was the first time that anyone saw us touching in public, a touching that was a continuous dance to many songs from Arch's jukebox. Later, by the swimming pool, Carter lectured that Amy and I were the most talked-about couple of the night. "I swear to God, it was embarrassing," he groused. "If you two don't have a baby out of all that rubbing up against one another, it'll be because one of you is sterile. I mean, I can appreciate a man being horny, and I think you know that. Talking to me about being horny is like talking to Noah about rain, but, my God, Bobo, the two of you turned on everybody in there, including Arch. I promise you, there're more backseats being used in Chevrolets tonight than at any time in the history of the Catskill Mountains. And there's another thing: I know you're a Georgia hick and you can't help it, but, Jesus, up here couples turn loose of one another occasionally. They don't dance to the sound of a quarter falling into a jukebox; they dance to music." Then he smiled. "I'm proud of you, boy," he added.

I had not intended to ask Amy for a date for Arch's Night, though I wanted to. I knew it would create gossip and I knew her mother was already watching me closely. Amy initiated it at lunch by saying to her mother as I was serving the entree, "Bobo wants to take me to the dance at Arch's tonight. Is that okay?"

I could feel a blush covering me.

Evelyn Lourie looked at me in surprise.

"Ah—" I said.

"Amy, are you saying that to embarrass Bobo?" her mother asked.

Amy giggled. "No. I'm just tired of waiting to be asked. I want to go and nobody will ask me, and you have to be asked unless you work in one of the resorts."

"Well, I think it's fine," Joel Lourie said. He looked at me. "Bobo?"

I stammered. "Uh, I—I'd be happy for Amy to go with me." I glanced at Carter. A gleeful grin was on his face. "With us," I amended.

"No, it has to be a real date," Amy corrected. "I've been coming here for years. I know the rules."

"I don't think you should pressure the young man like this," Evelyn Lourie said evenly.

"Then I think he should ask me," Amy insisted.

I stood in the horror of the pause. My hands were shaking. I had never known a person as bold as Amy Lourie. Her mother's eyes felt attached to my face.

"I think that's up to Bobo," Joel Lourie judged. He smiled and again said, "Bobo?"

"I—I would like that. Yes, sir."

"That's not asking me; that's agreeing," Amy argued.

Carter came to my rescue. He said, filling Amy's glass with water, "You know he's from Georgia. They don't ask girls for dates down there. They hit them in the head with a stick and drag them off by their hair."

Joel Lourie laughed robustly.

"So, I'll have to do it for him," Carter continued. "As an example of good manners." He looked at Amy with a preposterously affected gaze, like Clark Gable feeding on the eyes of Vivian Leigh. "Will you go to the dance with me—me, being Bobo—tonight at Arch's?"

Amy giggled again. "I'd love to. I didn't think you'd ever ask." She turned to her mother. "Is that all right?"

Evelyn Lourie's disbelieving stare moved from me to Amy. "I think it would be disgraceful not to go, after your behavior," she said stiffly. Then, to me: "I apologize for her, Bobo."

"There's no reason for that," I said. "It's fine."

I left the table and went into the kitchen and then into the walk-in cooler and stood, leaning on a crate of grapes, breathing deeply. In a moment, the door opened and Carter stepped inside. "Bobo, do me a favor. When you get ready to take her to bed, remember me. I'll be right there, in case you need a substitute." He laughed at his own humor. "Indeed, I will."

And so that night, I went to the lobby of the Inn and formally asked Nora Dowling to call Amy for our date.

"You behave with that girl," Nora warned. "Don't let anything happen."

"I won't," I said.

Amy bounded down the stairs, followed by her parents. She took my arm.

"Ready?" she asked.

I mumbled, "Yes."

She pivoted us to face her parents. "You know where we'll be," she said brightly.

"Don't be late," her mother cautioned.

"No, ma'am, we won't be," I promised.

As we walked away from the Inn toward Arch's, I knew that Joel and Evelyn Lourie and Nora Dowling were standing at a window, staring at us, wondering. And I did not blame them. I, too, wondered.

After the dance, with the ghost-heat of her body still pressing against me and the scent of her perfume rising from the collar of my shirt, I walked Amy back to the front porch of the Inn. Through the thin curtains of the window, I could see her parents playing bridge with another couple at a game table in the lobby.

"Are you going to kiss me good-night?" Amy teased.

"Are you crazy? Your folks can see us."

"I don't mind."

"You may not, but I do," I said.

She smiled softly. "What should we do? Shake hands?"

"Not even that."

She stepped toward me, her face lifted.

"Don't, Amy—"

"What if I sneaked into The Cave tonight?" she whispered.

"My God, Amy."

She smiled again. She reached with her hand and drew her fingertip down my forearm, tracing the muscle.

"I love you, Bobo Murphy," she said quietly.

"I love you," I told her.

"Thank you for tonight, Bobo."

15

Lila was waiting for me in the Inn, pretending to work behind the registration desk. She handed me a glass of wine and then lifted her own glass and tipped it to mine in a bell-ring of crystal.

"To good findings," she said.

"To good friends," I replied.

"So, that's your Amy," she sighed. She leaned over the desk and gazed at me. "I don't blame you for looking for her all those years, Bobo. She's so damn beautiful, it makes me wish I were gay." She sipped from her wine. "I hope you know I'm jealous."

"No reason to be," I told her. "You're still my favorite fantasy. By the way, thanks for lunch. It was good of you and Sammy."

"We enjoyed it," Lila said. "Anyway, I think Sammy's inspired again. You'll probably see something that's supposed to be Amy's face—or a mutilation of it—in a piece of rock before the week's over."

I laughed. Lila was right. If Sammy was inspired, and I was sure he must be, he would hammer away at a stone until he was exhausted. But Sammy would not understand that stone was too rough for Amy Lourie Meyers's face. Her face begged for the delicate touch of a brush from an artist of extraordinary talent, someone like Jean Archer.

"Tell me something, Bobo."

"Ask."

"Did you ever make love to her?"

"No, Lila, I didn't."

"Why not?"

"We were very young. It was different then, a different time."

"Did you want to?"

"I think so. Yes, I think so. I just remember being confused."

"Do you want to now?"

"Lila," I said with warning.

"All right, I won't ask," she said. "I think I know the answer, anyway. Oh, Carter called a few minutes ago. I told him the two of you were in your room and had the Do Not Disturb sign on the door. He wants you to call him when you're finished."

"You don't stop, do you?" I said.

She sipped seductively from her wine. "Never."

There was a schoolboy eagerness in Carter's voice. He demanded to know what had happened with Amy.

"Nothing happened. We took a walk and then sat on Avrum's bench for a few minutes and talked, and then she left."

"That's it?" He sounded disappointed.

"What did you expect? Front-porch fornication? She had to meet with some people who were working on her house."

"She told me about that," he said. "I know the place. It could use some work."

"Is your meeting over?" I asked.

"What meeting?"

"The one you were going to in such a rush."

"You dumb shit, I didn't have a meeting. I just wanted to give you some time alone. Christ, Bobo, are you ever going to quit being a redneck?"

"I guess not," I said.

"Well, if you had any sense, you'd be out buying her flowers, boy. Sending them in by the goddamn truckload. In case you missed it, she's not in the best marriage in the Western world, and you know what that means, I hope."

"I don't think I do," I said. "What?"

"You've got a second chance, and that's something that almost nobody gets. You blow it this time and you're going to wind up like Avrum, locked up in an old-age home, listening to the music of memory."

"You forget, Carter, I'm also married."

"Oh, yeah," he said. "I wondered why her story sounded so familiar. I've heard it before."

"Don't you think you could be wrong?" I asked. "Isn't it possible that she's perfectly happy, and I'm perfectly happy, and this is nothing more than a nostalgic look back on our youth?"

Carter snorted a laugh. "Shit. Remember who

you're talking to, Bobo. Did you ask her about the painting?"

"No."

"Why not?"

"It didn't seem the right thing to do, not at the time."

"Maybe tonight, then."

"Maybe. But let me do it. I don't want to bring it up until it's the right time."

Carter promised he would not say anything about the painting. He seemed more concerned with Libby. "I hope to God she's not intimidated," he said.

"I don't think that'll happen," I assured him. "After all, Libby is a few years younger and she doesn't look like the type to be intimidated."

"Don't start on the age thing, Bobo. Jesus, stay away from that. If it comes up, we were there in 1960. Remember that, and tell Amy."

I promised to protect his deception.

"You know, damned if Amy's not prettier now than she was at seventeen, and I didn't think that would be possible," he said.

"I can't argue with that," I agreed.

"All right, I'll see you around seven tonight."

"Seven."

"Oh, by the way, you did a damn fine job today with Avrum's service," Carter added. "Beats the hell out of 'This Little Light of Mine.'"

"I don't know," I said. "I didn't get a standing ovation this time."

"You didn't look as pitiful," Carter countered.

"Anyway, it was good. I had the feeling that old cockroach was sitting in there, listening to you."

"Maybe he was," I said. "Maybe he was."

After I changed clothes—from the suit I had worn for Avrum's memorial service to the ancient, out-of-style casual wear that I like, but Carolyn despises—I slipped out of the Inn without Lila seeing me, and I walked north to the cemetery. I could hear a dull hammering from Arch's and I knew that Sammy was at work, knocking away pieces of marble or granite in search of Amy's face, like some crazed surgeon trying to make life out of spare parts. Sammy would not stop to think the face from the stone. He would pound it out. I saw the young girl standing in front of the window, wearing the woman's dress hat, staring inside at Sammy. She seemed intrigued, or amused. She turned, as though she could sense my presence, and looked at me, then she turned back to the window.

My walks through the cemetery began the year that Nora Dowling died. While visiting her grave, I realized there were many names that I recognized, people who had been patient and caring. Each time that I returned, there were new names, new headstones with brief, coded stories of a life chiseled into the facing, like headlines from newspapers. Arch Ellis was the newest story, the latest headline. Amy said she had been to Arch's grave. When she said his name, it was with sadness and joy, and I knew that I would also feel that bewildering contradiction.

One year, Carter went with me into the cemetery and complained irritably about my solemn pauses at the gravesites. "They're dead, boy," he grumbled. "You're not going to talk them out of that ground and we both know it. But if you do, I've got a deal for you that you won't believe."

Carter did not understand why the cemetery visits were important to me. "Must be a Southern thing," he groused. "Some kind of redneck religion. Is that what they mean by 'The South's gonna rise again,' Bobo? Is that what your people do? Stand around the tombstones, hoping General Lee will come charging down off one of those monuments with Jesus on his right hand and Stonewall Jackson on his left? Is that how you Rebs are finally going to whip our ass, Bobo?"

I tried to tell Carter that being in the cemetery was a simple thing, that it effected memories of good people from one of the good experiences of my life. He denounced my argument as poetic bullshit. As always, he evoked the name of Amy Lourie.

"The person you're looking for is not in there, Bobo," he declared. "The only reason you come here is because every one of those piles of bones reminds you of something that happened with her. You're forgetting your Bible, my man: 'Why seek the living among the dead?' Or was that Shakespeare? Anyway, she's not out here, and if she were, it wouldn't do you any good, would it?"

I had never considered that I was looking for Amy in the cemetery, as Carter had accused, yet it was true that when I was there, I would sense her. Gentle thoughts, gentle moments. Like leafing through an album of old family photographs and pausing, with a tremor of gladness, over a smiling face from another, smiling time.

I remembered her at Ben Benton's grave. Remembered Ben's affable kidding about dating a rich Jewish girl from the city. Remembered his constant offers to let me borrow his garbage truck to drive her to some isolated country road to park and make out. "Won't nobody mess with you in my truck," Ben had bragged.

I remembered her at Nora Dowling's grave. Remembered seeing Nora Dowling's look of pride over my friendship with Amy sour into a frown of concern. "It's not good to be so close a friend with such a girl at your age," she had lectured. "She's pretty. Pretty girls leave their marks. And you are so different, Bobo. So different. It is not easy when you are so different, I can tell you. My late husband, he and I were different. It was never easy."

I remembered her at Harry Burger's grave. Especially at Harry's grave. At Harry's grave, I remembered his warnings about Avrum: "Avrum, he wants to make himself young again. . . . Amy, your Amy, she is lovely, yes, but she is not Amelita Galli-Curci. If you make her that, you will suffer."

Harry had been prophetic.

And, now, I remembered Amy at the grave of Arch Ellis, which was decorated with fresh flowers in a buried vase. There was no card, but I knew the flowers were from Amy. I stood beside the grave and remembered Amy's delight over Arch's stories, remembered her body against me at the dance on Arch's Night, remembered the covered touch of her hand on mine as we sat together in Arch's, in a booth, with Carter and Rene sitting across from us.

And I remembered the night, after work, when Joey Li, who had been hired to replace me as the dishwasher, came into Arch's and said, "Excuse, Bobo. Mrs. Dowling says you have a phone call."

"Are you sure?" I asked.

Joey bobbed his head, a reflex to the Chinese bow he always used in greetings. He answered, "Very sure."

I must have looked concerned. Amy said, "Don't worry about it. I'm sure everything's all right, or Mrs. Dowling would have come for you herself."

"Ah, it's nothing," Carter added casually. "Probably about his prize-winning pig having piglets." He grinned arrogantly.

"Be back in a minute," I said. I slipped from the booth and followed Joey back to the Inn.

The message was from Carolyn. I was to call her collect.

She said in a happy voice, "I've got a surprise for you."

"What?" I asked.

"I'm coming to see you."

For a moment, I said nothing, and then, "When? How?"

"With Raymond and Linda," she said excitedly. "Your mother and I are riding back with them when their vacation's over, and then we'll come back on the bus with you."

"Well, that's—I'm glad," I stammered. "When did this come up?"

"Your mother called me yesterday, to see if I wanted to go. I worked it out with Marlene."

"Who?"

"Marlene. She owns the dress shop. You do remember I'm working there this summer, don't you?"

"Oh, sure. I'm sorry. I forgot her name."

Her voice became soft and longing. "I can't wait to see you," she whispered. "I've missed you so much."

"Yeah, me, too."

"I'll write you about everything."

"Yeah, okay. Good."

"You don't sound too happy," she said. "Are you sure you want me to come?"

"Of course I do," I told her, forcing life into my voice. "I'm just surprised, that's all. But, yes, I want you to come. It'll be fun."

"I'll write tonight," she said. "I love you."

"I love you," I mumbled.

I walked back across the street to Arch's and sat beside Amy.

"Everything all right?" asked Carter.

"Fine." My voice quivered.

"What's wrong?" Amy said.

I glanced at her. She was more beautiful in that glance than she had ever been.

"It's really nothing," I said. "It was about my brother—when he's leaving to come back up here."

Amy blinked. A frown, a question, a doubt, swam across her eyes.

"That's all?" Carter said.

I nodded. I tried to smile. My face felt heavy and hot.

Later, Carter and I went to the swimming pool and sat in the lounge chairs and I told him the truth. He shook his head heavily.

"You've got to tell her," he said.

"I know. I will. But not right now."

He pushed his cigarette into the ground, then lay back against the chair and laced his fingers over his chest and gazed at the sky.

"You know what's about to happen, don't you?" he said quietly.

"No, I don't."

"You're about to see what it's like for a dream to become a wake-up. And, believe me, Bobo, it's the most beautiful dream you're ever going to have."

As I turned to leave Arch's grave, I saw the young girl. She was inside the stone fence that surrounded the cemetery and she was pulling buds from white rose bushes that grew wild and crawled over the stones like vines. She dropped the buds into the woman's dress hat. I watched as she filled the hat, moving casually among the bushes, stripping them. And then she began to walk among the graves, dropping a single white rosebud on each, like someone planting seeds. She glanced at me once. Her dark eyes were bright and daring. A strange, playful smile— almost superior—waved over her lips. She took a bud from the hat, held it over a grave, posed for a moment looking at me, then she released it. The bud fell into an open flower cup.

16

The more wine that Carter drank, the merrier he became. He sat on a large, thick-cushioned sofa in his den, with Libby leaning against him, and he laughed and talked about our summer together, weaving exaggerated stories from the thin, frayed cloth of memory. Amy and I sat in armchairs facing the sofa, with a small, antique table between us. Amy had her left foot tucked under her right leg, as she had often sat in the booths at Arch's. A weak fire burned in the fireplace, more for atmosphere than for the slight night-chill that always fell in the Catskills during the summer.

"You should have seen us, Libby," Carter would sigh. An impish grin would wiggle into his face and he would take another sip of his wine, and then he would point the wineglass to me or to Amy and he would say, "Do you remember . . .?" The question was never answered. It was not meant to be answered; it was only a prelude to another story.

He told of the morning that Mrs. Mendelson, in one of her befuddled moments, got up from the table and pulled her chair to the Lourie table and began to talk loudly of wedding plans between me and Amy, and how Nora Dowling had to leave the kitchen and come into the dining room and lead Mrs. Mendelson away, and how the occasion had embarrassed me so much that he—the busboy—had to serve the Louries their breakfast. It was a story that neither Amy nor I remembered.

He told of the swaggering, spoiled grandson of David and Judith Feinstein visiting for a weekend, and how the grandson had made advances to Amy, and how Carter had taken the grandson aside and informed him that Amy was secretly engaged to someone who worked in the Inn.

He told of the night that the steering rod on his car had dropped off when we were returning from a movie in Margaretville, and how he had forced me to call Ben Benton to come for us, and how we all crowded into the cab of Ben's truck, the girls sitting on our laps, and how Ben had splashed the cab with aftershave lotion to kill the odor of the garbage.

It was a story that Amy remembered with delight. "My mother was waiting up because we were late," she said. "She wanted to know why I smelled so bad. She thought it was from Bobo. I had to tell her that I bumped into a girl in the rest room as she was closing a bottle of cologne, and some of it spilled on me."

"I don't remember that at all," I protested, but I was lying. I did remember it. I remembered holding Amy in Ben's truck and Ben trying to be a clown about it. It was after that night that Ben began to offer me his truck to hide on some isolated road with Amy. "She loves my truck," he had teased. "I could tell."

Carter remembered the day that I left Pine Hill to return to Georgia. "We stopped traffic from both ways," he said. "And Ben Benton put Bobo in his truck and started at the top of the mountain and roared through town, taking him to his brother's house in Shandaken. Everybody was out on the sidewalks, yelling, 'Go to hell, Rebel!' and Bobo was waving out of the window, looking pitiful, as usual. The only thing missing was Amy."

"I heard about that," Amy said. "I'm sorry I wasn't there."

"And what about the night Eddie Grimes almost drowned, trying to save my life?" hooted Carter. "I know damn well you remember that, Bobo. You helped set it up."

I laughed and nodded and waited for Carter to tell the story.

Carter combed his fingers casually through Libby's hair. "Honey," he said, "that was a masterpiece, a work of art."

He told about Eddie Grimes from Queens in New York, a busboy who was lazy and irritating, and who invented outrageous stories about heroic acts that he had performed—children he had rescued from burning buildings, dogs he had pulled from the paths of speeding taxi cabs, fights he had had with armed street gangs because his mother had been insulted.

But Eddie's bragging was mild compared to his childish tricks. He put shaving cream on Carter's pillow, short-sheeted Joey Li's bed, shaved Ex-Lax into the morning hot chocolate of Walter Asher, who was an old and gracious guest. He sewed the sleeves of my waiter's jacket together, overspiked the fresh fruit cocktail with cognac, stuck chewing gum over the coin slot of Arch's jukebox.

Carter despised Eddie Grimes, and one morning after Eddie had reset The Cave's clock to alarm at three instead of five-thirty, Carter swore revenge. "That son of a bitch woke me up just as I was pulling Rene's panties off," he hissed, "and I don't care if it was just a dream, he's going to pay for it."

It took Carter a week to perfect his scheme.

He first befriended Eddie. It was a sickening, but effective, performance. Jokes shared privately between them. Gifts of cigarettes and milk shakes from Carter. Carter begging Eddie to retell his dramas with street gangs. Giggles about a Busboys Union the two were plotting. And during their togetherness, Carter confessed that he suffered from a baffling illness: he was a sleep-walker.

Eddie took the bait hungrily. "Don't worry, buddy, I'll watch out for you," he promised Carter.

"Just don't let anybody wake me up if I do it," pleaded Carter. "That could send me off the deep end, like my daddy."

Eddie was curious. "What about your daddy?"

"He lost his marbles, Eddie. We had to put him in a home. They just let him out a few weeks ago."

"Oh . . ."

And then Carter got his vengeance.

One night he began to moan softly in his bunk bed above me. Eddie sat up attentively. I pretended to awake from a sound sleep. "What's the matter with Carter?" I mumbled.

"Be quiet," Eddie commanded.

Carter moaned again. He began tossing wildly about, fighting with his pillow, and then he rolled out of bed and pulled on his jeans and opened the door and walked outside.

"What's going on, Eddie?" I asked anxiously.

"Sleepwalking," Eddie pronounced. "Don't wake him." He scrambled from his bed.

"Stop him, Eddie," I begged. "He could get hurt out there."

"He won't do nothing he wouldn't do if he was awake," Eddie declared. "I know about sleepwalking." He snatched a cigarette from the desk and lit it and then followed Carter outside, wearing only a T-shirt and his boxer shorts. He did not know that half the residents of Pine Hill were hiding behind the hedges, waiting and watching.

Joey Li and I quickly slipped on our pants.

Carter crossed the street in a strong stride and headed for the swimming pool with Eddie behind him, and with me following Eddie and with Joey following me.

"He's going straight for the pool," I called desperately.

"He won't go in," Eddie said with authority.

At the edge of the pool, Carter paused. He lifted his head as though sensing danger, and then he stepped into the pool and sank to the bottom. I yelled to Eddie, "He's going to drown! You've got to save him!" Eddie looked at me in shock. He was a poor swimmer and he knew it. "Eddie, do something," I begged. Eddie jumped into the pool, his cigarette still dangling from his lips.

I could see them in the pool. Carter was on the bottom. Each time Eddie would grab at him, Carter would swim away, and Eddie would bob up to the surface, gasping for air.

"Save him, Eddie, save him," I pleaded. "He's the only busboy I've got."

Finally, when he needed air, Carter permitted himself to be rescued by Eddie. Joey helped me pull both of them from the water. Carter looked at Eddie, who was soaked and shivering, and cried, "You saved me! You saved me!" Then he lifted his arms in a prearranged signal and those who were watching in hiding jumped from behind the hedges, cheering and applauding.

"I got the son of a bitch," Carter said smugly, pulling Libby to him.

"Carter, I think that's mean," Libby said playfully. She slapped at his dangling hand.

"Honey, it was one of the great moments in

the storied history of the Catskill Mountains,"
Carter told her. "Arch added it to his repertoire
of tall tales. You were there, weren't you, Amy?"

"I had to sneak out," Amy confessed, smiling
at the memory, "but, yes, I was there. And
Libby's right: it was mean, but it was also funny."

"All my life, I've been trying to match that
feat, and I never have," Carter said. "Closest
I've ever come is winning a court case one time
because of it."

"How did you do that?" I asked.

"I claimed my client was sleepwalking when
he was arrested for stealing a couple of tires from
a service station. Even the client believed it. He'd
been so drunk, he didn't know the difference.
They let him off with restitution and a warning."

Carter laughed softly and touched the wineglass to his lips, but he did not sip from it. He
gazed at the amber coals of the cooling fire, then
he turned his face to me and from me to Amy.
He said quietly, "I'm a happy man, my friends,
but I think that may have been the best year of
my life." He paused. His eyes began to mist. "It
was magic. *Magic.* Even then, I knew it was."

"Yes," Amy whispered.

"It was," I agreed.

"And here we are, back together," Carter said.
He lifted his glass. "To Avrum."

Amy and I stayed only a few minutes after the
toast to Avrum. All of us embraced as friends
embrace and we thanked Carter for the dinner

and the memories. Amy paused again at each of my paintings hanging in Carter's den. When she had first seen them—led to them by Carter—she had touched my arm and whispered, "They're beautiful, but I knew they would be." And she said again, as she wandered from painting to painting, "They're beautiful."

We drove back to Amy's summer home. She had given me a tour earlier. It was a small, cedar-board house with interior walls of paneling, giving it a feeling of warmth. It had a den with a large stone fireplace and one wall of bookshelves, but with no books in them. And, surprisingly, there were no paintings or prints hanging in any of the rooms. "It looks empty, I know," she had explained, "but I'm packing everything that belonged to my mother and moving it. I'll replace it with my own things."

There was no awkwardness at the door when we returned. Amy went inside and I followed. She asked me to light a fire while she made coffee, and she went into the kitchen. I was sitting on the floor, watching the fire build into flames, when she came back into the den.

"It's nice, isn't it?" she said. "Of everything in the house, I like the fireplace the best. The one we have in the city looks as though it would hate a fire."

She put the coffee on the stonework before the fireplace and took cushions from the sofa and sat beside me, pulling her knees up and wrapping her arms around them. The aroma from the coffee and the faint air of woodsmoke filled the room.

Amy watched the flames curling around the wood. Fingers of fire danced in the reflection of her eyes. She said after a moment, "I remember sitting in the Inn that night after the dance at Arch's, and there was a fire like this. My parents were waiting up for me, playing cards with another couple—the Traubs, I think—and I sat there, on the floor near them, wanting you to be with me." She looked at me. "You remember that night, don't you?"

"Yes, I remember it."

She inhaled slowly, as though inhaling the memory and the warmth of the fire, and then she said quietly, "I believe that was the night, and that was the place—there, in front of the fire— when I first knew that I really loved you. When I felt it, I mean. When it was more than just something I said because I was glad to be with you."

"Is that when you talked to your mother about me?" I asked.

She nodded and leaned her chin against her knees. "We'd talked before, a little. She had great instincts about me. I think she knew from that first morning, at breakfast, that I was interested in you. But she didn't say very much, not then. Little things, you know. Trying to pry out of me what I was trying to hide. But the night we really talked, and I told her how I felt, was that night, after we went to Arch's. We were in my room. She cried."

"Did I frightened her that much?" I said.

Amy reached for my hand, touched it, pulled her hand back. "It wasn't you, Bobo. It was me. She knew that I was growing up, that I was in that awkward girl-woman stage no one ever understands. Until that summer, I had had boyfriends, but they weren't really boyfriends. They were just wonderful little infatuations that would come and go like mood swings, and my mother had helped me through them with a lot of patience and a lot of caring. She knew it was different with you. She told me there was something about you that made her know it. And, believe me, Bobo, since I've been a mother to three daughters, I've learned a lot about the intuition of parents. You may not understand what goes on in your own life, but with your children, you know. You always know."

I thought of my own children and I understood.

"Tell me about your husband," I said.

She did not respond for a long moment. She gazed at the fire and the reflection of the fire waved in her eyes, flickered like candles. Then she said, "Peter's a good man. He cares deeply, I think. His work—" She paused. "I love him, but it's never been a complete marriage, and that's more my fault than his."

"Why?"

She turned her face to me. Her face looked like the painting in Jean Archer's bedroom.

276

"Don't you know?" she answered quietly. "When Peter and I married, I loved you. I loved you with the one thing I couldn't share with anyone else—with joy, Bobo. With joy." She blinked and her eyes were shining.

"It was that, wasn't it?" I said. "Joyful. That's the perfect word. I used to think I would split apart with joy."

She smiled and looked again at the fire. It was as though she could read the fire, the way she watched it shimmering over the wood. Then she asked, "Do you remember the day we said good-bye in Avrum's room?"

"Of course. Yes."

"I told you I wanted to make love to you."

"I remember."

"I thought about that for years," she said. "But I was never ashamed of that feeling. I wondered what would have happened if we had. But we couldn't, of course. Not in that time."

"No, we couldn't," I agreed.

She closed her eyes against the flames and she again wrapped her arms around her legs and leaned forward to rest her chin on her knees. She smiled again in memory. "The first time that I ever made love to anyone, Bobo, I said your name."

"That must have been interesting," I said.

She opened her eyes and laughed easily and nodded against her knees. "It wasn't with Peter, or with Adam. It was with a boy named Steven. We were dating just before I met Peter and it was something that happened. But it didn't last, not after that night. He couldn't get over being called Bobo, and I refused to tell him anything about you."

"I guess it's a good thing it wasn't Peter," I said.

"I was careful after that," she admitted. "But I did tell Peter about you. A little. Not everything."

"What does that mean?"

"I told him we dated during the summer, that you were from Georgia and had become a well-known artist. He didn't ask much about it. I think Georgia was like a foreign country to him, too far away for worry."

"Sounds mild enough."

She looked at me. "I mean for it to be." Then: "Have you ever been sorry that we didn't make love in Avrum's room?"

"I don't think I've ever said it aloud, not even to myself, but, yes, I have. Not then, but later, thinking about it, I was sorry."

"We did fit nicely, didn't we?" she said. "I really liked kissing you."

She reached for my hand and pulled it to her and kissed the palm gently.

"I probably shouldn't tell you this," she said easily, "but I have one of your paintings."

My look had to be a look of disbelief. She nodded against my hand. *"The Waiting Man.* Do you remember it?"

"Of course I do. It was sold at a charity auction. How did you get it?"

"I used to be on a procurement committee for one of the museums. We were always getting information about estate sales and I saw it advertised in a brochure from one of the auction houses in Atlanta. I made a couple of discreet calls, twisted a couple of very pliable arms."

"My God," I said. "That must have been twenty years ago."

She kissed my palm again. "I've had it for ten years."

"I'm stunned. Really surprised. And Peter let you keep it?"

"I don't think he's ever looked at it carefully," she said. "Why should he? He only glances at photographs of the family when we take pictures. Like I said, he's busy; he doesn't pay very much attention to what I do." She looked at me warmly. "I love it, by the way. You're a very gifted man, Bobo Murphy."

"No," I said honestly. "I'm a good painter, but not gifted. A gifted painter paints. I teach. Good painters teach, hoping to find someone who's gifted, someone they can belong to in some small measure. Gifted painters can't stop painting, and good painters never stop trying. I'm satisfied with that."

"And I believe the difference between good and gifted is what the artist leaves *off* his canvas, not what he puts there," Amy said.

"I think I hear the philosophy major speaking," I replied.

"Yes, you do. But I believe it, Bobo. When

you did *The Waiting Man,* you didn't leave anything off. It's the work of a gifted man, but I do have a question about it."

"A question?"

"I think the man looks a lot like you, and the bench he's sitting on could have been Avrum's bench. Was it a self-portrait?"

"I didn't intend it to be," I told her.

"But you didn't have a model, did you?"

"No. I just painted it. I didn't think I would ever finish it. That's why I donated it for auction, to make me stop working on it. I hope you didn't pay a premium for it."

"It wouldn't have made you rich, but you could have taken a comfortable vacation," she said. And then she smiled, as one smiles over a pleasant memory. "Do you know how parents teach children to believe in happy secrets? I've always thought of it as my happy secret."

"I'm really surprised you have it," I said again.

"Don't worry. You're going to paint another for me. For here. For this place."

"Gladly. What do you want?"

She did not answer for a moment. The amber of the fire coated her face. "I want what you feel when you paint it. Whatever that is. And I don't want you to leave anything off the canvas. I want you to be in it, Bobo. *You.*"

She stretched her legs forward and cupped her hands around my hand, kneading it with her fingers.

"And now what about us?" she said quietly. "After all these years, what about us?"

"I don't know," I answered.

"We're not teenagers."

"No, we're not, are we?"

"You were always a little afraid of me," she whispered. "Are you still afraid?"

"No," I said.

Her hands tightened on my hand. She drew herself to me and kissed me softly. And then she turned my hand against her breast and a soft whimper rose in her throat and slipped from her tongue into my mouth. I felt the heat of her tongue filling me as it did the first time we had kissed, felt her body turning to fit against me, felt the blood pumping in her abdomen, felt her hands stroking my back.

"I don't know why I still love you, Bobo," she said quietly. "But I do. I do love you. I always have. All these years, I've loved you. With joy, Bobo. With joy."

We made love—slowly, wonderfully, discovering one another with bodies that were young and powerful from the memory of another time. She was as giving as I had always known she would be. We moved from the den to her bed and we lay close and we talked and we touched and we did not sleep. She wore her silver necklace with the blue love stone. We watched the graying of morning from the window and we made love again.

As I was leaving, after a shower and breakfast, Amy asked, "Do you have any regrets?"

"No," I told her. "Do you?"

"No," she said. "I've wanted last night since we said good-bye in Avrum's room. I don't think that day has ever left me."

17

Lila was sitting on the front porch of the Inn, smoking a cigarette, drinking coffee, an eager smile set deep into her face.

"Well?" she said.

"Are you going to lecture me?" I asked.

"I don't know," she replied playfully. "Why don't you just lie to me and get it out of the way."

I sat in a lounge chair beside her, rooting my shoulders against the cushion. She poured a cup of coffee from the thermos she had with her.

"I'm afraid I fell asleep on the sofa," I said. "Too much wine, too much good talk. Amy threw a blanket over me and let me sleep it off."

Lila laughed and handed me the coffee. "Oh, that's good, Bobo. Very well done. I almost believe you. I don't, but I almost do. But I can give you some advice."

"I'm sure you can, and you will."

"If you ever try that same bullshit on Carolyn, don't show up with your hair still damp from the shower. In fact, don't even take a shower. I can smell the soap, and I know it's not the same cheap brand we supply."

I laughed. "I pity Sammy," I said. "By the way, where is he?"

"Still asleep. He worked most of the night and then waited up to show you his latest creation."

"Amy?" I asked.

"If it is, I don't think she's going to age very well. I took a peek this morning." She pushed her cigarette dead in the ashtray. "But speaking of other women in your life, I think you'd better get inside and give the one in Georgia a call."

I sat up. "Carolyn called?"

"Up until one o'clock. She wasn't a happy camper, Bobo."

"What did you tell her?"

She looked at me in astonishment. "I lied, of course. What kind of person do you think I am? I told her you were with Sammy at an art show in Woodstock, and if I were you, I'd stick to that story. I think she may have believed it." She smiled coyly. "When are you going to see Amy again?"

"This afternoon. We're going to drive up to Margaretville and have a late lunch and look through some antique shops."

"Ummmm," Lila purred. "Antique shops? I like that. Romantic. Now, go call Carolyn and get some sleep. You look a little like the stockbroker this morning."

If Carolyn had been distressed over not reaching me, she did not sound it. She was at work. I could hear laughter in the background.

She answered my apology, "No, I wasn't bothered. I just hadn't talked to you in a couple of days, and I wondered how things were going."

"We had the memorial service yesterday. It went well. A lot of people were there."

"Good."

We talked briefly about the children. They were well. Jason had called to say he had seen Dee Richardson's interview with me and was impressed. Rachel was upset that she had missed it. Lydia was trying to get a copy from CNN. There was no mail of significance. She'd had a good week at work.

"You sound worried about something," she said. "Are you sure everything's all right?"

"Everything's fine," I assured her. "I should have called you earlier. I'm sorry."

"When are you coming back?"

"Probably next Monday. Maybe Sunday. I'll let you know."

"All right. I've got to go. We're a little busy." I could still hear the laughter.

I sat on the bed, holding the telephone in my lap, waiting for the hammer blow of guilt. But there was no guilt. None. Only the sweet, remembered pleasure of the night. I put the phone on the nightstand and pushed off my shoes and lay back against the pillows and closed my eyes. I could smell the perfume of the soap from my shower.

It was a bothered dream. Quaint and bothered. I was sitting with Avrum on his bench, and then he was not there, but Amy was. She was holding my hand. The voice of Amelita Galli-Curci was suspended in the air. And then Amy was not there, but Carolyn was, and Harry Burger was standing beside the bench, dressed in his baggy pants and cardigan sweater, and there was a great sadness on his face. He shook his head and walked away slowly, dragging his feet in the labored shuffle of old age. And then Mrs. Mendelson crowed from across the street, from the porch of the Inn—*"Ja, ja. Ist gut. Ist gut"*. And Ben Benton passed by in his truck, twirling his bear-buckle belt from the window.

"Who are all these people?" Carolyn asked suspiciously.

"Friends," I said. "They're my friends."

"Funny group of friends, if you ask me."

And then the dream blinked, changed.

"I have to tell you something," I was saying to Amy.

"I don't think I want you to," she answered in a small, worried voice.

We were walking at the base of the Belleayre ski lift, her hands holding my arm. The night was cold, bright. Above us, stars sizzled like fireworks.

"I have to say it," I told her.

She stopped walking and looked at me. I thought she already knew. I thought that Carter had told her.

"Carolyn's coming to visit me."

She did not speak for a long time. She looked away, over the valley. She pulled her hands from my arm and pushed them into her coat pocket. Finally, she asked, "When?"

"The end of next week."

She still did not look at me. "How long have you known?"

"Since last week. Remember when Joey came into Arch's to tell me I had a phone call? It was Carolyn."

"Did you ask her to come up?"

"No. I didn't know anything about it. It was something my mother arranged. They're riding up with my brother."

She sniffed and turned her back to me. "I knew something was wrong," she whispered. "I asked Carter, but he wouldn't tell me."

"I'm sorry," I said, begging her to believe me. "I didn't expect it. It's not something I—"

She turned to me. She was crying.

"Will you hold me?" she said.

I embraced her. Her body shuddered against me.

"I'm sorry," I said again.

"You know I can't be here," she said quietly. "Not for that. I couldn't see . . . that. I couldn't."

And then I was standing in front of Arch's and I saw Raymond's car slowing to a stop on the street, and I saw Carolyn through the window of the car. She was waving and smiling happily, like a child arriving at a party. I saw her open the car door and rush to me. She threw her arms around me and crushed me with gladness. Across the street, in the doorway of The Cave, Carter smoked a cigarette and watched me. He wagged his head sorrowfully and spit the cigarette from his mouth.

Amelita Galli-Curci was singing. I could hear her voice rising in the air and I could see her standing on the porch of Sul Monte. Avrum was sitting on his bench below her, holding his bouquet of roses. His head was bent back, his eyes were closed, his lips mouthed the music.

Carter crowded close to me in the kitchen dressing room, which smelled of perspiration and body talc. He was whispering, "Bobo, I've got to tell you what you're going to see when you walk out in the dining room. You're going to see Adam."

"Who?"

"Adam. The old boyfriend. He drove up this morning."

"Why?"

"You dumb shit," Carter sighed. "You've got Carolyn coming up in two days. Amy told you she couldn't be here to see that. He's here to take her back to the city."

"When?"

"This afternoon."

"She's leaving today?"

"Bobo, remember what I told you about the wake-up from the dream? This is it."

And then I was at the Lourie table, numbly serving lunch. Amy did not look at me. Adam and Joel Lourie talked easily, laughed easily, ignoring my presence. Only Evelyn Lourie

288

seemed to understand what was happening, and to care. Her eyes said, "I'm sorry."

The dream blinked again, jerked forward. I was standing on the loading dock off the kitchen, watching Joel Lourie and Adam pack Amy's suitcases into Adam's car. They were still behaving like old friends.

Carter tapped me on the shoulder. "Avrum wants to see you."

I walked through the dining room and the lobby of the Inn, then out the front door and across the street to Avrum.

"I want for you to go to my room and bring me the medicine in the blue bottle," Avrum instructed. "On the dresser."

When I opened the door to Avrum's room, Amy was standing beside the window, looking out at the mountain and the birch tree where we met at night. She was dressed in the same blouse and skirt she had worn for the dance at Arch's. She turned and crossed to me and put her arms around me.

"I didn't mean for it to be like this," she said quietly against my chest. "I wanted to meet him in Kingston, but my parents—"

"It's all right," I told her.

"It was the only way I knew to go home, but I'm not staying with him, Bobo. I want you to know that. I'm staying with one of my friends. With Judy. I told you about Judy."

"Yes," I said.

She looked up at me. "Do you love me?"

"Yes. Don't you know that?"

Her eyes flashed tears. She smiled. "Do you know what I want to happen?"

I did not speak. I could feel the stinging of my own eyes.

"I want us to make love. Here. Today."

"Amy—"

She lifted her face to me, touched my lips with her lips.

"Why were so many things against us?" she whispered.

"I don't know."

"Will you remember, Bobo? Will you?"

"Yes."

"Do you know what's going to happen?" she asked.

"No."

"Everyone's going to tell us that this was just a summer thing," she said softly. "Maybe they'll make us believe it, or half-believe it. They'll say, 'That's over. Don't think about it. It's over.' But they don't know, do they?"

"Know?" I asked.

"The only thing that's over is the summer. I may never see you again, Bobo, but we're not over. Not us."

She kissed me again, tenderly, and then she reached into the pocket of her skirt and took out two small, blue stones shaped in ovals.

"They're love stones," she said. "Cut from the same piece. Put them together and they fit perfectly." She pressed one of the stones into my hand. "One is for you, the other for me." She touched my face lightly with her fingers. "I do love you, Bobo Murphy," she whispered. "I do." Her fingers brushed against my lips and then she turned and left the room.

I watched from the window in Avrum's room as Amy got into the car with Adam. I watched them wave to her parents as the car pulled into the street. I thought I saw her face turn to the window where I was standing. It was like a stroke of light. The ache of her leaving cut into me with its sharp, killing blade and I began to weep.

Beside the swimming pool, in a puff of afternoon heat that had driven the older people inside, Carolyn said, "You've changed. I don't know why, but you've changed." Her voice was bitter and accusing.

"Everybody changes," I replied weakly.

"I don't believe that," Carolyn argued. "It's being up here that's done it. It's almost like you think you belong up here, not back home."

A dream-blink and Carolyn was gone.

Amelita Galli-Curci looked down on Avrum from her porch at Sul Monte. He was offering the bouquet of red roses to her as hundreds of people, dressed for the opera, cheered wildly. She took the roses and angrily tore at the petals and flung them into the air. The petals rained down over Avrum like splattered blood.

Another dream-blink.

Amy gazed at me from Jean Archer's painting in Jean Archer's bedroom. A sunspot from the skylight, brilliantly hot, crawled in slow motion across her face and down to the bed. Amy was on the bed, nude, her remarkable body relaxed in slumber under the sunspot. Jean Archer was standing beside the bed, in front of an easel that held an empty canvas. She was painting furiously with brushes that grew from her fingertips, but nothing appeared on the canvas. Amy moved in her sleep and Jean Archer stopped painting and stood gazing at her. The sound of a heartbeat echoed in the room.

I awoke perspiring. Outside, I could hear the skipping rope of the young girl. Each slap of the rope on the sidewalk throbbed in my chest.

I rolled from the bed and removed Avrum's envelope of instruction from my briefcase, and I read: *Avrum Feldman's kaddish. To be opened six days after his death. A.F.* I wondered what surprise the envelope contained.

18

Sammy was in the lobby when I went downstairs an hour later. His hair was still dusted in granite powder, his eyes were red and swollen, but glazed with passion, or madness.

"Hey, Bobo, you got a minute?" he boomed.

I glanced at my watch. I was expected at Amy's house at twelve-thirty. It was twelve.

"A few," I said. "What's up?" I knew it was a wasted question.

"Come on," Sammy insisted, heading for the door. "You're not going to believe it, Bobo. I promise you."

Lila lit a cigarette from behind the registration desk. She rolled her eyes comically.

I followed Sammy out of the door, across the street and down to Arch's. Dan Wilder was sweeping the sidewalk in front of his coffee and pastry shop. He waved.

I saw the young girl next to Arch's, standing in front of the Mountain Guest Inn, which had been closed for two years. She was dressed in a woman's clothing—a sleeveless, grape-purple dress with fringes of tiny beads, a matching hat with a nest of black netting rolling from the top, and oversize high-heel shoes. She looked child-ishly cute, yet there was something strange about her: the makeup covering her face was flawlessly applied. Her face was the face of a sensuous woman. She posed boldly for us, her head lifted arrogantly, then she slowly turned back to the window of the Mountain Guest Inn and pretended to read from a menu that was still taped to the glass.

"You better get on home, Trinity, and wash that stuff off your face before your mother shows up," warned Sammy.

She flicked a haughty look at him.

"All right," Sammy said. "You know what she'll do if she finds you like that." Sammy opened the door and walked inside. I could hear him mumbling.

"What's that all about?" I asked.

He shook his head in despair. "She lives with her mother down the street—the old Harbin house. One of those single-parent deals. Her mother works for the state, something to do with the environment. Leaves the girl by herself most of the time. It's all right when school's in session, I guess, but in the summer, she's got nothing to do. Pisses me off. I feel sorry for the girl."

"She's a beautiful child," I offered.

Sammy looked out of the window. The girl was standing at the corner of the building, glaring at him, her sensuous face daring him.

"Yeah. She's pretty, but she pulls tricks like this just to piss off her mother. There'll be hell to pay down here tonight. Her mother's one of those New Age hippies with a short fuse. Can you imagine hanging a name like Trinity on a child? Why do people do things like that, Bobo? Do they think they're God? Anyway, she'll get her little ass torn up, but she won't cry a drop. Not one. And one of these days, when she gets old enough and her mother's off at work, she'll pack her bags and catch the bus to the city and that'll be that. She'll just disappear. Probably wind up as a hooker on Forty-second Street."

"Does she have any playmates?" I asked.

Sammy laughed cynically. "Good God, Bobo, there's barely any adults left around here and almost no children. I think of her as the only one, the last of us all." He shook his head again. "I know how she feels."

"What do you mean?" I said.

I could see a shadow pass over Sammy's face. He seemed far off, lost.

"I've been there," he whispered after a moment. He shuddered suddenly, then he said, "Aw, shit. Come on."

We went to the back of the room where Sammy worked. A stained towel was draped over a small piece of granite on one of the tables. Sammy glanced at me, grinned, and then pulled the towel away in a ceremonious sweep.

I was surprised. It was not a finished figure, not defined or polished, but there was something about it that could have been inspired by Amy, something in the soul of the stone that was her.

"That's good," I told him. "Very good."

Sammy touched the face. His hand trembled.

295

"You like it? I mean, you really like it?" he asked eagerly.

"I do, yes."

Sammy pulled his hand away and fished a cigarette from the package in his shirt pocket and lit it. He was watching my face.

"You know who it is?" he asked.

"Amy," I said.

I saw a flicker of shock leap into his eyes. He drew from his cigarette and looked at the face.

"You can tell?" he asked.

"I can. It's her, isn't it?"

Sammy nodded and touched the face again with his fingers. The look of shock was still in his eyes.

"Nobody's ever been able to recognize what I was working on, Bobo." He played nervously with his cigarette. "You don't mind, do you?"

"Of course not. Why should I?"

"Well, you know . . ."

"Look, she's a beautiful woman," I said. "I guess I've sketched her face a thousand times over the years. I don't blame you at all. Are you going to do anything else with it?"

"A little. I just wanted to get it started before you left. I want to take my time with it now. Think it out, you know. Let it show itself, little by little."

"I think I'd like to buy it when you finish," I said.

A grin cracked on his face. "Maybe I can ship it with the *Old Man* piece." He paused, then asked, "How can I do something like this, Bobo, and the rest of it's not worth a shit?"

I didn't know how to answer him, because I did not know the answer. Sammy had no talent as a sculptor, yet he had created a reasonably good work of art.

"Sometimes, it goes better than it does at other times," I suggested.

"I guess," Sammy muttered.

There were workers at Amy's house when I arrived. They were enlarging the back deck and cutting in for a hot tub—"To improve my love life," Amy teased privately.

"Sure," I said. "I knew something was missing."

She laughed and called to one of the workmen, "I'll be back this afternoon."

The workman waved acknowledgment and turned on his circular saw. The blade screamed against the wood.

We drove toward Margaretville and talked idly of the changes that had taken place over the years in the Shandaken Valley. Amy admitted that her husband did not understand why she wanted to keep the house she had inherited from her mother.

"He calls this the Valley of Death," she said. "It's supposed to be a joke, but it isn't. He never really liked it up here, even if he did pretend well enough to fool me for a long time. Maybe I shouldn't blame him, though. He likes skyscrapers and airports."

"He must have been surprised that you kept the house," I said.

"A little, I think. He didn't put up much of an argument. I think it's his way of saying that's he's given up the fight."

I asked what she meant.

"The marriage fight. You know—the little nicks and bruises of a relationship." She reached for my hand, touched it with the tips of her fingers. "The giving and taking that Avrum talked about, but with Avrum it was always romantic. In real life, it isn't always, is it?"

"I won't argue that," I said. Then I asked, "When did your mother buy the house?"

She was quiet for a moment, gazing out of the window at the distant scenery. "About five years ago. She said she needed the tranquillity."

"Did she find it?"

Amy pulled her hand away from mine and began to play with the collar on her blouse.

"Forgive me," I said. "That's a personal question."

"It's all right. I think she did. She seemed more at ease when she finally moved up here."

"What about your father? Did he like it here?"

She answered simply, without emotion, "I didn't tell you everything about them yesterday. They were divorced many years ago. In the early sixties. He remarried. She's a lovely, kind woman

298

and she's made him happy." She looked at me. "Do you know that he liked you?"

"He was very polite to me."

"I always thought it was my mother who knew how I felt about you, but my father did, too," she said. "In fact, the only real father-daughter advice he ever gave me had to do with you—at least, I think it was you."

"What was that?" I asked.

"It was the night before my wedding. He asked me to go for a walk with him. He told me then that he believed the most important thing in the world was caring for someone—really caring for them. He was honest. He said he wasn't sure I had the kind of deep caring for Peter that a marriage needed. I remember he said, 'Maybe that only happens once.' He gave me a hug when he said that. I didn't ask if he meant you, but I think he did. He used to ask occasionally if I knew anything about you, where you were, what you were doing. I could only tell him that I knew you were married and that you were an artist."

I drove in silence, remembering Joel Lourie, remembering the day that he saved me from embarrassment in the dining room of the Inn. A man was there with his family—not regular guests, but stop-overs for a day's rest on a tour of the mountains. As I was serving the man, I noticed a row of numbers tattooed on his arm, above the wrist, and I wondered why he had the tattoo, why the numbers. I was about to ask him about it when Joel Lourie called me to his table.

He motioned me close to him and he whispered, "Bobo, I saw you looking at that man's tattoos. Do not say anything about them. I will tell you later." After lunch, he came back into the dining room and found me and told me the tattoos were from one of the death camps in World War Two. "That man was a prisoner," he explained. "He was one of the lucky ones. He survived." Years later, I painted a portrait of a man with the tattoos and it was purchased by another man with tattoos.

"What are you thinking?" Amy asked.

"About your father."

"What he said to me," she questioned. "Do you think he was talking about you?"

"I hope so," I said.

She reached for my hand again, touched it again with her fingers. The way she sat, with her head up, peering at me, I thought of Sammy's rough sculpture of her and I wanted to tell her about it, but I did not. Sammy's sculpture was like the painting in Jean Archer's bedroom— something not yet ready to be shared.

"Are you tired?" I asked.

"I slept like a baby for two hours after you left," she said.

"Did you dream?"

"Beautifully," she answered softly. "We were seventeen and we were making love in Avrum's room."

We had lunch in a small restaurant in Margaretville and then walked to the Galli-Curci Theater, which had been gutted and transformed into an antique mall.

"It's not the same, is it?" Amy said.

"Not exactly," I agreed.

"Remember when we used to come here to see movies, and we'd sit and hold hands, and Carter and Rene would aggravate us? And—oh, God— the night Eddie Grimes was here with that pitiful little chambermaid and she started screaming because he was trying to take off her bra?"

I had forgotten about Eddie and the girl.

"You don't remember?" she said. "I thought Carter was going to kill him."

"Are you sure you were with me?" I asked.

She laughed playfully. "Now that I think about it, it wasn't you. I was with Adam. I always got the two of you confused."

"Who?"

"You know who."

"Oh, sure, I remember him," I said. "Ate with his fingers, if I recall. Had buck teeth and a drooping eye and the worse dandruff I've ever seen. Looked a little like Freddie, or whatever his name is, from those horror films. And broke. Always broke. I had to tip him when he had lunch with you and your folks. Whatever became of him?"

Amy laughed. "Adam? He became president

of one of the largest banks in New York," she said lightly. "Mr. Megabucks. I could have been Mrs. Megabucks, if it hadn't been for you."

"Me? What did I have to do with it?"

She led me down an aisle of furniture. "I told him about you on the drive back to the city that day. He was livid. He thought I'd contaminated myself by consorting with a Georgia plowboy." She smiled mischievously. "I hinted that I might be pregnant and he said it would look like a gargoyle if you were the father. I never saw him after that day."

I frowned. "You're kidding, aren't you? You didn't break up over me."

She giggled. "Come on, I want to find a dresser for my bedroom."

We strolled the mall and I watched Amy inspect rows of furniture, almost buying, then changing her mind, then retracing her steps to look again. She peered at displays of jewelry, clowned childishly with earrings and old hats and granny glasses and delicately woven shawls. Her laughter was like music.

And then she said, "Look, finally something for you."

A large display of paintings and prints in eloquently refinished frames was hanging from a corner section of the walls.

"Find something for me," urged Amy. "Something that would go well in the guest bedroom, but nothing that'll clash with the one you're going to paint for me—for free, of course."

"Do I have to frame it also? That's where the cost is."

"No, I'll do it," she teased. "I'm sure there'll be some scrap wood left from building the deck. For your work, that'll suffice."

She drifted away from me as I moved slowly along the wall, studying the display. The works were varied, from overly inspired copies of classic styles—da Vinci, Matisse, Rembrandt, van Gogh—to the dabblings of primitive art from the school of Grandma Moses. I found a watercolor of yellow and reddish wildflowers—evening primroses and bull thistles, I thought—from an artist named James Broadax that appealed to me. Its colors were vivid and happy, like children at play, and yet it was warmly contained against a backdrop of fields and woods.

I turned and called for Amy. She did not answer. I saw her standing at the opposite wall, staring up at a print. I crossed to her and looked at the print. It was of a young girl leaning against a walking cane, staring at viewers with a vacant, hurting expression. The print was from a limited edition of a painting by Jean Archer. The face of the girl was mesmerizing, but it was not Amy's face.

"Amy?" I said quietly.

She turned to me and faked a smile.

"You know," she said, "I think I will buy that walnut secretary we saw. Do you think we can get it in your car?"

19

Many secrets, even those that are sometimes dark and fearful, are like gifts from benevolent gods. They feed the soul with memories that are too grand to forget, but too risky to share. Still, we share them, or they do not live.

Avrum Feldman had such a secret, and one afternoon in 1955, annoyed by the taunting of Harry Burger over Amelita Galli-Curci, he shared it with me, making me vow never to tell it to anyone.

I reminded him that I had never broken any of the many commitments of silence that he had imposed on me.

"This one, this one is important," he urged. "For this, I could go to the jail."

"Then maybe I don't need to know," I told him.

He waved my protest away with his hands. "No, I will tell you. I want that you should know."

And then he began to talk, telling his story in a low voice, glancing around constantly and suspiciously for passersby.

The second time that he saw Amelita Galli-Curci was in November of 1921, he told me, when she made her debut with the Metropolitan

Opera Company of New York, singing Violette in Giuseppe Verdi's *La Traviata*. It had been three years and ten months since the voice of her music had changed his life, but Avrum had not forgotten her.

As Amelita Galli-Curci was being lifted to celebrity in the theaters of America by the strong hands of applause, Avrum was committing the only deliberate crime of his life. He was carefully, patiently, inspecting pelts of silver fox and sable and mink and all the other exotic animals that were shipped to Mendenhal's Fur, Ltd., where he worked. He was searching for perfection, and when he found it—a fisher—he tucked it under his heavy coat and took it from the company. Working in the small apartment where he lived, he fashioned it into a boa of exquisite beauty.

On the day following her debut in *La Traviata*, a performance that had made him weep unashamedly in the audience, Avrum appeared at the hotel where Amelita Galli-Curci was staying. He announced at the desk that he was delivering a gift to Madame Galli-Curci from a benefactor of the Metropolitan who wished to remain anonymous. Avrum insisted the benefactor had instructed him to present the boa personally.

He was led to her suite by the hotel manager. When she opened the door and he was introduced, Avrum bowed graciously as he had rehearsed hundreds of times before his mirror, holding the boa draped across his extended arms.

"Madame Galli-Curci," he said in a whisper.

When she saw the boa, she gasped audibly. She stroked it with her fingertips as Avrum held it, then she took it from him and lifted it to her face and held it tenderly, as a lover would hold a lover.

"Who made such a beautiful thing?" she asked.

"I am a furrier," Avrum confessed humbly. "It was I." He added, "On the instruction of your admirer."

"Then you are a man of great talent," Amelita Galli-Curci told him. "I must give you something in return. Tickets to a performance, perhaps."

"Thank you. You are most kind," Avrum answered, "but I have tickets, as always when you sing. Yet, there are two small things I would accept and treasure if you have them to offer."

"Please tell me," Amelita Galli-Curci said.

"A sheet of music—any music—with your name on it, and, if possible, a small trinket you might have worn in one of your performances."

The signature of Amelita Galli-Curci across the title sheet of *La Traviata* and a necklace of costume jewelry that she had worn in the performance, both kept in his mahogany candlestick box, were the most valuable items that Avrum Feldman possessed.

After his gift of the black boa, Avrum confided, he would stand on the street at the stage entrance when Amelita Galli-Curci performed and watch for her to exit the theater, and if she wore the boa, he was warmed with pride. Once he believed she recognized him. There was a look, a pause in her eyes, a flash of a smile.

Avrum shared the secret of the gift of the boa with me many times over the years, as he also shared the secret of his gift of the roses at Sul Monte. Joy and bitterness, he explained. He wanted me to understand the power of secrets.

"They lift you up, they bring you down," he said. "But you can do nothing about them. You can only remember."

I thought of Avrum and his gifts to Amelita Galli-Curci as I waited among the offerings of antique dealers in the Galli-Curci Theater for Amy to purchase a walnut secretary that was, I believed, an excuse to walk away from the print of Jean Archer's painting, and from a secret that was dangerous and clouded with regret.

I put the secretary into the car and drove back to Amy's house, forcing more idle chatter that we both knew was forced—Carter's romance with Libby, the frequent and funny fights between Carter and Rene, Joey Li's dream of returning to Taiwan and becoming a political power, the closing of the resorts. Chatter. I wanted to ask her about the painting hanging in Jean Archer's bedroom, but was afraid the question would make her flee from me, and there had been too much fleeing.

The workmen were still at the house. I helped her take the secretary inside and place it, and we agreed to have dinner at the Dollhouse Lodge and Restaurant at seven. I explained that I had to see Carter about Avrum's will.

"Tell him I'll talk to him soon," she said.

I asked if we should invite Carter and Libby to dinner.

"To be honest, I'd rather spend the time with you," she replied. "They'll still be here when you leave. I'll want to see them then."

"And to be honest in return, I'm glad you said that," I told her.

She kissed me lightly, out of sight of the workmen.

I did not know if Carter would be at his office, but he was, and he was eager to interrogate me.

"Tell me about it, boy. Don't leave out a thing, and I mean nothing."

"We're both getting divorces," I said seriously, settling into one of his leather armchairs. "And then we're going to get married and have a half dozen children."

Carter laughed. "What're they going to be— Jewish or Christian?"

"We're thinking Hindu."

"You asshole," he snorted. "You're not going to tell me, are you?" He handed me a cup of coffee and sat in his chair behind his desk.

"We had a wonderful evening," I said.

"Evening?"

"All right: night."

Carter leaned toward me. "That's better." He clucked his tongue. "Good, good. Tell you the truth, Bobo, I don't want to know what happened. If you had a chance to take that woman to bed and you didn't, you're either a eunuch or you're gay, and if that's the case, I'd have to kick your ass out of here." He leaned back. "You know what surprises me?"

"I'm sure you'll tell me," I said.

"Damned if she's not as beautiful as she was at seventeen. It's amazing. What is she? Fifty-five? She has to be. We were all the same age, but she looks thirty, at most. Good God, she's got a body for that age. She looks better than Raquel Welch, for crying out loud, and I dream about Raquel Welch at least once a week."

I wanted to tell Carter he would be stunned at Amy's body, but I knew that was what he wanted me to say. Instead, I said, "Talk to me about something."

He arched his eyebrows in anticipation. "The painting?"

"Yes."

"Did she tell you about it?" he asked.

"No. I didn't ask. It's funny. It just never seems the right thing to do, and I don't know exactly how to explain that. I've got a feeling she would go off screaming if I brought it up."

"There must be a reason, if you think that," Carter replied. "I mean, shit, Bobo, I may be a lawyer, but I do believe in instinct. It's gotten me into a lot of trouble over the years, but once or twice it's pushed me out of a bedroom window just as some irate husband or boyfriend was walking up to the front door."

I ignored the pride of his smile. "We went to Margaretville today," I told him, "to the antique mall, and there was a copy of a painting by Jean Archer. Not the one of Amy, but another one. Anyway, I caught her staring at it and her mood changed instantly."

Carter smirked in reaction. "What do you think?"

"I don't know. She changed. I don't know why."

"You need to ask her, Bobo. Or I do. I could do it, you know. Tell her that I'm handling the sale of the house and that I saw the painting."

"No, not now," I said.

"Then what?"

"I don't know. Maybe let it drop. I'll be leaving in a few days."

Carter propped his feet on the edge of his desk and looked at me with his lawyer's gaze. He said, "Are you in love with that woman?"

I hesitated, then shrugged to deflect the question.

"Sure you are," he said forcefully. "You always have been, from that first night in Arch's, the night I told you you would be. You've been in love with her, or the image of her, all these years. Maybe it's something you got from Avrum—the poor, disillusioned bastard—or maybe it's just something you can't help. Or her, for that matter. You've spent most of your life in a lie, wanting a woman you thought you'd never see again. And now you've seen her. You've made love to her, and I don't give a shit whether you admit that or not; I know you did. I knew you were there all night before I asked you about it. I drove by early this morning, just to see, just to be able to bust your balls about it."

He paused, sighed, shook his head, played with the coffee cup he held in his hand. Then he dropped his feet from the desk and looked at me. "And you're telling me that you're going to be leaving in a few days and that's it? You're going to leave it all behind you, like you'd just had a cup of coffee with a stranger? Bullshit. You're not giving it up now, not after all these years. Remember Rene Wallace? Your giving up on Amy would be like me giving up on Rene, and I didn't, if you remember. I chased that girl all summer, and finally made it. No, Bobo, I don't believe you're going to turn away now. I don't believe it and you don't believe it. And I also don't believe you can let something like a painting of her interfere with that."

I sat for a moment thinking about what Carter had said. I knew he was right, but still I was afraid of the risk.

"You know what's so shitty about marriage, Bobo?" Carter said quietly. "It's the biggest decision we ever have to make and everybody thinks we're capable of making it when we're twenty or twenty-one or twenty-two. Jesus, we're too young to make *any* decision at that age. We don't even

311

know how to buy a fucking car, or the right kind of shoes or ties that match our suits, but we're supposed to be absolute in marriage." He chuckled. "You get a bad car, you trade it in. You get bad shoes, you fling them to the back of the closet. You get a ridiculous tie, you give it away as a present the first chance you get. You get the wrong person in marriage, and you're expected to nobly bear that burden until you take your last breath, and that's just stupid. Just plain stupid."

"Maybe you're right," I said.

"Of course I'm right. By the way, I think Archer may be coming back up here this weekend. I got a call from her agent in New York, about someone wanting to see the house."

"Do you know when she arrives?" I asked.

"Sunday, I think."

"Avrum's kaddish," I said.

"What?"

"Nothing. Sunday's the day I'm supposed to do Avrum's version of the kaddish. God only knows what it'll be. Anything but Jewish, I'm sure."

"You don't know?" he asked.

"It's in an envelope. I'm not supposed to open it until Sunday."

Carter laughed pleasantly. "That old fart was one odd bird, Bobo. It wouldn't surprise me if he wanted midget jugglers and a belly dancer. Incidentally, I've looked into his affairs. He's leaving a good hunk of change, something over a quarter of a million."

"You're kidding," I said. "Where did he get that kind of money?"

"Bobo, you're getting old and forgetful," Carter answered. "Don't you remember those people we used to have in our dining room? Worked their ass off and saved everything. Splurged once a year, when they were at the Inn. Remember the Sterns? Mama and daddy and their son, Junior. Forty-two years old and spent his time cutting paper dolls. They made flowers out of crepe paper and sold them on the street. They made a fortune. And who was that asshole that had brandy for breakfast? Otto somebody. He bought Army-Navy supplies and peddled them out of the back of his car. He retired up here. I sold him the biggest house we had, and he paid in cash. Avrum was no different. He invested heavily a long time ago in some risky import ventures that paid off. Apparently, he didn't spend any of it, and he damn well had it long enough to make a profit. There's more splits in his stock portfolio than a Dallas Cowboy cheerleader pulls off in a double-overtime game."

I stood. "Well, that should make Sol Walkman happy," I said.

"So, what are you going to do?" Carter asked. "Or do you need me to repeat the lecture?"

"Right now, I'm going back to the Inn and sleep for an hour or so, then I'm having dinner

313

with Amy. And what happens—frankly, I don't know."

Carter smiled an understanding smile. "Don't let her get away this time," he said.

20

Before my mother and Carolyn arrived in the Catskills with Raymond and Linda, I asked Nora Dowling if I could invite them to the Inn for a meal.

"A meal?" she said energetically. "No, for your mother, we must have a party." And she rushed off to huddle with her sisters to begin the planning.

The party was a smorgasbord buffet of every specialty the Inn offered—steak tartare to roast duck, Wiener schnitzel to calves' tongue, soups to compotes, fresh fruit cups to butter cake. It was a celebration to honor the mother of her two Southern men, as she referred to Raymond and me. She led my mother from table to table, introducing her, lavishing praise on her in a loud, dominating voice, an English-Yiddish-German splintering of language. Carolyn sat in my dining room with Raymond and my sister-in-law, Linda, watching the spectacle with awe and bewilderment.

My mother bravely sampled each dish of food. The food had a strange, rich taste, she later told me, but she beamed with gladness over the attention, and in the tradition of the Southern woman, she stood before the guests of the Pine Hill Inn and responded with gracious appreciation for the "kindness extended to my sons" in a small village in the New York mountains.

Carter whispered that he had always believed Scarlett O'Hara was literary myth until he heard the gushing of my mother. I told him that Southern men took great exception to the slightest insult to their mothers and warned him that I would employ Ben Benton to whip his ass if I saw even a hint of a smile.

To Nora Dowling, my mother's comments were inspired. She hugged my mother and wept. "Such boys," she declared in a booming voice. "Such boys."

"*Ja, ja,*" the diners of the Pine Hill Inn sang in agreement.

"This Bobo, I taught him to be the waiter," Harry barked with pride.

The only people who did not attend the buffet were Joel and Esther Lourie. He apologized to me the following morning at breakfast, explaining a previous engagement with a couple they had met from the Greenleaf Lodge. I knew instinctively that the previous engagement was a convenient excuse to avoid making me, and them, uncomfortable. I did not tell him that Carolyn and my mother and brother and sister-in-law had sat at their table.

During the week that she was in the Catskills, I tried to be with Carolyn as much as possible. We went to a movie in Margaretville. We rode the ski lift on Belleayre Mountain to take pictures of the scenery. We walked in the hills behind the Inn, though I avoided the birch tree where I had spent so many hours with Amy. We went into Arch's for milk shakes and to hear Arch's stories. Carolyn said nothing, but I knew she was aware of the stares and the whispers. When I introduced her to Avrum, he faked his act of craziness and babbled about the new names he had ordained on immigrants at Ellis Island, and then he closed his eyes and pretended to be sleeping. Carolyn, like others, thought he was insane.

There were moments with Carolyn that were as warm and as tender and as full of wonder as the moments we had known in high school, but the aftermath of those moments carried a sickness of confusion. How can I do what I am doing? I wondered. How can I see only the face of Amy when I am alone?

Carter was conspicuously absent during Carolyn's visit. Always there was an excuse—problems with Rene, problems with his car, problems with his finances, the need to spend time with his parents in Phoenicia.

He talked to me only once about Carolyn, after I forced him to go with me to the swimming pool late one night.

"Bobo, I'm going to be honest," he said. "Carolyn's nice. She's one of the most pleasant people I've ever met, and she's pretty. You were damn right about that. God knows, it's a miracle she has anything to do with you. She's great, Bobo, but she's not Amy. You know that and I

317

know that. I also know you feel like shit. Amy's gone, and you miss her. Carolyn's here, and you're ass deep in guilt because of Amy, and you're also scared to death Carolyn's going to find out what's really been going on this summer. Well, I don't think she will. For some reason that totally escapes me, people seem to like you. You've got a lot of friends. They're not going to dump on you."

It was curious that I now thought of Carolyn from those few days in the Catskills. I wondered if it was a mind game. A turning of the tables. A payback. It was as though Carolyn was, for the first time, one of the ghosts who waited for me in Pine Hill, and thinking of her was the haunting of the guilt that Carter had recognized.

In an odd, disturbing way, I wanted to be with her.

Yet, it wasn't the first time that I had sensed the presence of Carolyn, or felt a need for her. There had been other moments, like some strange and disturbing echo from a voice that had once been as music, a call so distinct that I could not hear the hollowness of the echo.

There was a summer when I went away to the Outer Banks of North Carolina, to Ocracoke Island, to paint in isolation. An exhibit had been scheduled for October at a major gallery in Washington, D.C., and the teaching had taken its toll. Too few paintings were ready with too little time to prepare. "You should do it,"

Carolyn had encouraged. "Go. Forget about things here. It's important."

It was, at first, liberating. There was magic on the island, something that flowed like a mist off the skin of the Atlantic water. It was both energy and peace, long hours of work and quiet reflection. Images fluttered around me like playful and colorful birds. Each place I looked, I saw them and my hand remembered them for the brush.

Then one Sunday, almost two months after arriving on the island, I awoke with an overwhelming urge to pack quickly and to drive the long drive home. Carolyn could hear the longing in my voice when I called.

"Maybe you've been working too hard," she suggested. "Why don't you get away from it a couple of days? Just relax. Do nothing."

"I want to come home," I told her. "Now. Today."

"Then come home. But, why? I thought this is what you needed."

"I did, but I've been here long enough. I need something familiar."

Her laugh was light, surprising. "You mean you miss home."

I thought about her remark. Yes, I did miss home. I missed the chair that I loved. I missed the invasion of the children in my home studio. I missed the feel of my bed, the sound of Carolyn's breathing in sleep, the taste of breakfast coffee at my table, the yelp of the dog, the slope of the driveway that led from the street to my house, the annoying bubble in the screen of the high bedroom window—the screen I had vowed to repair for five years.

"Is that it?" Carolyn asked. "You're homesick?"

"I guess."

"Do you miss me?"

"Of course."

Her laugh was quiet, weak. "I'm part of the familiar, right?"

"Sure you are."

"Well, I suppose being familiar is better than being forgotten," she said. "Come on home. I think you just need a hug."

I did not paint again for three weeks after I returned. There was no magic, no images like playful and colorful birds. My eyes saw nothing, my hand remembered nothing.

It was like the misdialed telephone call.

How's everything?

Any mail?

Any calls?

Are the kids all right?

The familiar was too familiar.

I dreamed of the Outer Banks.

Because I did not want to face Lila's inquisition about the day with Amy, I went into Dan Wilder's Coffee and Pastry Shop when I returned to Pine Hill from my meeting with Carter. I sat at my table and had coffee and crumb cake and talked to Dan about the dying of the village.

"The way it's going, I'll be forced to close down myself," Dan confided. "Move down toward Kingston, and, tell you the truth, Bobo, I don't want to do it. I like it here. I like the way it feels when I walk outside."

"I thought your business was good," I said.

He rolled his massive shoulders in a shrug. "So-so. Good in the winter, in the ski season, not good in the summer. So it's so-so. I've got a few roadside stores and one or two resorts that take regular orders and I do a catering now and then, but that's about it. Not many people walk in anymore. It's like Sammy and Lila. I mean, God knows, they don't know a hell of a lot about running a resort, but even if they did, where are the customers coming from? That airhead broad and the stockbroker who show up once a month to play hide-and-screw?"

"You know about them?" I asked.

Dan laughed softly. "The only people who don't know about them is his wife and her husband—unless they're getting together in the city when the two of them are up here. But what do I care? They know I know and every time they leave they go with a special order—two dozen brownies for her and a pound cake for him. I think it's a hell of a good way to keep their spouses dangling. Stuff their mouths with sweets from Dan Wilder and they can't ask questions." He laughed again, then said, "By the way, Lila told me you had a good service for that old man."

"That's nice of her," I said. "I'm glad it's over."

He rubbed his hands down the front of his apron, smoothing it. "So, what else have you been doing?"

I told him about the trip to Margaretville and shopping for antiques in the old Galli-Curci Theater, explaining that a friend was refurbishing a home in Shandaken.

"Yeah, I like to go up there myself. Browse around," he said. "I don't ever buy much, but it's a good way to spend time. Just looking, you know. I always feel a little like an archaeologist. One of these days, I'm sure I'll open up an old trunk and find a pile of bones in it."

I do not know why I asked the question, but I did: "I saw a print from an artist that I'm told lives near Woodstock—Jean Archer. Have you ever heard of her?"

Dan nodded. "I know her. Catered a couple of her parties. Crazy damn woman."

"What do you mean?"

"Tough as shoe leather. If it's not the way she wants it, she's a goddamn maniac."

I smiled at Dan's candor. "What kind of parties did she have? Artist friends talking art?"

"Artists, my ass," Dan murmured. He snorted a laugh. "Bunch of freaks, if you ask me. One of them told me one night they were all models. Auditioning, or something. Said the Archer woman liked to see them in a social setting before she decided which one to paint."

"That's unique," I said.

Dan's smile and voice were teasing. "That's not how you do it, Bobo?"

"Never have."

"Well, damn, you've been missing out. I mean some of those girls looked pretty good. A little anorexic, maybe—especially for me." He patted his stomach proudly. "But a good-looking skinny girl needs as much attention as a plump one. Naw, Bobo, if I was an artist—I mean, like you, instead of in a kitchen—I'd hold so damn many auditions, they'd think Cecil B. DeMille had kicked off the dirt and pulled himself up out of the grave, and even if I didn't do anything but look, it'd be worth it."

"I'll have to think about that," I said.

"Want some more coffee?" he asked.

"I don't think so," I replied. "I need to get up to the Inn and take a shower."

Dan wiggled his eyebrows. "Got a big date tonight?"

"Dinner with a friend."

"Not Lila, is it?"

"Good God, Dan, of course not," I answered in shock. "Why'd you say that?"

He lifted himself from his chair and stretched. "Well, it's none of my business, but I think Sammy wonders about you."

"Me?"

"You, Bobo."

"Lila and I are just friends," I assured him. "And you know her. She likes to play games."

His face turned serious. He said in a quiet voice, "It's not Lila that I worry about. It's Sammy. I swear to Jesus, he's stuck between floors and the emergency bell's not working."

"Anything specific?" I asked.

He thought for a moment, inhaling deeply. "I don't know." He looked out of the front window and across the street to Arch's.

"Sounds like you do," I said.

He chuckled softly. "Hell, Bobo, we're all a little crazy up here. Don't you know that? Sometimes I think we're the last people on earth and there's not enough of us left to make any difference whether we survive or not. We kind of stand around watching one another, to see who's going off the deep end first. It's like that thing that nutty old friend of yours said when he was in here two or three years ago."

"Avrum?" I asked.

"Yeah. There were a bunch of people sitting around, mostly kids from one of the camps that used to be up the road. He scared the shit out of them."

"What did he say?"

Dan cocked his head in thought. "It had something to do with singing. Something like, 'She's going to sing again and you'll hear her. Just like me, you'll hear her.' Yeah, something like that. It's been a long time. He had this wild look about him and his voice was cracking. He sounded like static on a bad radio. Two or three of the girls started to cry and I had to hustle him out of the shop, and then I had to tell the kids that he was just a crazy old man who heard voices. But maybe he was right, Bobo. Maybe we're all just sitting around, waiting for somebody to sing again."

"Avrum could get that way at times," I said. "Especially over the last few years. But I think he did things like that just to play the role. People thought he was crazy, so he played crazy."

Dan reached for the coffee cups on the table. "Maybe so. Maybe so. But I've got to tell you, Bobo, I keep listening. I keep listening."

I left Dan and crossed the street to Sammy's workshop—to Arch's—and tried the door, but it was locked. I could hear the ringing of the hammer on the chisel, a true, light ringing, almost as delicate as the pinging of crystal, and I knew that Sammy was chipping carefully at the stone face of Amy Lourie Meyers.

If I take Sammy's sculpture of Amy with me, can I ever escape her? I wondered.

Carter spoke from an echo: "Your giving up on Amy would be like me giving up on Rene, and I didn't, if you remember."

Rene.

The face of Rene Wallace blinked in memory.

What Carter did not know was that, for one night, Rene had given up on him.

It was a night when she and Carter argued bitterly in Arch's over a guest at the Greenleaf Lodge, where she worked. The man, who was in his early thirties and married, had propositioned

Rene and she told Carter about it. Carter did not respond as she wanted him to—with empathy and warm assurances. He became enraged, accusing her of being suggestive around the man. I could not calm him and Amy could not calm him.

"Come on," Amy finally said to Carter, "you're going for a walk with me. You need to learn a few things." She looked at me. "Bobo, walk Rene home."

Carter slid from the booth and stormed out of Arch's. Amy followed him.

"Are you all right?" I asked Rene.

She was pale from the argument. She nodded.

"Come on," I said.

The Greenleaf Lodge was above the village, far off the road on a knoll of hemlocks and pines. It was a small, elegant resort with riding stables and tennis courts. Its clientele was younger than the residents of the Inn, and often, at night, we could hear the gaiety of their partying drifting down from the knoll.

The path from the road to the Lodge was through the hemlocks and pines, and at night it was a path of shadows, with pits of darkness under the umbrella limbs of laurel. Carter had jokingly called it the Make-Out Road.

That night, with Rene, I understood what he meant.

We were in the woods, between the road and the Lodge, when she stopped walking.

"Can we wait a minute, Bobo?" she asked. "I don't want to go up there with my eyes all red."

"Sure," I said.

She sat beside one of the laurel bushes, in the darkness, and dabbed at her eyes with a tissue. I sat near her.

"I hate him at times," she said after a moment.

"Carter?"

"He gets so mad so easy," she whimpered. "I didn't do anything to make that man come on to me, Bobo. I promise I didn't." She looked at me. I could see the dots of her eyes, bubbling from tears, and her puffed lips. "He's not like you," she added softly. "You're nice."

"Uh—thanks," I said. "Carter's all right. He's just a little jealous. It means he likes you."

Rene ignored my remark. "Sometimes I think about you like you're my big brother."

"Is that right?" I replied. I glanced through the underbrush of laurel and the wall of trees to the Lodge. I could see the silhouette of a man walking under a night-light. I wondered if it was Carter. Then I saw two children race to him.

"But I don't always think that," Rene added.

"I'm sorry. Think what?"

"That you're like my big brother. I only think that sometimes."

I felt suddenly uncomfortable.

"Sometimes I wish you were Carter," she confessed quietly.

I did not speak.

"Sometimes I wish Amy weren't here, either,"

she continued. "It's not that I don't like her. I do. I mean, she's really nice, but sometimes I wish she weren't here."

I did not understand what she was saying. "Why?"

She smiled sadly. Her voice was a whisper: "I shouldn't tell you this, since you and Carter are such big friends, but I think about it sometimes: if Amy weren't around, I wonder if I wouldn't be dating you instead of Carter."

"Rene, you shouldn't talk like that. You're right: Carter and I are good friends."

"So?" she said. She slipped closer to me. "What Carter doesn't know won't hurt him, will it?"

"Uh—look, Rene, I—"

Her face was almost touching my face. She whispered, "Have you ever made love to anyone, Bobo?"

I was astonished by the question. I shook my head.

"I didn't think so," she sighed. "I have. Not to Carter, no matter what he tells you, but I have."

She pushed her lips against my lips and she caught me in a powerful hug and pulled me to her. Her mouth crushed my mouth. She rolled, still holding me, and I was suddenly on top of her. She opened her legs and scissored my body and began thrusting herself against me.

"Make love to me, Bobo," she begged. "Let me be the first." Her mouth attacked me again.

I fought to free myself. "Rene, stop it. I don't want this. Carter—"

"I don't want to hear about Carter," she snapped. "Not now." She was breathing heavily. She looked at me from the dark burrow of the laurel bush and smiled triumphantly. She pushed her tongue from her mouth and slowly circled her lips with it, then she pulled open her jacket and slipped her sweater up over her bra. "Look, Bobo," she teased. She ran her fingers under the bottom of her bra and lifted it, freeing her breasts. Her breasts were full, her nipples erect. "Touch them, Bobo, touch them."

I wiggled away from her and stood. "Rene, I'm leaving," I said emphatically. "You're just trying to get back at Carter, and this is not the way to do it. Not with me."

Rene pulled her bra and sweater down. The smile vanished from her face. She began weeping again.

"I'm sorry," she murmured. "Bobo, I'm sorry."

"It's all right."

"I've made a fool of myself," she sobbed.

"No, you haven't. Things just got a little out of hand."

"You hate me."

I knelt beside her. "No, I don't, Rene. Sometimes big brothers and little sisters fight, but I don't think that means they hate one another."

A small smile played across her face.

"You're a good person, Bobo Murphy. I envy Amy. She doesn't know how lucky she is."

I hugged her lightly and left her and returned to The Cave. Carter was there, sitting on the edge of my bunk, smoking a cigarette. He was in a subdued mood.

"Is she all right?" he asked.

"She's fine. She was just a little upset, that's all. What about you?"

"Okay." He nodded and rubbed the palms of his hands together. "You're a good buddy, Bobo."

"Where's Amy?" I asked.

He motioned his head toward the Inn. "She went in," he said quietly. "She said she'd see you in the morning."

"Did she give you the business?"

Carter stared at his hands. "Yeah. Yeah, she did."

The following night, Amy and I went for a walk to the birch tree and Carter and Rene drove away in his car—"to see a movie," he said. When he returned to The Cave, very late, he pulled me from my bunk and made me dress and follow him to the swimming pool.

He flopped in a lounge chair and lit a cigarette and said in an astonished whisper, "I got it, Bobo. Right up there on Make-Out Road, I got it. Oh, man, it was great. She's crazy about me. First time I ever thought about marrying anybody, but she could be the one."

I stammered that I was glad for him.

He leaned his head toward me. "Tell you the honest-to-God's truth, Bobo, it was the first time for me."

He grinned at my startled look.

"Yeah, I know, I know," he confessed. "All those stories. So I lied. I'm a boy. Boys lie about things like that. But not tonight. Bobo, she was so turned on, I thought I was going to have to hose her down." He drew from his cigarette and whirled a large, blue lariat of smoke into the air. "First time for her, too," he added confidently. "I thought she was going to bleed some, but she didn't. Said she'd broken that thing—whatever they call it—riding a horse bareback. I don't care, though. That horse did me a favor. I'm telling you, Bobo, I don't know what got into her, but I'm glad it did. Maybe it was that old son of a bitch that came on to her."

I never told Carter, or Amy, about the night with Rene, and I do not believe she talked about it, either.

But it was not a secret.

Not as Avrum had described a secret.

It did not lift up and it did not bring down.

If anything, it was a childish lie for both of us.

21

The rabbi, a small, gentle-faced man named
Norman Gold, was sitting uncomfortably in the
lobby of the Inn, talking to Lila. His discomfort
was over Lila's dress—a white, low-cut pullover
with matching pants. The pullover and the pants
were as tight as a body stocking on Lila. The tops
of her breasts glistened from lotion.

The rabbi had been waiting for an hour to
speak to me, Lila explained, chiding me for being
gone so long. She excused herself and went into
the dining room to review the menus for the
weekend.

I apologized to Norman Gold. "I wish I had
known you were here. I've been next door, having
coffee with an old friend."

"Oh, please," he said, "it's I who need to beg
forgiveness, stopping by like this."

"It's fine," I told him. And then I asked the
unnecessary, but polite, question: "What can I
do for you?"

Norman Gold shifted on the sofa where he was
sitting. He lifted his chin and licked on his lips.

"I spent some time today with Sol Walkman
at the Highmount Home," he answered timidly.
"I try to stop by there a couple of times a week,
to see if I can be of any assistance."

I thought it would be kind to rescue him from further uneasiness: "You talked about Avrum Feldman's kaddish. Am I right?"

He nodded with relief. "Yes. That, as well as the generous gift from his estate to the Home. Believe me, it comes at a critical time."

"I'm glad he had the means to leave something substantial," I said. "And, to be honest, I think the Home deserves it. They took care of Avrum for many years and he was, at best, a difficult man."

Norman Gold smiled.

I thought about Carl Gershon and Leo Gutschenritter and Morris Mekel. "I know the Yiddish expression for the way he behaved. *Meshugge.*"

Norman Gold's smile became a laugh. "Mr. Feldman was unusual," he said. "We had many discussions about God."

"That must have distressed you," I replied. "His attitude about matters of religion was often very radical. I hope God has settled things for him by now."

"I'm confident of it," Norman Gold said.

"He was something of a prophet, though," I suggested. "He knew this visit would take place, that a rabbi would come to speak to me."

I could see a question twitch in Norman Gold's eyes.

"Do you know what he told me?" I said.

"I'm almost afraid to ask."

333

"He told me—no, instructed me—to ignore what the rabbi would say."

Norman Gold brushed his lips with his fingertips. He looked at me, waited.

"There's an envelope upstairs in my room," I explained. "I am to open it on Sunday, six days after his death. In it will be his directions about his kaddish."

A frown settled sadly into Norman Gold's forehead.

"I am not Jewish, Rabbi Gold, but I know what a kaddish is. And I know that what I am to do is not that. It has nothing to do with a sacred ceremony. The word was used by Avrum as part of his argument with religion—all religion.

"I don't know why he wanted me to wait six days to open the envelope, but I have a pretty good idea. He meant to pull my leg. He used to joke with me that if Christ could rise from the dead in three days, so could he. I'm certain that in the envelope upstairs, I'll find a comment, something on the order of, 'So, maybe it'll take twice as long for me.' Whatever it is, Rabbi, it will be a private thing between us, an old argument. I only know that I am bound, as a friend, to follow his wishes."

Norman Gold bobbed his head. "I understand. My concern is that the kaddish, or maybe the reverence for the dead, is not insulted."

"I respect that," I said.

"The sacred ceremonies, they mean much to

us," Norman Gold said quietly. "I wasn't sure you had ever attended one."

"Not many," I told him. "A few. The first one, in fact, was here, in this room."

"Oh? What was it?"

"A *bris*."

He laughed easily. "That must have been memorable for you."

"It was," I admitted. "It was the grandchild of a guest. The parents lived in Big Indian in a home too small for the ceremony."

"Then you know what I mean," Norman Gold said.

I remembered the *bris*. Amy had persuaded the grandparents—the Cohens—to invite Carter and me. At first, Carter had declined. He had been to a *bris*. "I don't care what they call it, to me they're cutting his pecker off," he had complained. "They get him drunk on wine sucked from a cloth and then whack away. Who wants to see that?" Amy had forced him to attend. "If you don't come, Bobo won't either," she had badgered, "and I want Bobo to see it." I had asked, "Why?" and Amy had answered, "I want to see you in a *yarmulke*." I had asked what a *yarmulke* was. "Didn't you ever see a Jewish base-ball team?" Carter had answered. "It's a baseball cap without a bill." At the *bris*, in a borrowed *yarmulke*, I had been pronounced exceedingly handsome by Amy. "It's a setup, boy," Carter had warned. "She wants you to know what you're going to go through when the two of you start having babies." The ceremony, I thought, was beautiful. There had been much laughter and many tears.

"Yes, I think I know how you feel," I said to Norman Gold.

He rubbed his hands together and smiled. "So, we will see. If you need me for anything, please call."

I promised that I would.

Norman Gold left a few minutes later, after casual talk about Avrum's passion for Amelita Galli-Curci. Norman Gold confessed that he, too, loved the opera and was familiar with the Galli-Curci legends. Other than for arguments about God, it was one of the reasons he had visited Avrum at the Home.

"At least, he knew about worship," Norman Gold said.

"Yes, he did," I agreed.

As I started up the stairs to my room, Lila stopped me.

"Thanks, Bobo," she said sarcastically. She was standing at the door leading into the dining room.

"Did I do something wrong?" I asked.

"You made me sit here half the afternoon entertaining a rabbi. I'm not used to that. Makes me squeamish."

"I think, Lila, that it was the rabbi who was squeamish."

She smiled, then did a seductive turn in the lobby. "You think this is too revealing for a man of the cloth?" She stretched her arms over her head. Her breasts lifted proudly.

"You're really shameless at times," I told her.

She giggled. "I put it on just for you. Since I found your magazine in the trash can this morning, I thought you might need some inspiration before tonight."

"I'm going to miss you, Lila," I said. "And, probably, one day, when I'm hobbling around on a cane, I'm going to regret not calling your bluff."

"I'll be waiting, Bobo. Even then."

She laughed and again twirled seductively. Then she pushed open the door to the dining room and disappeared.

In my room, I made two obligatory calls—to the school, explaining that I would not return to my classes until Tuesday, and then to Carolyn.

Brenda Slayton, the headmaster's secretary, assured me that an extra day would not be a problem. Since I had been on CNN, I had become a celebrity, she teased. "Celebrities get special treatment. Besides, it's summer, and you know how it is in summer around here. Everybody's as languid as the weather."

Carolyn was not so pleasant.

"I just talked to you this morning," she said irritably. "What're you doing? Checking up on me?"

A wave of guilt struck me. "No, I just thought

I'd call. Sammy and I may be going back to Woodstock tonight and I thought if—"

"What's going on over there?" she asked.

"Where?"

"Woodstock."

I swallowed a cough. "An art show."

"Well, everything's fine here. Do you know when you're coming home?"

"Monday, I think."

"I'll see you on Monday, then," she said nonchalantly.

I paused.

"Anything else?" she asked.

"I was thinking about something this afternoon," I said. "Do you remember anything about your visit up here?"

She laughed a short, cynical laugh. "I remember feeling like I was interfering with your life."

"That's it? Nothing good?"

"The trees were pretty."

"The trees?"

"What's wrong with that answer? I thought you liked the trees up there."

"I do," I said. "But I wasn't talking about trees; I was talking about us."

"Bobo," she said seriously, "what's going on up there?"

"It's just a question, Carolyn. I was just wondering about it. It was on my mind, that's all. I wondered if you ever thought about it, about us, I mean. You know, that summer."

I could hear her breathing. In the background, a woman's voice was speaking to Darby. The woman said, "I don't know what kind of software he needs. Why don't I have him call you?"

"No, I honestly don't think about that summer," Carolyn said evenly. "Not until you bring it up. If you want to know how I feel about it, I can only tell you that I loved part of it. I loved seeing you again, because we had been apart so long. But I didn't like the feeling of being an outsider, somebody that everyone stared at. I didn't like the feeling that you really didn't want me there."

"I'm sorry you felt that way," I said.

"You asked the question."

"And it's unfair of me," I told her. "It's just that this may be the last time I come here. There've been a lot of memories, that's all."

She was firm in her reply: "Well, enjoy them, because you're right, it is the last time you go up there, unless I go. I've had enough of that place, and everything about it, dragging you away from where you belong."

"My God, Carolyn, you won't ever understand it, will you?"

There was a pause. "Do you know something, Bobo, I could say the same of you, couldn't I? Call me before you leave," she said calmly.

From the manner that Maggie and Paul Charles greeted me at the Dollhouse Lodge and Restaurant, I was certain that Lila had called and alerted them. "The artist friend from Georgia," Lila would have said in reminder. "You can't miss his accent."

Maggie and Paul bubbled warmth. They embraced Amy as they would embrace an old friend and then guided her on a tour of Maggie's doll collection. The way they introduced the dolls—name, place of origin, age, costume, personality—made them sound like happy, make-believe parents from a children's book with bright illustrations and lyrical stories.

Amy was impressed and I imagined the three of them as good friends in the future, being together for dinners and concerts, for trips into the city, making late-night telephone calls with flutterings of distress or joy, joining in laughter on holidays, exchanging gifts for special occasions. I knew that Amy would lead her grandchildren on the same tour of dolls that we were taking. She would lift one and hold it gently and tell her grandchildren that this was her favorite, and she would tell them the story of the doll in whispered awe.

Maggie asked Amy where she lived and Amy told of the house she had inherited from her mother.

"Oh, I know the place," Maggie enthused. "You're having some work done, aren't you? I saw some trucks there a couple of days ago."

"It needs it," Amy said. She added, "I'll either move up here permanently one day, or I'll sell it."

"You must move here," Paul insisted in Paul's hand-taking way. "Here you can feel life. How can you do that in any city? Listen to me; I know. San Francisco, such a place. Wonderful. But it takes your life from you. Here you reclaim it. Come, come, sit. We must have a glass of wine to celebrate a new neighbor." He dashed away.

Maggie led us to a table near a bay window and Paul returned from the kitchen holding a bottle of wine that he proclaimed as a superior French chardonnay. "None of that water from California," he crowed as he opened the bottle and sniffed the cork in closed-eye delight. He poured a taste for Amy. She smiled agreement. "Wonderful," she said.

Dinner was to be the same as it had been with Sammy and Lila—the menu ignored. "Tonight, a lobster," Paul declared. "Yes?" He disappeared, his voice ringing in the restaurant, causing smiles from the three other couples already eating.

"They're fresh," Maggie whispered to us. "And he loves to do lobster, but if—"

"It's perfect," Amy assured her. She looked at me.

"I never argue with an artist," I said.

"Then I think I'd better go keep him under control," Maggie said. "He is French, you know. They do have a way of letting their passions get away from them." She swept away from us, pausing at each table of guests on the way to the kitchen.

"I like them," Amy said. "I'm glad you suggested this."

"Me, too," I told her. "I like feeling special."

Amy glanced at me, held the look. A smile trembled across her face. She reached for the wineglass, touched the rim of it with her fingertip.

"What is it?" I asked.

She continued to gaze at the wineglass, continued to stroke its rim with her fingertip.

"I was thinking how—how strange this is. How strange and, yet, how good," she answered quietly. "I never thought it would happen. Seeing you again."

"Me, either," I said.

"Avrum told me it would, though. He said I would see you again."

"He did?"

She pushed the wineglass away from her hand and picked up her salad fork and began to press the letter *R* into the white tablecloth. A playfulness glittered in her eyes.

"It was the last visit I had with him," she said. "A few months ago. I think he knew it would be the last time. He told me then that he was ready to die, that he had lived too long. And he started talking about you." She paused, turned the fork in her hand. "He really loved you, Bobo. I've never believed in surrogate parents or surrogate children, but he felt that way about you, that you were a son to him. And I think he felt that way about me to some degree. Or maybe he thought of me as a surrogate daughter-in-law. Anyway,

342

that time, that last time, he told me I would see you again and that everything would be right with us."

"He must have known his death would bring us together, somehow," I said.

Amy touched the R that she had pressed into the tablecloth. "I don't think you know how much I stayed with him that summer, when you were working," she said after a moment.

"I didn't know you did."

"Yes, a lot. It worried my parents. I cleaned his room for him, put flowers in it. He tried to teach me to play chess, but I was terrible at it. Mostly, he talked about you. I think he knew that talking about you was the best way to keep me around." She leaned toward me and whispered, "Someday I'll let you read the diary I kept that summer. All of Avrum's stories about you are in it."

"I'm not sure I want to see it," I said.

"You should," she teased. "Then you would know how wonderful it was making love to you that summer."

"You lied to your diary?"

She smiled. "No. I lied to me."

From over Amy's shoulder, I saw a woman nod to her husband and push away from the table where they were sitting. She hesitated for a moment, inhaled nervously, and fashioned an artificial smile on her artificial face, then she approached us.

"Excuse me," the woman said sweetly.

Amy looked up at her.

"I'm sorry to interrupt," the woman added in a rush, "but I was talking to my husband—" She glanced back to the man sitting at the table, then looked back to Amy. "Well, we were talking about how you looked so familiar. At least, I thought so. And he agreed." She laughed a silly, shrill laugh. "Anyway, we were sitting there, trying to place you."

"I'm sorry. I don't think I—" Amy began.

"Oh, no, we don't know you," the woman said quickly. "That's what we finally realized. We've only seen you."

"Excuse me?" Amy asked quizzically.

"The painting." The woman said. She paused, waiting for Amy to respond.

"Painting?" Amy said after a moment.

"Yes. The one in Jean Archer's home. We were there this afternoon. We're thinking of buying it."

Amy did not move her eyes from the woman, but I thought I saw her face quiver involuntarily. She tried to force a smile.

"There must be some mistake," Amy said quietly.

"Oh, but it couldn't be," the woman insisted. "Your eyes, your face, even the way you do your hair. It's you. We were very impressed with it. My husband wants to include it in the purchase agreement, if we buy the house."

"But I've never posed for a painting," Amy said evenly.

344

The woman blinked confusion. Her eyes flashed to her husband, then back to Amy. "But—"

"It isn't me," Amy said. "I really don't know what you're talking about."

"Oh—"

22

Amy tried, but she could not completely dismiss, or ignore, the woman who had seen Jean Archer's painting.

She had smiled pleasantly, accepting the woman's embarrassed apology before the woman returned to her table. To me, she had whispered, "I must look like someone," then she had detoured the conversation to the wine and a visit she had made with her husband to the wine regions of France. It was a rambling, fragmented story. I listened patiently, but watched her closely. I saw her eyes flit occasionally—almost necessarily—to the woman's table, then away. She smiled obligatorily when I made obligatory comments. And then Paul and Maggie ushered out the dinner in a performance so splendid it begged for applause.

It was as though the food was a diversion, and for an hour the specter of Jean Archer's painting was what Amy had tried to make of it—a mild intrusion, an odd case of mistaken identity. She laughed gaily. Her eyes sparkled. She drank liberally from a second bottle of wine, and when we left the restaurant, she was giddy, insisting that Maggie and Paul would visit her soon. Outside, in the parking lot, under the dimmed lamp of the moon, she whirled in a full dance step and cried, "Oh, God, Bobo, I'm happy!"

We returned to her house, and to her bedroom, and I relaxed on the bed as she lit candles and placed them on the nightstand and on the dresser. She opened the curtains of the windows.

"I know I'm slightly tipsy, Bobo, but I want to make love with the stars watching us," she said.

"The stars may not be the only eyes out there," I warned. "There's a road—"

"I don't care," she said. "I want them to see us. I hope they do. I hope the whole valley sees us. I hope God sees us. God and Avrum, stopping one of their arguments to watch. Would anything please Avrum more? I hope Carter drives by and looks in. Don't you think it would make him happy? I do." She glanced seductively over her shoulder. "Did I ever tell you he tried to make love to me that summer?"

I thought she was teasing. "Sure he did. Carter? Come on. He was the one who pushed us together."

She turned fully to me and began to unbutton her blouse. The light of the candles bathed her.

"Oh, he did. He was very ashamed," she said casually. "Remember the night he got into the fight with Rene and I made him go for a walk, and you walked Rene to the Greenleaf? It was that night."

I began to laugh.

"Do you think that's funny?" she said.

I motioned her to me on the bed. "I have a story to tell you. As Avrum would have said: 'Such a story.'"

We were like children in our gossip of Rene and Carter. As Carter had confessed to me about making love to Rene, Rene had confessed the same to Amy. "We were their inspiration," Amy declared. "Damn it, they got all the benefit." She rolled on the bed until her body was against my body, skin against skin. She whispered, "But that was then; this is now."

We made love freely, exuberantly, in the fluttering, amber light of the candles, with the night and all the eyes of the night watching us through the windows with the pulled-back curtains. Amy was like a sensuous, possessed dancer, moving with a music that consumed her. And then she fell asleep in the cradle of my shoulder, her hand resting on my neck. I lay awake watching her. The beauty that had always been a gift to her seemed even more extraordinary in sleep, and I thought, Yes, the woman and her husband at dinner had been as astonished by that beauty as everyone who sees her. Her breathing against my chest was slow and even, like the purring of a dozing cat, and her breathing coaxed me into sleep and into a dream of being in the restaurant of dolls, and of Maggie and Paul, and of Amy's laughing voice.

When I awoke, Amy was not in the bed. It was still dark and the room was chilly. I could smell the faint, pleasing smoke of burning wood, and I slipped from the bed and pulled on my pants and shirt and went into the den. Amy was sitting on the floor in a flannel nightgown, leaning against the sofa, staring into the flame that trembled out of the heart of the firewood. There was no other light in the room.

"Are you all right?" I asked.

She did not turn to my voice. "Yes," she said after a moment.

I sat beside her. "The fire's nice," I told her.

She leaned her head against my shoulder.

"I thought you were sleeping peacefully," I said.

"I was."

"A bad dream?"

She shook her head against me.

"Regrets?"

"Yes," she admitted. "But not for tonight."

"For when?"

"For then. Back then. Regrets that we were so afraid."

"Is that it? Really?" I said.

She did not reply for a moment. Then: "It's most of it."

"What's the rest? The woman at the restaurant?"

I could feel her body tense.

"Was she right?"

Her answer was like a sigh: "No."

"Do you know Jean Archer?" I asked.

She lifted her head from my shoulder and

pulled her knees up and hugged them. She continued to gaze at the fire.

"Do you?"

"No, Bobo, I don't. I know of her, of course, but I don't know her."

"Do you want to talk about it?"

She turned to me with a puzzled look. "No. Why should I?"

"Just wondered. Can I do anything?"

"Hold me."

"That's easy," I said. I folded her in my arms. Her face nestled into my chest. "Anything else?"

"Yes."

"Name it."

"Stop time."

"Not easy," I replied.

"I know."

"But if we can't stop it, let's make the most of it."

"How?" she asked.

"Make it worth remembering."

"Is that enough, Bobo?"

We returned to bed when the fire faded. We did not make love and we did not talk. Amy lay close to me, her back curled against my chest, her head resting on my arm, her hand laced into my hand. I did not know if she slept. Her breathing was not easy and purring.

At sunrise, she rose from the bed and tugged at me playfully.

"Come on," she said. "It's a new day."

"Where do you want to start?" I asked.

"You'll see," she answered. "Come on."

I followed her into the bathroom and we showered together in the large, claw-foot bathtub under a heavy, stinging spray of heated water that billowed steam. The steam coated our bodies like smoke gliding across wood. She pulled a large, soft towel from a hanger and draped it across the back of the tub and urged me to lie down, and there, with the water raining on her hair and shoulders, sliding from the tips of her nipples and swirling into bubbles that splattered across my face and chest, she opened her legs and knelt over me and, with her hands, guided me into her. She tilted her head back and closed her eyes. Her mouth parted slightly, and the water and steam spilled across her lips. Her body rocked gently against me, slowed, stopped, quivered. She looked down at me. The water trickled over her face in narrow veins, like rivulets from crying.

"Two more days?" she asked.

"Two," I said.

We were eating breakfast when Carter called. He spoke briefly with Amy, saying something that made her laugh, then she handed the phone to me.

"Surprise," she whispered. "Carter found you."

"I don't want to hear about it," Carter said before I could speak. "You're not eloquent enough to do it justice. Just let me imagine it."

"Good morning to you, too. What's up?"

"Not the same thing that was up with you last night, I'm sure," he replied. He snickered.

"Clever. And very much you."

"Yeah. I thought so, too. Wit as well as intellect. Aren't you impressed?"

"Overwhelmed, but my coffee's getting cold."

"Okay, okay," he said. "Forget the wadded sheets. Can you tell me what happened in the restaurant last night?"

"What are you talking about?"

"Maybe you can't talk now. Just say—ah, that you'll have to think about it, if you want to call me later."

"Well, first, I'm confused," I told him.

"I got a call last night," Carter explained. "A couple named Fergis. They told me they saw the woman in Jean Archer's painting at the restaurant, but she denied it was her. They wondered what was going on. Nosy shits, but they like the place and I'd like to unload it before I have to deal with Archer for the rest of the year. What happened?"

I glanced at Amy. She was clearing the plates from the kitchen table.

"Well?" Carter pressed.

"Let me think about it. I'll get back to you."

"Not the right time, huh?"

"That's correct."

"Okay. Call me when you can. Tell her anything. I'll cover." I heard the click of the hangup.

"Problems?" Amy asked when I replaced the telephone in its cradle.

I invented a story about loopholes in Avrum's will.

Amy shrugged. "It's just lawyer talk, but you'd better get used to it. It's their game. I listened to it for so long, I don't hear it anymore."

"I suppose," I said.

She poured another cup of coffee and sat at the table across from me. "Obviously, Carter knows about us. Is he having fun with it?"

"I think he's happy for us, like you said. Maybe a little concerned, but happy."

"Concerned? Why?"

I wanted to guard the answer. "You know Carter," I said casually.

She poured cream into her coffee and stirred it. I knew she was thinking, selecting words to make certain they were the right words. She said, after a long moment, "I do know Carter, Bob. And I know that what he just asked you had nothing to do with Avrum's will." She flicked a smile. "But it was about me, wasn't it? Or, maybe about us?"

I nodded. I wanted to look away from her eyes, but I could not.

"It's all right," she said quietly. "But I think you should tell me—unless it's one of Carter's bedroom stories."

I thought: Be careful, be careful.

"Okay, we were talking about you," I admitted. "But that's nothing new. I think that at least seventy percent of the conversations I've had with Carter since the first night I met you in Arch's have been about you, and on that night he could have stood with the great prophets."

"Ummm, I like that," she mused. "But you're being evasive, and I know that trick. I'm a woman, a wife, and a mother. There are some things that become obvious."

"But it's true. You should hear some of the stories Carter tells about us. Frankly, I never knew he was in your room all those nights when we were making love, with your folks next door, and I always thought he was asleep when you sneaked into The Cave."

Amy laughed. "God, I hope you're telling the truth. It would mean that at least one person I know had the same thoughts I had. But you're still being evasive."

"Will you go for a drive with me?" I asked.

"Will it answer my question?"

"I think so," I told her.

I did not understand why Amy avoided talking about the painting in Jean Archer's home. She had denied knowing about it in the restaurant, and sitting in front of the late-night fire, she had brushed away my question about it. Her behavior made me remember the night that Carolyn, on her visit to the Catskills, asked me about Amy, though she did not know Amy's name, or anything about her. We were in a coffee shop in Margaretville, and the waitress, who had seen me

often with Amy, said to her, "Oh, you're new."
It was a simple statement, but enough to begin
an inquisition. What did she mean? Carolyn
wanted to know. Why did she say that? Was she
accustomed to seeing me with someone else? I
tried to dismiss it as waitress talk. "We come here
a lot," I told Carolyn. "Me, Carter, some of the
kids who work at the other resorts. I guess she
knows us pretty well by now. She just hasn't
seen you, that's all." I knew by her expression—
a frown of doubt—that Carolyn did not wholly
believe me. I asked, "Does it bother you?" And
she replied, "No. It just seems funny. Everybody
up here looks at me like they're trying not to say
the wrong thing. Everybody but that waitress."

I sensed some of the same discomfort that
Carolyn had experienced when I thought about
the painting of Amy. I did not want it to appear
on my face, but I could feel the mask of doubt.

Amy did not press me about my conversation
with Carter, and she did not ask where I was
taking her, though she knew we were driving
toward Woodstock. She wore the face of a good
mood, of someone whose spirit matched the
vibrancy of the day.

She wanted to know if we could browse
through the shops in Woodstock after we were
done with whatever it was we were doing.

"Sure," I told her. "I drove through with
Carter earlier this week, but we didn't stop. The
place has changed."

"I know it has," she said, "but I still like it.

Do you remember the first time we drove over that summer, with Carter and Rene? We met that man who made bracelets from airplane metal."

I confessed that I remembered the trip, but not the man or his bracelets. "Unless I'm wrong, that was the first time we went anywhere during the day, and I was more than a little worried about getting back to the Inn on time for dinner."

"That's what you said," she corrected. "But that wasn't it. You were worried what people would think if they saw us together." She leaned quickly to me and kissed me on the corner of my mouth. "I wanted to do that on that trip." She glanced out of the window. "In fact, I think we were at this exact spot when the urge struck me."

"Good try, but I doubt it, since this is a new road. It's a good thought, though."

She laughed and sat back against the seat and stared out of the window at the mountains and the orchards that seemed to rotate around us as we rode past them. She said, "Do you know what I'd like, Bobo? I'd like for you to meet my children."

It was the first time she had mentioned them since the lunch in the Inn.

"I'd enjoy that," I said. "Tell me about them."

She was silent for a moment before answering. "They're very sweet, very close. Sometimes they remind me of the daughters in *Fiddler on the Roof*, but they're also very spoiled in a way. They know how to play me against their father and their father against me, and that gets tiresome."

"I know," I said.

"It's that way in your home, too?"

"From their first temper tantrum."

"In our home, Peter can buy their attention, and does. I don't believe in that. But they would like you." She looked at me. "In fact, they already do."

"Should I ask how?" I said.

"A few years ago, when we were all together on vacation in Maine without their father, it began raining one night and we were all tucked inside a cabin talking girl talk and they asked me about the boys I'd dated. I told them about you."

"Everything?" I asked.

"Enough for them to understand. They were envious. They wanted to know why it only lasted for a summer."

"What did you tell them?"

"What they wanted to hear. That it was the perfect summer and then it was over."

"That sounds a little tragic," I suggested.

She smiled warmly. "Oh, no, Bobo. To girls, in a cabin in Maine, in a rainstorm, it was romantic." She paused, remembering the cabin and the rain and the circle of daughters cuddled around her like pillows. "It was nice. Really nice. Cindy—she's the youngest—wanted to know why we didn't get married. She said she'd love to have a father who was an artist, someone to draw pictures for her."

"That must have been hard to explain," I said.

"Jeannie and Meg had a great laugh over it.

They tried to tell Cindy why that wouldn't have been possible, but I don't think she understood. Not then."

"They sound like good kids."

"They are," she said. Then: "They think I'm losing it."

"Why?"

"They call it the Project—meaning the house up here. They're afraid I'm getting ready to leave their father and become a hermit."

"Are they right?"

She laughed again. "I don't know." She turned her face to me. "I think about it sometimes, but I don't know if I have the nerve. Could you leave Carolyn?"

I shrugged.

"Tender subject?" she asked.

I shrugged again.

"So many years, Bobo. So many years. Right?"

"I suppose."

"Have you ever discussed it?"

"I think every couple does, at least once or twice. It's been a few years with us, though. I don't even remember why it came up. Something to do with how different we were. The only thing I remember was the reaction from Jason, our son. He told me privately that he'd overheard the argument and that he wanted me to know he and his sisters would understand if we divorced. He said none of them thought we were very compatible."

"The permission discussion," Amy said. "I

wonder if every parent gets that. My daughters have all said the same thing. Of course, there were enough tears to make me realize their understanding might have had its limits. I've always thought of such talks as playing adult."

"Maybe," I replied. "Children can be perceptive, though."

She pulled her knees up in the seat and leaned her head against my shoulder like a teenager. "So, where are you taking me?"

"We'll be there soon," I said.

"We'd better, or I'll be asleep." She yawned, wiggled her head deeper into my shoulder. "You're keeping me awake at night." She closed her eyes.

She sat up as I slowed the car and pulled into the road leading to Jean Archer's house. I knew immediately she had never been there.

"Is this the house the woman talked about?" she asked.

"Yes."

"You've been here?"

"With Carter. He's handling the sale."

I could hear tension in her voice: "Bobo . . ."

I stopped the car in front of the house. "Come on," I said.

We got out of the car and I went to the rock and took the key and led Amy to the front door. She glanced about with apprehension.

"It's all right," I promised.

I opened the door and we entered the house. She stood, hesitantly. Her eyes scanned the great room, pausing on the paintings. An uneasy expression was on her face. I took her by the arm and led her to the stairs.

"I think we should leave, Bobo," she whispered.

"Not yet," I said. "It's upstairs."

I held to her arm as we went up the stairway to Jean Archer's bedroom. When I opened the door, I stepped back. She saw the painting instantly, and the force of seeing it made her tremble. She paused, then moved toward it. She stood at the side of Jean Archer's bed for a long time, staring at the painting, and when she turned, her face was damp with tears.

I moved to her and held her. She tucked her head into my shoulder. After a moment she whispered, "It isn't me, Bobo."

"It has to be," I said.

"No. It's my mother."

23

Amy did not speak again until we were in the car, driving back toward Woodstock. She sat, tucked into the seat, leaning against the door, gazing vacantly at the landscape. Finally she said, "I wonder when it was painted."

"A number of years ago, I'd judge," I told her.

"It's so strange," she said. "Seeing it. I can understand why you and Carter and the woman in the restaurant thought it was me. At first, I thought so, too. I thought she had taken a photograph of me and painted the face from it, but it's not me. It's my mother."

"Did your mother know her?" I asked.

She muttered something I did not understand. "She did?" I said.

Amy turned to face me. "She may have. She told me once about a fund-raiser she helped to organize, something for displaced Jews. It was an art auction and one of the contributors was Jean Archer. I remember it because my mother told me about the painting Jean Archer had offered. It was of children in one of the death camps. My mother said people wept when they saw it, that it was so real it frightened them, and no one bought it. It was finally sold to a museum in Pittsburgh."

"That was the only time your mother ever mentioned her?"

"Yes—no. One other time. We were in a gallery in New York and there were two or three of her paintings on display. My mother stood for a long time and looked at them, then she said something like, 'She's remarkable.' I remember her voice. It was a whisper, like—like worship. She was in awe."

"She had a right to be," I said. "She was looking at talent. When was that?"

"I don't remember. Ten years ago. Maybe longer. I thought about it when we were in the antiques store yesterday and I saw some Jean Archer prints."

"Could your mother have sat for a portrait when she was working on the fund-raiser?" I asked.

Amy was silent for a moment, then she said, "I don't know. I was young—fourteen or fifteen. I was so busy with my own life that I didn't pay very much attention to what was going on around me. She could have, but I don't know why she never mentioned it, unless—" She paused.

"Unless?"

"Unless it was because of my father."

"Your father?"

"I never really understood it, but my father always objected to my mother's activities in the arts. He believed too many of the people she knew had more talent for taking than doing. He called them moochers. It was the one thing they

362

disagreed over. I sometimes wonder if that wasn't the reason for their divorce."

"It's not a new story, Amy. There's someone in Atlanta who has something of the same opinion about her husband's friends, who happen to be artists for the most part. And, in fact, she's right about a few of them."

She smiled sympathetically and reached across the seat and let her hand rest on my arm.

"I'm sorry," I said. "Bad joke."

"It's all right," she replied. "I'm just confused, that's all. My mother was a private person. Maybe she did have a portrait done by Jean Archer and was afraid to bring it home, but if she did, I wish she had told me about it. The truth would help now."

"I read something once," I told her. "It said: 'Truth becomes heaviest when someone tries to help you carry it.'"

"Do you believe that?" Amy asked.

"No," I said, "but I think that's what people are afraid of."

She slipped close to me and took my hand and kissed it. "I think that's the way I feel about us. I've always wanted to tell Peter everything about you, but I couldn't. I couldn't expect him to understand. Even when I've thought about it over the years—and I have, often—it's more like a childish dream than a reality."

I thought of Avrum's warning: *It is painful to love someone and believe you can never be with them.*

363

I asked if she was sorry that she knew about the painting.

She did not answer immediately. Then she said, quietly, "No. It has love in it."

We stopped in Woodstock and had a light lunch, but we did not browse the shops as Amy had suggested earlier. She was not angry or sad, but I knew she still saw the painting in her mind, and I believed she needed to be alone. I told her I wanted to check with Carter about the disposition of Avrum's will, and she agreed to dinner at her house. "I make a fettuccine *al pesto* and a spinach salad you won't forget," I promised.

She smiled warmly. "Sounds wonderful. And I think you should tell Carter about the painting."

I assured her that I would. "If I don't, he'll drive us both to insanity."

I called Carter when I returned to the Inn. He was not as amazed by the news of Jean Archer's painting as I thought he would be, vowing he had often confused Evelyn Lourie for Amy. He laughingly remembered an incident during the summer before I arrived to work at the Inn. "I saw her mother by the pool, in a bathing suit. She was laying on a lounge chair with an umbrella shading her. I swear to God, Bobo, I thought it was Amy. I whistled at her and shouted something stupid like, 'Why don't you wear that to dinner?' And then she stood up and I saw who it was. Don't think I've ever been that embarrassed, and I've had a lot of opportunities to top it. I promise you, she had the body of a sixteen-year-old. I even dreamed about her."

"Somehow, that doesn't surprise me," I said. "Anyway, Amy wanted you to know."

"That's good. I can call the Fergis couple and tell them it was nothing more than a coincidence, but I'd sure like to know how the painting got there, if Amy knew nothing about it. That's a hell of a secret to keep—having a painting done by one of the great artists of the world."

"I think Amy feels the same way," I told him.

"So, I don't suppose you're free for dinner tonight, are you?" Carter asked.

"Good try, Carter. But, no, I don't think so. Amy and I are going to rent a couple of wheelchairs and roll down memory lane together."

"Sounds kinky," Carter replied. "But, what the hell. Couldn't be much worse than the back-seat of my old Chevy. Just don't roll over anything dragging the floor, Bobo, and give me a call tomorrow."

I could hear his laughter in the click-off.

There are look-alikes.

In Atlanta, there is a man who so resembles me, people who know me are startled when they see him. I have never met him, but I know of him and he knows of me. He likes art and often attends exhibits sponsored by galleries. Many of the owners of the galleries tell me they have mistaken him for me, and are stunned when they learn he is only a look-alike. They say he takes it all in good stride, vowing that, some day, he is going to call me for a meeting. If I had his name, I would call him.

Fern Weisel was a woman who had looked remarkably like Amelita Galli-Curci. Avrum had pictures of both women, and one day, sitting on his bench with a photo album that covered his life in a tale of austere but stiffly smiling faces—staring as unmoving for the camera as they might have for an executioner's gun—he had put the pictures of the two women side by side and asked if I could pick out the real Amelita. I couldn't. I thought they were of the same person and that it was another of Avrum's tricks.

"So, you see," Avrum proclaimed triumphantly, "the eye is a liar." He tapped his chest with his forefinger. "Only this knows."

And then he told me of Fern Weisel.

He had met her while working as an interpreter at Ellis Island. It was a stunning thing, seeing her across a crowd of people, believing that she was Amelita Galli-Curci. When he learned that he was wrong, that he was merely seeing a look-alike, he made his way to her and introduced himself.

She became his lover.

It was, after so many years, a laughable matter to Avrum, but he confessed that he had tried to fashion Fern into Amelita. He purchased dresses for her that resembled costumes Amelita Galli-Curci wore in her performances. He forced her to listen to his records of Amelita Galli-Curci. He encouraged her to sing. She was tone-deaf. Avrum's effort was a failure. "She was like my wife," he lamented. "She did not love the music. She loved only the gifts and the bed." He smiled merrily when he spoke of the bed. "*Ja*. Her music was in the bed."

The liaison lasted only a year, Avrum admitted. He could not abide an imitator, even if it was he who had created the imitation, and even if the imitator was a lover worth bragging about.

"Only this knows," he said again, again tapping his chest with his forefinger.

When I thought of Fern Weisel, I could see her clearly in the photograph that could easily have been Amelita Galli-Curci, and I could imagine Avrum urging her to dress as Violette from *La Traviata* or Gilda from *Rigoletto* or Lucia from *Lucia di Lammermoor* or, of course, Dinorah from *Dinorah*. There would have been nothing perverted about his behavior, regardless of how it might have appeared to Fern Weisel, or to anyone. Avrum's longing was obsessive, but not dangerous. Still, sometimes I wondered if that was why he quarreled with God: he could not, himself, be God.

Fortunately, I did not suffer an inquisition from Lila about another late night away from the Inn and I did not have to follow Sammy to his shop to judge his late-night work on the bust of Amy. They were busy with thirty guests from a

Dutch Reformed church in New York, away on a weekend retreat intended to revive the passions of their marriages. The only thing Lila said to me from behind the registration desk was a whispered, "All they need is a good roll in the sheets." Then she smiled and winked and added, "Maybe you could testify for them, Bobo."

I slept for a short time, then showered and dressed and drove to the Highmount Home for Retired Citizens. Because I wanted to be with Amy, I thought it would be my last opportunity to visit Sol Walkman, and, too, there was a tug of guilt about Avrum, that in being with Amy I had compromised the mourning of his death, even if his philosophy had been a blunt "Dead is dead."

Sol greeted me enthusiastically. He had been working on new financial projections that included the gift of Avrum's estate, and he jabbered about plans to add an exercise room and indoor walking track. "It'll give most of our people something to do other than watch television and play board games," he explained, "and that's what they need—to know they can still do things. Otherwise, all they're doing is putting in their time before they die."

He asked my advice on being more aggressive about securing donations from families whose relatives had spent their last years at the Home, but fretted that he knew the response.

"They'll think they've already paid enough," he reasoned. "It's sad. It's damn sad, but a lot of them can't wait to tear open the will and find out what they've been left, and they're not about to give any of it back to the Home."

He wanted to show me where the exercise facility would be, and I followed him down a corridor that had fading snapshots of residents and their visitors thumbtacked to a corkboard wall. I paused before a photograph of me with Avrum, taken perhaps ten years earlier by one of the orderlies. Avrum was smiling a crooked, silly smile.

"I'd like to have that one blown up and put in the exercise room," Sol said. "In fact, I'd like to call it the Avrum Feldman Room, if you don't object."

I wondered if Carter had negotiated the idea despite my disapproval. Probably. Carter had liked Avrum and Carter liked such touches. It was his practice of quid pro quo.

"I don't mind," I told Sol.

He saw me looking at the picture of an old and shriveled man in a wheelchair, his head bent permanently forward over his chest. A young woman was kneeling beside him, preening into the camera. It was the judge's wife, the stockbroker's lover.

"Do you know her?" Sol asked suspiciously.

"I met her briefly at the Inn, earlier this week," I said.

"I suppose you know the story, then? About her lover."

"I think everybody up here knows," I

answered. "Lila, Sammy, Dan Wilder, Carter, the woman in the flower shop in Phoenicia, you, and, somewhere, somebody in a wine shop. It must be the most celebrated and open affair in America."

Sol laughed easily. "Could be, but she won't have her excuse much longer. Her uncle is in his last weeks, the doctors tell us."

"If she needs an excuse, why don't you take advantage of it?" I suggested.

"How?"

"Make her the chairlady of something—maybe the Pledge Committee."

Sol's eyes narrowed in a pleased thought. "Good idea."

I stayed with Sol for an hour, listening to him, watching his flashing hands draw images of equipment and space as he enthused about improvements to the Home. He promised to correspond about the work and he invited me, in good humor, to also belong to the Pledge Committee. I thought of Amy and, in good humor, agreed. Before I left, he gave me a small, sealed box that contained Avrum's ashes. The box had been delivered by the crematory on Friday, he explained.

"I don't know what you plan to do with these," he said, "and I don't think I need to know. I'm sure that was something personal between the two of you."

"It was," I told him. "It's kind of you to understand."

He shook my hand vigorously at my car and thanked me again for the contribution of Avrum's estate. I expected him to ask about the kaddish, but he did not. Sol Walkman understood the art of negotiation. He had dispatched Norman Gold, the rabbi, to voice his concern, as Avrum had predicted. The negotiation was finished. He would not risk his gift foolishly.

"You've been a godsend," Sol said gratefully. "A godsend."

When I drove away, watching him fan the late-afternoon air with his waving, I believed what Sol really meant by his godsend comment was that God had finally tilted things in his favor to compensate for all the years of tolerating Avrum Feldman.

The sun was disappearing, leaving its skid marks of color, like the smear of finger paints, on a wall of clouds that rolled up from the collar of the mountains. I thought of Arch Ellis. It was the time of day that Arch most loved, and the reason he always swept the sidewalk in front of his store at that hour. "A man who sees a sunset in the Catskills and doesn't believe in God is a man condemned to hell with his first breath," Arch would thunder like a street preacher of the South. I had learned from Arch there was nothing wrong, or weak, in letting beauty have its way with you. If anything was worth shouting about, it was beauty.

And that, too, was a ghost of the Catskills.

Amy was outside, working in a flower bed, when I arrived. Her jeans and frayed oxford shirt were stained with dirt. Even in the cooling air, a narrow ribbon of perspiration laced her forehead. She had the blushed, happy look of a child who has played to exhaustion but has ignored the call to come home. If she had been despondent over seeing a painting of her mother in Jean Archer's bedroom, she had buried it in the rich garden soil.

"Oh, God," she exclaimed. "What time is it?"

"Who cares?" I said.

She pulled the work gloves from her hands and wiped at her forehead. She kissed me easily, naturally.

"I'm filthy," she said. "I need a shower."

"I won't argue that," I told her. "But I'm early. Thought I'd stop by and see what we need from the grocery."

"Let's look," she said. "I have a refrigerator full of things I really don't need, which means I'm always throwing things away, but I don't care. It's my way of declaring my independence." She led me into the house.

I did a quick inventory as Amy showered. She had boxed fettuccine and spinach and parsley and grated Parmesan cheese, but no basil or walnuts or olive oil or cream. She came from the bedroom, wrapped in a towel, as I was completing my list. Her hair was glistening from the water.

"You're doing that on purpose, aren't you?" I said.

A smile played across her face. "I don't know what you're talking about. Doing what?"

"Tempting me."

She leaned and kissed me. "Do you know that I used to model?"

"Did you?"

She did a model's turn, like a dance step. "For charity, of course." She pivoted again, turned her back, tilted her head over her shoulder as she had posed before the opened curtains in her candlelit bedroom. Then she opened the towel slowly and turned seductively to face me. Her body was like an erotic painting.

"It won't work," I told her.

She feigned a pout.

"I don't know what time the grocery closes," I said.

She folded the towel around her again and settled into my lap. "I just want to be foolish, Bobo. I love being foolish, and I never am. I always think someone's watching me—except when I'm here. Not in this place. I think I'm safe here, but to be honest, I don't care who sees me with you. I want them to. I want Carter to know that we've made love, that tonight we'll sleep together again and tomorrow we'll have breakfast together." She rolled her face against my face and her damp hair fell against my temples. "I know," she whispered. "Let's invite Carter to breakfast."

"Are you sure?"

"Absolutely. I think he needs to be here. He was the first to see what would happen between us." She leaned back and took my face in her hands, like a child wanting attention for a sudden thought. "Do you know what he told me the night I met you—I mean before you came into Arch's?"

I mugged a no.

"He told me that I was going to be really impressed, that I'd probably fall in love with you and spend my life on a farm in Georgia, raising chickens and children and singing in the choir of a Baptist church."

I smiled at the thought. "He was busy that night."

"What do you mean?" she asked.

"That was the same night he warned me that I would fall in love with you and become an idiot. He said you were the most beautiful woman I would ever meet."

Amy giggled. She slid from my lap and did her model's turn.

"Do you still think so?" she said.

I gazed at her. She was not the girl of the Catskills, yet her body was still slender and firm and athletic, the body of a woman in her midthirties, and it was as beautiful as the face that looked at me. I reached and pushed open the towel and touched one of her nipples.

"Yes," I answered. "Yes, you are."

She stepped into my hand and rubbed her

breast against my palm, then she took my hand and lifted it to her mouth and she began to kiss the tips of my fingers, to suck gently on them.

"Amy . . ."

She pulled away and tugged the towel back around her body.

"Go," she said softly, "before I get too greedy to let you leave." She turned and went back into the bedroom.

There was a small grocery in Phoenicia that had fresh herbs and a surprisingly good selection of wine. I quickly found what I needed and was waiting in line at the checkout counter when I glanced through the store window and saw the woman from the restaurant coming out of an ice cream shop with Carter. They had ice cream cones and the woman was laughing. One of Carter's remarks, I thought. A good one. They stood for a moment on the sidewalk and talked. The woman smiled uncomfortably at Carter and then she looked quickly away, as though searching for someone. Carter leaned to her and said something that would have been spoken in a whisper, and she looked at him, hesitated, then nodded. Carter spoke again and again she nodded, and then she walked away, flicking a small wave of her hand to Carter. Carter watched her leaving, the smile never wavering in his face. And then he took a satisfied lick from his ice cream and strolled across the street to his car.

"Is that all?" the clerk asked.

"Yes," I said. "I think so."

As I drove out of Phoenicia, I saw the woman in a small park beside the Esopus Creek. She was sitting at a picnic table, watching a group of teenagers floating by on tubes. She seemed deep in thought.

Amy had dressed in clean, snug-fitting jeans and a pale blue oxford shirt while I shopped, and she had started a small fire in the fireplace. She was pouring two glasses of chardonnay when I went into the kitchen.

"Is this okay, or do you want something stronger?" she asked.

"It's fine," I told her. "I picked up a cabernet for dinner."

She took the bottle of cabernet that I fished from one of the grocery bags and examined the label. "Nice, but not as nice as we'll find when we get to France."

"You have the tickets, I suppose," I said.

She began helping me take the groceries from the bags. "I can get them in a day," she replied easily.

"You sound almost serious," I countered.

"I am."

I said nothing for a moment. The thought of being with Amy in France, in the small villages and on the magical night streets of Paris, flashed like a begging.

"That would be good," I said.

She took the olive oil and opened a cabinet

and placed it inside. "I could do it, Bobo, but it would be easy for me. Not so easy for you. I told you my family already believes I'm in a delayed midlife crisis and anything I do that's flighty, but relatively sane and harmless, is fine with them. With Peter, it would be, 'France? Sounds great. Want me to call my travel agent for you?' With the children, it would be, 'Have a great time, Mom. Don't worry about anything here. We can take care of everything, including Dad.' And they would all see me off, waving like a pack of wild cheerleaders at a football game, acting as though they had planned the whole escapade."

She paused and smiled foolishly. "I put the olive oil away. You need that, don't you?" She opened the cabinet and took out the olive oil. "Maybe they're right. Maybe I am losing it."

"Maybe it's just the opposite," I said. "Maybe you're finding it."

She kissed me lightly on the cheek. "Thank you. I'll accept that. Now, cook. I'm hungry."

We prepared and cooked the dinner together and made make-believe plans for a make-believe trip to France and Germany and Italy. We were performing a game that both of us knew was merely a game. Amy plotted that we would be like lovers who meet in Paris on the Champs-Elysées, drinking wine at a sidewalk café. Both divorced, she projected casually, both eager to put their pasts behind them and to begin new lives with new lovers, or maybe with old lovers newly found.

"Then we rent a car—a Mercedes—and we begin driving," she added enthusiastically. "No maps, no plans. We just drive and we stop where we stop. And maybe we stay for the night, or for a week. We stay as long as we want to stay."

"Who drives?" I asked.

"We both do."

"I've driven in Europe," I objected. "Cruising at a hundred miles an hour is not my idea of relaxing, even in a Mercedes. You can drive."

"Fine. But we have to rent a convertible. I love the wind in my hair."

We talked of stopping at roadside rest stops and eating sandwiches purchased in small villages from small delicatessens, and drinking the wine of the region out of crystal glasses that we would buy in Paris and carefully pack after each use. We talked of visiting art galleries and ancient churches, of festivals and pageants, of reading histories from monuments and plaques. We talked of lovemaking in the sparse rooms of cheap boardinghouses and of partying with strangers in strange taverns.

The only thing we did not talk about, the only part of the game that we did not perform, was the return to reality, because we both knew that reality was always the last night for lovers and no one speaks of the last night until it is necessary.

We had finished eating and had washed and put away the dinnerware and were sitting on the floor before the fire, leaning against the sofa and drinking cognac warmed over goblets of hot water, and we were talking about my years as a painter and teacher—steady years, but not as distinguished or as exhilarating as I had dreamed, or wished, I confessed—when the doorbell rang.

Amy's eyes flickered in surprise.

"Are you expecting anyone?" I asked.

She shook her head as she stood. Then, as though to assure me: "I talked to Peter while you were shopping. He's in Washington."

I stood beside her. "Maybe it's Carter," I suggested.

Amy did not reply. She went to the door and opened it. A stately woman, dressed casually, her steel-gray hair swept back as though it had been brushed only with the wind and her fingers, stood in the doorway.

"Yes?" Amy said.

The woman did not speak for a long moment. Her azure eyes were locked on Amy's face. Then she said in a quiet voice, "Yes. Unbelievable."

"Excuse me?" Amy said.

I moved to Amy and took her arm.

"Amy, this is Jean Archer," I told her.

24

We sat in the kitchen, around the table, with coffee and cognac, and we talked—or Jean Archer talked, answering questions from Amy. I had volunteered to leave, but Amy insisted that I stay. I saw doubt in Jean Archer's eyes, but she said nothing.

She confessed that she knew about Amy from the couple who were interested in buying her house, and she knew that Amy had inherited her mother's summer home.

"I took a chance that you would be here," she said to Amy. "I had to see you, to know, to look in your face. Many times your mother shared photographs of you, and always it was the face of your mother that I saw."

We told her about going to her house without permission, and about seeing the painting that I, and Carter, had believed was a painting of Amy.

She said nothing about our entering the house, though her body tensed in objection.

"It was my doing," I emphasized. "And I hope you forgive me. It was an impulse." I did not tell her about being there alone, at night.

"It doesn't matter," she replied coolly.

And then Amy asked the question that she had

not been able to answer for me: "When did my mother pose for the painting?"

Jean blinked. A film of moisture seeped into her piercing blue eyes. "When you were very young, in your early teens, I think. She left you and your father for a few weeks. Do you remember?"

"Yes," Amy answered.

"She was with me," Jean said.

I could see Amy's face pale.

"When we knew she was dying, I told her I would find you, and tell you," Jean added evenly.

"Tell me?" Amy said quizzically.

Jean paused. Her body became proudly, defiantly erect. "Your mother and I were lovers, Amy."

Amy slumped, but her eyes did not leave Jean Archer's face. I reached for her hand and held it. Her grip on my fingers was like a voice holding a scream.

"I'm sorry to shock you," Jean said calmly. "I believe in truth and the truth has been hidden long enough." She looked at me. "This man, he is your lover, isn't he?"

Amy did not respond and I did not respond.

Jean turned her eyes back to Amy. "I know about him. Your mother talked about him the summer that you met him and then again before she died. She remembered that she was afraid of him, afraid of how he could hurt you because you were so different. She was thinking of us, of course. How much hurt our relationship would

381

cause if anyone knew." She paused and inhaled. "I disagreed with her. I disagreed, Amy, because I loved her as much as you love this man, and we were as different as people could be. But I knew that I could not live without her and she knew she could not live without me, no matter how hard either of us tried to stop it."

Amy whispered the question: "Does my father know?"

"Yes," Jean answered. "That was the reason for the divorce. Someone who knew about us told him."

"But—"

"He never said anything to you. Yes, I know. Your father is a very dignified man, a wonderful man. I have always hurt for him, but I could not stop loving her."

"Have you ever spoken to him?" Amy asked.

Jean nodded. "A few times. When Evelyn—your mother—died, he called me. He asked that I not attend the funeral. He was very kind about it and I understood."

Amy pulled her hand from mine and lifted the glass of cognac and held it and gazed thoughtfully at the rim of the glass. After a moment she said, "Tell me about it."

"Are you sure?" Jean asked.

"Yes."

The story that Jean Archer revealed agreed with Amy's suspicions: her mother had met Jean in New York at the fund-raiser for displaced Jews. Their affair had begun immediately and had continued—with lapses created by Jean's famous anger and occasional infidelities, and by Evelyn Lourie's seizures of guilt—until Evelyn's death. It was the reason Jean had purchased a house in the Catskills: to be near Evelyn.

"You may not understand this," Jean said softly, "but until I met her, I never knew who, or what, I was. I had tried to hide my sexuality, which I felt even as a child in the ghetto at Lodz. After I met her, I couldn't deny it. Until I knew your mother, until I had that love, I was only a person who drew lines on paper; after that, I became an artist. She *was* my art. I wanted to die when she died." She paused. "I even tried to."

I listened without interruption, feeling uncomfortable, but in the way the mind plays tricks, I also imagined Evelyn Lourie making love to Jean Archer, her body moving submissively to finger touches as delicately stroked as a painter's brush, and then reaching to pull Jean Archer's face to her and to feed hungrily from the flicking nipple of her tongue.

And for a reason that only the trick-playing mind understands, I remembered Kelly Pender, a shy, cautious woman who taught English at the school where I was employed. One night, when we were chaperoning a dance, Kelly confided to me that she was a lesbian—"because I trust you, Bobo, or maybe because I have to try the truth out on someone, since I don't think I can live a lie much longer." And I listened to her story as we patrolled the dance, prying apart adolescents whose hormones were boiling like lava, and, later, as we drank coffee at a coffee shop. Her lover was a former student who was then in graduate school at a nearby university. I knew the girl. She was Scandinavian—personable, bright, talented, remarkably blond, remarkably beautiful. When Kelly described their lovemaking, she spoke of gentleness, of softness, of caring. "With men it's always get it and go," she said bitterly. "And you know what's funny, Bobo? I used to dream of making love to men and I'd wake up angry. Now, I don't dream of making love to men at all. I dream of making love to her. Only her, and that's why I think I have to accept the truth."

It was late when Jean Archer rose from the table to leave. We walked her to the door.

"I had to see you tonight," she said to Amy. "Tomorrow, I am leaving and I will never again return here."

Amy stepped to her and embraced her warmly. "I'm glad you came. I'm glad you told me."

"Do not let what I have said hurt the love you have for your mother," Jean advised. "Believe me, because of how deeply she cared for you and your father, our relationship was painful for her."

"I won't," Amy said.

"Good. Now, there's one other thing: the painting. I will not sell it, but I will give it to you if you want it."

Amy shook her head. "No. It's beautiful, but I can't take it. It's yours."

The film of tears again glittered in Jean Archer's eyes. She raised her face and closed her eyes for a moment, then she looked at me.

"I'm glad we met," she said.

"Me, too," I told her. "I feel privileged."

She folded her arms around Amy, held her for a trembling moment, then she turned and walked away from the house.

We watched her drive away and then Amy closed the door.

"Are you all right?" I asked.

She nodded.

"Do you want to be alone?"

She turned to me. "I want to go to bed. I want you to hold me."

I did not ask her to talk about her mother and Jean Archer. In bed, she curled into my body as a child who needs comfort curls against a parent, and she slept. I do not think she dreamed. When I awoke in the morning, she was still against me, still curled.

I slipped from bed and went into the kitchen and made coffee. It was early—the morning before morning. Outside, the black of night was fading against a promise of light. I could hear a bird fussing energetically, as though it had decided to quarrel with the laziness of the night, and I remembered that it was Sunday—the day of Avrum's kaddish. I went to my briefcase and took out the envelope that he had marked for me as *Avrum Feldman's kaddish. To be opened six days after his death. A.F.* and I opened it. His instructions made me smile. Not even Sol Walkman, or the rabbi, would object.

I put the envelope back into my briefcase and sat at the kitchen table and had coffee and listened to the fussing bird and watched the bluing of morning, and again I thought of Kelly Pender. Soon after her talk with me, and on my advice, Kelly had admitted to the headmaster that she was lesbian and her contract was not renewed. I wanted to advocate for her, but she would not permit it. "Don't you see?" she argued. "It sets me free." And she had been right. She had become an activist in the gay rights movement and was often quoted by the media. One night, in a restaurant on Highland Avenue, Carolyn and I saw her with the woman who was her lover. Kelly bounced across the restaurant and threw her arms around me gladly, causing Carolyn to burn with indignation. On the drive home, Carolyn blurted, "How can you be friends with someone like that?" Her question stunned me. "How can you turn your back on a friendship, for God's sake?" I snapped. Carolyn sat against the car door, glaring at me. After a moment, she said, "I can't believe how much you've changed."

I poured a fresh cup of coffee and returned to the bedroom. Amy had rolled to the spot on the bed where I slept. She turned on her back and peeked at me.

"Coffee, please," she said. She pulled up in the bed, pushing the pillows behind her back, and she leaned against the backboard. The covers fell from her breasts.

I gave her the cup and sat on the bed beside her.

"What time is it?" she asked.

"A little after six-thirty."

"Do you always get up this early?"

"Most of the time."

She sipped from the coffee. "Ummm, good."

"Are you okay?" I asked.

She touched my lips with her fingers. "Yes. I'm fine."

"You want to go back to sleep?"

She smiled. "When we go to Europe, I insist on sleeping until at least eight o'clock—every morning."

"Maybe in Paris."

"Especially in Paris," she said.

She put the cup on the night table and moved over in the bed and took my hand and pulled me to her.

"We forgot something last night," she whispered.

"Did we?"

"You can't be that old," she said. She nuzzled my chest with her face. "But we don't have a lot of time to make up for it."

"Why don't we?" I asked.

"Carter will be here at seven-thirty. I called

and left a message for him when you were shopping. He called back just before you got here."

We made love hurriedly, but with passion that was of muscle and soul—strong, uninhibited, giving. It was more than sex. It was an exorcism of everything that had ruled us, every pressure, every prohibition. Amy cried aloud in the final, rushing convulsion and then she threw her body against me and held me. "My God," she whispered. "My God." We showered and dressed. When Carter arrived, we were in the kitchen preparing breakfast.

He was in Carter form. It was in his grin and in the light of his eyes.

"So, here we are," he enthused with a sweep of his arms around the kitchen. "This is great. Little mom-and-pop scene. Real homey, Amy. Real homey."

"I think so, too," I said. "I just got here."

Carter laughed his evil laugh.

"Both of you, stop it," warned Amy. "I heard enough of your little-boy jokes when you actually were little boys. Carter, pour yourself some coffee and get some orange juice if you want it. Where's Libby?"

"Still asleep, I guess," Carter said. "I didn't even tell her about this. She's too damned young to appreciate it, which is the only thing I despise about youth. If I'd known where to find Rene, I'd have invited her, but anybody else would have been an intrusion."

I looked at Amy and smiled. She fought not to laugh and lost the fight.

"What?" Carter said. "What did I say?"

"Nothing," I told him. "We were just talking earlier about the four of us being together, and you mentioned Rene. It's just funny."

"Not without a Bloody Mary or two," Carter countered. "You sure you guys haven't been celebrating without me?"

Amy turned to me. "Do you want to answer that?" She laughed again.

"Forget it," Carter said. "I withdraw the question. It was stupid." He pulled a chair from the table and sat. "I'm hungry."

We ate breakfast leisurely. Carter directed that I serve and he would clean the table and Amy would leave a generous tip. It would be like retired baseball players playing in an old-timers' game, he reasoned. Going through the motions for the sake of memory.

"And that's how I plan on handling the tip—going through the motions," Amy told him.

"Suits me," Carter replied. "Bobo always got most of the money anyway, and somehow I think he's had enough reward for his miserable display of work."

Amy flashed a look at him. "You wouldn't believe it," she said in a teasing voice.

"Jesus, Amy, don't do that to me," Carter sighed.

After breakfast, Amy opened a bottle of champagne and we sat at the table—still uncleared by Carter—and made toasts.

"To childhood," Carter proposed.

"To adulthood," I countered.

"To now," Amy said.

We toasted Rene and Joey Li and Nora Dowling and Ben Benton and Harry Burger and Eddie Grimes. We toasted Arch and Avrum.

"Ah, yes, to Avrum, who pulled this little party off in his own oddball way," Carter said. "If I didn't know better, I'd think the old cockroach had it planned all along. I think he knew his dying would bring the two of you together." He tipped his glass toward us.

Amy raised her glass. "To Avrum."

"To Avrum," I said.

"Who did we leave out?" Carter asked. He let a smile build on his face. Then he said dramatically, "To Jean Archer, who knows beauty when she sees it."

Silence struck the table like a sudden blow.

Carter was holding his champagne glass in front of him. "Did I just hear the fall of a lead balloon?"

"Ah—" I began.

Amy interrupted. "No, Bobo, let me."

Carter pulled his glass back. "What?" he said.

"Jean Archer came to see us last night," Amy replied calmly.

"She did? Why?"

"To tell me about my mother."

"Your mother?" Carter asked.

Amy paused for a beat, then she said, "They were lovers, Carter."

And then she told Carter about the affair between her mother and Jean Archer. Carter listened intently. The frown on his face was not his lawyer's frown, but Carter's frown, the one he wore when he cared and when caring made him ache.

"Amy, honey, I'm sorry," he said when Amy finished her story. "God knows, that must have been hard to take."

"It was, but it's all right now. At least, I finally know what my mother was going through. And the funny thing is, I think I understand." She reached for my hand and held it across the table. She said to Carter, "You know that I love this man, don't you?"

Carter shrugged. "Of course I do. I've always known it. I know it better than the two of you do."

"I think that may be true," Amy said. "He and I have today, and tonight, and then we may have nothing, ever again. In twenty-four hours, he'll be gone. I don't know if I will ever see him again, but I do know I will forever keep these past three days in my life, and I know that nothing will, or can, take them from me, or make them cheap in any way, or make me regret them."

"Regret?" Carter argued. "My God, I don't want to hear the word."

"You wanted me to call him before he married," Amy said. "Do you remember?"

391

Carter bobbed his head. He glanced at me, then back to Amy.

"Maybe if I had called or written, our lives would be different. Maybe we would have been together all those years. I don't know." Her hand rubbed my hand. She leaned toward Carter. "But, Carter, those are all maybes. And we can't make our lives out of maybes. Living needs more than that, just as it needs more than boredom or routine. I don't know how it's supposed to be done in order to be perfect, but I do know that anything that's truly grand, wonderfully grand— even if it's only a few hours—is worth a lot of pain.

"I think that's what my mother discovered," she added in a whisper. "And that's why it's all right—her life, I mean."

Carter's voice cracked when he spoke: "Goddamn it, I love the two of you." He stood at the table and opened his arms and motioned us to him, and we stood and let him swoop us into an embrace. "Damn, I love you," he said again.

25

I walked Carter to his car after our breakfast. He had a meeting with Joe and Anne Fergis, he explained. "The right nudge and old Joe will reach for his checkbook and it'll be done. No more Jean Archer for any of us."

"Are you sure it's a sell?" I asked.

"The wife loves the place," Carter replied confidently. "Especially loves the fact that somebody famous owned it." He smiled. "People," he added, clucking his tongue. "They do fall for the sizzle, don't they?"

I thought of Carter with Anne Fergis in front of the ice cream shop. "I guess they do."

Carter glanced at his watch. "Gotta go. Joe was supposed to get back this morning."

"Who?" I asked.

"The man with the checkbook. Had to go back to the city yesterday to juggle some money."

"And he left his wife alone with you?" I said lightly.

A blush, like a red shadow, swept across Carter's face. He covered it with a wink. "Yeah. Man's a fool, ain't he?"

"Be careful, old friend."

"Don't worry," he said. "What's on the agenda for you today?"

"Just a couple of things to take care of, and then I'm off early tomorrow morning."

"Will I see you before you go?" he asked.

"Maybe. If not, I'll call."

He embraced me. "You've got another reason to come back now."

"I don't know," I confessed. "Maybe this is all it was meant to be."

Carter looked toward the house, then he opened the door to his car and slipped inside. "I don't believe in that kind of thinking any longer, Bobo. I used to, but I don't now. When you met Amy, I knew how you both would feel. I don't know why, but I did, and I thought it would be an impossible relationship." He shook his head in wonder. "Jew and redneck. God, what a mix. I was right then, but none of that matters now. I think things are what you make them. Listen to me, old friend, you've always been too practical. Sometimes you need to put it all on the line, and now's the time. Do this one right, Bobo. Do it right."

Avrum told me in 1977 that he would be cremated when he died.

"And I will show you what you are to do with the ashes," he said.

He took a small box from the closet of his room at the Home and handed it to me.

I asked, "What's this?"

"Ashes," he said.

"Where did you get them?"

394

He looked at me incredulously. "The fireplace," he snorted. "What do you think? I burn somebody? Now, come, let me show you."

He instructed me to drive him to Pine Hill, to his bench.

"Go, go. Find a shovel," he ordered.

I borrowed a shovel from Arch and returned to the bench. Avrum was sitting in the same spot where he had sat for years.

"Now, dig," he said.

"Where?"

He jabbed a finger toward the ground, between his feet.

"Why here?" I asked.

He lifted his head and closed his eyes, as I had seen him do many times when he listened to Amelita Galli-Curci.

"It is my place," he said simply.

He pulled himself up from the bench and stood aside as I dug.

Gut, gut," he said after a few minutes. "Now, the ashes."

He watched as I poured the ashes into the hole.

"Should I say anything?" I asked.

A wrinkled smile crossed his face. "*Ja.* 'There goes Avrum.'" He giggled an old man's giggle. "Now, cover it up."

A puff of ash billowed from the hole when I pushed the first scoop of dirt into it.

"There go my toes," Avrum said gleefully.

We went to Margaretville after the burial of the fireplace ashes, and we stood in front of the

Galli-Curci Theater for Avrum to gaze at the name that sustained him. At dinner, in a small restaurant, Avrum ate heartily and joked with the waitress about being old enough to be her great-grandfather. The waitress thought he was funny. She asked him, "How old are you, anyway?"

"Ninety-one," he replied proudly.

"No," she said in genuine awe.

Avrum bobbed his head. "Maybe I will live to be a hundred, maybe two hundred."

"Well, you may at that," the waitress said.

"When I die, this man will bury me," Avrum told her.

The waitress looked at me with surprise. "Oh," she replied.

I did not tell Amy that I needed to be alone to bury Avrum's ashes and to prepare for his kaddish, or what he called, in mockery, his kaddish. I told her only that there were some details that I had to attend to before leaving, and she understood. I promised to call her in the afternoon.

"It won't be late, will it?" she asked.

"No," I said.

"We have so little time left," she said. "I don't want to lose any of it."

The impression, driving into Pine Hill, was that the village had been invaded, or that a festival was taking place. Couples strolled the street and sat in the chairs on the front porch of the Inn.

They were wandering into and out of Dan Wilder's Coffee and Pastry Shop, and, surprisingly, a few were standing at the opened door of Arch's. I could see Sammy inside as I drove by. He was waving his arms dramatically toward a display of his sculpture.

I parked my car on a side street and went into the Inn. Lila was behind the counter, working furiously at a calculator. She seemed relieved to see me.

"Jesus, Bobo, where have you been? I could have used an extra waiter this morning."

"That's why I stayed away," I told her.

"You're a lot like another man I know," she said. "You're all worthless, even the best of you."

"How's it going? You look busy."

"Like the only whore at an all-male convention." She pushed the calculator aside. "Do you think these love-ins work, Bobo?"

"For some, I suppose. Carolyn and I tried it once. We went to a place called Callaway Gardens with a group from the church. The azaleas were on fire. It was beautiful."

"And what happened?"

"We argued all the way home," I said.

Lila laughed, then apologized for laughing. She leaned across the counter, toward me, and whispered, "If I had to put up with some of the idiot women with this group, I'd put my ass on the road and never look back."

"That bad, huh?" I said.

"Bobo, compared to some of the bitching I've

heard over the last twenty-four hours, PMS is nothing but a mild headache. If they think God's paying any attention to them, they're in for one hell of a shock when they turn up their toes."

"Maybe they're all looking for a miracle," I said.

"Aren't we all?" she sighed. "What are you doing here, anyway? Amy get tired of you and kick you out?"

"No. I came to bury Avrum."

"Jesus, Bobo," Lila whispered in shock.

"I need to borrow a shovel."

"Where are you going to bury him?"

"Under the bench he used to sit on."

Lila glanced out of the window. A middle-aged couple were sitting on the bench, holding hands and grinning foolishly.

"Are you out of your mind, Bobo? What're they going to say when you stick a body under their feet?"

"It's only a few ashes, Lila. I'll explain it to them and ask them to move."

Lila lit a cigarette nervously and spit the smoke over her head. After a moment, she said, "I have to look at that bench every time I sit on the porch, Bobo."

"What are you saying?" I asked.

"If that old man starts showing up out of the blue, I'm going to come to Georgia and rip your balls off."

"Are you afraid of ghosts, Lila?"

She looked at me through narrowed eyes.

"When I start believing in them, I'm sure I will be, Bobo. But I also think if I lived in the middle of a cemetery, I may start believing, and what you're doing is putting a cemetery across the street from me."

"You don't have to watch," I said.

"I don't plan to," she snapped. "The shovel's under the back deck."

I turned to leave and she stopped me.

"I forgot. Carolyn called about an hour ago. I told her you were out walking."

"Thanks," I said.

"She must think something's going on between us. She sounds pissed every time I talk to her."

"I told her about you," I said. "Even drew a sketch of you in the nude to show her. She hates you."

Lila murmured, "Asshole." She smiled. "I wish I didn't love you."

I knew the moment that Carolyn answered the telephone that I would have to wait until she was ready to tell me whatever it was that bothered her. Her voice had a gay and lilting manner. Her talk was the talk of chatter. As I listened, I remembered an artist friend from New York who once grumbled that he despised talking to Southerners because it took them forever to get to the point of a conversation. He recalled being in Washington and visiting a senator from South Carolina with a woman seeking federal funding for the Arts Council of Columbia. "They spent an hour talking about crops and cousins and aunts and uncles," my friend said. "I thought I'd go crazy. I wanted to yell at her to ask for the damn money." I tried to explain that it was important to listen to what he considered rambling. "It's not *what* Southerners say," I emphasized, "it's *how* they say it, what tone they use. If you listen carefully, you can tell by the tone if what you are about to hear is serious or not." He looked at me in disbelief.

I knew by Carolyn's tone that she was bothered; she was much too friendly not to be. And, after a few minutes of prattle about work and about the children, she said it:

"Oh, by the way, before you get back home and hear it from some gossip, you should know that I had dinner last night with Kenny Carpenter."

"Really?" I said.

Kenny Carpenter was a neighbor whose wife had been dead for four years. He operated the service station where we bought gasoline, and he was, as the neighborhood ladies had observed around the community swimming pool, Hollywood handsome for a man in his midfifties. Of the men I knew, Kenny Carpenter was the only one who might have coaxed Carolyn into bed. The yes was in her face, like a sign, whenever she saw him. He was like Carter in a curious way. There was something about him, a roughness, an edge, that made women blink in surprise. With Carolyn, the blink had always been an answer, a code, even if she did not know it. I had watched her many times talking to him as he worked in his backyard. Another neighbor had once joked, "You better not let old Kenny get too close to that wife of yours. Poor son of a bitch drools every time he sees her."

Carolyn rushed her explanation. "It was totally unexpected. I was shopping at the mall—there was a sale at Rich's—and decided to stop in at Ruby Tuesday's for dinner. He was there, by himself at a table, and he invited me to join him."

"I think that's nice," I said. "I don't see anything wrong with that."

"We talked about his kids," she rattled cheerfully. "He's worried about David. You know, the one that dropped out of college to join the Army. Now he wishes he'd stayed in school, and he's always after Kenny for money."

"Well, I'm glad Kenny had a chance to get it off his chest," I replied.

"I just wanted you to know," Carolyn said. "Hilda Sain was there with one of her daughters, so I'm sure it's all over the neighborhood by now. She pretended not to see us."

"Don't worry about it. If anybody says anything, tell them it was an act of retaliation. I was with two women last night."

There was a pause. When she spoke again, her tone had cooled. "Really? Who?"

"A very famous artist named Jean Archer and an old friend named Amy Meyers."

"Oh—"

"My God, Carolyn, don't you think we're old enough to enjoy life without always looking over our shoulders?"

"I suppose so," she said. Then: "Will you be home tomorrow?"

"In the afternoon. I'll call you from the airport when I get there."

"Fine. I'll see you."

"Give my best to Kenny," I said lightly.

She did not appreciate the feeble humor. She hung up without replying.

26

Lila was waiting at the bench, impatiently pacing on the sidewalk. A slip of warm air slithered down the street and seemed to curl around her face. She watched with disgust as I walked up with the shovel and the box containing Avrum's ashes.

"I didn't think you wanted to see this," I said.

"I don't," she grumbled, "but somebody has to make sure you do it right. Anyway, I had to get the lovers off the bench."

I asked what she had told them.

"That I had a man from the water department looking for a water main under the bench." She glared at the box I held. "Are they in there?"

"Yes."

She stepped back. "God . . ."

"It won't take but a minute," I assured her.

"Don't you need a rabbi, or something?" Lila asked.

"No. It's not a ceremony. It's carrying out the wish of a friend."

I placed the box on the bench and began digging in the same spot of the rehearsed burial. The girl on the bicycle rode in her figure-8 circles on the street in front of the bench. She wore a garish orange scarf around her neck and again her face was covered in makeup, but not perfectly applied as before; it was caked, with freckle dots of lipstick across her cheeks and the bridge of her nose. She had the look of a circus clown who had been hired to perform some comic pagan ritual for the burial of Avrum Feldman. The wheels of her bicycle hummed monotonously.

Lila watched and talked nervously, as though she were participating in an act of desecration. Why did he choose a sidewalk bench as his resting place? she demanded. Why didn't he have his ashes scattered across the stage of the Metropolitan Opera House if he was so damned obsessed with opera? How could I seriously honor the ravings of a man who obviously was loony? And how could I possibly blame Carolyn for being upset each time I left home to escape to the Catskills if the reason was to visit Avrum?

"I'm having a really hard time with this, Bobo. I think you need help when this is over. You need to talk to someone qualified to lead you out of this pile of bullshit you've been wading in for all these years."

I paused in the digging. "Look, Lila, why don't you go inside and I'll be finished in a few minutes."

"I've stayed for this much of it, I'll see the rest," she declared. "God knows, you may need a character witness when they try to commit you for such absurdity."

I finished the digging and took the box from the bench and opened it. The ashes were inside in a plastic zip-seal bag. Lila peeked over my shoulder.

"Oh, shit, it's a sandwich bag," she moaned.

"I think it's just an example of keeping up with the times," I said.

I started to open the bag.

"How do you know it's him?" Lila said. "Maybe it's nothing but cigar ashes. Maybe they sold his body to some medical school, or something."

"It's him."

"Wait, wait," Lila whispered. She moved quickly around to the front of the bench and knelt beside me and fanned open the bottom of her skirt, shielding against the breeze.

"What're you doing?" I asked.

"Christ, Bobo, you don't want ashes blowing all over the place, do you? Now, get it over with."

I poured the ashes into the hole and watched them slowly settle, as Avrum had settled into his place on the bench. I whispered, "There goes Avrum."

"What?" asked Lila.

"Nothing," I said.

I gently pulled the dirt over the hole and covered it and packed it down with my hands, and then I stood and Lila stood with me. She tried to strike a mourner's pose. After a moment, she whispered, "Is that it?"

I nodded.

"Don't you think you should say something?"

"I did."

"You did? What?"

"I said, 'There goes Avrum.'"

"Jesus, Bobo . . ."

The girl on the bicycle rode away, her garish orange scarf fluttering in the wind.

The burial of Avrum's ashes had been observed with mild curiosity by the hand-holding couples of the Dutch Reformed church strolling the narrow sidewalks of Pine Hill. Lila's lie about searching for a water main had been murmured among the guests and was sufficient to prevent questions, though I was an unlikely looking maintenance man. Lila had a response prepared if anyone inquired, however. "I'll tell them you're a politician tired of my bitching," she said. "That's exactly what you look like."

We went back into the Inn, to the dining room, and after scrubbing her hands thoroughly, Lila poured coffee for us. She seemed pleased that she had helped me dispose of the ashes, even if Avrum's choice of what to do with his body repulsed her.

"When I die, Bobo, I don't want to get near fire, not even a cigarette lighter. I want to be pumped full of wax and sealed in an airtight tomb. A thousand years from now, I want somebody to find me and go ape-shit over how gorgeous I was."

"I'll see to it," I promised.

"Maybe, by then, they'll be able to fit me with

some spare parts and get my motor running again."

"I don't think that's what's meant by eternal life," I said.

"Eternal? I wasn't talking eternal, Bobo. I was talking second chance."

"I may be wrong, but I think that's something you have to do by yourself," I told her.

She gazed at me over the rim of the coffee cup she held to her lips. "Yes, it is, isn't it?" she said pointedly.

"I'm sure there's a message in that, but I'll think about it later," I said. "I need another favor."

"What?"

"I need to borrow a few things."

"Borrow what?"

"I wish you wouldn't ask. I wish you'd just trust me."

Lila leaned dramatically back against her chair. Her great breasts pushed against her blouse. "All right, Bobo. Take whatever you want. You know where everything is, anyway."

"*Merci,*" I said.

"And don't try that on me. The one thing Southerners can't do is speak French."

In my room, I took the envelope containing Avrum's instructions for his last rite from my briefcase and read again from it: *Take the candlesticks and place her picture against them and set out the music sheet and the necklace, as I have shown you. . . .*

I opened the mahogany box and removed the candlesticks and put the white candles into them, and then I placed the candlesticks on the night table beside the bed and I leaned Amelita Galli-Curci's photograph against them. I placed the sheet of music in front of the photograph and then I laid the necklace of costume jewelry over the sheet of music. I read her signature. It had been hurriedly scribbled across the sheet, like a lashing whip.

Only one other thing to do, I thought, but it must wait.

I went to the window and looked out. The strolling couples from the Dutch Reformed church were like standins from a scene out of 1955. Their walk was slow-moving—a few steps, then stopping to examine something that had caught their attention. Couples huddled together in pools of sunlight. Their easy talk and laughter rose up from the street and sidewalks.

I saw among them a younger couple, perhaps in their early thirties. Both were blond, with the kind of athletic bodies that pose for fashion catalogs. They wore matching tennis shirts and shorts. Their legs were muscled and tan. And I wondered why they were there. Was their marriage so fragile that it needed a retreat? Did they touch only when they were posing in their fashion-catalog poses? Had they had affairs?

They were talking to an older couple, who

408

seemed uncomfortable in their presence. Even from the window, I could see the expressions on the faces of the older couple. It was as though they had comic-strip balloons over their heads, with hand-lettered words telling their thoughts:

What do they know, these young people?

They're children.

They don't have the first idea what marriage is about, how mean it can get.

If they've got any sense, they'll get out while the getting's good.

The younger couple walked away—paraded away on the runway of the sidewalk—and I saw the old man's eyes lingering on the slender body of the blond woman.

Damn, I'd like to have something like that one time before I die.

The older woman jabbed at her husband with her hand and he turned his head away from the blond woman with the slender, remarkable body. I could see the older woman lean to the older man and hiss something. He snarled like an irritated animal and stalked off, leaving his wife to glare bitterly at him.

And I suddenly remembered the night that Jimmy Crenshaw—Whistling Jimmy, a waiter for a short time during the summer of 1955—tried to kill Dave Klein with a knife used for slicing cheese.

Dave Klein was the wealthiest and most demanding guest of the Inn, even more wealthy and more demanding than Harry Burger. He also imagined himself a ladies' man, an illusion that Harry promoted because, to Harry, it was great humor.

One evening, Dave became annoyed with Jimmy because Hilda Klinger, a woman he was trying to impress at Harry's urging, was last to be served on the service rotation. He began to shout at Jimmy, insisting that Jimmy serve Hilda immediately. Jimmy quietly tried to explain the rotation to Dave, but Dave refused to listen. His shouts became more belligerent, more insulting. And Jimmy finally broke. He grabbed the knife from the cheese tray and bolted across the room, shouting, "You old bastard, I'm going to kill you!"

Carter dumped a tray of dishes on the floor and turned the tray up like a shield and slammed it against Jimmy. We dragged him out of the dining room as he screamed threats that made Dave turn the color of ash.

It was, as Harry later described it, the most excitement in the Pine Hill Inn since old Abe Brumfeld was caught screwing a chambermaid named Elsie while his wife played bridge downstairs in the lobby.

"Abe said it was the first woman he'd been with in thirty years," Harry vowed. "Said it was worth every penny he had if his wife wanted a divorce."

Now, I watched the older woman turn and, with practiced dignity, walk back toward the Inn. The balloon over her head carried the words:

You son of a bitch.

I went to my bed and stretched across it and studied the picture of Amelita Galli-Curci leaning against the candlesticks on the night table. Avrum had thought she was beautiful. I did not. There was nothing soft about her face. It had the expression of arrogance, of a complaining queen who tormented her servants with needless orders. But I had heard her voice from Avrum's records and her voice was as commanding as Avrum said it was. I believed it was her voice that Avrum loved, because he loved the music that it created.

I looked at my watch. It was just before noon. In twenty-four hours, I would be on an airplane, skimming clouds toward Atlanta, toward home. So little time before this ends, I thought. And I remembered Avrum's proclamation about the one grand, undeniable moment of change, a change so apparent and consequential that it never stopped mattering.

Amelita Galli-Curci had been Avrum's moment.

Amy Lourie had been my moment.

I rolled to the side of the bed and lifted the telephone from its cradle and dialed Amy's number. She answered on the second ring and I knew instantly that something was wrong.

"Oh, hi," she said brightly. "How are you?"

"Fine," I said. Then, after a beat: "What is it?"

"I just had a surprise," she answered, her voice still bright.

411

"Really?"

"Yes. Peter, my husband, drove up. He got in about thirty minutes ago." She did not pause for me to reply. "He finished his business in Washington last night and flew to Newburgh this morning and rented a car."

"That's—that's good," I mumbled.

I could hear a man's voice in the background. "Who is it?"

Amy answered so that I would hear: "It's the woman from the antique shop in Margaretville. She called to say she thinks she's found the coffee table I was looking for."

The man's voice said, "That's good."

Amy spoke into the phone. "If it's all right with you, I think I'll drive up and take a look at it. My husband wants to get a short nap, and if it's what I want, I don't want him standing around objecting."

"Yes, please," I said. "I'm at the Inn. Room twelve."

"Great," Amy said. "See you shortly, then."

"Sure."

I sat on the side of the bed for a long time. I did not tremble because of the risk of Peter Meyers appearing unexpectedly. There had been moments with Amy when I wished for him to open the door and to find us in her bed. It would have been an honest discovery, and it would have settled the confusion for all of us. But I knew those were moments of bravery, or foolishness.

What I felt, sitting on my bed, was an overwhelming sadness.

I pushed from the bed and went to the window and looked out again. The street and the sidewalks were deserted except for the girl that Sammy had called Trinity. She was sitting on Avrum's bench, staring at the freshly turned earth beneath her feet. Her bicycle was leaned against a tree. Sammy had thought of her as the only child in the village—"the last of us all." She seemed to sense me watching her. She raised her head slowly and looked toward the window where I stood. In that moment she appeared to hover over Avrum like a protecting angel. A shiver clawed at my shoulders and I had a thought, a sensation, of the girl being the angel of death, waiting patiently. I moved my body to calm the shiver. Or perhaps she is not that at all, I thought. Perhaps she is the angel of mercy, watching over us. She smiled toward me.

I stepped back from the window.

From the hallway, I could hear voices and the movement of people, and I remembered hearing the hollow ringing of the lunch bell as I sat on the bed. In winter, Lila used the bell to call skiers from the slopes; now she used it to call people trying to survive bruised marriages.

I will miss this place, I thought.

There was a light tapping at the door and, from outside, Lila's voice: "Bobo?"

"Come in," I said.

She opened the door and stepped inside. She

413

immediately saw the candlesticks and the photograph of Amelita Galli-Curci. "Who's that?" she asked.

I told her without explaining Avrum's ritual, or the instruction for his kaddish.

She crossed to the picture and studied it.

"My God, Bobo, she's ugly."

"I'm sure you remember the old line about beauty being skin deep," I replied.

"Well, love, she needed some new skin," Lila said, "and some new bones." She turned to me. "Are you having lunch with us?"

"No. I'm expecting Amy."

"Good."

"I don't know," I said. "Her husband showed up this morning. She manufactured some excuse to get away."

"Oh, shit, Bobo, I'm sorry."

"It's all right. I just want a few minutes alone with her."

Lila touched my face gently with her hand. "Don't worry. I'll keep Sammy busy." She smiled weakly. "And I'll behave. I promise."

"I know you will," I said. "But thanks, anyway."

"You know, Bobo, in a way I envy her, but in another way, I feel sorry for her," Lila said quietly.

"Why?" I asked.

"My mother told me something once, just before my divorce, when I was trying to make sense of wanting to live with Sammy. It may be the only good thing she ever did for me, but I've never forgotten it. She said, 'Nothing is worse than not having what you want when what you want is so close to having.' I know it sounds confusing, but when you think about it, Bobo, it makes sense."

"I guess you're right," I said.

"No, Bobo. You *know* I'm right," Lila countered softly.

Amy arrived fifteen minutes later. I watched from the window of my room as she parked her car on the side street and hurried into the Inn from the front porch, and I went to the door and waited for her. She linked her arms around my waist when she entered the room.

"I'm sorry, I didn't know he was coming," she whispered.

"I know you didn't," I told her. She released me and I closed the door and locked it. "Why is he here?"

"He said he wanted to surprise me," she answered bitterly. "Said he'd been thinking about it—how he'd ignored my enthusiasm about having the home up here. But that's not why he's here; it's only his story. He wants me to sell the place. Thirty minutes after he arrived, he was telling me he knew someone who wanted a home in the mountains. He had even talked price with them, the son of a bitch."

"It's your place, isn't it?"

415

Her eyes burned with anger. "And it's going to remain my place," she said evenly.

"How long will he stay?" I asked.

"Tonight. He'll be back in his office tomorrow. He's never missed a day of work. Never."

"I think we should call Carter and tell him," I suggested. "To prevent one of his well-meaning blunders."

"I did," she said. "I stopped at a pay phone. He wants you to call him later."

She looked around the room and smiled softly. "Do you know what's funny about this?"

"What?"

"This was my room that summer."

"Are you sure?"

She crossed to the window and looked out. "Of course I am. I used to stand here and watch you and Carter going to the swimming pool at night. I always wondered what you were doing."

"Talking," I explained. "That's where we went when Carter wanted to tell me something he considered serious."

"I spent that entire summer trying to tease you up to this room, and now we're here," she said. The trace of a smile slipped over her lips. She looked around the room again and saw the candlesticks and the photograph of Amelita Galli-Curci. "The ceremony," she said quietly.

"Yes. You know about it, don't you?"

She nodded. "He would do it for me when I visited. He said you were the only other person who had ever seen it." She turned back to me. "Do you have a picture of me?"

"Yes," I said. "The one you gave me for the drawing I did. It's in my briefcase, with the stone. Do you want to see it?"

She hesitated for a moment, then signaled a yes with her eyes.

I opened my briefcase and took out the photograph and stone and handed them to her. She closed her hand over the stone and gazed at the photograph.

"I was so young," she whispered.

"We both were," I said.

She smiled. "I still have the drawing you did. I had it laminated a long time ago."

"I thought you may have burned it," I told her.

She handed the picture back to me, but kept the stone, massaging it with her fingers. "Burn it? No. I would never do that. Sometimes I take it out and look at it and remember."

"I've done the same thing," I confessed. "I think Avrum taught us well."

She looked at me. "It has nothing to do with Avrum, Bobo. Not for me." There was surprise, and hurt, in her voice.

"I didn't mean that I—"

She interrupted: "I've wondered about that, Bobo. It worries me sometimes. How much he might have manipulated you."

"Avrum?" I said.

"Yes. I loved him dearly, as you did, but he was a manipulator. You do know that, don't you?"

"He was just different," I said. "He had an obsession. Most people didn't understand that."

A puzzled frown swept her face. "Obsession? It was more than that, Bobo. It was also deception."

"I don't understand what you're trying to tell me," I replied.

"The story about the fisher boa that he made for her. Do you remember it?"

"Yes," I answered with surprise. "But he told me I was the only one who knew that story. He made me promise—"

"No, not the only one," she said. "He also told me, that same summer. I made the same vow you did—never to say anything about it, even to you." She paused. "But it was a lie, Bobo. It didn't happen."

I was stunned. "How do you know?"

She went to the night table and picked up the sheet of music and looked at it.

"This is not Amelita Galli-Curci's signature, Bobo. That other woman, the one who looked like her . . ."

"Fern Weisel?" I said.

"Yes, Fern Weisel. She signed it."

I could not believe what Amy said. I took the sheet from her and stared at the signature.

"You didn't know, did you?" she said quietly. "I thought perhaps you did, but you really didn't, did you?"

I shook my head.

"He admitted it a few years ago only after he knew that he had to," she explained. "I saw Amelita Galli-Curci's signature once, when my mother and I were in Margaretville. An antique dealer had it in one of his displays. It was her autograph on a program about the opening of the Galli-Curci Theater. It didn't look at all like this. And then I visited Avrum—the next day, I think—and I told him about seeing her autograph. I thought it confused him. He didn't say anything for a long time, and then he asked me to give him his box. He took her picture out of it and sat, holding it, and then he told me the truth. The story about the boa, about her autograph, about the jewelry—it was only something he wished he had done, Bobo. He had to have such a story to make him feel romantic and brave, so he invented it. He wanted to be a hero, and in that story, he was. Even the theft of the pelt was heroic to him. He told us about it because he wanted us to believe in him, and then he told me the truth because he wanted me to think about you."

She laughed softly, sadly. She looked at the stone, rubbed it between her fingers. "And it worked. I did think about you." She turned her eyes to me. "When I left that summer, I knew I would have to put you out of my life. It took years for me to manage that, Bobo, but I did. Sometimes, you would pop up, totally unexpected, but I could manage it by making myself busy, by telling myself you were just a memory.

419

And then Avrum told me the truth about the boa and the signature and the jewelry, and you came flooding back, and I couldn't control it. And then he died and you were here."

I sat heavily on the bed, near the night table with the candlesticks and the photograph. I could sense something leaving me, something falling away.

Amy sat beside me. "Does it matter what Avrum did?" she said. "I don't think it does. That's why I haven't said anything about it. It wasn't really a lie; it was an illusion. And that's all right, I think. Don't we all do that?"

"I used to do the same thing with your picture," I confessed. "I had my own ritual. I imitated him."

"And he would have loved it," she said. She took my hand and slipped the stone into it. "He believed in magic. So do I."

"I'm not sure I do," I told her.

She slipped from the bed and moved to the window, and she stood for a moment gazing out of it. Then she looked back at me. "What do you think magic is?"

"I'm not sure," I answered honestly. "Something we can't explain, maybe."

"I think it's making things happen that we're afraid of," she replied gently. Then, after a moment, she said, "Bobo, I want to tell Peter about us."

She lifted her hands, with her palms toward me, to stop my words.

"I thought about it driving up," she said in a rush. "I could hear myself saying it. I could hear the words, Bobo. I said to him, 'There's a man that I've loved for a very long time, and I thought I had lost him, but I found him and if he leaves, I'll never see him again.'" She looked at me with pleading. "I could hear myself. It was so easy to say. I could imagine sitting at the table with him, telling him. I could see the whole thing, like it was a scene from a play and I was high above it, in a balcony, looking down, watching my lips move, listening to the words." She paused and stepped toward me. Her voice became calm. "Do you know what was funny about it? My mother was in the balcony beside me. I could sense her, sitting there, and maybe that's why it was easy. It's what my mother did, isn't it?"

"It wasn't easy for your mother," I reminded her.

"But she did it," Amy argued. "She did it. Can't we do that, too, Bobo?"

I shook my head. "I don't know."

She did not speak for a moment and then she asked, softly, "Do you want to do it?"

I did not answer.

"You're afraid, aren't you?"

"Yes. Yes, I am," I admitted.

"Is it our age, Bobo? Do you think we're too old, that we've waited too long?"

I shook my head again. "I don't know."

"Damn it, Bobo, we're not too old," she said desperately. She began to pace the room. "We're

421

fifty-five. What are we supposed to do—live another thirty years like we are now? Do you want to do that? Do you want to live another thirty years like this, accepting what we are because that's what's expected of us? Thirty years, Bobo. Think of it. I don't want to do that. I don't want to spend my time going to proper little parties and serving on committees for black-tie dinners that are supposed to be charity events for the homeless, but are nothing more than excuses to parade around comparing designer gowns." She laughed sadly. "I don't want to stay awake at night making retirement plans and worrying about wills and burial plots. Damn it, Bobo, I want to live. I want *us* to live. I want us to make love like teenagers. I want to go to Paris with you. I want to sit and watch you paint. I want to lie beside you in bed and hold your hand. I want to *feel* you, Bobo. So many good years. Why can't we have that time?"

I saw her tremble. She moved back to me and took my hands and urged me up from the bed and she held to me.

"Will you think about it?" she begged against my chest. "Will you promise that much?"

"Yes," I said.

"I don't want to hurt anyone, Bobo, and I know we would. We would hurt Peter and Carolyn and our children and our friends, but I don't want to live the rest of my life wondering what might have been, and wanting what I didn't have. I've spent too many years wondering that."

She pulled her face from my chest and looked at me. She closed her eyes slowly, and when she opened them again, the expression on her face had changed. She was calm, resolved.

"I'm sorry," she whispered. "You can't do it, can you?" She touched my face with her hand. "No, you can't, and it's wrong of me to ask you. But I understand, Bobo. I do. This morning, I couldn't have done it, either, no matter what I said. I can now, and I don't know why. It's not Peter being here, and it's not knowing about my mother. It's just something I know I could do, something I want to do."

She kissed me gently.

"Avrum didn't mean to lie," she added. "He wanted to tell the truth, but he couldn't *do* the truth. I'm not angry with him for that, and I'm not angry at you, or at us. If we can't do the truth, at least we know it."

She smiled radiantly and stepped away from me. She looked once around the room and crossed to the door, then she turned back to me.

"I love you, Bobo," she said tenderly. She opened the door and walked out of the room.

27

When pain first strikes, the body and the soul do not ache in the same way.

The body screams, surrenders, begs for injections to kill the agony.

The soul anesthetizes itself, turns itself numb, deceives itself into believing there is no pain. The soul becomes dazed.

I did not remember walking to the window of my room to watch Amy cross the street back to her car. Yet, I watched her. I stood at the window, holding the stone, and I watched her. She did not look back at the Inn.

I went to the telephone and dialed the 800 number for a hotel near the airport at Newburgh and made a reservation, and then I left the Inn and walked to Arch's, in search of Sammy. He was in his workshop, moving pieces of his battered-rock sculpture from the back of the store to display tables near the front window. He had sold a piece—*World in Turmoil*—that resembled a basketball marred by a scar like the rip of an earthquake. The buyer was from the Dutch Reformed church, a woman who wanted to celebrate her newfound love for her husband by presenting him with a work of art. To Sammy, it was not the most appropriate of his pieces for such a gift, but the transaction had inspired him to offer a special sale on what he considered his carry-home pieces.

"You know, Bobo, Dan may be right," Sammy enthused. "I clean the place up a little and put in some good lighting and do the right kind of promoting out on the highway, I think I could move a few pieces. Maybe bring in some arts and crafts from some of those shops up in Fleischmanns and Margaretville. You know what I'm talking about, don't you? Tie this business and the rooming business together. Maybe specialize in these church marriage-renewal things. I mean, shit, it sounds like they're talking about renewing a driver's license to me, but if that's what works, then have at it. Hell's bells, I'll even give away free vitamin E tablets and bring in a strolling accordion player if that helps get the juices flowing. Or maybe I'll put in some of those closed-circuit porn movies, like they've got in some of those motels I've been in."

I knew that Sammy's blithering was intended, in part, to distract me, to keep me from thinking of Amy. He could not know what had happened in the room, but Lila would have told him of Peter Meyers's sudden appearance, and I was certain that she had warned him against trying to advise me.

"So, what do you think?" Sammy asked, forcing an eager smile.

"Sounds like a good idea," I said. "Maybe

that's what the village needs—a specialty, like it had in the fifties when all the refugees were here."

"Yeah, that's what I was thinking, too."

"Look, Sammy, I wonder if you'd do a favor for me," I said.

"Name it."

"I will later, but it's not complicated."

Sammy's eyes blinked a question, but he did not ask it. He shrugged and said, "Sure."

"I've decided to drive back to Newburgh today and spend the night there. I've got an early flight out in the morning," I told him.

"Hate to see you go," Sammy said earnestly. "Damn it, I wish you lived up here. I always do my best work when you're around."

"You don't need me or anyone else," I replied. "You just need yourself."

Sammy tugged at one of the pieces of sculpture on the table, rearranging it. After a moment, he said, "Thanks, Bobo."

"I'll see you a little later. Okay?"

"Sure, I'll be here. I've got a couple trying to decide which piece they want—*After the Bomb* or *Dead Volcano*." He swept his hands proudly over the two pieces. They looked very much the same.

I left Sammy and walked through the village a last time, past the cemetery, following the path of walkers long dead, the path that Amy followed when meeting me at the birch tree. The tree was gone, but I knew the spot where it had stood. There was a stone the size of a fist lodged in the grass and ground, and I remembered the day that Amy had angrily buried the brochure about interfaith marriages. The earth had taken the brochure, had swallowed it, digested it.

From the hillside, I could see couples from the Dutch Reformed church packing their cars for the trip back to the city. For a moment—from the distance—the village seemed to be the village of 1955. I sat in the sun where Amy and I had sat under the shadows of the birch, and I watched the cars pull away, leaving the village deserted except for the girl named Trinity. She rode her bicycle up the street and turned and rode back and turned again. Up and down she rode, as though reclaiming her place, and I wondered if she would be there when everyone else had died, or moved away, and Pine Hill itself had been digested by the earth. I wondered what the sound of her voice was like.

I sat for a long time, thinking of Amy. Avrum had said that my being with her was meant to be, that, as with my meeting of him, it was destiny. He had tried to persuade me that it was the same as his experience with Amelita Galli-Curci—an ordination, not to be questioned. The way Avrum had said it, it *was* magical. And, for thirty-eight years, I had believed him.

I thought of the people who knew him, or thought they knew him. They had called him crazy, an old fool preoccupied with romantic nonsense.

"Take care, take care," Harry Burger had warned. "Avrum, he likes to pull the strings."

"He's using you," Carolyn had insisted. "If you think he's hearing opera, you're as batty as he is. All he's doing is pretending, so you'll pay attention to him."

I felt foolish and angry. And used.

I left the mountain and returned to the Inn and called Carolyn from my room to tell her that I would be staying the night in Newburgh.

She wanted to know why.

"I thought I might get an earlier flight," I said. "I think there's one that leaves around six in the morning."

"You don't have to go by the school tomorrow, do you?" she asked.

"No. I just thought I'd get in as soon as I can."

"Are you all right?" she said.

"I'm fine. Why do you ask?"

"You don't sound fine. You haven't all week." She paused. "Something's happened, hasn't it?"

"It's like I told you earlier," I countered. "Memories."

Again there was a pause. I could hear a sigh and then the sound of tapping, and I knew she was playing with the pen she used for taking messages. It was her habit when she was annoyed.

"I'll see you tomorrow," I told her.

"Wait a minute," she said. "I want to say something."

"Go ahead."

"I don't want you to come back unless you've

worked out everything up there," she said deliberately. "I mean it. I'm not asking for you to tell me anything, but I am asking you to be honest with yourself. I don't want anything lingering when you come home this time. I won't take that anymore. I can't."

"Carolyn, I don't know what you're talking about."

"Yes, you do."

I leaned back against the bed. I remembered something she had once said to me during an argument: "You may not think I know how you feel, or that I know very much about what you do, but I know you. Don't you ever forget: I know you." And she did. She knew me well.

"May I ask you something?" I said.

"I'm listening," she replied.

"Do you love me?"

Her response surprised me: "I love you, Bobo, but that can't be the answer for everything. It's not a cure-all. I don't want to play games anymore, and I don't think you do, either. We're both too old—and still too young—for that."

"All right," I said after a moment.

"I'm here," she said evenly.

The door to Arch's was unlocked and I went inside and called for Sammy, but there was no answer.

I called again: "Sammy."

Still, he did not answer.

I walked through the shop, among the blocks

of stone. It was eerily quiet in the place where Arch Ellis had told his stories to applause. I stopped at one of Sammy's half-finished busts. The primitive image of a man's face seemed to be lodged in the stone. It was a proud and defiant face, and I imagined it was inspired by the giant Indian, Winnisook, and that Arch would have been pleased with Sammy's finding him and releasing him.

I wandered to the room where Arch had kept his stock stored and I knocked lightly at the door.

"Sammy?"

He answered from inside: "Bobo?"

"Yeah," I said. "It's me."

"Come on in."

I opened the door and stepped inside. The room was empty except for a sofa and a scarred coffee table sitting in front of it. Sammy was stretched out on the sofa, his feet crossed at his ankles. I could smell the sweet odor of marijuana.

"How's it going, Bobo?" Sammy asked lightly.

"All right," I said. "You?"

Sammy smiled foolishly. "Great, old buddy. Great. Just relaxing a minute." He swung his feet off the sofa and sat up. "You found me in my hiding place."

"Looks that way," I said.

"It's where I get my ideas, Bobo. Right here. It's my thinking place." He patted the sofa with his hand and nodded satisfaction. "One or two hits on the forbidden weed, and the ideas roll out, but I've got to be by myself. You ever get that way?"

"All the time. I stay away from the hits, but I like some time alone before I start work."

"Don't tell Lila," Sammy cautioned. "She thinks I come down here and pound away over a pile of rocks. She had any idea I like being by myself, she'd go bat-shit crazy."

"Maybe she'd understand," I suggested. "Maybe she likes a little time off to herself, as well."

Sammy looked at me thoughtfully. "Let me tell you something about Lila," he said, "something very few people know. She's a basket case waiting for the fruit to fall out. Has this phobia about being alone. She's all right if I'm close by, or if somebody else is around, but if she thinks she's completely by herself, she's as wacky as Daffy Duck." He laughed wearily. "I tell everybody we moved up here so I would have the peace and quiet to work on my art, but that's just a bullshit line. I could do what I do in a goddamn alley in Brooklyn in the middle of a mugging—in fact, it might improve things having a few bullet nicks to work with. You and I both know that. No, Bobo, we came here because of Lila. It's why we run the Inn. We thought there'd be people around all the time."

"I didn't know," I replied. "I'm sorry, Sammy. That's got to be pressure."

He stretched his arms above his head like a man waking from sleep, then he rubbed his eyes

431

with his fingers. "It's not bad. She came from real blue blood. Queen of the ball. The son of a bitch she used to be married to could buy and sell third-world countries out of his change pocket. She took it as long as she could and then she snapped, and she's been just the opposite ever since." He paused, laced his hands behind his head, and looked at me. "She dresses like a whore most of the time now," he added easily. "Acts like one, too, I guess. But she used to look like a *Vogue* model and she could have had tea with Alistair Cooke and made him feel like one of the Three Stooges. You heard her speaking French, didn't you? You saw her that night. That was a glimpse of the old Lila."

"What happened?" I asked.

Sammy did not reply for a long moment. He gazed at me sorrowfully, then he said, "She got pregnant and her ex-husband made her have an abortion. He didn't want kids. It almost killed her. She was hospitalized for a month and then institutionalized for another year. That's where we met. I was working in the institution as an orderly and going to school at night."

He smiled and shrugged.

"I'm glad you told me, Sammy," I said. "I'm glad you think that much of me."

He stood, unfolding himself from the sofa like an old man. "I wanted you to know. I want you to come back. You make Lila feel special, the way you treat her. Like a gentleman, I mean. You make her remember the good part of her life."

432

"She is special to me," I told him. "Both of you are."

"Can I ask you something, Bobo?"

"Of course."

"Do you think I'm crazy to do what I do?"

"No," I said. "No, you're not crazy."

Sammy smiled. "You ready for that favor?"

"Yes," I answered.

The door was partly opened to my room and Lila stepped into it without knocking. She sniffed the air dramatically and said, "I knew it. Sex. Definitely sex, and that's against the rules. I'll have to ask you to leave."

"That's not musk you smell," I said. "It's dust."

She laughed and sat on the bed next to my suitcase. "Did you get everything done?"

"Yes. Sammy's taking care of the last thing for me."

"Oh, that's what he's doing?" she said. "I saw him leave, but he didn't say where he was going."

I thought of Sammy's warning about Lila's fear of being alone. "He won't be gone long," I told her.

She picked up a shirt I had stuffed into my suitcase and began refolding it.

"So, Bobo Murphy, is this the last time I see you?"

"I doubt it," I said. "I'm like a migrating bird. Every couple of years, I hear something calling from up here and I have to find some wings."

"Amy?" she asked quietly.

I took the shirt from her and placed it in the suitcase and closed it.

"I'm sorry," she said. "I shouldn't ask. It's none of my business."

"Yes, it is your business," I replied. "It's Amy, yes, and it's you, and it's Sammy, and it's Dan and Carter and that little girl who keeps riding up and down the street on her bicycle and never speaks. It's Avrum. And Sol Walkman, and all those old people at the Home. There's something about this place that affects me. Avrum used to tell me this is where my life changed, and maybe he was right, even if he was a dreamer."

Lila looked at me quizzically.

I sat on the bed beside her and took her hands. "Look, I care for Amy," I confessed. "Maybe from the first moment I saw her sitting in Arch's with Carter, or maybe it's just something Carter made up and I came to believe it. It doesn't matter. I wish I knew the answer, Lila. I wish I could find whatever's missing. I only know that something is over, in one place or the other."

"At least you had some time together," Lila said gently.

"Yes, we did. And do you know what was beautiful about it?"

"Tell me," she said.

"It was exactly what I knew it would be."

"Doesn't that tell you something, Bobo?"

"I don't know," I answered. "Maybe it should, but I don't know."

★ ★ ★

I asked Lila not to walk with me to my car and she understood.

"I want to sit on Avrum's bench a few minutes," I said.

She kissed me tenderly. "In the next lifetime, Bobo."

"I promise it," I said.

I put my suitcase and hang-up bag in the car and crossed the street to Avrum's bench and sat. It was five minutes before five. *Do it at five o'clock,* Avrum had instructed in the note on his parody of the kaddish.

A cooling wind stirred the limb-tips of the hemlocks and oaks and birches and pines, fanned them like waving hands calling for a gathering. And as I sat and waited, they began to appear. Harry Burger and Nora Dowling walked down the steps of the Inn. Ben Benton drove by in his truck, stopped it on the street, and got out and began walking toward me. Arch Ellis came from his store, sweeping the sidewalk with his broom. Mrs. Mendelson waddled across the lawn, her head bobbing with her step. Evelyn Lourie stepped from beneath a table umbrella at the swimming pool. Joey Li and Eddie Grimes leaned against the door of The Cave. Carter and Rene stood beside an oak, holding hands. Avrum was sitting beside me on the bench, smiling proudly.

"Listen, listen," Avrum said. He closed his eyes and tilted his head.

Amy had said that magic was making things happen that we're afraid of.

"Do you hear it?" Avrum whispered.

And then the first note from the voice of Amelita Galli-Curci, singing the "Shadow Song" from *Dinorah*, floated in, grew stronger, swam through the valley below Highmount. It was surprisingly clear from the tape player and the speakers that Sammy had taken from the Inn to Sul Monte.

Play from Sul Monte the music I most love, Avrum had written.

I saw Lila open the front door of the Inn and walk to the porch. She sat in a chair and listened.

Dan Wilder stood very still in front of his coffee and pastry shop, his head lifted.

Trinity—the girl of the jump rope and the bicycle and the bouncing ball—held to her bicycle on the sidewalk. She looked up and searched for the music with her eyes.

Avrum leaned to me on the bench. Again, he said, "Do you hear it? Do you?"

I could feel the voice of the music touching me.

"Yes," I said.

"Then you know, *ja*? You know."

"Yes."

"Go, go," Avrum urged.

I stood and crossed the street to the Inn.

"What is it?" Lila asked.

"I want to use the telephone," I told her.

She smiled and closed her eyes and rested her

head against the cushion of the rocker. The brilliantly clear music from the throat and soul of Amelita Galli-Curci drifted across the porch.

Inside, I dialed Amy's number. She answered immediately.

"Tell him," I said.

"Do you mean it?" she asked. Her voice quivered.

"Yes," I answered. "Yes."

IF YOU HAVE ENJOYED READING THIS LARGE PRINT BOOK AND YOU WOULD LIKE MORE INFORMATION ON HOW TO ORDER A WHEELER LARGE PRINT BOOK, PLEASE WRITE TO:

WHEELER PUBLISHING, INC.
P.O. BOX 531
ACCORD, MA 02018–0531